"Catherine Brakefield transports fans of historical romance to an earlier time and lets us experience the sorrows, but also the joys of life as it was!"

—RICK BARRY, author of *The Methuselah Project*

"Catherine Brakefield has woven an interesting tale of love gained and love lost, life and death, war and peace throughout a tumultuous time of American history. Her characters draw the reader deep into the story as they journey through the stresses and joys of their lives."

— MARCIA MITCHELL, author and minister

"Although the story takes place over one hundred years ago, it's relatable today. Catherine's characters are real-life, and the story is a hard won maybe happily-ever-after ending. I haven't read a family saga in a long time. Now that I've read Destiny's Whirlwind I need to follow the family to the conclusion. Beautifully-written."

—CINDY ERVIN HUFF, author of *Secrets & Charades*

OTHER CROSSRIVER BOOKS
BY CATHERINE ULRICH BRAKEFIELD

DESTINY SERIES

Swept into Destiny
Destiny's Whirwind
A Destiny of Heart (coming late 2018)
A Waltz with Destiny (coming in 2019)

OTHER TITLES

Wilted Dandelions

Destiny's Whirlwind

Blessings in Christ's love!
Catherine Romans 8:28

CATHERINE ULRICH BRAKEFIELD

CROSSRIVER
BREWSTER, KANSAS USA

"From the chamber of the south comes the whirlwind." Job 37:9 NKJV

Is it fate, ourselves, or an omnipotent God that guides
our destiny and the destiny of our children? Or was it the
heartbeat of a race, nurtured on the milk of their Savior's
words that brought this nation safely through the battles of time?

This book is dedicated to today's and tomorrow's patriots.

"...then the Lord answered Job out of the whirlwind." Job 38:1 NKJV

Acknowledgments

In 1976 I won a trip to the Decision School of Christian Writing. I was pregnant with my first child. Two months after my daughter's birth, my grandmother came to live with us. My writing took a detour into the inner recesses of my file cabinet and was replaced with bottles, diapers, and doctor visits.

Little did I know at the time that I was now enrolled in God's School of Christian Learning. From those twelve years Gran lived with us, the inspiration for my first novel *The Wind of Destiny* evolved. I thought the legacy of this part of my life was closed until I met my agent, Cyle Young of Hartline Literary Agency, and the dedicated staff at CrossRiver Media Group.

I had given Tamara Clymer a copy of the out-of-print novel *The Wind of Destiny* and a recent copy of my new manuscript. She proposed a redo and tying my past novel in with my new manuscript. CrossRiver editor Debra Butterfield agreed. Hence, this four-book series evolved. *Swept into Destiny* was the first book of this Destiny series. *Destiny's Whirlwind* is book two of the series.

"Commit your works to the Lord, and your thoughts will be established." Proverbs 16:3 NKJV

Tamara Clymer, this speaks to me about you. Thank you for your insight, unfailing encouragement, and your beautiful cover artwork.

"The heart of the wise teaches his mouth, and adds learning to his lips." Proverbs 16:23 NKJV

Debra L. Butterfield, you have added learning to my words, enriching my writing skill and wisely smoothing out the rough edges of *Destiny's Whirlwind*, making it shine with truth and vitality.

"A man's heart plans his way, But the LORD directs his steps." Proverbs 16:9 NKJV

Cyle Young, your support continues to inspire me. Your dogmatic persistence in attaining this Destiny contract and your belief in my writing talents is an encouragement to me.

To my husband, Edward Brakefield, your faith in me, your patience, and your understanding help me persevere throughout the many phases and hours of writing and rewrites.

Thank you Marcia (Mitchell) Lee for your keen wit and your insight. Rick Barry, for the time you take reading my manuscripts and your expertise and honesty. Cindy Ervin Huff, for your valuable time and wisdom.

Margaret Bowyer, did you know you and your family have encouraged me for over a decade? Your continued excitement with every new book I produce encourages me to persevere throughout the rewrite stages!

To Zander and Logan, may you come closer to knowing your roots and this great nation you may need to serve someday. To Annabelle and Willow, thank you for your patience during the trials and hour-crunch of my final rewrites. May you acquire wisdom and discernment in picking the right husbands someday by reading this book!

To you, my precious readers, I pray *Destiny's Whirlwind* will guide you into the truth as to our historical roots of our beloved nation that God forgives daily and beneath which His guiding hand is divinely present.

Dear readers, I pray Collina, Franklin, and Ruby will carry you into new depths and visions as to the knowledge of Christ's unending and enduring love. God bless and to Christ Jesus be the glory forever!

"If ye have faith as a grain of mustard seed...nothing will be impossible unto you." Matthew 17:20

Chapter 1

"… taking the shield of faith…" Ephesians 6:16

March 1, 1898, Emerald, Kentucky

Snow slapped her face, but it was the townspeople's taunts that hurt the worst.

"Smallpox carrier Collina May, go away. We don't want you or any McConnell to stay."

It had been two weeks since the McConnells had come down with the pox. She had come to town to get hay and a thousand pounds of feed for their livestock. Mother said to stop at Doc Baker's to pick up more salve and not to forget her father's medicine.

"Tell Doc I need him to come tomorrow." Mother would say no more, only that Collina, in spite of the storm, must go today.

"Smallpox carrier Collina May, go away!"

Her thoughts chilled her more than the boys' hateful remarks or weather ever could.

Joseph McWilliams rode up. He'd helped her load the supplies. He rode his sorrel gelding next to her wagon, scowling at Emerald's townsfolk, his fiery-red hair and thick beard adding to his frightful appearance.

As the two made their way to Doc Baker's, store clerks sweeping the wooden porch leading to their doorways paused in midstride. Children stopped their snowball fights. Three men outside of Jim's Mercantile halted their chatter.

A woman from the crowd of bystanders who had congregated on the mercantile porch ran down the steps like a passel of hornets was attacking her, hauled her boy up by the inside nape of his collar, and glared at Collina. "Pox May go away!"

"No, ma'am." How could she ever face the townsfolk again? Did they truly think she gave her people the smallpox?

She pulled her team to a halt and jumped down. Her boots slammed up the wooden steps of Doctor Baker's office, and she pounded on the door until the prickly pin needles of pain from her cold hand made her stop. No answer. As she prepared to leave, her boot hit the package marked Collina McConnell. It sat like a forlorn pigeon on the threshold, covered with snow. Where could Doc be?

She snatched the package, then took the steps down two at a time.

Joseph jumped off his horse and barred her escape, his large hand like an iron anvil weighing her shoulder, his red head as alert as a bird dog's on a sudden shift in wind. "What you fixin' on doing, drivin' your team home in a snowstorm just cuz some mama boys called you a name who ain't got nothing better do with their day than pick on a lone woman?"

"Let go, Joseph." She yanked away from his grip. "I can handle myself and my team as good as any—"

"Man? When you going to realize God made you a woman for a reason? You just say the word and those gents won't feel like singing anymore."

Her puckered eyebrows met his scowl.

"Seems like yesterday you were just a freckle-nosed kid, kicking that big Macintosh boy in the behind cuz he'd muddied up your stockings."

"Wasn't just the Macintosh boy that got my boot, I'm recalling. And it looks like I…" She looked away. Joseph heard plain enough. Now she knew what a leper must have felt like back in Jesus' time. No matter, she needed to get home with this medicine.

Joseph's six-foot build had a width of shoulder that won him easily every arm wrestling fight from Kentucky to the Tennessee border, but he let go of her without a struggle. His arms fell to his sides as he hunched his muscular shoulders against the north wind. "These are truly bitter days in more ways than a thermometer can record."

"I'll be all right," she whispered, swallowing down the lump that followed, seeing the pity in Joseph's eyes.

"Take Haggerman Road, not that lane you came in on. I'd go with ya, only Pa's come down with a bad case of gout; I've got to tend the store."

"Too long that way. The lane will cut two hours off my trip. When Doc comes back, can you please tell him to come to Shushan first thing tomorrow morning?"

"Sure."

She mounted the wagon; the seat was cold and damp. She clutched her red-plaid blanket. Thick white flakes of snow flew gracefully downward, as if they'd sprouted wings. Wet and pearly white, they rested on her lap blanket like tiny flies—little snowflies. Just a passel of fly-flakes. She could make it through the pass. Pa always says a person can make good of any situation.

"You might cut two hours out of the trip, but you risk getting stuck or worse yet, busting a wheel or an axle. That lane is hard to navigate in good weather—"

"I'll get through." Her hand rested on the package. Mother wouldn't have sent her out in a snowstorm unless her father needed this medicine.

Joseph swept his hat off and wiped his brow. "Someday someone will come along and make those stubborn feet of yours want to follow. But I sure pity that gent's toes before you learn the step."

She chuckled. "You're not bad lookin' from up here. You might even be powerful handsome if you ever took a razor to those whiskers you call a beard." She laughed as deep crimson spread across his face like a signpost telling of his adoration for her.

He bent forward, resting on his strong forearms, his voice low and masculine. "Most girls tell me I'm handsomely appealing."

She knew that to be the truth. She couldn't figure why he bothered looking her way. She bent down and cupped her hand lightly on his upturned cheek. "Don't forget your promise. Find Doc."

"I'll hunt him down like a hound on a coon; don't you worry about that. Doc will get your message before nightfall."

Joseph's word was as good as the US Treasury. She never held much store in the prating tongues of the townsfolk. So she'd not miss anything losing their friendship. She had the friend that mattered. She slapped the reins. "Giddup."

If the townsfolk want something to gawk at, she'd oblige. "Yah!"

Her six white horses picked up the pace to a trot. She gave the clucking sound and with heads arched, her horses went into a high-stepping gait. The ground beneath the wagon pounded their rhythmic beat.

"Yeehaw, Collina, you show 'em." Joseph hooted.

She grinned. Every storeowner's nose was pressed to the window pane.

The harness and breast plate buckles jingled in unison like bells on Santa's sleigh. The ice and snow wasn't so bad. The ground was soft, and taking the lane meant she wouldn't have to endure the townspeople's gawking stares. Like Joseph, Pa had warned her not to, said you never know what's lurking around a bend in the lane, but Pa hadn't heard the townsfolk's new song about them, either.

She burrowed into her wool collar. The snow blanketing western Kentucky had put everyone in a bad spirit. January had started out cold and stayed that way. It being the first day of March, surely the worst was behind them. What more could happen?

The wind picked up as she made her way home, and so did the snow. Flakes blew about her team like dandelion seeds. She wished it was dandelion seeds and not a storm she had driven her horses into.

The horses strained against their harness, heads bent low to the ground, their strong hindquarters digging into the hill as they pulled the heavily laden wagon through the rutted and snow covered lane and up the steep hillside.

She couldn't see for the blowing flakes. Then just as suddenly as the storm had begun, the wind seemed to sweep the snowflakes away. She could see now that the stars were just appearing in the new night, and through the scurrying clouds that swept the sky like grey ghosts, the soft, mellow rays of the full moon suddenly lit the snow-covered pathway before her with a luminous glow. The words of Matthew 17:20 came to mind. "If ye have faith as a grain of mustard seed, ye shall say unto this mountain, remove hence to yonder place; and it shall remove; and nothing shall be impossible unto you." Lord, please get me and my team home safely is all I'm asking. But if You feel like moving something, please take this smallpox plague off the McConnells' shoulders.

The old vagrant Mother and Father had fed and clothed during the winter months gave the McConnells the smallpox. That old vagrant who lost his home and family after the Civil War always wintered in the McConnell's sharecroppers' cabin. Mother nursed him and Father buried him. Mother said she'd do no different even if she had known the outcome. Nine of the McConnells had contracted the pox. Only she and Mother had proved immune.

She hunched her shoulders to ward off another blow from the chilling wind.

What is the matter with me? Mother always said never to look back at trouble or else it was sure to follow you around like a long tail to a hound dog!

The left front wheel of the wagon rolled into a rut with a jolt. "Whoa, Daisy. Easy, Jude." Collina braced her boots against the bumper panel, her lap blanket falling to the floor. Daisy fell to her knees, then Jude. She could feel the hay on the wagon shift. Daisy neighed, whipping her head from side to side, fighting to free her front leg from the crevice.

Collina jumped down from her high seat and worked her way to the lead mare.

Daisy's nostrils glowed red in the darkness. Collina blew on her hands, willing her cold fingers to become nimble, and tried to loosen the taut leather straps. Daisy snorted, neighing her fright to the others, and fought to free herself.

She heard an answering neigh, then a man rode up.

"What—"

"You hurt?" A pair of strong, hardened hands wrapped themselves around hers. "Are you hurt?"

The wind whipped away her words of gratitude as a blowing snow squall peppered her eyelashes. The stranger wore brown trousers and leggings tucked in his shiny black boots. A uniform with brass buttons, collar, cuffs, and an epaulet in yellow gold that matched the brass eagle insignia on his shoulder straps temporarily mesmerized her. She glanced up. He scowled back.

Her smile wilted like last year's roses, replaced with a grimace to match his. "Just who are you, and why are you riding Pa's stallion?"

"Guess that means you're not hurt," the man yelled over the howling wind. "Can you hold the harness taut?"

She nodded. He grasped the slippery strap, then motioned for her to take his place. Daisy, feeling the slackened pressure, struggled to rise, thrashing out wildly with her foreleg. Collina clung on, digging her fingernails into the wet leather.

"You've got as much strength in those arms of yours as a fly does to lift an elephant."

The wagon moaned, swaying and twisting like a ship lost on a billowing wave. Flakes of timothy hay flew about their heads. She coughed, spewing fragments of the hay from her mouth. Another of her horses reared and the front wheels bounced from the force, causing pressure on the shafts of the last four horses.

"Get out of here," he yelled.

"No!"

The man's large hand gripped her shoulder like an iron vice and shoved her nearly two yards across the mud and snow.

A groan escaped her. She'd hit the ground hard. Her tongue tasted blood from a gash in her lip. She stumbled to her feet, wincing with pain.

The man threw his hat to the ground. His straight dark hair shone blue black in the moon's rays. Placing his broad shoulder underneath the cross bars, the glint of his steel knife shone in the moon's light.

"A knife? Don't cut that harness. It's from London, England!"

The soldier glanced up.

She gasped at the boldness in his eyes. The blade of his knife gleamed in the moonlight at her to beware. Recalling her shotgun on the floorboards of the wagon, she inched toward it. Daisy jumped to her feet.

"Shove that rock behind the front wheel…Good, now you take the mare and bring me back that gelding."

He hooked up Jude, kicking the rock away from the front wheels. "Yah! Yah!" He guided horses and wagon safely onto the high side of the lane. "Only right thing you did was hitch up enough horses to pull this overburdened wagon."

He hitched Daisy to the one remaining strap, then retrieved his hat. The inside lead rein dangled like a disjointed rudder on a ship.

"Thank you for your help, mister." She marveled at his tenacity. He could have ignored her scream. Charles Dana Gibson could have acquired his inspiration for his Gibson Man from him. His cavalier pride was as evident as the coat he wore proudly about his broad shoulders.

"Franklin Long of the 1st Volunteer Cavalry, ma'am, at your service." He swept his cavalry hat off his head.

That didn't say much about his trustworthiness. She reached into her buckboard and cradled the shotgun in her arms. "And where were you heading with our stallion?"

His eyes sparkled into hers. "Looking for you, ma'am. Say, just how old are you?" He could barely contain his humor. "Your mother was worried you might have gotten yourself in trouble; she gave me permission to ride the stallion when Doc Baker told me to fetch you."

"She did? Our home's under quarantine. How do you know Doc?"

"We were on the same polo team back in Long Island. Only, seems I've been enlisted by Doc Baker as a medical dispatcher for the McConnells."

Looks like Doc came a day early. That should please Mother. She placed the rifle back onto the wagon floor. After all, if he wanted to do her harm, he'd have tried to by now.

Franklin, hands akimbo, studied her. "Your lip is bleeding a little, right there."

"If you recall, I encountered a nasty fall." Her hands felt gritty. She wiped them on her riding skirt.

Iron black brows knitted together; a half-smile teased the corners of his mouth.

"Here," he said, extending his handkerchief. "A young girl like you shouldn't be out alone."

"I'm old enough."

"I apologize for that tumble I gave you." His fingers wrapped around her hand, as if seeking solace for his actions. "Your hand is cold. Take my gloves."

He was too forward to suit her. She yanked her hand away. "I'm fine."

"Couldn't be helped…you did a foolish thing taking this lane tonight."

"I cut two hours off going this way."

"Good thing Doc warned me not to expect the expected from you."

It was on the tip of her tongue to call him a liar. Doc Baker would never say such a thing about her—would he? The gall of this man. "I almost made it. This was the last big hill. After this one I'd have been home in half the time it would take going down Haggerman Road."

"I'd just hate to see that pretty head of yours crushed beneath your wagon bed." Franklin's thick brows arched in deep angles above his troubled eyes. He raked his fingers through his hair. "You've got more gumption than most men I know. Now, I need to get you home, girl. Take the stallion. I'll bring the wagon."

"Quit referring to me as a girl. I'll have you know I'm full grown."

"Sure, kid. Doc Baker wrote me how hard it's been. How you and your mother have been doing all the work on your farm. I'll stay on until I get my orders. You're going to need help now that your father—"

"Do you even know what you're volunteering for? Lincoln freed the slaves some time ago. It's not the glamorous Old South of yesteryears and hardly as adventurous as riding off to some exotic country in a shiny uniform."

His mouth contorted into a grimace. Collina met his scowl with one to match. "Then there's the smallpox. Some believe I'm a carrier. Even after Doc explained to everyone in town about smallpox, people still part like the Red Sea whenever I walk down Main Street. I can't blame them. Smallpox leaves terrible pit marks on your face. No, you go back to your make-believe war and allow the rest of us to live in the real one."

Her hand gripped his handkerchief. She had the very thing that would crumble that proud and arrogant face. "Here's your handkerchief, Mr. Long. But are you sure you want it back? Some of my blood's on it."

His eyes turned an icy steel-blue color.

She shivered. She'd hate to meet that gaze when he was toting a gun. His fingers wrapped around her hand and she felt the strength of them.

"Yes, some of your blood is on it." He lifted the soiled cloth to his lip. His eyes never left her face. He wiped his mouth. "Girl, you've got a lot to learn. Now, get on this horse. I'll follow you with the wagon."

Her shotgun was in that wagon. She didn't know this stranger well enough to leave him with her team and a loaded shotgun. She turned to climb onto the seat. He restrained her from mounting the wagon.

"Let go of me." All she could sniff was his aftershave, which reminded her of what she must smell like, thanks to her horse. Her arm felt like it was caught in a vice. She kicked him in an effort to free herself. What has he got for arms, lead? "Let me go this instant!" She kicked him again.

"Ow!" He let go of her arm. "Get on that horse, or I'll place you on him myself. You can ride, can't you?"

She swung at him. He ducked, holding her at arm's length. "I see I've got my hands full of one spitfire tonight."

"You're a bully. Picking on a defenseless—" She kicked him again.

"Ow...defenseless...you?"

She took the remaining steps to Raymar at a run and jumped into the saddle.

"Just as I suspected, you straddle a horse like a man." Bending over, he rubbed his leg. "And you have a wallop like a boxer. Now go. I just hope you're not too late."

"Late?" She'd totally forgotten. "The medicine." She galloped Raymar toward the wagon, grabbed the package and tucked it into her coat, then turned Raymar sharply toward the lane. He did a half-rear.

The clamor of her horse's hooves matched beat for beat the pounding of her heart. Was that soldier being overly alarmed? Still, if Doc had asked a perfect stranger to fetch her back to Shushan, something must be seriously wrong.

The moment Collina entered the house; she realized why she had felt uneasy earlier in the day. A heavy foreboding hung in the air. The large oak doors of her parents' chambers rested partly open. She gave them a thrust and stepped through. In the kerosene lamplight, Mother's big mahogany furniture etched jagged shadows across the Indian rug; the fire on the stone hearth shone crimson hues of light. Collina crossed the small parlor and entered the bedroom quarters. Like silent sentries, the McConnells stood around their parents' big four-poster bed.

Her mother's walnut-colored hair tinged with silver was swept into a coiffure. A wan smile creased her lips. She walked toward Collina with a regal poise that always flowed invisibly about her countenance, that impeccable grace that always claimed recognition.

"Collina," her mother whispered. "Your father's been asking for you."

Doc Baker's graying hair appeared more silver in the lamplight, and the shadows etched deep lines around his forehead and beneath his eyes, making him appear older than his forty-odd years. Taking the stethoscope off her father's chest and clicking the earpiece out of his ears, he rested them around his neck. "Did Franklin find you?"

Collina nodded. Pa looked so pale, so tired.

"Good. Your father's sleeping now." He slapped his bag shut and started toward the open door, then stopped, glancing toward her mother.

"His heart's worn out, Maggie, too much for it to handle, what with the sickness. Told him before to stop harboring every tramp from here to the Tennessee line." His voice quivered, then grew gruff. "I told Ben, I warned him, he needed a rest. Told him the work would always be there, but he might not."

"He's a hard one, my Ben, could never stay still for long."

"I'll be downstairs if you need me."

"You children go with Doc Baker. I'd like to talk to Collina alone," her mother said.

Collina felt like someone had punched her in the gut. She blinked away her tears, hurried to the large brick fireplace, and laid a birch log on the hot ashes. A popping noise, then a meowing wail followed as dying embers encircled its prey with hungry fingers, consuming the white parchment with an unquenchable appetite.

"What…what happened? Father appeared in good spirits when I left."

"A blood clot somewhere caused it."

Her father stirred.

"Come, child." Maggie rose tiredly from the large Bentwood. "Death never waits on convenience."

"Pa?" Collina bent low toward the still form.

Her father's eyes opened, fluttering for a moment. His lips worked their way into a crooked grin. "You got that hay and grain from the McWilliams okay?"

"With the usual measure of trouble thrown in."

His lips creased into a smile. "It's the pepper sprinkled on our table meat that gives it flavor. What's the date? Are we still in February or—"

"No, Father, it's March and would you believe, I just rode our whites through what felt like a blizzard."

"It'll not last. Hard times never do…Hardened people…nursed on God's Word…endure. Collina, above all, ye must take up the armor… the shield of faith…to quench the fiery darts of the wicked one…"

"Father, you're going to lick this—"

"My journey's done…I'll be…present with the Lord soon." His lips struggled to form the words. He coughed. "But yours is yet to be. Your mother, she'll have a lot to do…with tending to your younger brothers and sisters." He forced his eyes to stay open, breathing deeply. "You could manage, Collina, without me. You turning just sixteen worries me, but then you were born old. Like my dear departed father fulfilled his vision and I be the product, I knew when I first laid eyes on your wee face you'd be my Joan of Arc, my Esther of Shushan."

She swallowed. Painful tears blurred her vision. She blinked, willing them to retreat. They fell, unheeding her wishes.

His forefinger touched one tear as it lay on her chin, then stroked one long dark curl. "I'm sorry, lassie. I'm putting a lot on such thin shoulders." Her pa gasped for air, his mouth making a hissing noise. He coughed. Mother brought him to a sitting position. "We've come through worse. Promise me, never forget Shushan. You understand, daughter?

"Oversee the fields and the breeding, and not allow…the legacy of Shushan to end." His eyes closed.

Was Pa dead?

His eyelids quivered like a window shade blown by a breeze. His dark eyes penetrated hers, seeing into her soul. "Our Lord will walk with ye, directing ye."

"But why not Chester or Jessie?"

"Chester's married and his place is with his family," her mother interceded. "Jessie's just fifteen and Robert's thirteen, both are too young and headstrong for the job."

"They can take over when they're mature enough, if you think they can handle the farming and the breeding. But Shushan, it's more than a place…" Ben gasped for air.

"Pa, I—"

"Daughter, I always told you, you should have been a boy. What with all that ambition, you could have been someone…Maggie." He placed a hand on his heaving chest. "Who blew the lamp out? Everything's so dim." His hand waved the air and her mother grasped it gently, guiding it to her lips.

"My darling Maggie, what…would I have…ever done…without you? I'll love ya always."

"Yes, my darling, and I'll always love you." Maggie's tears fell on Ben's hand unnoticed. "Yes, my love, you go home now, we'll be together soon."

Collina stumbled out of the bedroom, feeling more than seeing her way down the stairs. Doc was saying something. She felt his hand on her shoulder.

"Collina, did you notice? I had Robert take down that yellow flag. If the McConnells can lick the smallpox, they can lick anything."

"Pa's dead."

"I know. There wasn't much hope," Doc said.

Collina blinked back her tears. Franklin stood next to Doc. He glanced away, but not before she saw the pity in his eyes.

"Why didn't you tell me?" She glanced down at her hands. "I guess it was best this way."

"Collina." Doc gently shook her. "Franklin is offering you his services until he receives his orders. He's willing to work for a bed and his meals. That is, until Roosevelt sends for him. But that could be six months down the road."

She felt the knot in her throat growing. She dared not speak. She nodded and fished in the large pockets of her riding shirt for that hankie, but all she could find were a few bits of grain. She stared down at them. They're all dried up. No use to anyone.

"Here." Franklin held out his linen. Her fingers again felt the warmth of his.

"I'll tell you, Franklin," Doc said. "You won't find a better family to stay with, never a harder working, long suffering..." Doc paused, clearing his throat. "Here, let me have that dang hankie."

Chapter 2

*C*ollina was deceiving herself to think anything would grow for her like it did for Pa.

The open grave, awaiting her father, gaped back at her.

Big Jim McWilliams and Joseph had come, so had Mary Baker Blaine, Doc's baby sister, and Mary's husband, Austin. Doc, his son Luke, and his daughter Rose; Jacob, his wife Prudence, even that new clerk named Clem was there standing next to Collina's sister Myra. Practically all of McDuff County and Emerald City, too, stood some fifteen feet or so away. Most likely afraid to come near me.

There stood Lawyer Farlin, big as life and twice as mean. What was he doing here? He'd sworn to get even with her father after he'd made a mockery of Farlin's crooked scheme to get a widow's homestead. Would he seek his vengeance on them now?

Franklin shuffled closer. His face immobile, like it was carved out of the very stone that marked Pa's grave.

Doc Baker motioned the townspeople closer. "The quarantine is over. There's no fear of contracting smallpox from the McConnells."

"What about Collina May? Isn't she a carrier?"

Joseph stepped before her and frowned at the man. Doc slapped his hat on his pants. "I told you people before, you can only contract smallpox if the person has the virus. It's been over three and a half weeks now since the last case. So come on in folks, don't be afraid. Say goodbye to Ben. He was a good neighbor to you all."

The preacher stepped forward, a giant of man who had earlier been a professional baseball player. Father and Mother had heard him preach once in Garner, Iowa. When Mother learned he was in town preaching on his way to Paducah, she had asked him to come.

Billy Sunday didn't believe in tiptoeing when it came to Christ's salvation message. Collina grinned. Sunday and her father had a lot in common.

"Your reputation is what people say about you. Your character is what God and your wife know about you.

"Mrs. McConnell told me Ben was a good provider and a God-fearing man. Ben had accepted his Savior, Christ Jesus, at a tent revival in Tennessee and had been healed from his affliction. Ben knew heaven awaited him. A lot of you here think to yourself, 'I'll accept Jesus later, when I get closer to the end...' But deathbed repentance is burning the candle of life in the service of the devil, and then blowing the smoke into the face of God.

"I have seen multitudes of saved people, but I have yet to see one who did not get his salvation by believing on Christ. Find the place in this world that comes the nearest to being like hell itself, and you will find it filled with those who are haters of Jesus Christ. You can't argue it. Go into saloons, gambling halls, and such places, and the people you find there are all haters of Jesus Christ, and the more of them you find, the more the place in which you find them will be like hell itself.

"Ben didn't allow the devil a foothold. He knew that temptation is the devil looking through the keyhole. Yielding is opening the door and inviting him in.

"Remember the parable of the sower in Luke 8:5? You farmers know how important the soil is to grow a crop. Well, this soil is the state of our heart, and the seed is God's word. How you deal with God's salvation message is up to you. You have choices. God doesn't take away your ability to make your own choice.

"Like that seed you sow and then water and care for. Well, this is your heart our good Lord is referring to." Billy slammed his fist into his palm. "Now let me read you something Ben wrote in his Bible along the margin about this parable. 'You must read your Bible, choose godly pursuits, your actions will show which book you are following, the Good Book or your I Will book. Be careful, your I Will book will take over your life faster than weeds in a wheat field.'

"Folks, Ben is right, your lifeline to heaven is proved by your choices and actions.

"But that on the good ground are they, which in an honest and good heart, having heard the word, keep it, and bring forth fruit with patience."

Pa's words echoed through Collina's mind: My journey's over, but yours is yet to be. Help me, Lord. Help me harvest a good crop of Your fruit like Pa did.

The wooden casket closed with a thump that reverberated through her body like lightning in a thunderstorm. Then her father was slowly lowered in the ground. Big Jim shouldered his bagpipes. The Irish patriotic song, "Minstrel Boy," that haunting melody, echoed throughout the hillside. Pa often sang the lyrics accompanying Big Jim's bagpipes during a funeral. "In the ranks of death…One faithful harp shall praise thee."

The first shovel load of dirt hit the casket. More followed. She heard Lawyer Farlin chuckle. Her younger sister Ruby sobbed. Collina wrapped her arm around her. Her littlest sister Bugie whimpered like an animal caught in a steel trap, jumped off Mother's lap, and held out her hands to Franklin. He swept her up, cradling her in his arms. She buried her face into his shoulder and sobbed.

Farlin's low chuckle was like a menacing snarl. Franklin glared back at him. The promises Collina made to her father echoed in her mind. "Do not let the legacy of Shushan end."

Collina greeted their friends, but felt she was performing her duties like a puppet in a minstrel show. A shiver started at her shoulders then passed down through her spine despite the heat radiating from the mammoth stone fireplace.

Farlin is not going to let his vendetta die with Pa. Then the lyrics of a song coming from the kitchen fell on her ears like the welcoming strains of a nightingale on a cold night just before dawn.

"That's Bugie, tell her to stop," her eldest sister Myra said. "People are trying to talk." Myra brushed aside a strand of blond hair that had managed to loosen itself from the cascade of curls carefully done up in a sweeping coiffure. Her powder-blue crepe de chine dress brought out the deep aqua of her eyes.

Collina rolled her eyes at her and whispered, "Where are you going so fancied up? Aren't you afraid of what the neighbors might think?"

Myra shrugged. "Father said he didn't want us to wear black at his funeral because death for a Christian wasn't the end, but the beginning. Second Corinthians 5:8, 'willing rather to be absent from the body, and to be present with the Lord.'"

The gigot sleeves and high broached collar with a bodice trimmed in white satin complemented Myra's creamy complexion. The wide satin sash that belted her stomach and streamed down the back of the dress enhanced her slender waist. "So Clem's taking you for a buggy ride later?"

"Yes, but…there goes Bugie again. Tell Mother to make her stop."

Collina hurried into the kitchen. She enjoyed her little sister's exuberance; however, others might have a difference of opinion, like Myra.

"Oh, a raccoon has a ringy tail, a possum's tail is bare. A rabbit has no tail at all, but a little old bunch of hair." Bugie's short legs waved the air, pumping out the words in rhythm to her swinging feet.

"Bugie darling, sing a little quieter."

Bugie picked up the ends of her starched Gretchen apron and flapped it. "Okay. I was getting tired anyways."

"Mother, Farlin was at the funeral."

"So? Maybe his conscience was prinking him."

Mother carefully kept her black velvet cuffs away from the hot iron skillet and the hissing bacon grease. She had a skill of staying clean, no matter what task she turned her hand to. "The McConnells will get through this, just like we've done other hardships before."

"Yes, Mother." Collina shoved back a lock of curls that had fallen over her forehead. Mother looked lovely. Her black serge dress discreetly peeked from beneath her embroidered bretell apron and made a soft rustling sound on the oak floor. She went about her chores, as if Pa was just in the next room, not buried in the family cemetery.

Bugie snatched another handful of beans, her hair moist from the steam of Mother's pots. "Got most of them snapped, see?" Bugie pushed aside one curly black ringlet. "Are all the people in our parlor going to eat with us?"

"Yes, and you are doing a fine job." Mother wiped a stray tear off her cheek.

Bugie's little face beamed up at her.

Mother bravely chooses to tuck aside her mourning for our sake. Collina choked back a sob.

"Oh, a raccoon has a ringy tail, a possum's tail is bare. A rabbit has no tail at all but a little old bunch of hair!" Bugie's curls bounced about her head to the tempo of her song.

The sudden hissing coming from one of Mother's pots sent her rushing to her stove before the boiling pot spilled its precious cargo.

A knock startled them, drawing their eyes toward the back door. "Come in."

"Howdy do. Hate to be bothering you at a time like this," Uncle Charlie said. "But we've got to start burning our tobacco beds, if we want a good crop."

"Well, tomorrow's Friday, and Monday I expect our lawyer will want to have Ben's will read. Some might need a time to mourn. Best make the crop planting a little later in the week," her mother said.

Collina chewed on her bottom lip. She'd never done that planting before. Wednesday would be the ninth of March. "How about Wednesday or Thursday?"

"Sure. I got Franklin Long bedded down in the sharecroppers' cabin. He tells me he knows about plantin' tobacco, so might be he'll lend an arm."

Bugie glanced up. "Uncle Charlie, are you really our uncle?"

Uncle Charlie smiled. "No child, but I'm your uncle in spirit."

"You staying for supper? You and your daughter are welcome," Mother said.

"No, ma'am, you've got plenty to feed as it is." Uncle Charlie looked at Collina. "I'll meet you Wednesday morning by the tool shed and we'll get started early." The door slapped its frame redundantly on Uncle Charlie's exit.

Her mother sighed. "I just don't know what's going to happen. This has become a torment. How am I going to raise you to be a young lady a gentleman will want to marry with you working in the fields like a hired hand?"

"Father spoke true; I should have been born a man."

"I don't want to hear such talk, you hear? God made you a woman for a reason."

"Mother, I think I know best."

"I see that temper of yours still flares out at anyone who says what don't suit you. I had hoped you and Myra would outgrow that, but I guess it will take the Almighty to tame it out of you." Her mother took her by the shoulder. "He made you a woman, and He made us all in His image, and He alone knows what's best for us. Now, I plan for you to go to Rose's debutante ball next month....Don't go making that face at me, daughter."

She missed Pa and she didn't like dances. Mother drew her close.

"You'll do fine. You see, I was a lot like you." She smiled. "I preferred riding horses and going against the norm. I taught Irish immigrants and slaves alike to read and write, not so popular back in the 1850s."

"But Myra says Doc Baker is going all out. That it'll rival the derby in popularity this year. Rose went all the way to New York to purchase her dress. And I don't have anything to wear."

"Your sisters will help. Ruby has a knack with the needle, even at her young age. She's going to become quite the little seamstress. That ball is over six weeks away. There's time."

"I'd rather muck stalls than be poked and led around by some man."

"I don't care if you stomp the ground like a Cherokee brave on the warpath; you're going to that dance. Get used to the idea."

"Humph. It looks to me like it's Farlin on the warpath for McConnells' scalps."

"Don't worry about him; we've got God on our side."

The noise from the parlor sent her mind spinning out of control. A passel of folks were looking for dinner, and she wasn't sure if God was fixin' on blessing her planting. What if she wasn't made of the right soil?

The clouds chased one another in befuddled disarray as the wind blew over the hilly countryside. Collina wrapped her red plaid scarf about her hair and tied it firmly beneath her chin. She would have to hurry; the afternoon shadows were growing long. Dusk was approaching, and the blackness of night would follow swiftly on its heels.

She lit the lantern Father kept inside near the barn door and looked about the whitewashed walls of the stable. Harnesses and breast straps hung neatly arranged on their pegs. The smell of saddle soap and leather, horseflesh, alfalfa, corn, and molasses intoxicated her nostrils. They were the smells she had grown up on, drinking like a babe its milk, the sweet flavor of abundance and of plentiful harvests, those smells that lingered on Pa's coveralls.

She reached for her mare's bit and for her saddle from its peg on the wall, then spotted the small leather pouch of Pa's that had lain alongside. He always kept the pouch close and usually wore it around his neck. He had probably removed it when he did the chores. They had been the last things he'd done before falling ill.

Why had God taken a father with nine children? What sin led Pa to this early grave? She'd been taught that God loved them, and according to Proverbs 3:6 He directs each Christian's life. How could a loving God do this? Pa's death made no sense, no sense at all. He read his Bible, prayed over the table and over his fields, what more could a man do to please God?

Collina snatched the pouch from its peg, feeling its contents. If this was God's doing, she wanted no part of Him! She wasn't close to being the Christian her pa had been, never would be. She'd show God what she thought of His love. Metal stirrup against her leather boot, she felt the solidity of her fluid movement as she sprang into her hunt saddle.

As she galloped across their land, the rustling trees swayed to the soundless voice of the wind that swirled the leaves and flakes of snow beneath her horse's hoofs into a whirlwind of flight. Magic snorted.

"Easy, girl." She stroked her horse's velvet-smooth neck.

The cornfield lay just ahead of her. Disheveled and rough, like an unmade bed, the harvested field stretched out before her. She dismounted, tying Magic's reins to a low-hanging branch before walking to the disarrayed rows of cornstalks. The broken and beaten stalks of corn lay crushed on the very soil that had once nurtured it. It was hard to believe that once straight and tall, they had thrived in the warm breezes and gentle rains of summer. Those were happy days.

The wind whistled about her form. She shivered, wrapping her scarf closer around her neck. The sun, taking its leave, lit the winter sky with one last glow of color. Deep aqua and fuchsias streaked across the horizon as its rays illuminated golden arches of light across a blackened border.

Bugie's only four, will she remember Pa? Collina sighed. Bugie would never know him like Collina had, sitting at his desk with the Aladdin oil lamp shining down on his figures, working over the accounts long into the night. Bugie would never hear his roaring laughter reverberate across the hillside, see his ruddy face and laughing eyes that were always merry, no matter how tired he may be. Never know his strong, yet patient hands encouraging, consoling, guiding.

"I can't stand it!" Her nails clawed with the rage of a wild animal at what remained of the broken corn stalks. "You did this. You did this," she screamed, looking up toward heaven. But only silence answered her accusations, a thickening, unbearable silence. She covered her ears and rocked to and fro.

"Why, oh why?" she cried. But there was no explanation to be found in the dark swaying forms of the trees probed by the chilling strokes of the wind. No explanation in the rows of lifeless stumps that had once known the greenness of life. The wind blew the trees above her, and withered leaves fell silently about her.

Here, I will scatter them here. She reached into her pocket for the pouch. Magic gave out a loud whinny, pricking her ears toward the direction of the path.

"Hello…who goes there?" a man's voice questioned.

On queasy legs she hastened to the edge of the cornfield. Magic neighed. Branches snapped and an answering neigh broke the stillness. A horse jumped a fallen log and crashed into the clearing.

"If you had stayed on the lane for another yard, you would have come out on the clearing made by Pa's wagons. Don't you see, you've taken a wrong turn?"

"When you've taken as many as I have, what's one more?" Franklin Long lifted a gloved hand to his hat, removed it, and was off Raymar in one sweep. His lips were smiling, but the brows above his troubled eyes told her he'd heard her scream. "You shouldn't be out here alone."

"I, I needed to check my girth." She lifted her leathers and adjusted the buckles up another notch. "There, see. It was loose."

"You'd best clean your face; your company might wonder what happened to you. At the funeral today, I couldn't help noticing you took the preacher's words pretty hard."

She swiped one cheek with her dirt-stained hand, and intertwined her fingers in Magic's mane with her other. "I'll just tell them I had a nasty fall."

His arm restrained her. "I meant to ask you; Shushan, that's a funny name for a farm."

She forced her voice to remain calm. "It's from the Bible, the book of Esther. Pa often quoted 8:6, 'For how can I endure to see the evil that shall come unto my people? or how can I endure to see the destruction of my kindred?'"

"Yes, I remember the story."

"Pa named our plantation Shushan on the eve of Lee's surrender to Grant to remind him of the destructive nature of war and how God alone could heal our land and our hearts."

He studied her. "Esther was the queen of King Ahasuerus. She took the chance of losing her title and her neck for her kindred…strange."

"All I remember was that Pa said we ought never to lose heart, and he'd quote Esther 9 something and told us not to forget, and I already have." Her voice broke. She closed her eyes tightly, blinking away hot tears.

"Look, I can help."

"What could you possibly say that could help me?"

His hand tightened firmly around her arm, forcing her to turn and face him.

"I envy you. You see, I never knew my parents. I lived in an asylum up in Cuba, Canada, until I was twelve. You couldn't be much older than I was when I lit out on my own."

She thrust her chin up. "I'll have you know I'm now sixteen."

"Really? You act more like you're ten."

"That's a big help." She reached for her stirrup. His hand wrapped around her arm, his concern evident.

"I know how confused and worried you must be. It's a big responsibility managing a spread like Shushan."

How could he know? How could this stranger understand what she was feeling? Pa was gone. How could she hope to fill his shoes? Her family was depending on her. Franklin's face contorted in agony, as if reading her thoughts.

"After all you're just a girl."

She tried to shake herself free of him. "I don't need your help. Let me go." His sympathy angered her. "How could you of all people know what I'm feeling? Why you don't know nothing about a—"

"Family?" He let her loose then. His square chin jutting out, his shoulders straight and unyielding, wearing his uniform like a knight would his armor.

"No. I mean, yes. Look, I don't know what I mean. I'm just sorry that you never had anyone. But how could you understand, not having a father is…" She gasped, reliving Pa's last breath, his eyes gleaming, unseeing into hers. "Dear God, help me."

The rough wool of his coat felt warm to her cold, wet cheek as she buried her head in his shoulder and cried. The ache for Pa crushed her like a boulder. Never to have known Pa, never to have had a family that cared for you and you for them, never to have known that love, would be a worse fate.

"Here." He placed something soft into the palm of her hand.

"I see it's a fresh one." She wiped her eyes with the cloth.

"Keep it. You need it more than I."

"I'm sorry. I'm not usually much of a crier. I—"

"I know; anyone who would come all the way out here." A flicker of comradeship lit the depths of his eyes. "Don't worry. Your secret is safe with me. I should have said something earlier. I'm always too late to be of much help to anyone." Franklin turned and grabbed a branch off a nearby tree. He broke it, the sound echoing in the night air. "I should be getting you home. It's much too cold and damp for you to be out."

"I'm not going back, not yet," She felt for the pouch in her pocket. "You go ahead. I'll be along shortly."

"I'm not leaving you here."

Her heart leaped against her rib cage. Why was she drawn to him? But she was not the only McConnell. Her youngest brother, Scott, followed Franklin's steps about the large house like a lost puppy, and little Bugie had more than once climbed into his lap. They knew so little about him. Was it true, had he grown up in an asylum? "Did you contract smallpox while in the asylum?"

He hesitated, pushing his bottom lip forward in thought. "Yes, a smallpox epidemic hit while I was there, but I never got it. I had a natural immunity, like you."

"You've probably noticed Robert's face. I don't know why he got it so hard when the others hardly have a scar. Bugie had only one pox on the heel of her foot. Is that the way it was in the asylum? You can't imagine how hard Mother and I had to work to keep Bugie in bed. Doc said the young'uns had a harder time recuperating."

Franklin reached up, wrestling another limb to the ground. He turned toward the empty field that lay beneath the star-drenched sky.

Only the wind running its fingers through the trees causing their branches to chatter like dried-up old bones broke the silence. She listened to the barren sounds, the blankness, dark and deep, the solitude of a winter's eve drawing them together, comrades of fate.

"Who was it, a girl friend, someone special that you lost?"

A smirk curved around the hard lines of his mouth. "Yes, a little girl. Your little sister, Bugie, brought the memory of Sara back. She was your sister's age when she died. She liked to pretend I was her brother. Hatfield, the superintendent of the asylum, didn't like the urchins, as she called us, getting too close to each other. So she put Sara in the left wing of the asylum.

"When the smallpox hit, I was sent to her ward to help tote out the dead, and that's where I found her. Her sweet face covered with hideous, oozing sores. The only comfort I could give her came after midnight. When the nurses and staff were asleep, I'd tiptoe in and hold her. She died that way, wrapped in my arms. Our funerals are not like yours. They used barley bags for the little ones. They made me put her in that bag, carry her to the hole I'd dug and lay her in it alongside the others."

"But some of you must have had parents, sisters or brothers, someone that cared." She cringed before his stark gaze.

"Yes." A bitterness she had not heard before encased his words. "Worlds apart are we." His face contorted into an agonizing pain, like a person who'd just been shot in the gut. He moaned. "How I long to be rid of this devil of the past. I've seen what hate can turn a man into. What that preacher said, do you believe him? Could I be letting the devil have his way with me?"

She rested her hand on his shoulder and whispered, "Go on."

"There were two hundred or so of us. Some retarded, others deranged, a few mangled by the war, but the rest were us half-breeds, unwanted and rejected children. It wasn't uncommon to find a basket on the doorstep with a dark-skinned infant inside. Hatchet Face told me my half-breed mother had handed me over to them when I was two, said she had consumption and couldn't keep me.

"There were always a lot of Indians roaming the streets, homeless, broke and drunk, eating what the dogs wouldn't. I'll never forget one of them. She came every Sunday and hung a trinket over the doorstep. My friend, David, said it was meant to ward off evil spirits, that it was sacred. She was asking the Great Spirit to protect those who dwelled there. Mike, David, and I started to watch for her.

"Tall and thin, she'd be wrapped in her colored blanket. Her thin moccasins moved slowly, and I often wondered why she bothered to walk the three miles of winding trails to the asylum. Then, when I lost David and Mike to the typhoid, she stopped coming." Franklin shrugged. "Most likely she got the fever. But I don't even know if what Hatchet Face said was true or not."

"Why?"

"Hatchet Face was mean. She did and said things to break your spirit. If she could claw your heart out, I believe she would. After David and Mike died, every night she'd come to my bed just after lights went out, her breath reeking with whisky. 'You'll be next,' she'd whisper. 'I'll be sewing thread over ye face closing that burlap tight around ye ugly head soon.'"

Collina shuddered.

"Fear's no longer your enemy when you've bunked with him as many times as I have."

Her fingers clasped the leather purse. "You weren't too late for Sara; you were there to give your love. And I'm grateful to you for sharing your story. It's not too late for you to stop allowing the devil to have his way with your life. And it's not too late for me to ask God's forgiveness for listening to that devil. I looked up in the Bible what Pa said just before he died and still I feel like a rotten apple wastin' away in my grief! 'Wherefore take unto you the whole armour of God, that ye may be able to withstand in the evil day…Above all, taking the shield of faith wherewith ye shall be able to quench all the fiery darts of the wicked.'"

The cold, damp ground worked a chill through her knees to her shoulders. She clasped her fingers tightly, her tears wetting her cheeks. "Lord, forgive me my sins, I ask this of Thee. I do believe You died on that cross of wood to pay the penalty for my sins so I could receive peace from my sorrow. And this be my peace, that I will see my pa again in a life never-ending, filled with contentment and joy. Amen."

She stood and turned her face toward the full moon. "No, it wasn't a coincidence you coming here. Pa always quoted Matthew 17:20, 'If ye have faith as a grain of mustard seed...nothing shall be impossible unto you.'" She drew out Pa's leather pouch and the seeds that lay within. "These were a gift to my pa from his dad who left everything he loved in Ireland to give his son a better life in America. You made me realize that Pa left a little of himself in everything he touched."

Reaching for his hand, she laid the seeds in his palm. "Here, you take them. I was going to throw them away. I don't understand what Pa meant about not letting the legacy of Shushan end, because, truth be known, I don't know what that legacy is?" She swept her hand over the desecrated cornfield. "Is Shushan meant to be bigger than this?" She shrugged. "The answer will come, I've got a feeling, when I need to know.

"If you hadn't stopped by, I would have thrown those mustard seeds away. I realize now, I would have thrown away what Pa believed in. I needed someone to point me in the right direction. You were God's messenger. But what I don't understand is why did God send you?"

Chapter 3

The McConnells' mourning had ended. The reading of Pa's will and testament went according to everyone's wishes. Each child received a token of Pa's love, and Mother got the house, all the acreage, and out buildings. The McConnells were pleased and accepted Pa's wishes. Or so everyone thought until Clem, who'd been waiting in the foyer to take Myra on a buggy ride, stormed into the room.

Red-faced and swearing, Clem blurted, "There ought to be a law against giving a widow all this and not sharing the wealth with her children!" He reached for Myra's hand.

She pushed him away. "Pa was right to give Mother what they worked together for."

Clem threw up his arms and stormed out the front door.

That was last evening's problems; this morning a whole new set of worries stood before Collina.

She sighed. Now came what she dreaded, planting the tobacco crop. She thought baring her soul beneath that moonlit night in the cornfield would give her supernatural power. Instead, it felt like the devil had stepped up his attack on her.

Franklin wasn't used to taking orders from a woman, or as he put it, a girl. He had an opinion on how everything should be done, and she could sense her brothers doubting her authority. Who would oversee Shushan when Franklin rode off into the sunset if her brothers didn't think she could handle the job?

Now, what all did she need to plant the tobacco beds? She quickly checked them off her list: rakes, hoes, seed, and cheesecloth. She just hoped she purchased enough. Cheesecloth was vital in protecting the tobacco seeds, which resembled finely ground pepper.

Franklin strutted out of the kitchen chewing on a piece of bacon. Thank God for Uncle Charlie, whose credibility no one dared argue. He had burned the beds yesterday.

The kitchen door slammed sharply behind Uncle Charlie. "Robert, go to the tool shed and find as many rakes and shovels as you can. Now, I want one of you men at each corner."

Men? Where did Uncle Charlie want her?

The smoke from the embers of the fire from yesterday sent up ghostly spirals in the cool morning mist. Collina, Scott, and Franklin started at the far end of the section, and Uncle Charlie, Robert, and Jessie started at the other. The boys wanted a race. The last to reach the middle would have to feed the livestock. Mother came out with her mustard plants.

Scott's blond head looked up for a minute. "You say go, Mother."

Joseph's large shoulders appeared around the corner of the tobacco shed. "Need any help?"

"I claim Joseph for our side," Robert yelled.

"That's not fair," Scott said.

"Uncle Charlie," Mother said, "why don't you help me with the mustard plants, and leave the raking to younger backs?"

"Does that appear fair to you all? Collina, what do you think?" Uncle Charlie looked at her for approval.

Collina troubled her bottom lip. Joseph was worth two in the fields, and neither she nor Scott knew if Franklin ever held a rake, let alone knew how to use one. He could be all talk. Part of her wished he was. "Let's give it a try."

The grueling and backbreaking work consumed their energy. Only the sounds of the big iron rakes running through the smoking ashes and their heavy boots crunching the ground beneath filled the cool air as the morning shadows disappeared into high noon. Collina had never seen her brothers work so hard. But Franklin surprised her the most. She and Scott were actually slowing him down.

Belle rang the dinner bell, creating a welcomed reprieve.

Robert and his crew were first to reach the kitchen steps. He opened the door for Belle and cried, "My back has a kink in it. Belle, do me a favor and rub it."

"You can do your own rubbing, Robert Dennis. I toted all this wood in myself. Someone forgot to fill the crib."

"Here comes soldier boy," Robert whispered.

"He's not a bad guy," Jessie said. "In fact, he's a hard worker."

"Day's not over yet, we'll just see what he's made of," Robert said. "One thing's for sure. I ain't losing to a dandified soldier, a boy, and a girl."

Collina smirked. "We'll see about that."

Joseph was silent, his large hands flexing and relaxing themselves.

"I hope the three of you lose your shirts." Belle turned from the stove, using her wooden spoon as a teacher would a pointer to an unruly student. "You should be ashamed of yourselves."

Joseph slapped the table with his hand. The noise echoed like a Cherokee war drum. "You going to let a half-breed beat you?"

"What?" Jessie said.

"He couldn't say for sure himself, cuz he doesn't know his heritage," Joseph said.

"You don't know for sure," Collina said.

"He's an orphan; just ask Doc Baker." Joseph's eyes were burning a hole through her face.

When the shuffling of Scott's and Franklin's feet came from outside the kitchen door, Collina put a finger to her lips. How had Joseph found out about Franklin? He'll think I told him.

"Sis, you shouldn't work so hard. Your face is sweaty. Just look at your hands. Your nails are all split." Compassion lit Belle's soft blue eyes. "I'll feed your team first."

"Belle," Robert complained.

"Don't start with me, Robert."

"Belle," Jessie said, "can I help it if I got picked for Robert's team? I'm still a growing boy, and a starving one at that."

Robert's face turned red as he watched Franklin enter the room.

Belle placed the food on the table. "All right, it's every man for himself." Belle stepped out of the way as her brothers rushed to the table. "Prayers first!"

Collina said grace and Franklin snatched up the food with zeal and accuracy. He slapped down chicken and biscuits on her and Scott's plates.

"Golly," Jessie groaned. "He can even eat better than us."

"Mmmm," Franklin muttered between mouthfuls. He stared at Joseph and Robert chewing thoughtfully. "Ah, do you boys want to arm wrestle for the last biscuit, or do you want to hand it over here nicely?"

Robert's pockmarks showed white next to his angry red face. He bounced up. Joseph shoved him down.

"I'll wrestle ya." Joseph rolled up the sleeve of his shirt, displaying his muscular biceps. "But we need to talk first. I want to wrestle for more than a biscuit."

Joseph and Franklin were eyeing Collina. She'd been caught consuming an oversized mouthful of food. "So I'm hungry." She bit into a piece of chicken, then realized they were still staring at her. "I don't know what mischief you two have concocted, but if you're not outside in ten minutes then you both forfeit the bet and get to do all the chores, including the pigs."

"Come on, Joseph, we can talk privately in the parlor," Franklin said.

She gulped down a glass of milk, watching their retreating backs.

"Joseph has a terrible temper and is forever picking fights," Belle said. "Are you sure Franklin won't get hurt? After all, he is our guest."

Before Collina could make it into the parlor to break up any potential tussle, Joseph and Franklin were back in the kitchen.

Franklin rolled up his sleeve, his expression masked, staring at Joseph, who sat across from him. They locked their fingers in a crushing grasp.

Collina rested on her rake, breathing in a deep breath of the pungent odor of burnt grass and fresh crisp air. Franklin didn't pause, his rake scraped through the ashes and red dirt, his legs swaying with a grace, almost a oneness with the earth. Where did he learn to work the ground like this?

She flexed her wrists and leaned over the rake, pushing it through the ground. Just a little further and they would be to the halfway mark. Mother's mustard seeds were planted and she had filled the sprinkling cans. They stood waiting, like tin dolls, along the edge of the field, running over with their precious seeds. She couldn't help but feel proud of what they'd accomplished. Yes, they were going to finish today after all. Franklin ran to pick up his can. Her brothers scrambled to grab their cans brimming over with the little pepper-like seeds.

Long sheets of cheesecloth, which would protect the seeds from harsh sunlight, heavy rains, and possibly late frost, were spread over the newly sown field and fastened firmly in place. The young seedbed stretched out in the dusk of the new evening like a white shrouded mummy against the painted horizon. The first planting of the year was behind them.

"We won! We won! Hurray!" Scott said, his young face beaming with joy. He looked up at Franklin with newfound admiration. "Where did you learn to use a rake like that?"

Franklin gave Scott's blond head a tussle. "In the summers, I was hired out on a farm when I was little."

"How did you learn to arm wrestle like that? Boy. You sure impressed Robert. Say, what did you and Joseph wrestle for?"

"Scott, don't you ever get tired of asking questions?" Collina said.

Franklin, with a twinkle in his eyes, said, "I'll tell you later, Scott. Now, we'd best give your brothers a hand—I feel bad about this."

"Why? We won fair and square," Scott said.

"It wasn't a fair match. See, I didn't know."

"Didn't know what?" Collina aksed. "I worked just as good as the two of you."

He laughed. "That's just it. You surprised me. I thought for sure you wouldn't be able to hold up and here you gave me a run for. Why do you think I worked so hard? I couldn't let a girl beat me."

"Why you—"

"Sis, you'd better not."

She lifted her arm to him like she would to one of her brothers. Franklin caught it, his grasp firm. She was struck anew of how blue his eyes were, as deep as the sky. The crimson rays of the setting sun shrouded his broad shoulders like a cloak, and she noticed his bronze arm and hand that wrapped her wrist.

"I hear there's a dance at Doc's, you going with anyone?" His voice was low and soft, almost musical. His eyes held hers.

"Collina? Who'd want to go with her? She can't dance." Scott laughed.

She blinked.

Avoiding Franklin's face, she wished she could dig out that stone her foot had found and hide in that hole.

"I would," Franklin said. "How about it?"

Her pride wounded, she retorted. "Scott's right; I don't like dances."

"You'll like this one."

For the first time in her life she wished she could dance and do all the things girls her age accomplished easily. How could she tell him the truth—she didn't know the first thing about dancing. "I have plans."

Robert was there with Jessie. "I knew she'd say that," Jessie said.

Robert dug his fists deep into his pockets. "Go on, Jessie; tell the rest."

Jessie looked from Robert to her. "Why is it I always get the shoveling detail? Look-a-here, Sis, we think you should oblige one of them. Who will it be? At least we're giving you a choice. That's more than what Franklin and Joseph were going to do."

Joseph, smiling broadly, rotated his arm carefully. "Best arm wrestle I've had for some time. Hate to be a poor sport, but if you want to go with me, I'd be honored."

"I could nail the coffin closed on the lot of you."

"Now, don't get your war paint on; it was purely innocent. See, I was sure I'd win," Joseph said. "How did I know Franklin had an iron arm? So who's it going to be, me or him?"

She could hardly talk over the thumping of her heart. "I guess Franklin. It would be unsporting of me to renege." She clinched her fists at her sides. "But I've got something here I need to give my—"

"Sis, this time it's not our fault." Her brothers took a wayward step away from her.

"Sis," Belle said, running forward. "Rose Baker is here and asking to see you."

"Me?"

"Least you're going to Rose's ball." Joseph smiled. "Now, don't let her back out of it, Franklin. Save me a dance, Collina."

"Dance?" She squeaked out. Oh, I just wish I could box his ears proper. Franklin laughed, his deep baritone filtering through the air with blithesome gaiety.

The idea of being led around by either of them was unnerving. Men, what did the female population see in them? Walking to the house with Belle by her side, she said, "I'll find a way out of my promise somehow."

"Not this time, Sis, Franklin's not the type of man who will take your bullying."

"I have six weeks to think of something."

"Collina?" Rose placed a white-gloved hand to either side of her rouge-tinted cheeks, "Why is your face so red?"

"Do you know what Joseph and Franklin did? They arm wrestled— arm wrestled to see who would take me to your ball."

"Oh." Rose placed her gloved hand to her purple frieze wool coat with double-breasted buttons. "How barbaric. I can't believe Franklin would have a part in that."

"Believe it." Collina dismissed their boyish prank with her usual indifference. "What do you have on? It smells nice, doesn't it, Belle?"

Rose's hand went to her light brown hair that surrounded her heart-shaped face and ivory complexion, giving it a pat. "My new perfume from Paris, do you like it?"

"Yeah." Belle chuckled. "Sis could use some."

Rose's delicately arched brows rose in alarm. "I…see what you mean." Rose stepped away from her.

Collina chuckled. "Don't worry, Rose, my stench don't rub off that easy. Come in." They entered the kitchen and she closed the door behind them.

"It's good to have you back from Lady Augustine's Finishing School," Belle said.

Noise at the front entrance said her brothers had entered the house.

"Bring Franklin down a dry shirt," her mother said from the stairway. "The one he's wearing looks like it's been doused in the creek."

"I've got wash still on the line outside." Belle hurried out the back door.

"Sure, Mother," Scott said, and three pairs of heavy boots now climbed the stairway.

Walking through the entranceway, Collina nearly bumped into Franklin. She avoided the confrontation and yelled up the staircase. "Mother, we've got company. Rose Baker stopped by."

Franklin put a finger to his ear in mock alarm.

"Whatever." She shrugged him off and walked back into the kitchen, pumping the kitchen spigot with vigor. Cool water came bubbling forth. After filling a tall glass, she drank long gulps, ignoring the spills that fell past her lips to her chin. Then, taking water from the spigot, wiped it across her forehead. "That feels good. Would you like a glass of water, Rose? Some tea?"

Franklin rested his tired body on the walnut-finished entranceway, the clean shirt across one shoulder. He couldn't help smiling as he observed Collina and Rose unnoticed, one hand playing with the smooth, sweet-smelling bar of soap Maggie had brought him. Rose was impeccably dressed from the top of her tiny hat to the bottom of her shiny patent leather pumps. She was a tiny thing and barely came to his shoulders. Her New York creation fit her curves like the feathers on a dove.

Collina was the direct opposite. Tall and lanky, her oversized dress hung over her curves like clothes on a scarecrow. Yet, there was simplicity of style that surrounded her like a halo on an angel. Her hair shown like the wing of a black bird, glimmering blue-black, and her sparkling green eyes shone with vitality of spirit that would thrill any knight. She reminded him of a young filly he'd train, full of fight, spirit and eagerness.

"Who is taking you to my ball?"

"I am," Franklin said, as he entered the kitchen.

Rose glided off her chair with one sweep.

Collina didn't break stride, not even recognizing he'd said anything. She placed her glass on the wooden counter and reached for a towel.

He was brought back to the issue at hand when Rose pinched his arm. "Ow..." Hadn't she ever seen biceps before?

"You...you mustn't work so hard. You'll be leaving if—well, I don't understand why you enlisted in Roosevelt's cavalry in the first place. You'd think Roosevelt had enough to do being Secretary of the Navy and not looking for a war." Her reddened lips pursed in pretended disapproval.

"Why do you stay here when Collina works you so hard?" she whispered. Her large liquid eyes stared back into his.

She would never understand. But he would try. "I enjoy work, Rose, the harder the better. I enjoy pushing myself to the ultimate physical experience and then going a yard farther." He tilted his head. "Now let me get a good look at you." His eyes were appraisingly frank. "You must be careful; don't get too close. I've not cleaned up yet, and I might get those lovely clothes of yours smelly."

Rose blushed.

Franklin hoped to see a bit of jealously playing across Collina's face.

Collina was saturating a small hand towel, totally oblivious to him and Rose. She rung it out and applied it to her face and neck, then sighed with satisfaction. "If I remember, Roosevelt wrote something about America expanding its horizons?"

Franklin smiled. "Exactly. 'No triumph of peace is quite so great as the supreme triumphs of war.'" He glanced at Rose. "If you recall, when

Teddy took the Secretary of the Navy position, he said, 'The diplomat is the servant, not the master, of the soldier.'"

Collina nodded. "The triumphs of war and then with—"

"The USS Maine sunk by an explosion in Havana Harbor, Teddy wrote us to be ready. We don't have a regimented uniform, not yet, but Teddy sent me a sketch of his uniform and what he wants his officers to wear."

They thought alike, he could feel a kindred spirit igniting with Collina. Rose was completely oblivious.

Collina frowned. "Put a shirt on, you'll catch your death. It's still too cold for that."

He reached for the towel. "Thanks, need to wash a bit before supper."

"That's my towel." She tried to wrestle it out of his hands.

"Why don't you come on out and join me. We can share the towel and wash up together."

Her glance swayed from the towel to his face. Her full lips pouted. She was losing the battle and didn't like it. "No. I, I'd rather stay here and keep Rose company. Let go."

"Rose wouldn't object, would you, Rose?"

Rose giggled. "A little soap wouldn't hurt you."

"Thanks, Rose, but I take my sponge baths alone," Collina said.

He stepped closer. She released the towel and stepped back.

"Then I'll be on my way." Her towel slung over his shoulder, he reached his hand toward her.

Collina jerked back, hitting the edge of the counter. "Ouch." She placed her hands in the small of her back; she'd hit the wooden edge hard. Her large green eyes swept his, as if trying to read his intentions. Shyness veiled her visage and she shoved him away.

"I was just trying to wipe away that smudge." Franklin placed his hand softly on her cheek, stroking an imaginary spot. "What's the date for your ball, Rose?"

Chapter 4

April 19, 1898

ollina didn't feel well. How was she going to get through the day? Every time Franklin got close to her, her heart fluttered like the wings on a canary. It was confusing. Her emotions had overtaken her good common sense. Myra had fallen in and out of love a half-dozen times. Collina never gave it a thought—until now. And to make matters worse, tonight was Rose Baker's debutante ball. Mother assured her this ball would become an evening she would never forget.

It would be memorable all right—a memorable nightmare with her making a spectacle of herself. She wanted Ruby to come. But Mother said Ruby couldn't attend any balls until her fifteenth birthday. Collina remained adamant. Stephen would be there, and he'd be a good person for her sister to get to know. So Mother had agreed.

Myra with Luke Baker, Belle and her beau, Bo, Ruby, and Collina and Franklin were going in Doc Baker's fine heirloom coach, and pulling it would be the best trotters in the state of Kentucky.

Collina hurried through the chores. Then came the final hours of preparation for the event the county had been talking about for months. Would her ball gown fit? What would she do if it did not?

The ten yards of taffeta clung fashionably to Collina's waist, sweeping gracefully to the floor. The mutton sleeves of silk moiré tapered down to her arms then fastened snugly about her slender wrists with pearl buttons. Her timid fingers followed the lace trimmed, boned bodice of Ottoman silk that dipped just above her bosom and met the silk moiré that ran around her waist. Standing before the mirror, a lady she didn't recognize reflected her image back to her. A lady with a sloping neck and shoulders adorned in a gown that dipped just above her bosom. "This is much too low." She lifted the soft silk folds of fabric about the bodice. What would Franklin think? "Oh my!" she softly gasped, envisioning his look.

"You're too simple for words," Myra said, coming through the door, swirling from one side, then to the other. Catching her eye, Myra said, "What do you think about my dress?"

"You know what I think. It looks perfectly gorgeous on you. Everything you wear looks beautiful."

Myra laughed, her voice rich in mirth. Thick, sooty lashes veiled her luminous blue eyes. The sea-blue taffeta flowed about her well-curved figure gracefully. A cascade of roses and foliage fell from her bare and tapered shoulders back and down the side, and long, pale cream gloves complemented the slender fingers they adorned.

Myra turned her gaze on Collina, placing one tapered finger on her full lips. "Ruby, we forgot about Collina's hair. We've got to hurry. Our escorts will be here any minute." Myra's talented fingers started to work at Collina's braids.

"Really, Sis, you're much too old to always go everywhere with your hair braided."

"Here, Myra," Ruby said, holding up a brush.

Myra gave the long dark tresses a fast brushing, which made Collina's thick hair fly about her face and neck.

"It'll be in my eyes," she complained, looking at Myra's golden locks she'd dressed into a pompadour in the front and taken up in a chignon at the back. It showed off her long, slender neck to perfection. She couldn't help envying Myra. "My hair isn't like yours. It's too thick."

"What I'd give for hair like yours." She brushed a strand of curls about her shoulders. "I wish Chester wasn't working two jobs besides working his own farm and could help us at Shushan." Myra hugged her. "So, you, my dear sister, could learn the art of becoming a potential bride to some deserving gentleman."

"Sarah wants Chester to add another room onto their house," Ruby said. "More likely he'll be taking Jessie and Robert over to help."

"Pa needed to have his sons before his daughters. I never thought it fair the way he had Collina working alongside of him in the fields," Myra said.

Collina surveyed herself critically. "No, Pa did the right thing. I prefer to work outdoors. I love seeing the sun come up on a newly seeded field." She tried to grab the ribbon away from Myra and frowned. "And the practicality of nature, I like practicality—and this isn't—my hair is going to be in my eyes. Let me have my brush."

"Practical. Who needs practical when you're going to a ball?" Belle chimed as she came waltzing through the door of their bedroom. She did a series of spins, and her emerald green satin gown billowed like a gentle breeze on a sea of grass.

"Beautiful, Belle, simply beautiful," Myra said. "Now can you help me with this wayward damsel?"

"Belle, tell me seriously," Collina said. "Does this look right?" She pointed to her bodice.

Belle tipped her head from one side to the other. "Do some twirls. Don't look so stiff. You resemble that mannequin in Eve's Dress Shop."

"Twirl? No thanks." Collina rushed to leave. Her sisters stopped her.

"She's serious?" Belle said. "I think Sis might have found her heart."

"Franklin?" Ruby said.

Myra nodded. "And I think she needs you know what."

"Would it be okay with Mother?" Belle said.

"I know it will, if it will give Collina some confidence."

"Okay. Ruby, would you get it, please?" Belle said.

With a rustle of Ruby's powder-pink gown sweeping her slender ankles, she went to do her eldest sister's bidding.

Belle grasped Collina's shoulders firmly. "Now close your eyes real tight. Ruby, hurry up, you know Sis can't stand still for long. Don't worry. I'm just going to lead you over here a little bit. Hurry up, Ruby."

Collina felt something fastened around her neck.

"Sis," Myra said, "I want you to pretend you don't know the person in the mirror. Look at her like you've just met her for the first time. Now promise."

Myra's hands lifted from Collina's shoulders and she felt fingers fluffing up the sleeves of her gown. She opened her eyes slowly. A green-eyed, dark-haired lady with an upsweep of silky thick hair, long slender arms, a tiny waist, and a deep crimson dress, stared back at her. Around her neck was grandmother's heirloom necklace. A delicate pearl resting on a handmade chain of gold nestled in the gentle curve of her breasts just above the Ottoman silk.

"It's lovely."

"Girls," Mother called from the hallway, "your gentlemen friends have arrived."

Collina glanced down the long stairway and whispered to Ruby, "It never seemed that steep before."

"Sis," Myra said. "This is going to be a night you'll never forget."

"If I ever make it down those steps with these high heels and long skirts, you mean." Collina watched as Belle walked down gracefully. Bo smiled proudly up at her, waiting just below the last step.

Ruby gave Collina's arm an encouraging pat. "I'll be right behind you, Sis."

Myra fidgeted nervously with the pearl buttons on her glove. "I meant to tell you before now, but I guess now will just have to do." Myra exhaled. "I've got to follow my heart. Right or wrong, one can't always help falling in love."

"Myra, what are you saying?" Collina stared at her, bewildered. All of MacDuff County knew how Luke Baker felt about Myra. He was crazy in love with her. If not for the fact that the university had first bids on two more years, he'd have proposed to Myra four years ago. Myra had it all, all Collina could only dream of, beauty, grace, and an adoring beau.

"Try to like Clem, for me. If you do, I know the rest of the clan will accept him," Myra whispered, then began her descent. Her heels barely touched the steps, her billowing dress gracefully fluttered about her as beautifully as the wings on a dove.

"Ruby, what do you make of it?" Collina said.

"Mother's totally against her marrying Clem, and when have you known Mother to be wrong about anything?" Ruby said.

Luke stepped forward and offered Myra his arm. It would devastate Luke if Myra didn't marry him.

Franklin stepped forward. The buttons on his uniform shone in the sunlight from the oval windowpane, as did the gleam in his eyes. Tall, distinguished, he oozed confidence from every pore.

Oh dear, she should have picked Joseph. How will she ever get through this evening?

Collina gasped. The high-polished wheels shone radiantly in the sunlight. The black leather seats set off the fine old carriage as warmly as any heirloom of the rich days before the Civil War could. As Myra and Belle exclaimed over the beautiful crimson lining inside set off with squabs of morocco leather, Collina ran toward the two dark bays impatiently pawing the ground, snorting and flinging their fine arched necks in protest of being halted for such a length.

"I've never seen anything so beautiful!" She stroked their outstretched necks. "Are they hard to drive?"

"No," Luke said, smiling at Myra. "Collina, would you like to drive my father's team? I'd rather enjoy the company of your irresistible sister."

"Are you sure she can handle them? They gave you quite a test around the bend," Franklin said.

"I'm sure I can." Collina's eyes pleaded. A spark of interest flickered in Franklin's gaze, his eyes appraising. "What happened to your braids, and what did you do with the girl I once knew?"

"There was never a girl there, Franklin," Myra said.

His blue eyes held a strange gleam in their depths, and his straight black hair shone beneath the sunlight. He took a firm step toward her. "I never could refuse a beautiful lady anything."

Collina gulped. She'd been queen in her fields, but now her senses warned her that soon she'd be treading on unfamiliar ground. Did she want Franklin looking at her as a man would toward a woman?

The weeks of hard work had only encouraged Franklin's inherent hardness. His muscles noticeably rippled beneath his uniform. He had her around the waist, and before she could even mutter a response, lifted her high into the air, setting her slowly down on the carriage seat.

"That was unnecessary," she said, her heart beating as if she'd just run a mile.

"After seeing you descending those stairs earlier, it's safer for you to not attempt these tiny steps." His eyes twinkled. "I sure hope you can dance better than you can climb down stairs."

So that was the reason for his sudden spurt halfway up the steps. A high burst of laughter from the group seated in the carriage made her bite down on her bottom lip in humiliation.

"That's all right," she said with a toss of her curls. "I'll just chalk that experience toward this memorable evening I'm never to forget."

Bo stuck his head out of the carriage just before Franklin closed the door and said, "You up to the challenge?"

"Challenge? Humph." Collina retorted, giving the reins a shake. She wanted to climb down from that coach right that minute and get out of this tight-fitting corset. But then she wouldn't be allowed the opportunity of driving the coach. The attention her attire had attracted from Franklin was flattering, but definitely unnerving. She smiled. Most likely the only memorable event I'll recount will be these trotters.

Franklin climbed up onto the seat, then opened the glass window, encouraging communication with the passengers in the carriage.

"I'll try to make up for lost time." She removed the whip from its holder and cracked it sharply over the trotter's spirited heads. They jumped against their harnesses with a start.

"Oh dear," Myra exclaimed. "Franklin, we're holding you responsible. You'd better get a hold of her reins, or none of us will ever see the Bakers."

There was a loud burst of humor from Luke and Bo with more winks in Franklin's direction.

Collina pretended she didn't notice. She had her hands full

admiring the horses. "Relax, Myra, I promise to get you there, one way or another."

Velvet and Jasmine were every bit the horses Collina had anticipated. Their long, slender legs moved in simultaneous rhythm to the unwritten tune their hooves played on the hard, clay bridle path that connected the farms. She held the fine leather reins carefully, inviting more speed down the winding dirt road. They took her challenge eagerly.

Franklin unfolded his long arm across the back of her seat. Bo picked up the earlier conversation from in the foyer. "Franklin, I'm glad to see Roosevelt's planning on defending America's rights after what those Spaniards did to our battleship."

Franklin shrugged. "Only there's no proof Spain sunk the *Maine*."

"Still, you think McKinley will declare war on Spain?" Luke said.

"Roosevelt is planning on being prepared for the worst."

Collina breathed deeply of the blooming fragrance of the dogwood trees and honeysuckle vines, absorbed in the realization that the rolling countryside was budding with new life. Franklin seemed to be enjoying the serenity as the conversation rose and fell behind them.

"Franklin," Belle said. "Are you part Indian? Robert said Joseph told him you were."

Franklin's profile stood out clearly in the afternoon sunset, his pronounced cheekbones, square chin, his skin deeper than normal in contrast to his white broadcloth shirt.

"Even though Franklin does not know his parentage," Luke said, "it is evident in his features that he is."

Franklin didn't look at Luke or Belle. He simply removed his arm from around the back of Collina's seat and gazed out at the hills of Shushan.

What had gotten into Luke to make such a statement? "So what do you have against Indians, Luke? Our grandmother was part Cherokee. Nationalities never change the character of an individual. It's what's inside that counts. Besides, I've never seen an Indian with eyes as blue as Franklin's."

"Aw, Collina," Luke said, "you're always a surprise. I never would suspect you ever noticing a man's eyes. Bet you couldn't tell me the color of mine?"

So what if she hadn't noticed the color of Luke's eyes. Mmm, probably brown like his hair. "Brown, of course."

There was a volley of laughter behind her.

"I know Collina better than she," Luke said.

"We can't allow Franklin to leave. Seeing how he's the only fella Sis's ever noticed," Myra said.

"Or took the time to dress up for," Luke said. "Clothing may not change a woman's personality—but it does accentuate her attributes. Hooray! I've just won this argument."

She felt a flush rise to her cheeks. "The way you're rattling on you'd think I'd made a—"

"My eyes are hazel, Collina."

"Humph," she muttered, "Just wouldn't you know." She urged the horses into a faster trot. "I apologize for that, Luke. But I'd like you to recollect, for future reference, how I encouraged you to lose your uppity Yankee ways and acquire some of the traditional culture of our fine hills."

"Yeah, right, I truly appreciated you allowing me the privilege of being a part of that hog killing five years ago."

Another volley of laughter swelled behind her.

"I do declare," Belle said between peals of mirth, "my eyes are going to look like I've been peeling onions."

"Most likely be the only amusing time we'll experience this evening," Collina said.

"Franklin, I don't envy you. You've got your work cut out for you to be sure," Bo said.

The big white four-pillared house loomed into view, and Collina applied a steady pull on the reins. Velvet and Jasmine snorted, tossing their fine heads in defiance, bent on getting to their stalls as quickly as possible, their clipping pace making the small carriage bump hard on the ruts and stones in the road like a ship caught in a storm. Those blasted snaffles. Why hadn't she thought to bring her leather gloves? She could feel the reins dig into her palms, blistering them through her silk gloves.

"Sis, slow them down please. Ow. My head," Myra said.

"We're bouncing all over the seat back here," Belle said.

Franklin's arms were suddenly about hers, his large hands entwining the reins. Strongly, his fingers pulled on the lines. "Whoa. Whoa, I say." Again he pulled, pulling her into his broad chest.

"Don't you just love these light snaffle bits?" He whispered, his lips entwined in her hair.

She tried in vain not to feel his arms encircling her—glad only that the others in the carriage were too busy fighting to remain seated to notice what was happening in front. The two horses came down to a clipping jog. She could feel his chin against hers. He was so close she was afraid to breathe.

"I could have done that," she said. Then, realizing what she had implied, said, "Not that I purposely…I needed my gloves."

A half smile lifted the corners of his lips. "Indeed." He inhaled deeply. "Mmm, what's the name of that perfume?"

"Perfume? I'm…not wearing any."

His lean muscles next to her arm tightened. She released her hold of the reins. "Here, you take them."

Doc's stableman, Jacob, came forward and took hold of the reins, noting with dismay the heaving flanks of his trotters. "Master's not going to like this." A smile formed on his lips as he peeked into the chaotic array of pink, blue, and emerald skirts askew on the black leather seats. "I can take it from here, Mr. Baker."

"Thank you, Jacob," Luke said.

"Enjoyed the ride, Collina," Bo said, smirking broadly, his good-natured face holding his humor in check while Belle descended the carriage steps.

"Bo, I need to use the powder room," Belle said.

"I think this will have to do for my memorable experience," Myra said. "I'm sure I couldn't handle another like it in the same evening. Luke, promise me you'll drive us back?" She gave her ball gown a shake.

Luke sent Collina an encouraging wink. "Sure, if it's all right with your sister."

Ruby's laughter split through Myra's next words like sunlight through storm clouds. "It was wonderful fun. I can't wait for the trip home."

"Ruby, I knew you'd boost to my spirits." Collina exhaled and watched the couples walk up the steps of the mansion. "I don't think Belle or Myra want to ride back with us."

Franklin chuckled, covering his mouth. He wasn't fooling her. She'd seen the grin tickling the corners of his lips.

"I don't care if you laugh."

He swung her down from the high seat and said, "Yes, ma'am."

"I still think they need to put a sharper bit in those horses' mouths."

He nodded, his eyes void of humor. "They're not the only ones in need of that this evening."

Chapter 5

*O*h, dear." Collina clung to Franklin's arm nervously. "I'd be more comfortable in the stables with those trotters than here." She turned. The townspeople's taunting words on that wintry day seven weeks before was a wound that hadn't fully healed. Franklin's arm held her firm.

The foyer and ballroom entranceway gaped at her as if daring her to step a foot inside. Its large oak doors, wedged on each end with shiny brass horse heads, stared back at her. While she fidgeted with the folds of her dress, Dr. David and Martha Baker approached her and smiled.

"My, you are a vision of beauty this evening, Miss Collina."

She curtsied. "Thank you, Doc and Mrs. Baker, for your gracious invitation." She stole a deep breath as the kind doctor and his wife moved forward to welcome another couple.

Then a noise like geese in flight captured Collina's attention to her left. A winding staircase with dove-white, delicately hand-carved spindles gracefully wove its way upward to the second floor. Ladies adorned with silk fans cradled in their immaculate white gloves gently grasped the rosewood handrail with their free hand as they appeared to float downwards on a shimmer of taffeta and giggles. Collina swallowed. Burying her not-so-white glove behind her back, she whispered, "No wonder I thought of a passel of birds gibbering to one another."

Franklin chuckled. "You'll have a fine time this evening. Just relax and allow that to happen. You're dressed for the part. Now all you need is confidence in yourself to be like those other ladies."

He surveyed the room. "Doc's home is a page out of what I envisioned a southern plantation to look like. He did confide to me that he hired an English craftsman from New York to handcraft every spindle of that stairway. Still, Baker's home glistens with impeccable taste and Southern charm."

David and Martha Baker surveyed their guests at Rose's debutante ball, then nodded. "Gather your ladies fair. The ball is about to begin."

Collina smiled as Joseph approached her. She couldn't believe the change. "You should shave more often, I hardly recognized you."

He grasped her hands and spread her arms wide, his eyes sweeping her appraisingly. "My, my, you clean up well yourself. And I shall add, the most beautiful lady present." He bowed and kissed her hand. His hair was neatly trimmed and displayed a widow's peak on a well-defined forehead. His short-jacketed suit and waistcoat of pearl-grey gave his broad shoulders an even larger dimension. His glance swerved from her to Franklin.

"About that day we planted the tobacco crop, I apologize for the way I behaved. Now, like I was saying, I—"

Franklin put up his hand to halt Joseph's next words. "All that was needed to be said was said."

Joseph stepped forward, his hands puckered into fists at his sides.

Collina stepped forward. "Joseph, remember, you're a gentleman."

Unguarded, Franklin's glance met hers. Was that a spark of jealously she'd seen?

Franklin and Joseph were both twenty years old. But his heritage made him feel many years Joseph's senior. Franklin bowed to Collina, reaching for her hand and giving it a light kiss. "I need to speak with our host. My preference is the waltz. May I have the honor of the first?"

"Waltz?"

He noted with pleasure a warm flush rise to her cheeks. Just as he had suspected, she knew nothing about waltzes. She probably could handle a jig, even a reel, but a waltz, no. It would be his pleasure to introduce her to her first of many new experiences.

"I shall return momentarily." Franklin clicked his heels sharply and bowed, strolling toward the edge of the ballroom to the study.

Doc cleared his throat. "Franklin, this just came for you. Or should I be addressing you as Lieutenant Long?" Doc held out the envelope. "A messenger has just dropped this off. It's from Washington."

"This might be the orders I've been waiting for."

"Father, is that what I think it is?"

"Yes, Rose, most likely Franklin's dispatch papers."

Rose's fingers clung to Franklin's sleeve like a burr on a saddle blanket. "If anything happened to you I don't know how I would—"

"Now Rose." Doc Baker coughed, noting her pouting mouth. "Let's not get carried away." He turned to Franklin. "You had better watch out for this one, or she'll wrap you around her little finger like she has her brother and me."

Franklin unfastened her hand from his arm, brought it to his lips, and kissed it lightly. "Don't go worrying your lovely head. Just remember to save at least one dance for me over your many admirers."

"Yes, a waltz for sure, and I've got something special to tell you."

Doc gave Franklin a wink. "Wonder what that could be? Now, if it's a proposal, just tell her the truth. She's got a lot of growing up to do before she'll make anyone a good wife."

Rose stamped her foot. "I'm hardly a child."

Noting his daughter's heightened anger, Doc stopped his jesting tone and as he pivoted his daughter toward the ballroom, said over his shoulder to Franklin, "I'll talk to you later."

Franklin closed the door of the study and plopped down in the overstuffed burgundy leather chair. The fire in the stone hearth warmed the sudden chilliness he felt. He ripped open the seal and read.

"Lieutenant Franklin Long, return to your post in 48 hours. Congress passed joint resolution today, April 19, asserting Cuba's independence. War eminent. Arrangements being made for all Rough

Riders to meet at Fort Sam Houston in San Antonio, Texas, for training. Troops departing San Antonio May 29 en route to Tampa, Florida, to await embarkation to Cuba. Lieutenant Colonel Theodore Roosevelt." He opened the study door a crack. Seeing Collina's slender profile, he felt a flush work its way to his cheeks. How her smile could work its will on his heart.

His fingers clasped the small box in his pocket. He crushed the telegram, then wadded it into a ball. His heart beat in time to the thump of his steps; he paused before the stone fireplace and tossed the ill-fated parchment into the fire.

He stared as the flames consumed it, mingling with the black ashes of the hickory. Smirking, he watched the flames lick the spot where the white paper had once been. Who was he duping? He'd found the family he'd longed for amidst the McConnell household. The soulmate he desired to share his life with at Shushan. He laid his head on his arm as it rested on the mantel and closed his eyes. "Lord, I hardly know You, but please give me strength of character, a will of iron, to do the right thing.

He could not burden Collina or her family with the added weight of a soldier going to an unknown destiny. The soft notes of a violin echoed through the doorway to him, whispering of fleeting hours too few.

Chapter 6

hirty pairs of men and women swayed and dipped to the eloquent tempo of the music. Collina watched Franklin's broad shoulders maneuver gracefully around the dance floor with Naomi. Her quick, agile feet kept in perfect step to his.

"Collina May?" Joseph said.

She was immediately alert. Joseph only used her formal name when he was very upset with her. "Yes?"

"Could you do me a favor?"

Her eyes left his face for a flutter of a moment. Franklin was taking Naomi over to the punch bowl.

"Of course." They were partners of fate, an inseparable team that continuously pulled together against the unfairness life often bequeathed them.

Joseph's Adam's apple worked overtime. "There's going to be a war with Spain. I want to be one of those Rough Riders. I've asked Franklin to put in a good word for me, but he's put me off. Said it wasn't my fight. He could get me in; his word is well received in the Army. He knows Roosevelt. His orders have got to be arriving soon. Doc had a telegram for him not more than an hour ago. Could you ask him? Find out where they'll be assembling?"

"Joseph, what makes you think he'll do it for me?" Her gaze unconsciously fell on the two by the punch bowl.

Franklin glanced up from Naomi's face. Their eyes met and caught, his eyebrows rose in obvious pleasure.

Collina groaned, turning away.

Joseph grimaced. "He'd be a fool not to."

"I'm not keen on the idea of you leaving for some foreign place." His arm tightened around her waist. "I thought that's what the girls liked, a soldier beau. All the ladies here are standing in line to dance with the gallant soldier decked out in his uniform."

"He reminds me of a peacock. And with Naomi and Rose making such a fuss over him, there's no telling how big his head's going to swell. Joseph, you're different. You're not like Franklin. You've got roots, people depend on you, and you'd be sorely missed if you leave. Franklin's been a great help, but I've always known he wouldn't be around for long. You belong here."

The lines of Joseph's mouth drew into sharp edges. "I need him now, but don't think I'm giving you over to the likes of him. You're too good for a fatherless no account."

"Joseph, he can't help what he was born into." Franklin's sincerity, his desire to help the McConnells and seek the truth about Christ Jesus had impressed her, just as Joseph's loyalty had. "You two are alike. Why, you even argue like brothers. Remember a name doesn't make you what you are.

"Sometimes the deck we're dealt in life isn't fair. We have no control over what we're born with or into. But we can determine what we do with what we're born with. Franklin's got a way about him. I don't understand it, but I feel God's going to use him. Even though he doesn't know his Savior well enough yet, some day he will. Then God will enlist Franklin in His army to perform that task only Franklin can accomplish. Does that make sense, Joseph?"

He smiled down at her affectionately. "All right. Only for you, I promise to treat Franklin like I would a brother. So will you put in a good word for me?"

"Yes. But only because I worry about you. I know sure as I'm standing here, you'll find a way to join those Rough Riders. I'm going to ask Franklin to watch over you, Joseph McWilliams. You're too stubborn for your own good."

His eyes were bright. "We've got something in common, then."

"Collina McConnell, is it truly you?" A slender man with soft light hair stared down at her.

"Stephen Meir, I haven't seen you in ages."

"I've been at the University of Louisville," Stephen said. "What about it, Joseph, is it okay if I take your girl around for a whirl?"

"Collina isn't my girl, though can't say I'm not wishing." Joseph handed her a glass of punch. "Only, be forewarned, she likes to lead."

"Come on." Stephen tapped his feet to the banjo player strumming a few notes. He took the glass of punch from her hands and placed it on the table. "The song is about to begin."

"Grab your partners for a good old-fashioned reel."

She kept step to another reel or so she tried. Stephen proved to be a cheerful counterpart to her governing feet, and they laughed at each other as they flew about the room. Seven years her senior, Stephen had been Luke's best friend and her staunch supporter during squabbles with her brothers. Good-natured, strong Christ-like values, genteel, and handsome as well, Stephen would make a perfect dancing partner for Ruby this evening. "Have you met my younger sister?"

Stephen cocked his head, his full lips forming a round O. "Not the sister who liked to eat dirt for breakfast?"

"Silly! No. She wasn't eating dirt; she was making mud pie. Now stop your laughing and listen. I'd like it if you could show her a good time tonight. This is her first dance."

Stephen stood a head taller than she, so he easily scanned room.

Franklin flew by with Rose pivoting gracefully around the floor, her sky-blue gown swaying in happy counterpart to Franklin's careful guidance, her eyes looking into his adoringly.

"Some girls have all the luck," Collina said. "Beautiful, petite, and an accomplished dancer. Is there anything Rose can't do?"

"Rose is crazy in love with Franklin Long."

"Don't say that, unless you know for sure."

"Luke told me that very thing this evening. But I'm not sure Luke approves of him. He thinks Franklin might be leading his sister on, you know, because Doc is so well to do."

"What do you mean?"

"Luke seems to think he's a fortune hunter. Said that up in Long Island Franklin led Doc to think he was a self-made man. Rumor goes he bought some kind of run-down business in Detroit and came here to ask Doc to help finance him. Franklin doesn't own anything but the shirt on his back, but that's not the worst. He's illegitimate and a half-breed."

The music ended and the dancers made their way to the punch bowl.

"Stephen, I have never met a more hardworking and honest man as Franklin Long. If he wanted handouts, why didn't he stay with Doc Baker and not at my sharecroppers' cabin working blisters on his hands? If he was trying to get a handout from Doc, why didn't he stay with him and woo Rose Baker? Why did he choose to labor in the hot sun when he could have rested beneath the shade trees at Doc's mansion, sipping brandy?"

Stephen's eyes played across her face. If he was thinking about laughing…he'd better think twice. She was mad enough to spit nails.

Stephen chuckled. "Save me another dance? Sure like it when you pepper your common sense across my dense thoughts."

"That is, if she's got any energy left after she's danced at least a half dozen with me," Franklin said.

She jumped at his sudden nearness. Had he heard?

"Darling, you look lovely this evening," Mary Baker Blaine said. Mary's arm was wrapped around Ruby's.

"Mary, it seems like ages when last I saw you." It felt like Christmas, seeing all her loved ones beneath one roof. Hugging her close, Collina turned toward her younger sister. "Ruby, meet Stephen Meir, and Franklin, allow me to introduce Doctor Baker's baby sister, Mary Blaine. Mary, this is Lieutenant Franklin Long."

Mary laughed, patting her bulging stomach. Her golden hair resembled woven silk with their cascade of miniature roses entwined within their locks. Her long tresses swirled upwards in regal style over her slender arched neck, like a golden crown, and complemented her high cheek bones, large sapphire blue eyes, and ivory complexion.

"You're still the loveliest woman in MacDuff County," Collina said. Mary pointed to her cane. "See what Austin made me?" The varnished cherrywood was carved with intricate designs. "Isn't it beautiful?" Collina exclaimed over the walking stick and noticed the unmistakable gleam of interest in Stephen's eyes lighting on fair-haired Ruby.

"My, you have grown up. I…I can't believe the transformation. Must have been all those mud baths you took."

Ruby tilted her head and gave him a cheeky grin. "And you're the boy that was afraid to get his hands dirty."

He laughed, extending his bent arm, and they were instantly in deep conversation, as he led her toward the punch bowl.

Mary continued to speak, slightly out of breath, with Franklin.

Collina noticed the flush in her friend's face. "Mary, are you sure you're feeling well? You might need to sit down. Franklin, let's find her a comfortable chair. This settee here will do."

"No, that's for two lovers."

"Your stomach is big enough for two. Sit," Collina said. Overhearing Franklin's chuckle, she replied, "If Mary isn't the epitome of love, I'd like to know who is."

Mary laughed, laying Collina's hand on her cheek.

"Collina, I hardly recognized you. You sure look different without your horses and plow." Austin Blaine always walked soft of foot for one so big, bearing himself with the proud grace of a backwoodsman.

His ancestors had been some of the first on Kentucky soil, making their marks right along with Davy Crockett's as they blazed the trail for the first settlers to follow. He was rugged of face with thick hair that waved about a generous forehead. A wide mouth set off with dimples on either side gave him an appealing edge with the ladies. She found his bold eyes offensive and returned his look with one of her own.

Doc Baker had been against his sister marrying Austin, and it was public knowledge that Austin kept Mary pregnant when everyone knew she was too frail a woman to be birthing so.

"You did a good job on Mary's cane." Then she turned her back on him, placing a hand on Mary's shoulder. Yes, everyone knew Mary's two little girls would likely be the only children God would ever grant her. For every time she tried another pregnancy, the newborn ended up stillborn.

"You look quite the lady," Austin said.

"Can I get you anything, Mary?" Collina ignored Austin's remark.

"She is, Austin, clear through," Mary said. "Clothes never make a lady. Never will. The quality comes from within, and Collina has inherited Maggie's grace." Mary smiled, patting Collina's hand. "Austin will tend to my needs. You go now and have some fun; you deserve to. Ah, there's Myra."

"I thought I'd introduce them to your cousin Clem, Austin." Myra tucked her arm into Collina's and pulled her over. "Franklin, Collina, may I introduce Clem Cass?"

Clem reached for her hand and shook it exuberantly. Dressed in a black suit with a short lapel set off by a white cuffed shirt and matching cravat, he cut quite a figure with his striking black mustache and curly dark hair.

"Myra's been telling me a lot about you." Clem smiled back, looking about the small crowd gathering around them.

"Belle, Bo, this is Clem Cass." Myra tapped Clem's arm. "Clem, tell them about the business you want to start here."

"I'm planning to start a mercantile. It will be like my store in Detroit."

"Would you ladies like a glass of punch?" Bo said.

"Luke's getting us some," Myra said, fidgeting with her earlobe.

"Detroit's a nice place, becoming a city for industry," Franklin said. "I've recently purchased a shop off Mill Street."

So what Stephen had told her was true. Collina asked Clem, "Why did you leave Detroit to come here?"

"Kind of a long story, but now that I've been down here for a while I've grown to love it. In fact, we've decided to stay, right, Myra. We'll have our own little store right here in Emerald."

"We?" Belle said.

Myra cleared her throat. "Clem's proposed, and I've accepted."

Clem's arm encircled Myra's waist. "We're planning on having the wedding this June."

"Mother wouldn't approve. It's much too soon," Belle said.

Before Clem could reply, Luke arrived with their refreshments.

"Here, Myra." Luke handed her a glass of punch.

The murmurs of the other dancers filled the silence between them. Collina could hear clearly the unspoken thoughts of Belle. Myra and Luke had been sweethearts since childhood. How was Luke going to handle this?

"Clem, isn't it?" Luke said,. "You work at the mercantile, don't you?"

"It's better than farming." Clem appeared somewhat offended at being called a simple clerk in a store. He continued in his offensive tone. "I never did understand how anyone could grub around behind a plow day in and day out and find hog killing and mucking out cattle bins an exhilarating occupation."

Myra shifted from one high-button shoe to the other. "Clem, please. I asked you not to say that."

Belle never lollygagged around the truth. So, like an avenging angel, she heralded out the news from the top-most peak of her irate voice. "Luke, Myra and Clem are engaged to be married."

Luke's mouth gaped opened, minus the finger cake that dropped to the floor.

Franklin bent over to rescue the lost pastry.

Luke looked at Myra for an explanation. She removed her laced glove. A small diamond ring on her finger twinkled in the candlelight. "I...I couldn't wait for you any longer, Luke."

A small disturbance of Jake wheeling his chair to the front, with his musicians following, caused everyone to look toward the stage. "Okay, ladies and gents, grab your partners and listen close. We're going to have a contest. Which is going to be the lucky pair to win these?" Jake stretched his long arms into the air, holding two gleaming silver goblets, trimmed in gold.

Murmurs rippled throughout the large room.

"Do you realize how much they're worth?" Clem glanced about the group. Then, noticing their indifference, said, "They're probably nice fakes."

"They're real." Luke's eyes locked on Clem's in open warfare.

Clem chuckled. "Hate to win them. Just to find out they're fake."

Bo glanced at Belle. "I don't mind sitting this one out." Reaching into his pant pocket, he produced a handkerchief and patted his forehead. "I haven't worked so hard since Pa found out I went fishing instead of going to school. Luke, you and Belle go. I've got two left feet, and no matter how I try, Belle doesn't stand a chance winning with me."

Luke made a hasty bow. "Belle, there's no one I'd rather dance with. Nothing would be more of an honor. But duty must win over pleasure for a time. I beg to be excused. Father has been called away, and I must reside the rest of the evening as host. In fact," he looked pointedly at Myra, "the reason for my appearance. I am glad to see you will be taken care of, Myra." He took her hand in his, lightly kissing it. "Farewell."

Jake's fingers gently stroked his bow on the violin, and the soft melodies of a Strauss waltz drifted across the room, hushing voices and stilling laughter.

Belle sighed. "I just love the way Jake plays. Don't try and back out, Bo; you're dancing." Taking Bo's arm, Belle led him to the dance floor.

Franklin then offered his to Collina.

"Uh…I'm a little tired."

His brows rose in jocular alarm. "I find that hard to believe." A smile creased his lips. "A lady never goes back on her word."

"Ladies and gentlemen, we'll begin our Johann Strauss waltz gala."

Franklin's eyes commanded her as he took her right hand in his left, then moving his right arm about her waist, said, "Beware, fair damsel, I refuse to allow you to lead."

"Well, I'm glad my little secret is out. Only, I don't know any other way to dance."

He chuckled deep down in his throat. "Those heels of yours have a surprise coming their way tonight."

With the first strum of Jake's violin singing the melody of the soft notes of *The Emperor*, she knew she was in trouble. Bravely, she ignored Franklin's determined shoes pushing hers aside as hers seemed always to be in the wrong spot. Without a loss in tempo, Franklin proceeded to do a series of spins about the large crescent room, his long legs gracefully keeping in step with the music. His fingers commandeered a stronger hold on her waist as he pirouetted her.

"Franklin," she tried to act nonchalant, "Joseph wanted me to ask—"

"No."

"You don't know Joseph the way I do. He'll find a way of becoming part of Roosevelt's new cavalry. Take care of him, Franklin. He needs looking after bad. Joseph will be sorely missed. I just don't want it on my conscience. Why, if anything should happen to him, I don't know what his Pa would do."

"What about yourself?" His eyes were penetratingly bright. "Weren't you his girl before I showed up?"

"Whatever put that notion in your head? Joseph's like a brother to me. Big Jim, Joseph's Pa, lost his wife and daughter to typhoid a few years back. Big Jim doesn't say it, but you can read it in his eyes; he's scared to death something like that will happen to Joseph."

"Big Jim loves his son that much? Well, I wouldn't understand, not knowing my parents…"

She felt terrible. "I didn't mean to say that you would not be missed if—the McConnells would consider it an honor for you to become a member of our family."

"There are several matrimonial invitations floating around tonight."

"I wasn't…"

He laughed. "Being an adopted brother, or an adopted uncle, like Charlie, is typical of the McConnells."

"Whether you choose to believe or not to believe, we consider you a member of our family and are praying for your safe return."

Franklin looked away. "Your family doesn't need more worries heaped on their plate. That's what I would become. I understand your attitude regarding soldiers more than you realize, and I respect it. Some soldiers do carry to war high ideals about the allure of military adventure. That is smothered on the battlefield. Do you realize I may lose my arm or leg to some sword-happy Spaniard? Only God knows if I'll even come back. Those Spaniards can swing a sword as good as your brothers swing an ax."

She gasped. "You've heard something. Joseph said a telegram arrived. That telegram was for you, wasn't it?" Anger tinged her words. "Why didn't you tell me?"

"I'm leaving tonight, after the dance."

She tripped over his feet and blinked away the maze of tears that clouded her vision.

"Listen to the flow of the music and let me do the leading." His voice was suddenly gentle.

This was their last night together. She wasn't going to spoil it.

The soft enchanting notes of *The Emperor* mellowed away, and the lovely *Blue Danube* began. This was one of Mother's favorites; she would hum it about the house when she did her chores and because Mother liked his music Pa took her one summer to New York to hear Johann Strauss in person. Her parents had been so happy together. Could she ever hope for such a love?

"Collina," Franklin whispered, breathing heavily. He knew it wasn't from dancing. Annoyed more at himself than her, he fixed his jaw in determined lines as he concentrated on making his arm rigid, willing it not to tighten uncontrollably around her slender waist. "We're going to get through this. Those silver goblets were meant for you, to be caressed in the hands of the most beautiful lady I've ever had the good fortune to meet."

"Then you've forgotten those awful things I said that night on the lane? I don't believe soldiers are all—"

"No, never. Never ask me to. They're you, honest and straightforward, not afraid to face your mistakes, yet determined not to give up because of them. It's a good trait to possess." He pirouetted her about. The beautiful notes of the tune floated around them.

Perhaps it was the gentle notes of the song that encircled the room with its charm. Perhaps she was just getting accustomed to his commands, for suddenly she was responsive in his embrace, obeying willingly the nudging of his arm about her. She gazed up into his eyes. "Do you think Myra's making a mistake marrying Clem? Mother is against the union."

His eyebrows rose quizzically over alert eyes.

"She can't be in love with Clem when everyone thought she was going to marry Luke."

He drew her closer. He could feel her breath on his face. "Don't ever take love for granted, true love especially."

"Does one always recognize true love?"

"No, not always. Love is like a rose bud. Though at first glance, it is lovely, you really can't see or feel the true flower, not until it blossoms— you have to be patient and wait. That's the way it is with true love."

As the gentle notes of the song moved the young dancers about the room, Franklin felt the eager movement of her graceful form blend into the rhythm of his own.

He murmured in her ear. "You're like the duckling that just learned it was a swan." He rested his cheek for a moment on her soft hair. "Are you happy?"

"Yes. I've never heard anything so beautiful."

His arm pressed her gently and she responded in perfect step. It was as if she had grown wings. No, not wings, it was the billowing taffeta that dipped and swayed in perfect rhythm to the soft, sweet notes of the waltz. He closed his eyes for a moment, hoping the notes could live on endlessly. War was a dream. This was real.

Chapter 7

Franklin borrowed Doc's small buggy to carry Collina back to Shushan, big enough for only the two of them. "You've got to see this. I've been waiting for weeks to show it to you." He pulled off the main road and drove Doc's gentle black mare down a small, one lane path. He stopped the horse, jumped over the buggy step, then led the mare along the banks of Lady's Lake, where he threw out her tending line. "Did you know how this lake got its name?" He walked around the carriage to Collina and extended his arm.

"No, though I often wondered why such a peculiar name, Lady's Lake. Must have been a woman who named it."

He smiled. "No, Doc told me it was because it resembles another lake, Loch Katrine. Sir Walter Scott used it in his poem *The Lady of the Lake*. Loch Katrine lay in a lovely valley region called the Trossachs in Scotland. This little lake reminded the homesick Scots that settled here so much of Scotland, that they named it Lady's Lake."

"I never noticed before how beautiful it was here." She looked out over the still waters with only the moon's rays touching its gentle depths.

He observed her silently. "Do you believe fate rules our lives, or Divine Providence?"

She turned, her eyes unabashedly searching his. "Divine Providence."

Recalling that night in the cornfield, it seemed decades ago, he shook his head. "I never believed in Providence or Jesus, until I met you." He reached into his coat pocket and laid a small box in her hand.

"What's this?"

"Open it and see."

A heart shaped locket fell from the box. She gently undid the latch to find a tiny seed encased in glass. She looked up, puzzled.

Around his neck he pulled out of his shirtwaist a glass-cased mustard seed on a rough chain. "We shall always carry this and have in common Matthew 17:20 and this secret of the mustard seed. 'If ye have faith as small as a grain of mustard seed…nothing shall be impossible unto you.' Treasure this, as I shall mine." He took her hand in his and led her along the banks.

"Franklin, what the Spanish did to our battleship, killing 260 people, was outrageous, but you're not going to bring them back to life by losing yours. So why must you go? I don't see why America needs to get involved. President McKinley has managed to pressure Spain into granting Cuba limited self-government. But they want total independence. Then let *them* fight for it. How can Cuba expect our men to go over there and shed their blood for a cause that doesn't affect Americans?"

The moon glowed on her high cheekbones, the strong, determined chin and fiery green eyes, an uncompromising face. He knew just the words to say to win his argument. "What if you lived there, wouldn't you like help to win back your freedom?"

"The United States should not get involved."

"You wouldn't fight for your freedom?" he said, folding her arm into his and leading her farther along the lake.

Her lips parted, displaying even white teeth that shone in the moonlight. "You know me better than that, but America has its own problems, and it can ill afford to send her most prized possession—her sons and sweethearts—away to die on foreign soil. Why would any man choose to live here knowing it could cost him his life?"

"There was never a doubt in my mind that here is where I should be. When I left the orphan asylum, I headed for the border. The only ones that ever showed us any kindnesses had been charities from the United States. I figured if they had so much food and clothes to give away, then if I was willing to work for them, they wouldn't mind me living there."

"You've never told me. Where did you go? How did you live with no family or friends to turn to?"

His eyes couldn't get enough of her. He wanted to memorize every part of her face. He'd shared his innermost soul with her and she had accepted him, good or bad, right or wrong, she had accepted him.

Her eyes looked questioningly into his.

"The New York factories I worked in as a boy were terrible. They were frigid in the winters and boiling in summers. I'd work a twelve-hour shift yearlong. Never saw the sun some days. Then I would have preferred the farmlands of my homeland. Though the fieldwork was backbreaking, at least I was outside. The Irish lady running the boarding house I stayed in took me under her wing.

"She made sure I ate properly, giving me choice meat and plenty of milk. One Christmas she even gave me a lamp to do my studies by. She called me her 'newly found son.' She'd raised six of her own, yet, she took time to teach me manners, how to dance, 'How to become a proper American gentleman.' She helped me adapt into the right kind of society. I found that strange. She was content to be what she was, a widow, and an Irish immigrant on top of that, taking in boarders and doing laundry to make ends meet, yet wanted more for me.

"Irish immigrants off the boat were treated badly, you'd think they'd be bitter, but America blows its breath of hope on everyone. When Teddy Roosevelt approached me after a polo match and asked if I'd join his cavalry, I was proud to. Proud to give a little back of what I was given."

"God gave us the oceans to separate us from the rest of the world. America didn't see fit to help the Irish when Britain was hanging them for wearin' of the green…so why now?" She stopped and faced him, determined to have him see her rationale. "My father came over to America to get away from tyranny. He would probably agree with you, but I don't! We don't need the world or their problems. We have enough of our own."

"True, but the world needs Americans. They need what America represents. They that first settled her gnawed their teeth in her belly, dying for their convictions. Christians settled the United States, for Christian principles."

He spread his arms wide. The moon cast its gleam on his outstretched palm. "The entire world will look to her someday for guidance amidst the chaos." His emotions overwhelmed him. He turned. A passion for her, for his adopted country, had overpowered his senses. Only God knew if he'd return. Looking over at the lake, its tranquil beauty comforted him.

"I'll never forget the first time I laid eyes on the Statue of Liberty, her right arm holding a great torch raised high in the air, her left arm grasping a tablet symbolizing the Declaration of Independence. I read the Declaration and what stood out to me was, 'with a firm reliance on the protection of Divine Providence.' Only a boy of twelve, I said those words repeatedly to myself.

"I found comfort in them, though I never fully understood or believed it. The day of your father's funeral, then that night in the cornfield—I know now God did guide my life. He was just trying to find a way to tell me. Shushan, a strange name for a farm, but it has come to mean much more than buildings and barns to me. Those mustard seeds your father held so dearly are like a promise of faith and commitment to God. I don't know much about the Bible, haven't even mussed the pages of the one you gave me, but I know I'll find the comfort I need for the journey ahead."

"Franklin, I don't know how you choose to accept Matthew 17:20, but I know how I shall. I will pray God does the impossible and brings you safely home, wherever He destines that to be."

Her thoughts were only of his well-being. And she knew now he was bound elsewhere. "My little factory in Detroit is doing a nice profit, I might add, thanks to my dedicated foreman."

"All I care about now is—"

"What?" He eagerly anticipated her next words.

"Live in Detroit, just be happy and most importantly, safe. And remember, you don't have to prove your thankfulness to America, no one else does." She laughed. A melody that rivaled the sparrow's awakening songs. "We just take it for granted. It's really become the American way."

He shook his head. "How long do you think America would last if everyone just took for granted she would always be there?"

A disgusted frown filtered across her pretty face. "I can't understand this determination of yours to be a part of the destructive nature of war. You and your causes. If you must go, take Raymar. He'll take care of you. But if it's all the same to you, I'd like to have you stay around for a little longer."

"Why?" She could be infuriating at times. Doesn't she care at least a thimbleful about him, a man wanting a woman?

She looked away. Then with her eyes shining brightly, one teardrop making its way down her gleaming cheek, she softly whispered, "Because I'd hate to lose my dancing partner."

Franklin reached for her and caressed his lips against hers. With regret, he released her.

She pressed her trembling fingers to her lips. She didn't have to say it. That had been her first kiss. Did its warmth linger on her lips like it did his?

"Our paths would not have crossed if not for Roosevelt's cavalry. Whatever is in God's plan for us, Franklin, I pray God will guide you in your quest and you find what you are seeking."

Why did she look at him that way? Was it only the shadowed moon, or were her penetrating eyes conveying to him a premonition of doom for them both?

Chapter 8

May 28, 1898

The light from their kerosene lamp burned below. Unable to sleep, Collina had noticed the light. She crept downstairs. Her mother knelt before the parlor window that faced the eastern sky, her delicate hands clasped in prayer, tears wetting her cheeks. "Dear Lord, watch over Myra. She's a bit headstrong, but she's one of Your sheep, Lord. Please have her husband, Clem, be a good God-fearing man. Bless their marriage, Father, though it was hasty in its conception. And if there is some way my family can help Myra, show us."

Suddenly the golden rays of sunlight gleamed through the darkness. Night no longer labored to give birth to a new day. The deep aqua blue of the sky appeared as if from nowhere as the sun's rays rose above the horizon and shone into the long windows.

Upstairs the cries of Bugie reached Collina's ears, and she hurried to grab the child. Mother needed her alone time with Jesus.

"There, there." Collina picked up Bugie who promptly fell back to sleep on her shoulder. She tiptoed to the bedroom of her brothers. Scott slept peacefully, his blond hair flung carelessly on the goose-down pillow. Though only ten, Scott was determined to be like his older brothers and slept just in skivvies. She covered his bare back with the handmade quilt that served as his spread.

Her finger traced one of the bridal ring patterns, the velvet of the blue riding habit. Mother's favorite and her father's lifeline when he'd gotten snake bit in a swamp in Tennessee.

Franklin's face came before her mind's eye as he did in her nightly dreams. She yearned to say so much—would she ever have the chance?

She peeked into the closet, looking for dirty overalls to wash. On the peg in the far corner was a pair of Chester's old coveralls. She grabbed them. Laying down the sleeping Bugie, she hurried to her room. There were too many chores to do to waste away the morning.

"Jessie, stop," Belle said as Jessie's burly frame came bounding into the kitchen with another armload of kindling wood.

Collina hovered around the corner, beneath the stairway, where she could hear and see everyone but not be seen. Nervously, she readjusted the bib on Chester's discarded coveralls. Anticipating, yet dreading the opinions of her outspoken siblings.

"Belle," complained Jessie, "it's a cold morning, and we gotta make this here kitchen warm for the little uns."

Belle lit the last burner on the stove, placing the heavy iron skillet full of thick slices of bacon. "You bring just one more cord in this kitchen, and I'll show you just how hot I can make it in here." Belle's blue eyes flashed her displeasure. Her thick blond hair, braided from the night before, rested heavily down her back.

"Jessie? Whatever possessed you to bring in so much wood?" Mother said as she entered the room from the root cellar.

"You won't need any for Sunday." Robert grabbed a biscuit fresh out of the oven.

"Robert Dennis!" Belle went after the stealing arm with a flipper, but missed, flapping the air.

"Got to get faster than that, Sis." Robert tossed the hot biscuit from one hand to the other.

"Be only fitting if it burned those big paws of yours," Belle said.

Robert spread butter on a biscuit, then shoved half between his teeth while fanning his mouth.

"If it don't do a work on his hands, it surely will burn that stealing tongue of his. I do declare, I have to cook twice the amount whenever Robert Dennis gets here ahead of the others." Belle flipped the popping bacon, her mouth drawn in a fit of anger.

"Mother, can I take the wagon to market today?" Jessie said.

"Yeah, me too," Robert said between gulps. "I'm as tired as Jessie of all the chores about the farm, and market would be more of an adventure than mucking out stalls."

Mother placed Bugie in her chair. "You're both too young to go alone."

"Aw, Ma," Jessie complained, "I am not."

"And I'm already taller than Jessie," Robert said.

"Tallness has got nothing to do with it. Collina should go. She's always been level headed and—"

"And I guess I'm not," pouted Jessie, following his mother to the big iron stove.

"You boys are all so headstrong. Once you get something in your mind, it takes a crowbar to pry it loose. Whatever Collina says. I believe I grow another grey hair every time I argue with you."

Scott's face lit up like a jack-o-lantern. "I'll ask her." He nearly upset the eggs Belle had retrieved from the ice box. "Sorry, Belle." He ran through the doorway at full speed, sliding to a halt before the staircase. "Sis?" Scott's already large eyes widened. "What are—"

"Chester's coveralls," she whispered.

"Wait till Mother sees you."

Collina stood taller, adjusting the straps tighter. She heard the rapid descent of slippers on stairs, then Ruby's large eyes danced into hers.

A chuckle escaped Ruby's lips. "You leave Collina alone," she chided Scott, giving him a soft shove with her hand. "I think she looks modern."

"Overalls modern?" Scott said. "That's a girl's thinking for you."

"Sis, wait. I've got something real important to ask you," Scott said.

What I have to do is important, too. Collina set her jaw in firm lines and entered the kitchen.

"I declare!" her mother said. "Daughter, you march right back up those stairs and put on some decent clothes."

"But, Mother," Robert chimed in, "they're decent, just big."

Collina sat down at her accustomed place at the table. "I can't work all day in the fields with a dress on. It just isn't practical."

"Practical? God made you a woman and women wear dresses."

"Women don't work in the fields. They stay inside and cook and sew doilies." Collina fingered her silverware. This time she wasn't going to give in. "When I retire from the fields, I'll wear dresses."

"Why don't you let the men of the family handle the outside chores?" Robert said.

"If Collina and Mother left it to the two of you to get done with the planting, it most likely wouldn't get finished," Belle said.

"Belle, I've got a good mind not to eat your food."

She turned from the stove and walked toward Jessie. He picked up his plate before she could snatch it from him. "Can't you take a joke?"

"Pa never let Collina do heavy stuff, nor work too long in the hot sun. We could hire some help," Jessie said between mouthfuls, reaching for another biscuit, even though he still had a half spread on his full plate.

"We can't afford to, Jessie," Collina said. "Besides, I don't care what people think. I'm just tired of bruising my legs."

Mother stroked her cheek. "I thought of disguising myself for the Underground Railroad. Sometimes hard times demand us to do the unthinkable."

"You…did." What Mary Baker Blaine said at Rose's ball came to her thoughts. Clothes never make a lady. Never will. The quality comes from within, and Collina has inherited Maggie's grace. Collina kissed her mother's outstretched hand. "Thanks, Mother." Was what Mary said true? After working like a sharecropper, could Collina become a lady like her mother? Franklin had opened her heart to a yearning she never knew existed before.

"Okay, my darling, wear your coveralls," Mother said.

"Okay?" said the vociferous Belle. "She looks terrible. You wouldn't catch me in something like that."

"Something like that wouldn't fit around those big hips of yours." Jessie nudged Robert.

A knock on the back door brought a moment's lull to the laughter.

"Come in, Uncle Charlie and Katie." Bugie yelled.

Katie was first to emerge through the back door. Her thick wire rim glasses she held up with an index finger. She squinted at Jessie, then at Robert. "I swear, I can't tell the two of you apart anymore."

Robert laughed, touching unconsciously the pockmarks on his face. He offered his hand to Katie. "Just look for the tall, handsome one and it'll be yours truly."

Katie blushed, clutching her other hand to her chest. "I swear, Maggie, this one's going to be a ladies' man if I ever met one."

"Uncle Charlie," Collina whispered from across the table, "I need to talk to you right after breakfast."

He nodded, his grey hair falling across his forehead.

Mother turned from the stove. "Sun came up clear. We can probably get most of our spring plants in before the real hot weather gets here."

"But you said we could go to market," Jessie complained.

"I said to ask Collina," Mother said. "Your pa's last request was for Collina to manage you boys and Shushan. I don't like it, but I guess there's no changing what must be. Without your pa, it's going to take everyone doing more to make up for that."

"No market this Saturday." Collina spread butter and honey on her warm biscuit. "Figured we could hold off this week and sell our dairy products to the neighbors around close. Uncle Charlie can take the dairy products over to Bill's store on Monday, and we can get more planting done today."

"Gee, Sis." Robert complained. "Pa didn't work us this hard."

"I'm glad Pa didn't pick me for that hot field work," Belle said.

Jessie looked up from his plate, eyeing his sister. "There's no way, Sis. You're just not built for it." He gave Robert a nudge and chuckled.

Belle closed her robe tightly about her. It accented her curvy waist and full chest even more. "Mother, you make them stop teasing me."

Uncle Charlie rubbed his gnarled hands together. "You have any more biscuits? It looks like we got a busy day ahead."

Collina rose, her slender profile looking even more boyish in her brother's coveralls.

"Are you losing weight? You look—"

"Thin. Mother, this field work isn't good for Sis," Belle said.

"I'm fine." Collina forced some eggs down to her knotted stomach.

"Looks to me like someone hasn't been getting enough sleep?" Uncle Charlie said, the wrinkles across his brow creasing deeper than normal, his voice soft, full of caring.

She pushed herself and her brothers close to exhaustion each day. Still, no matter how tired she was, Lieutenant Franklin Long came like a ghost to haunt her dreams. Somewhere in the blackness, in the wee hours past midnight, she would awaken and pray for him and Joseph, not understanding her heart or the man who had captured it.

Only through Joseph's letters had she learned that he and Franklin were as close as homeboys could be far from home. And the more letters she received from Joseph, the more aware she was of his strong affections toward her. The last thing she wanted to do was hurt Joseph. She wanted him to come home safe. She couldn't stand the thought of breaking his heart with the truth that she was in love with Franklin and not him.

Chapter 9

June 20, 1898

*C*ollina, startled out of slumber, listened. There it was again. With the moon's rays shining through her bedroom window, she descended the stairway rapidly. The frantic pounding on the front door had awakened someone else, too. She turned.

Mother descended the stairway and held up her lamp.

"Who is it?" Collina said.

"Austin Blaine."

Collina opened the door. Austin's dark hair shone in the moon's rays. His shirt was dangling about his large shoulders, fluttering in the cool breezes of the night as loosely as on a clothesline.

"Maggie," Austin said between pants, gulping down large mouthfuls of air, "Mary's started labor, she wants her brother."

"Doc's in Hillsdale. That's twenty miles one way. You'll never make back in time."

"She won't have it any other way."

"How was she when you left?"

"As good as can be expected, but I don't like the idea of leaving her alone." Turning to see what his horse had snorted about, he spun back around. "Mary wants Collina to come and be with her."

As much as Collina loved Mary, the pressing need to see to their crops made her hesitate. "Maybe Belle could go."

His dark eyes grew larger in the flickering lamp light. "Mary wants you. I'll help you get caught up with your fieldwork." His arms were taut. His fingers formed into strong fists by his side, his distaste in asking for help obvious. "Seeing how we're related by marriage you can't turn down kin, now, can you?"

"What?" Mother said.

"I thought you knew, Clem's my second cousin. He came and stayed with me when he lost his job up in Michigan."

"Now really, Austin, you needn't think we'd shirk our neighborly duty. We've known Mary ever since she stepped off that train from Long Island. But we're still suffering over Ben's death."

Austin looked down, as if ashamed of the predicament he was placing the McConnells' struggling household in. "But Mary needs Collina's strength. I know she'll rest easier if she's there."

"Mary's mind will ease if her wishes are met. I'll come over after I've taken care of my chores here, daughter."

Austin's eyes rested on Maggie. "Are you sure she'll go?"

Maggie moved her lamp toward Collina.

Collina stepped into the shadows of the room. "I'll need to get dressed first."

"Daughter?" A puzzled expression crossed mother's face. "Why do you have your coveralls on?"

Collina looked down, rubbed her hands down the coarse leggings and ignored the question. "Can Ruby come? She'd be a help to me, especially with Mary's girls."

"Look, maybe I'm asking too much," Austin said.

Collina's eyes fell to his clenched fists. "Don't you forget your promise. With such strong arms, I expect double work out of you."

"I promised Mary I'd keep my temper in check and do all your biddings, and I've wasted enough time trying to prove it." He turned and ran to his horse and sprang up as agile as a mountain lion. "I'll be back before supper."

"Merciful Savior, he'll kill that poor beast for sure," Mother said.

The bright rays of sunlight and clouds stretched lazy shadows onto the rolling hillside. The day was a warm one. Still no sign of Doc or Austin coming up the winding drive. What could have happened? Mary needed a doctor bad.

Collina's right arm instinctively shot behind Mary's shoulders in time to catch the floundering woman before she toppled off the bed.

Mary glanced out the small window of her bedroom. Her tongue moistened her dry lips. "My brother is later than I expected."

"It shouldn't be long now." She rested Mary back on her feather pillow and reached for a basin of water. "I'll just sponge you off a bit."

The small room, barely large enough for a bed, had grown warmer throughout the day. The stale odor of dust and remnants of last year's winter smoke mingled with the heat of the sun baking the hand-sawn shingles of the roof. The combined smell gave the room a rancid odor.

Perhaps she could open the window again. But then there was no way to control the flies and gnats that buzzed their irritating wings on Mary's sweating body. Desperate for fresh air, she tried.

"Ugh." Swarms of insects flew their little winged bodies into the open window. She slammed it shut.

"Austin's planning on using that manure pile for our vegetable garden. He's been so worried about me; he just hasn't gotten around to planting it."

Collina continued to brush her hair.

"He's a good provider." Mary's hand went to the soft strands of her hair absentmindedly, twirling a strand around one index finger. "You know, I was frightened of him when we first got married. He had such an awful temper. But he's so handsome, and he's got a way of looking at you that makes you forget all the bad times."

Avoiding Mary's nervous fingers, Collina concentrated on gently brushing out the tangles, recalling how Mary had looked the night of Rose Baker's ball. That night seemed but a dream, a fairy tale. She looked so very different now.

Mary's face was chalky white, with delicate blue veins lacing intricate patterns down her neck. Abhorrence, not admiration, swelled in Collina's chest. Austin didn't possess anything but arrogance. The shocking reality that Mary had found so many good qualities in her husband's character astonished her.

Mary reached out for her, and they clasped hands, entwining their fingers like threads on a quilt. Another contraction racked its will on her tired body. If Collina could take her pain, or infuse her strength into Mary, she would do so willingly.

"My back. When I push it hurts so down my lower spine. I never had one before to hurt like that."

"Don't push. Your contractions aren't regular enough." She patted Mary's sweating brow with a moist cloth. She'd helped many a cow to calf and mare to foal and noted with dismay that Mary's contractions, oddly staggering, were wearing on her scant supply of strength and doing nothing.

Mary would need her energy later. Breach? It was a word that brought fear to a midwife's heart. She'd lost a calf because of breach. Her father and she had worked all night, only the calf birthed dead. The cow, her bloodied entrails ripped, soon followed her ill-fated offspring. When will this nightmare end? Oh, please, Lord, help us. Please send Doc here soon.

A weak smile came to Mary's lips. "You're praying for me, aren't you? You've a good heart; you're always thinking about the other person. Would you do something for me, if I asked you?"

"Of course." Rhythmically she massaged Mary's shoulders and the tight muscles across her back, encouraging her to relax.

"Something's wrong. I can feel it." A tear trickled its way down her cheek. "I knew it when I sent Austin for my brother." She wiped at her eyes roughly. "If I should die, give Austin a chance. He'd make you a good husband."

"None of this. You're going to be fine." Collina reached for another pillow, propping Mary up to a half-sitting position. The last person on earth she'd marry was Austin Blaine.

Mary gave her hand a feeble pat. "I loved him in the good and bad times. Every minute I spent being his wife was exciting. He's as hard as granite on the outside, but gentle like a newborn puppy on the inside, and only he will let you in to see." She wrapped her arms about herself and giggled like a schoolgirl. "He can be oh so very charming, if he has a mind to be." She looked up at her, then tilted her head and smiled knowingly. "Collina, if he gets a notion to have you...he shall."

"Mother's here," Ruby announced from the bedroom doorway.

Collina clasped her hands together and looked upwards. "Thank you, good Lord." She patted Mary's hand. "Mother's probably delivered more babies than she can count. We're going to have us a little baby here soon; you just wait and see." Collina bolted out of the room as if Goliath was tramping on her heels."

"I'm sorry I took so long coming, but Scott had the croup this morning. Knew he'd come down with it, sleeping without anything on his chest that way."

"Mother, Mary's very weak. She's talking foolishly." Collina drew her mother toward the bedroom. "Planning if she should die." Humph. Marry that arrogant backwoodsman...when acorns rolled uphill.

"Give me a chance to get my hat off." Shaking Collina's hands off her arm, she reached up to undo the hatpin of her Sunday go-to-meeting hat. "There. Now it's normal for woman in labor to carry on so, though I'd expected better of Mary. I've forgotten just how far apiece it was coming here. Do you girls have any coffee made?"

"Mother, you got to come now." Collina pushed her toward the bedroom.

"My gracious sakes, what has come over you?"

Mary's thin body hardly made a wrinkle in the sheet. All anyone first saw was her huge abdomen and large grotesque swollen legs resting on the feather bed. Her mother gently patted Mary's thin shoulders and said, "Mary dear, how are you feeling?"

"Kind of poorly, Maggie, but now that you're here my spirits have perked up a bit."

"Should I warm the broth you brought, Mother?" Ruby said.

"We'll need some kindling. I'll get it," Collina said. "We'll have to start supper soon, but there isn't much in the way of food."

"I brought plenty of food. It's in the buckboard." Mother rested her hand on Mary's forehead. "My, you're burning with the fever."

Collina hardly knew when her feet felt grass. She was as dazed as a deer trapped in barbwire. Mary was just five years older than her. She looked forty. Exhaustion gave way to anger with every chop of the axe. How could such a thing be? She carried the wood back into the house and dropped it next to the stove, shoving the sticks into the burner. She jabbed and poked at the dying embers of the potbelly until the fire felt like it was burning her face. Mary had been the prettiest girl in the county. If that's what marriage does to you, she'd have no part of it.

She ran out the front door and banged her fist on the buckboard. The mumbled voices of Mary and then her mother filtered through the window to her. "Child, you hardly have enough flesh on you to keep your bones…You shouldn't have let yourself get this way."

"Collina, Mother needs that soup she brought warmed," Ruby said from the front porch. "And Mother wants some herbal tea brewed."

Mary got that way because she loved Austin, of all people. Collina loaded her arms with the provisions Mother brought, kicking the squeaking door open with her foot.

Her dress clung to her chest and arms from her sweat. Her skirt was dirty from chopping wood, as were her forearms and hands. She would need to wash up before starting supper. The sink gaped back at her. She'd forgotten—Mary didn't have a pump in her kitchen. Looking beneath the curtain, she drew out the last pail of water. She'd have to have Ruby or the girls go down to the creek for more. Carefully, she poured some of the water into a basin and washed.

She put the soup on to warm. Diced potatoes, carrots, onions, and beef found their way into the large kettle. She sucked on her index finger, which had come into contact with her flying knife. She'd need more biscuits; she had a half dozen left from breakfast, but she needed more for her bread pudding.

The front oak door banged opened, knocking against the walls of the cabin with a loud thud. Austin stood like a colossus in the entrance, the setting rays of the sun etching a shadowed portrait against the floor of the cabin.

She rushed forward. He just stared down at her.

"David wouldn't come."

She stared at him in disbelief. Mother hurried from the bedroom.

"There's an epidemic in town, Mrs. McConnell. Typhoid. He's not far. I went with him as far as Emerald City. How's Mary?"

"Her condition hasn't changed," Mother said.

His long legs covered the distance between door and bedroom quickly. He was gone for a good while, then reappeared only to plop down into a wooden chair at the table. "She's pretty bad." He rubbed his bloodshot eyes with his dirty hand. "She told me to tell you all not to worry, that she'd try and get some rest now." He stared straight ahead, his eyes bloodshot and puffy, his big fingers ruffling his thick, dusty black hair.

"I'm going to go out and get a breath of fresh air. It looks like a long night." Mother was nearly knocked over when the girls came running in from the creek.

"Pa, Pa!" cried the girls in unison, running over to him and plopping themselves on his lap. "We've missed you."

His hand stroked first Susie's then Becky's hair. "What did my two favorite girls do today? Did you help the ladies?"

"We helped sweep and dry dishes and eat. I liked the eating part best." Becky said. She reached one small finger to the crease in Austin's cheek. "Tell Miss Collina how come you've got those dimples there in your cheeks."

"I'll tell her, Pa," Susie said. "Someone busted him on either side with a store-bought ring!"

"Humph. Most likely he had it coming," Collina muttered.

A wry smile curved beneath his mustache. He'd heard. "What else did my favorite girls do?"

"We played with Ruby. She's lots of fun," Susie said.

"Why don't you two go out and play now? I promised your mother I would help the ladies." Then spying the wood shavings on the floor, he said, "Looks like I should have been here sooner."

"We're hungry," Susie said.

"I'm making dinner now." Collina turned back to her pots, stirring the stew.

"Come to think of it," Austin said, stepping toward her, "so am I."

She wiped her forehead with the back of her hand. He was beside her now, sniffing the aroma of her stew.

"Smells good, huh, girls?" Susie and Becky took hold of his hands. their little eyes gazing up at him adoringly.

"It's been a hot spring, for sure, and it's hot enough by this stove." Austin's dimples played across his cheeks. He was known for his feisty dimples and good looks, and he knew it.

Dimples never held any allure for Collina. All she saw was Austin's conceited opinion of himself. "I could use some water." She stepped away from him and removed a damp strand of hair off her forehead.

Austin's brows knitted themselves over questioning eyes.

"Girls make yourselves useful." Austin handed Susie and Becky the pails. "I'd better go and take care of Buckshot." He paused before going out. "Looks like rain tonight. Clouds coming over in the west could bring a storm. I'll get in some more kindling, too."

"Hurry, girls." Ruby said, setting the table. "When you return, we'll eat."

Collina turned. "But Doc, when did he say—"

"He's not coming." Austin slammed the door behind him.

Collina groped the edge of the sink. Doc had told her at the ball, "I'm concerned about my sister. I've warned her that another pregnancy like the last might kill her."

Mary wanted to give Austin a son, but for the past four years had been unable to. The last two babies had been stillborn.

"Collina," Mother said on entering the doorway with the girls, "I want you and Ruby to take Susie and Becky home. Ruby, you can stay there with them till I return."

Ruby's face broke into a tired grin. Turning to the two girls bringing the water into the cabin, she said, "And you can play with Bugie."

"Then, Collina, I want you to saddle up Magic and ride to town. Tell Doc to come quick. I never dreamt Mary was this bad. Don't you come back here without him."

"Don't worry, he'll come, if I have to tie him to Magic's saddle."

"Go get your things together." Ruby gave the girls a little shove, her worried eyes jumping from Collina to Mother.

Becky grabbed her sister's hand. "Come on, Susie, before they change their minds."

Watching the girls go to the far side of the room to collect their clothes, Collina wondered if Austin would approve.

Mother plopped down in one of the chairs and wiped her brow. Susie was soon by her side with her small bag of clothes carefully wrapped in her arms, followed by Becky.

"Put them by the door, girls, then come sit down to eat. Susie, you best go get your Pa and tell him dinner is ready." Maggie stroked the rich walnut-brown hair as the solemn, doe-eyed Becky stared back at her adoringly.

Collina realized Susie had her mother's blond hair and blue eyes; however, Becky had her mother's gentle temperament.

Ruby and Collina hurried to get the food on the table. She placed the small bowl of bread pudding on the table, looking at it proudly.

"What's that?" Becky said, placing an inquisitive finger on the bowl.

"Why that's bread pudding. That's the only dessert Collina ever found the patience to learn how to make."

"Mother," Collina said, "why did you have to tell her that?"

Mother laughed, winking at Ruby. "I guess cuz it's true."

Ruby smiled, turning to the wide-eyed Becky and placing a finger to one of the ruffles on the little girl's apron. "If you had waited for Collina to make anything as fancy as ruffles, you might as well wait for the judgment day."

"But if you want a piano moved," Mother said, rocking Becky on her lap, "just call on Collina."

Her sense of humor, slightly tarnished from disuse, soon was laughing along with Mother and Ruby, then she was suddenly the only one laughing. She turned to see Austin and Susie standing in the doorway. Austin's brows were drawn low, his lips in a scowl, which made his face look meaner in the half-light.

"We were kidding Collina about her housewife abilities," Maggie said.

Ruby shifted in her chair nervously.

Collina met Austin's scornful face with an expression that matched and placed a bowl of stew at his place. "It doesn't concern you. Eat."

With that she sat down across the table from him and filled her plate.

He sat down and picked up his spoon, emptying it a half a dozen times. His eyebrows rose in surprise. "It's good. Can't believe I'm saying that."

Does he really think I care if he likes my cooking? He can starve for all the matter it is to me.

His dimples played mischievously. "Where's your coveralls?"

"I only wear them in the fields."

Austin chuckled. "And to bed."

Maggie cleared her throat. "Austin, I think we're in for a long night with Mary. Will you allow the children to go home with Ruby tonight?"

He shook his dark head. "I don't see the need."

Collina frowned back. "It's been arranged, and Susie and Becky are looking forward to it."

He set his eyes on her and she stared back.

Mother gulped down a bite of stew. "I'm going to have Collina go for Doc. It wouldn't hurt—"

"Mother, I'm going with or without Austin's permission."

He rolled a piece of food around in his mouth, then swallowed. A half smile formed across his exhausted face. "Yeah, with those daggers you call eyes you shouldn't have any trouble at all convincing David."

"And Susie and Becky are leaving for Shushan," Collina said.

He slammed his big hand down on the table.

Maggie and Ruby jumped, grabbing their plates that had nearly landed in their laps.

Leaning over the table, Austin's eyes gleamed into Collina's. "Yes. Now, may I finish my dinner in peace? Or is there something else you'd like to tell me?"

Chapter 10

*C*ollina pounded on the rough boards of the door. Shivering beneath her slicker, she buried her head deeper within the folds of her hood as the rain now fell in earnest. How dare he? She wouldn't marry Austin if he was the last man breathing on earth.

She raised her clenched fist. "Doc Baker, it's Collina May McConnell. Open up." No answer. She'd been to town and had missed Doc by two hours. This cabin, nestled high on one of the hilltops, had been unknown to her and she'd no idea of its inhabitants, but Doc's horse was in their shed, and she wasn't leaving without him.

The heavy door creaked open. "Sickness here; go away." The person on the other side did not wish to be seen, for the cracked door did not produce a face behind the words.

"I'm not here to visit; I came for Doc Baker."

"Let her in, Skeeder," Doc's tired voice said. The door did not move.

She didn't wait for the faceless listener to respond. She shoved the door open with her riding boot.

Losing his balance, the thin boy fell. His dirty white teeth snarled back at her. "Why, you—"

"Enough of that. I warned you to be quick about it, didn't I?" Doc Baker's tired eyes winked at her. "Kind of like the boy the calf ran over, huh, Collina? Skeeder, Collina's probably the first lady you've ever met who can work a combine as good as any man."

She offered the young boy a hand up. Skeeder ignored it. She shrugged. Weren't enough minutes in her day to play a cat and mouse game of hurt feelings. "Doc, you've got to come quick. Mary's in labor, and she's having a hard time."

"Hmm, so Austin said. He was mighty worried, but a little too late if you ask me. I told him not to let her get in that condition for a while. I warned him."

"It's good you did. But she's that-a-way again and needs your help." She walked about the cabin, collecting Doc's black bag, hat, and coat. He may not know it, but Doc was coming. Mary needed him.

"Told Austin when he came to fetch me that I wasn't coming." This quarrel was worse than she thought. "You don't mean that. Mary hasn't a bad thought, nor a hard word for anyone. If there was a body ready for the hereafter, it would be your baby sister. Only, we need her goodness here, so she can rub some of it off onto us. Here's your hat."

"Is she really that bad off?" Doc said.

"When Mother gets worried, you know it."

"Son, go pour me another cup of that coffee on the stove." Doc rose from his chair, then swayed a little, placing a hand to his temples. "I'll just sit down for a minute."

She rushed over to the cook stove, seized the cup from the slow-moving boy and hurried to Doc. "You look like you haven't slept for days."

Doc looked up at her through blood shot eyes. "What day is it?"

"Monday."

"The last day I was home was Thursday." He gulped the coffee down. "Get me some of that bread Martha left, just a small wedge."

She nearly knocked the boy down in her haste.

"This typhoid's wearing me out. I sent Martha home. She was ready to drop." Doc took the bread from her outstretched hand.

She drew out a brown paper from one of her deep pockets. "Eat this with your bread." Unwrapping it, she offered Doc a piece of jerky.

The boy eyed it hungrily.

"Girl, you're a life saver. This poor family's been down with the fever for nearly two weeks, hardly has any food left on the place."

She walked toward the mattress sitting on the dirt floor in the corner of the room. There between the coverlets lay a woman and two young girls.

"Every day brings more sickness, more folks needing help," Doc said. The woman's curly black hair was moist on her perspiring forehead. She opened her eyes and stared at Collina. "Would you like me to bring you some homemade chicken soup?"

The woman smiled and nodded.

Collina patted her thin arm. "I'll bring you some clean things, too."

"We'd best get moving," Doc Baker said.

"You mean you're leaving us this a way?" Skeeder said.

"I've done all I can for now. I'll be back tomorrow. Here," he said, "give this medicine to your ma and sisters three times daily." He picked up his coat and bag. "The thing they need right now is some good food, and if I was you, I'd take Collina up on her offer."

"Here," she said, thrusting the package of jerky to Skeeder.

"We don't need your charity."

"It's not charity, boy. Collina could use a strong back like yours right about now," Doc said between mouthfuls.

"When Pa comes back, he'll need my help more, I reckon." The thin youth, dressed only in a pair of old coveralls, now shuffled his bare feet about the dirt floor, then reached down to throw another log into the hot embers of the cook stove. "I'll make some herb tea. Ma will like that."

"I'll drop the food and clothes off tomorrow. No need to worry about repaying it." She held the wrapped beef out to him again. Skeeder buried his dirty hands farther into his coverall pockets. She laid the meat on the stove and walked out into the darkness.

"How are they keeping body and soul together?" she asked as she helped Doc harness up his horse.

"Don't know," he said. "These hill folk are a breed all their own. Good lot, though, every one of them."

"Did Skeeder say where his pa was?"

"He didn't know. His pa's got a whisky still up in the mountains." Doc nodded his head toward a hand-dug cave chiseled into the hill. Don't understand why there wasn't any meat on the place. Tie Magic behind the carriage, and ride in here out of the rain."

"There's plenty of game in the woods." She climbed into the carriage. With his tongue, Doc made a clicking noise that moved Lady into a trot down the muddy road. "The man's probably on a binge. Those kind do that when times get hard."

"Why, the coward." She couldn't hide her distaste.

"You'll run across more cowards than heroes in your lifetime, and you'll probably not recognize the difference between the two until their character is put to the test."

"But what makes people that way?" She looked out over the bleak countryside, her thoughts on Austin. Had she judged him wrongly?

"There are only two alternatives in life as I see it." Doc gave a snap of his whip to his lagging horse. "Either you face your destiny, or you run from it. It's harder for boys like Skeeder to succeed."

"Why?"

"Because he has one mark against him. There's no role model to fashion his life after. What the Bible says is true, 'A good tree cannot bring forth evil fruit, neither can a corrupt tree bring forth good fruit. Every tree that bringeth not forth good fruit is hewn down and cast into the fire. Wherefore by their fruits ye shall know them.'"

"Then he hasn't got a chance."

"No, I didn't say that. It's just harder for them," Doc said. "He didn't run off with his pa; he stayed there. And you know what he said to me after you left the cabin?"

"What?"

"For me to tell you thank you and that he'd be down your way to help with the crops soon as his ma and sisters were better. Looks like a new tree has been planted, and with a little water and nourishment, it just might bring forth some good fruit."

She pondered Doc's words, staring ahead into the steady stream of rain falling off the buggy's fringed top.

"By the way..." Doc didn't take his eyes from the road. "Rose got a letter from Franklin. Said he was well and would ship out soon to Cuba. Rose has got a good heart in her; though he hasn't written but one or two letters, she still keeps on corresponding with him. She wanted me to ask you, has Franklin written you? She thought maybe, well, seeing how he took you to her ball."

"Not a word." She felt the necklace she now wore around her neck and touched her lips, recalling Lady's Lake. No, he hadn't written her a line. So, he's been communicating with Rose.

"Franklin's an example of what I've been saying. Had it worse than Skeeder could imagine, and he turned out a mighty fine man to my estimation. Rose considers him highly. He's already proved to me that he's got grit. I wouldn't mind calling him son one day. Have you heard from Joseph?"

"Yes. Joseph and Franklin have become good friends."

"So Joseph's been writing you?"

She turned her face away so Doc wouldn't see her tears. Dear Joseph, is that the reason why he'd been writing her so faithfully? Because he knew Franklin's affections had altered course? Rose was beautiful and so refined. She couldn't blame Franklin.

"Big Jim will be glad to hear that. Said he's gotten one hastily scribbled paragraph in the past two months. He's been pestering me for news about his son. I'll just send Big Jim your way when he gets to be too bothersome. How is Myra doing?"

Collina swept her face with her hand, recalling Luke's trepidations over Franklin's zeal for material success. So she'd been duped by him. Rose could have him. That would be the last tear she'd shed for the likes of Franklin Long. "We haven't heard a word from Myra. Mother is growing worried. I just can't understand her running off with Clem when there's Luke who's—"

"You can't make someone love you if they don't. And you don't always fall in love with the right one. I told Luke not to worry. Maggie's got two fine girls his age, the one sitting next to me being my first choice."

She looked sideways at him. Doc Baker hardly conversed a half-dozen words to her in their times of conversation. She understood now what sparked the sudden change. A smile escaped through the corners of her lips. Doctor Baker never needed to disclose his off-time hobby of matchmaker before.

"I know what you're thinking, but a father wants the best for his children. I've thought about it, and I've told Luke he doesn't have to wait until after his internship to marry. It was wrong for me to expect him to wait four years." Doc paused, then said, "We try to do right by our children, but we're only human. Parents make mistakes, too."

Deep puddles, ruts, and oozing mud perforated the steep hill leading to the Blaine's homestead. Doc's big bay sank down to her fetlocks on many an occasion, but relentlessly plodded on, pulling the big wheels of the carriage through the thick red gravy that now coated the once clean carriage.

Seeing Austin emerge from the cabin, she yelled over the heavy downpour. "How's Mary?"

Doc was off the seat in one bound, his leather bag clasped in his fist. Austin turned to block his way into the cabin.

"The baby, a boy, came breach and stillborn. Mary's dead."

"What!"

"Say it, and get it off your chest, David. Mary wasn't good enough for me. But whether you choose to believe it or not—I loved her!" Austin set out toward the barn.

Collina covered her mouth. Did Mary have a premonition about her death? Mary would want her to tell Austin how much happiness he'd given her. That the love Austin had for Mary had been enough… enough to die for.

Austin was half way to the barn. She needed to get to him before Doc did.

If anything ever happened to Franklin, she'd want to know the truth.

Chapter 11

June 22, 1898. Daiquiri, Cuba

The rumbling waves hit the makeshift wooden planks of the bridge at Santiago de Cuba with force, then retreated slowly, pulling the guidelines beneath its grip like a serpent would its prey. Franklin was sandwiched between men and horses. A sorrel mare shied at the spewing salt water erupting through a gaping hole that one of the weaker planks had vacated.

"Easy, big fella," Franklin spoke soothingly to Raymar, then turned to Joseph. "This bridge isn't going to last much longer with this undertow."

"Watch out, another wave!"

Franklin braced for the worst, and as the wave rolled past, glanced over his shoulder to thank the Good Samaritan. His gaze was met with a pair of dark slanted eyes the color of pitch. The large, muscular man wore a black felt hat that displayed straight black hair tumbling beneath its brim and a fringed, fawn-leather jacket, belted at the waist and fastened with a large Bowie knife. His deeply tanned face bore a jagged scar that wove down at a diagonal from his eye to his nose. His attitude did not allude to an overly zealous sentiment of neighborliness. Franklin coughed and said, "Much obliged," anyway.

Joseph nudged his side. "That's Joe. Did you get a look at his squaw and papoose?"

"Nah, they wouldn't let a woman come here," Franklin said.

"Joe was Roosevelt's chief scout during the time he had his ranch on the Little Missouri River in North Dakota and hunted buffalo. Joe's quite the fighter. Only, he wouldn't come unless he could bring his family, so here they are."

Straddling a large paint, a small woman of medium build with large brown eyes and high cheekbones stared back at him. Two braids of long black hair rested on either shoulder. A sling of cedar boards bound in leather stays laced about her back and chest, and the small black head of an infant turned solemn dark eyes to him. Joe glanced toward Franklin then, his eyes widening in surprise, he jumped onto his black horse.

A huge wave rumbled its way toward them, sweeping the water beneath and picking up speed, heading straight for their ship. No way will this bridge hold. The Indian was right. Franklin nudged Joseph. "Get on your horse."

"What?"

Grabbing his own bridle, he swung himself up. They had a better chance of surviving now. He knew his big chestnut could swim it. "Men, those who have horses, get on them and swim toward shore."

Like a volcano, spewing debris of planks and cargo blew like meaningless pieces of kindling swelling about the five-foot high waves. The flimsy makeshift bridge spanning the gap between the large battleship and the Cuban shoreline was now only a tattered piece of driftwood in the stormy sea as soldiers and horses tried desperately to make it to shore.

Franklin spit out a mouthful of salt water, narrowing his eyes before the onset of another wave, and leaned over Raymar's neck, murmuring reassuringly, heading him away from the debris at a diagonal against the strong current. He heard Joseph yell and looked back long enough to see that he was safe, clinging to his gelding's neck. Franklin motioned for him to follow at the same diagonal.

Then, out of the corner of his eye, he spotted the pinto, thrashing in the waves. Its legs appeared to be caught. Then Joe's black was caught. It looked to be fishing nets. Franklin headed away from the trouble, not wanting to take a chance of any harm coming to Raymar.

But his newly found conscience pricked his heart sorely. *How could I open my Bible again knowing I didn't try to help them?* That girl with the baby strapped to her back had a thread's hold on surviving in these waves. He reached for his knife and turned Raymar toward the struggling horses. The waves fought with increasing fury against Raymar, whipping him in the face. Franklin tied Raymar's reins about his horse's neck, heading him in the direction of the shoreline, then took a deep breath and dove deep into the salty foam.

The pinto's legs thrashed about. Franklin was hard pressed to make sure his knife didn't slip and gorge a leg instead of the slippery netting. Joe was working furiously at the other end. Both men sensed the woman bravely holding onto her pinto might any minute become caught within the grasp of the furious waves and undertow.

Franklin came up for air, then plunged beneath the surface again, knifing the netting stubbornly as one by one the intricate web was severed of its bounty. As if his prayers had reached the ears of God, both horses' legs broke free, their heads instinctively rowing forward, lunging with what little strength they had left. Joe's black followed the paint with the woman, the child still bound to her back. Only Raymar remained.

"Joe, Joe!" The woman screamed.

Joe was gone. Franklin dove down beneath the turbulent peaks. His hand touched an arm caught in the fishing net, like an octopus would its prey. Slitting the netting with his sharp knife, he grasped Joe by the nap of his shirt and with his last ounce of strength swam back up.

Joe coughed up salt water and then drank in big gulps of the salty air. Together they swam toward Raymar.

"Can your stallion handle the added weight?" Joe said in pants.

"We'll find out. Here, get on, I can always hold onto his tail." What had beguiled the stallion to stay and not follow the other horses?

"Come on, Raymar," Franklin, short-winded from his dive, gasped out the command as the strong undertow dragged them farther and farther away from the safety of the shoreline.

With one lunge, Raymar cut through the wave about to wash across his back. Another lunge brought him even farther away from the deadly undertow. His shrill neigh split the morbid sounds of squealing horses and crashing waves, and Raymar's muscular neck laid over the waters as his strong legs propelled them toward the shoreline.

Lieutenant Colonel Theodore Roosevelt gave Franklin's shoulder a hardy slap. "Fine work, Franklin. So glad you made it. Because with Troops C, H, and M being left behind, I need every able-bodied cavalryman I have."

"Yes, sir."

"As I always say, in any moment of decision, the best thing you can do is the right thing. The worst thing you can do is nothing." Roosevelt adjusted his pince-nez glasses. "You have yourself a good-looking animal here. I understand he's from a breeding farm in Kentucky? Mighty fine present, I'd say. Someone thinks highly of you."

"Thank you, sir." He sent a sidelong glance in Joseph's direction.

Raymar chose to shake himself vigorously then and whinnied loudly at a mare passing by. As if to say "Hello there, did you happen to catch that I just saved my master?"

"He's certainly a fine looking animal."

Raymar raised his head, his ears pricked forward, nostrils flaring, as another mare trotted by him, flinging her tail; he let out a shrill neigh.

Roosevelt chuckled. "Nothing like being the only stud on an island full of mares." Roosevelt hit his riding crop on the calf of his boot. He swept the perimeter, scanning the soldiers and horses. Spotting the person he sought, he yelled, "Joe, come here."

Joe complied.

"Joe, can we make this horse his own livery?" Roosevelt asked.

Joe nodded.

Beneath Roosevelt's bushy mustache, his mouth curved into a large grin. "Good." Slapping Joe on the back, he extended his hand and gave Franklin's a hardy shake. "I met Joe in South Dakota. He's a Native American." He chuckled. "Yes, we are all Americans; free born and free bred, where no man is our superior, except for his own worth, or as our inferior, except for his own demerit."

"Sir?"

"Yes, yes, soldier, lead the way, son." He turned to follow the young soldier, his fringed jacket bobbing with every energetic step of his quick legs.

Joseph crossed his arms, his red hair gleaming in the sunlight, watching the imposing stature of the man walking down the wake. "The soldiers here who served under him before respect him, not because they must, but because they admire him. You know what I heard him mumble as he watched you fighting for your lives? 'There is no effort without error…and if they fail, at least they fail while daring greatly.'" Joseph turned and frowned. "You were safe, so what happened? One minute I was following you and the next—"

"So you can tell the whole camp about it?" Franklin said gruffly. He was embarrassed everyone had watched their heroic actions, but unwilling to reveal it.

Joseph grinned. "You know me better than that. I only tell my friends." Joe extended his hand. Franklin responded automatically.

"Say, look at that." Joseph pointed to the cuts on Franklin's forearms.

"Looks like I missed the rope a couple of times."

Joe turned his forearm over. "More than once."

Joseph pointed to Franklin's and Joe's arms. "You have the same skin tones. Maybe you two are of the same tribe."

Franklin chuckled. "The all-American tribe, right, Joe?"

Joe placed Franklin's arm with the knife cuts upon his. "Now we are true brothers." Without another word, Joe strolled after Roosevelt.

"That beats all." Joseph fingered his sprouting red whiskers. "What do you make of that?"

Franklin looked after the retreating form, then turned a wary eye on Joseph. "Just how is it that before I get to shore, everyone knows my life story?"

"Guess I did let a few things slip. If it'll get you out of this brooding state you've been in lately, I'll put in a good word for you to Collina."

"You'll what?"

"You mean she didn't write you like all your other fair damsels? Did you really expect her to?" Joseph studied his face. "I can see it does bother you, what with that stubborn chin of yours jutting out just asking someone to punch it."

"So that's the way the breeze is blowing. Like I didn't know all along you and Collina were sweet on each other. I take it she's writing you."

"Haven't you been writing to Rose?" Joseph said.

"Rose does most of the corresponding." Franklin was used to having women write him. In fact, he'd gotten other letters, some from a Naomi McCancy, who for the life of him, he couldn't recollect.

"Have all the ladies you like. Only, you'll find out Collina's different. Can't ever be another woman like her, cuz the good Lord broke the mold after He made her."

"You're in love with her."

"Yes, I am. But Collina's happiness comes first, and she has taken a liking to you. Told me the night of Rose's ball that 'God was going to use you for His grand purpose.'"

"She said that?" Franklin asked.

"It's every man for himself, and I'm just telling you like it is. If you want a letter from her, you need to write her first. I'm only asking for one favor in return."

"What's that?"

"That you get me off this sorry island in one piece and not in a coffin."

Chapter 12

July 1, 1898

This hill was different. Raymar felt it. Franklin felt it. The battle at Las Guasimas would be child's play next to this. Horses and foot soldiers pressed them on either side, fighting for a place in the front alongside their leader who through the weeks of battles, they had all come to admire. "Teddy," as the men now referred to him though only behind his proud back, was a dynamic and powerful commander.

He paused now and the men grew silent, waiting for his next words.

"Soldiers, it is far better to dare mighty things, to win glorious triumphs, even though checkered by failure, than to take rank with those poor spirits who neither enjoy much nor suffer much, because they live in the grey twilight that knows neither victory nor defeat." Roosevelt smiled and placed his hat on his head. "Now that I have delivered my little speech," he raised his sword and shouted, "charge!"

Raymar took the steep hill in leaps, his strong shoulders never tiring, never failing to give more to the pressure of Franklin's heels.

Roosevelt's closest patriots tried to protect him as much as humanly possible; however, he would always maneuver himself away, yelling the words, "Remember the *Maine*!" His men had grown to love him and never failed to take up the chant, as they did now.

"Remember the *Maine*! Remember the *Maine*!" Among the thundering hooves, the clanging of swords, and the cries of the men, there was no room for fear for oneself. But fear for their fellow patriots—that was different.

Franklin's sword went deep, deep into the Spaniard, and he belched out blood. As he withdrew his sword, blood dripped onto the Spaniard's red coat. He'd watched his friends fall beneath the Spaniards' vicious sabers, and killing them didn't bother him. This war had to end.

Foot soldiers crumbled onto the blood-soaked earth. A big bay horse jumped over a lifeless form, then tumbled into a heap, head first, as a gun blasted part of her chest away. He hated to see that happen. What was the name of this hill? He tried to think of it as a bullet whizzed past his ear, then he sunk his saber into his opponent's chest. San Juan, that's it. How could he have forgotten? Roosevelt said they had to take this hill.

"Charge!" Roosevelt's cry could be heard ahead of him.

The smothering heat and hazy gun smoke permeated the air, giving off an odor of sulfur that mingled with the stench of horseflesh and dying men. Joe's black horse ran past Franklin, riderless. The bay mare and the man lying dead beneath her belly flashed before his mind's eye.

Joseph was beside him now. "I can't find Joe."

Ever since that fateful day in the Atlantic, Joe and his wife Jane and their daughter, Dawn, had become close, like family, to Joseph and him.

"Watch your flank. You hear! Don't turn back, no matter what happens. I'll find Joe and catch up to you later. Now stay alert and follow Roosevelt."

"Where are the guns they promised?" Joseph asked. "They were supposed to give us some cover. We're already outnumbered three to one. We need their cover to win this hill."

Franklin glanced toward the Atlantic and the harbor. Where were the battleships? Not wanting to let on to Joseph how worried he was, he said, "They'll come."

Franklin spun Raymar around, scanning the battlefield. The cries of dying men and animals mingled with the screaming voices of "Remember the Maine! Remember the Maine!" His horse lunged, his ears laid flat against his head, his mouth open at the approaching mount. "There." Franklin yelled. "This is for Joe." The Spaniard fell forward, and his mount on loosened rein galloped into the smoke of the battlefield.

Then he saw him. "Joe!" Racing toward the form, Franklin sprang from Raymar. He uncapped his canteen with the preciously small supply of water.

Joe lay sprawled in a mud of his own blood, split open like a watermelon by a Spaniard's sword. Franklin unfastened his belt, wrapping it around Joe's middle, then carried him to a nearby tree.

"I…knew…you'd…come."

"Take a sip." Franklin held the canteen to Joe's lips.

"No…you'll…need." Blood trickled like a brook onto the earth Franklin knelt on, an ever-widening pool of Joe's dwindling life. Only a spark of light glinted beneath the depths of Joe's falling eyelids. "Jane, Dawn, you take care?"

"Of course I will, Joe. We're blood brothers, remember?" When had this bond between them grown so strong?

A faint smile creased Joe's purple lips. His hand rested on Franklin's. "Good friend, do not be sad. It is good to finish life so…thanks to blood brother I now know Jesus. Tell my Jane…see…later. Jesus here to take me…home." His head fell forward. Lifeless.

"No, no." Franklin looked at the lifeless face of his friend and, suddenly, his deep-throated scream split the sodden air. "No!" Jumping onto Raymar, he urged his steed forward.

Before his eyes, the ground became strewn with men and horses. The air reeked with blood, but still no thunder of guns. The bodies of his outnumbered regiment lay strewn on the bloodied ground. Out of nowhere Franklin saw a Spaniard's sword aimed for his chest. Suddenly Joseph was there, slamming into the Spaniard's mount. They toppled together to the ground. Franklin plunged his sword into the Spaniard while Joseph remounted.

"Wasn't any action up front. Thought I best get back and see what kind of trouble you've got yourself in."

"It took you long enough."

"Joe?" Joseph asked.

"Dead."

They fought until the air around them smelled of sweat and the stench of blood and dead corpses rotting in the sun, and still they came. Then seemingly out of nowhere a Spaniard's sword went deep into Raymar's chest. Raymar fell to his knees.

"No!" Pain shot through Franklin's thigh as he felt the Spaniard's hot breath on his neck. Still he fought as he felt Raymar struggle, then sink slowly to the ground. Franklin slid from his mount, raising his sword, the sun momentarily blinding him. The Spaniard's face was over him— his dark face and black eyes, smiling, his left arm raised above his head.

Joseph jumped on the Spaniard and wrestled him to the ground. He and Joseph fought side by side. But now they were at a disadvantage, for they were looking up into the fast steeds of the Spaniards. Pain coursed through the nerves of Franklin's right arm, so he swung his sword to his left. Joseph's cry split the air, tearing into the very cords of Franklin's chest. He lunged out blindly, blindly into the darkness he felt himself falling into.

"Jane." Franklin reached for her hand. "Where am I?"

"In hospital. You left for dead. I found."

"Joe…Jane, I was there when Deerhawk…" Franklin cried. "Did Joseph make it? Of course he did. He's been plaguing me with his foolish jokes while I slept."

"No," Jane said.

"That can't be." Sobs racked through his thin body. "I can't believe it. I kept hearing Joseph's voice. Last thing he said just before I woke was, 'God wants me to listen. He has a special mission for you.'"

"You awake, soldier? We thought you planned on sleeping through the next war, too." The Cuban doctor showed his pleasure on seeing Franklin awake and alert. He leaned over, listening to Franklin's pulse, his heartbeat. "Nurse, get this soldier something to eat."

"My leg." Franklin moaned, for just that small amount of movement had sent shooting pain from his leg clear to his chest.

"Yes, your leg." The doctor removed the bandages and began

probing it with his index finger. "Your woman's been using some kind of hocus-pocus on it. Must admit it's working. I was going to cut it off, but she wouldn't let me."

"Joe?" Franklin looked at Jane questioningly.

Jane put a finger to her lips and touched her neck.

Franklin's hand went to his throat. His tags were gone. Only the chain with the mustard seed remained.

"Roosevelt said some of those Indian concoctions work. He certainly knew what he was talking about, though I wouldn't allow use of them on a white man."

"Ted? Where is he?" Franklin looked around bewildered.

"Here." Roosevelt walked over to him.

"How did the battle go?" Franklin said.

"We won. Santiago surrendered on July 17. Our causalities in the field were high. We lost around 1,600. As soon as Santiago came under siege, the Spanish fleet made a run for it. But Commodore Schley sank or beached every one of those Spanish ships. Schley only lost one sailor." Roosevelt looked down at his hands, then said, "Wish I'd only lost one at San Juan Hill."

"You did your best. With you screaming like a crazy man and waving that ridiculous sword of yours, I'm surprised the Spaniards didn't hightail it!"

Roosevelt laughed. "You mean I got a little excited, huh?"

"That's saying it mildly. Why do you think we rushed up that hill like that—you thought we were after the Spaniards? No, we were running after you, trying to shut you up."

Roosevelt's booming laugh filled the small room. "Bullish, simply bullish. Say, Major Miles wants to leave for Puerto Rico next week. Do you think you'll be up to it? We may go clear to the Philippines before it's all over. We're planning to knock on the doors of Manila itself," Roosevelt said.

"Wild horses couldn't keep me here," Franklin said, looking around at the unsanitary conditions.

Roosevelt turned. "Doctor, when can this soldier leave?"

The surgeon walked over and shook his head. "That Spaniard didn't

CATHERINE ULRICH BRAKEFIELD

leave you much. He nearly cut your leg off with his sword. Your woman did a good job stopping the infection, but the real test comes when you try to walk on that leg."

Roosevelt glanced at Jane and cleared his throat. "Oh, yes, a major mistake has been made here. This is Lieutenant Franklin Long. Please make the necessary changes on your papers as I shall mine."

The doctor looked at Jane questioningly. "Oh, I understand now. It was Joe that died and..." He glanced down, changed the name on his papers and shrugged. "Major ligaments have been severed, Lieutenant Long. I would recommend you go back to the States and plan on extensive bed rest. Find a good hospital that has a first-rate therapy program. That is your only hope for you to walk again and live a normal life."

Chapter 13

August 13, 1898

Clammy with perspiration, Collina's arms felt like they weighed a ton. She walked into the shade of the barn. It felt ten degrees cooler. She turned, looking for her brothers and their wagon returning from town.

The dusty lane to Shushan that wound through the stately arched trees on either side were all that met her gaze. *I wish I hadn't allowed the boys to go to market without me. They should have returned hours ago.*

She chastised herself for thinking her brothers couldn't handle the marketing of their produce. After all, someday her brothers would shoulder the responsibility of Shushan, and she needed to show confidence in their abilities. "Now, where could Jessie have left it? Ah, there you are." Picking up stool and pail, she walked toward the first cow.

Most everyone in her household was well and healthy, not like the McWilliams. *What will I do without Joseph?* Big Jim had been beside himself the day of the funeral. It was hard to watch. She never realized how much she depended on Joseph's helping hand until he was absent. Collina swiped her face clean. *No matter now.*

Rose had heard no news about Franklin. It was as if that Cuban dirt had swallowed him whole. Collina continued to pray for his welfare and had stepped up her prayers for him, urging her family to pray as well. "All-knowing Lord, keep him safely in Thy keeping."

She swatted at an obstinate fly and leaned her head on Betsy's side. The day was both hot and humid, a combination only the insects relished. Her hands pulled rhythmically, first one teat, then the other. The white milk, foamy and warm, made a shiss, shiss noise as it hit the sides of the metal bucket.

Her mind recollected the strewed pieces of her day. The thermometer on the back porch had read 110 at high noon. The sun baked down on her and Uncle Charlie's heads relentlessly as they worked silently down the rows and rows of tobacco plants, pulling off the dreaded sphinx moths and larvae. Sweat poured down her forehead beneath the brim of one of Father's old hats to the point that she, tired of wiping it, wrapped her bandanna around her forehead, blinking only now and then when the sweat still filtered down through the folds of cloth. She'd let Uncle Charlie leave early, and he'd shaken his grizzled old head at her. "You'll wear yourself out, girl, then you'll be no good to anyone."

"Someone has to do it," she muttered to Betsy. "I won't allow a passel of bugs to ruin my crop. We've just got to have a good one this year." Even the soft udder of the cow did not ease the ache in her arms. It was so hot; her tongue felt fuzzy, that agonizing thirst on her again. She'd get the milking done before she'd allow herself the luxury of another drink.

Feeling the stinging sensation of the liquid coming in contact with her open calluses, she remembered Uncle Charlie's words: We need more bodies to help with the crops.

Clem's haughty face came to mind. "He's got plenty of time to help, but who needs his meanness." She remembered Emma Glaser whispering that Clem had been seen at Lawyer Farlin's who carried a grudge a mile wide for Father. "I'd rather work alongside a snake. Betsy, just look what Clem's done to Myra." Myra's large blue eyes appeared even larger in the thin face that smiled at them during church last Sunday.

Myra had been pregnant and had morning sickness bad, then she miscarried. She looked so pale and thin that Mother insisted Myra come home for a while so she could 'fatten her up' on ham and biscuits. Clem's face had frozen into an angry mask, and Collina worried Clem would stop Myra from coming. Her mother's firm hand restrained her from saying what was on her mind.

"Clem, you're always welcome in our home," Mother gently said.

"I don't mean to separate the two of you. I just feel that my daughter needs some bed rest for a while. I know how much the two of you want a baby. Ben and I felt the same. I miscarried my first three, so I know what Myra is going through."

Clem and Myra had stayed for six weeks. Then Clem got an itch to his foot and decided to go to Detroit.

"How Mother could be nice to that man is beyond me."

The first bucket was nearly full. Collina paused. Voices and the plodding hooves of a horse approached. Sounds like my brothers are home. The buckboard came to a halt in front of the barn entrance.

"Whoa, you sorry nag." Robert said.

Collina stopped in mid rhythm.

"Sis, you in there?" Scott said.

Daisy's ears pricked forward; she neighed, a low sorry "Guess what I did" type of neigh. Her mane was all askew, and in between harness and horse lay an assortment of carrot stocks, cabbage leaves, onions skins, and turnip greens. Jesse, Robert, and Scott, too, were a maze of auburn and blond heads that smelled strongly of onions and greens. Their clothes were torn, stained, and maimed with tomatoes, beans, and cucumbers.

Collina laughed. "What happened?"

Jesse rested one tomato-stained elbow on his smeared overalls. "We were on our way real nice like down Brier Lane, when out of the blue, old Daisy here got spooked. Robert thought he could do a better job of controlling her, so I gave him the reins."

"You threw them at me," Robert said, his face growing as red as his tomato-stained shirt.

"It didn't help our situation none with the reins slapping Daisy on her rump, so she ran across old Tom's meadow. That's when we found out that Old Tom's got a heap of briers on his place." Jessie rubbed his dirty arm across his scratched face.

"That's when we figured out how Brier Lane got its name," Scott said.

Robert and Jesse looked at him tartly. Scott shrugged his shoulders, still grinning.

Robert continued. "Part of the time I was in the seat, and part of the time Jesse was in the seat and I was in the bed and—"

"You kept falling on me. Now I reckon I know what Mother's pin cushion feels like," Scott said, and gave him a shove.

"Ouch! My ribs are still sore from me bouncing out of the wagon." Daisy perked up her ears and whinnied.

The old barn rafters rang with their laughter. They laughed so hard, tears formed.

"And just look at this," Jessie said, reaching into his overall pockets and producing the cash box. "All the ladies bought from our wagon."

"Yeah," Scott said, "they were all so nosy—each had to hear the story themselves."

She looked into Jessie's outstretched palm and gasped at the wad of greenbacks. "You mean you sold all the vegetables? And it looks by that wad, they tipped well."

"Yeah. Sold everything but what we were wearing."

"Collina, you got time to talk?" Doc said, turning the corner of the barn, his hands embedded in his suit pockets. "Why, what's this?" He chuckled at her comically arrayed brothers. "Just when did it become fashionable to start wearing your food?"

"When it produces such a profitable return. Just look," Collina said.

Robert opened the box full of cash.

"You may have stumbled onto something, boys. I wish more of life's problems could end up as pleasantly."

Collina took a good look at Doc's face and led the way down the lane between the rows of apples and pears. She wanted seclusion before Doc released the heavy burden he was carrying onto her shoulders.

The gaily clothed cardinals, amidst the patchwork shadows of the bent fruit trees, pompously flaunted their brilliant red coats before the discreetly clad sparrows. Barn or blossoms, the sparrow, though imitated by their more popular counterparts, sang just as sweetly. If only we could find such contentment within.

"Rose received a letter she wrote Franklin some months back, unopened. Then I got this addressed to me." Doc held out an envelope.

"You open it."

Collina tore at the envelope with her dried and dirt-stained hands. Out fell a chain. Oh, dear God, don't let it be the mustard seed.

Doc bent down to recover it. The small piece of metal lying in his palm had Franklin's name on it. "He's got to be dead. How am I going to break the news to Rose? She's such a sensitive child. I just heard from my friend in military personnel that Santiago surrendered July 17. Roosevelt's Rough Rider regiment could be heading back to the States now, or else they may go with Major General Miles to invade Puerto Rico."

Collina looked down at the name engraved into the metal in Doc's palm, blinking hard. Franklin Long. "We prayed at Joseph's funeral that by chance Franklin had somehow survived. Now this."

"Big Jim told me how broken up you were about Joseph."

Collina couldn't believe she'd never see Joseph's smiling face again. She'd cried when Big Jim had told her. How could she ever forget him? He'd been the only friend the McConnells had during the smallpox.

"Here's the letter that came with Franklin's tags, you read it."

She fumbled with the envelope, tearing open the seal, unfolding the parchment.

This is to inform you that the cavalry officer Lieutenant Franklin Long was injured severely during the battle of San Juan Hill. After a life-threatening coma, he has pulled through, but with severe injuries to his face and leg. He is now at the division hospital in Jacksonville, Florida. Colonel Theodore Roosevelt.

She bowed her head and gratefully thanked God. "He's alive. Franklin is alive." They laughed and wept openly, and she felt a new surge of hope coursing through her veins like spring dew on winter wheat. Doc wiped the tears from his face. "Collina, could you go with Rose and me to Jacksonville? I'll pay all your expenses. I think Rose would like it if another woman went with her. No telling what she'll see with Franklin so wounded."

Collina gulped, the truth hitting her in the face like a twin-barreled shotgun. Franklin was Rose's beau, not hers.

"How is Myra doing?" Doc said.

"She's…" Collina fought against the urge to scream out that Franklin was her beau. "Myra's staying at our house while Clem is in Detroit."

"I'm glad. Luke's still away at school. Just between the two of us, I'm afraid of what he'd do to Clem."

Doc talked on happily. It would do neither of them any good to disclose her feelings.

"That boy Skeeder is in a bad way. They lost their home place. Remember, the boy whose pa ran off when his mother and little sisters came down with the typhoid? You think you could put them up in your empty sharecropper cabin, the one Franklin stayed in while he was here? Skeeder might prove to be a good worker given half a chance."

The recollection of working side by side with Franklin was almost too much for her to bear. She sought refuge stroking the grass with the toe of her boot as tears swam before her eyes. "Tell him and his kin to come, no use letting a good roof go to waste. I've got lots to do if I plan on going with you and Rose."

She turned away, walking toward the house, her tears blurring the ground before her. How would Franklin greet Rose? She envisioned his strong arms embracing Rose and gently kissing her lips just like he had hers at Lady's Lake.

Chapter 14

September 10, 1901

The three years that followed became as blurred as had that fateful day in August when Collina watched Franklin's face light up on seeing Rose and Doc. She had stood in the shadows, and when Franklin did see her, it was hard to tell just what his emotions toward her were. Recognition, joy, shock...guilt, or a combination of the four?

He was thin as a willow, his face bruised beyond recognition, with a deep gash from his eye to chin. His arm looked like it had been gouged, his left leg so badly maimed, it was impossible for him to rise. Even raising his arms sent him into spasms of panting, as he whispered to her his deepest apology for Joseph's death. "He died in my place, Collina. Can you ever forgive me? I wish to God it had been me. I deserved to die, not Joseph. I...I am plagued constantly with that truth." He fell back on his pillow and pinched his eyes shut.

Rose rushed to his side, kneeling at his bedside. "Oh, Franklin I could not have endured life if you had died."

Collina chewed on her bottom lip. She and Doc exchanged glances. Each knew Franklin wasn't far from dying himself.

Rose bustled about, getting him water and food. Doc made the necessary arrangements to have Franklin transported to a rehabilitation hospital in Detroit.

Collina would never forget Franklin's compassionate look to Rose. It felt like a knife—right through her heart. But her love for him outweighed the pain.

Because of Rose, Franklin would have the best of medical care. Doc Baker was rich; he would make sure Franklin had the choicest doctors. There would be no limit to the care he would obtain with Rose by his side. Yes, it was well with her soul just knowing this.

She looked out the barn door and sighed. The rain on the tin roof made an awful ruckus. She thought Franklin and Rose would have married by now. Oh well. She had enough to think about without brooding over someone else's decisions.

More rain than they could handle kept them from harvesting their crops on time last year, followed by a bad winter that had depleted their staple crops and made them scramble to get in an early hay harvest. At least their tobacco crop had done well.

Just when things were in the black, the biggest blow came one afternoon in August. It nearly knocked the wind completely out of the lot of them. Papers had been served to Mother contesting Father's will. Mother assured them their pa's lawyer would handle that and not to fear. Only, Collina wasn't so sure.

As for Franklin and Rose? She hadn't heard. The McConnells had not been invited to too many balls lately, nor dinners, not even an occasional tea. She sighed. There wasn't much time for those things anymore. This year had been a powerful year for America.

She'd read in the paper that President McKinley had been shot on Friday. This being Tuesday, she hadn't heard how he was doing. Hopefully, he'd pull through, or else Vice-President Theodore Roosevelt would become their new president. He'd come a long ways from establishing the first volunteer cavalry, the Rough Riders. It seemed ages ago. She wiped at her eyes. That had been another lifetime. She had no time to think of past loves.

No, all there had been time for was keeping up the estate, paying the bills, birthing calves, foals, and, of course, planting and harvesting. Chester had helped out a few times. Amazingly, it had been Austin Blaine who had become her right-hand man now that Joseph… He never failed to appear just at the time she needed a strong shoulder to tote a load too heavy for her arms to bear. He exemplified a good role model for her rambunctious brothers. Austin's amusing wit and entertaining antics eased the tension between her and her brothers when she pressed them into working too hard or long.

He'd draw her aside at such times and confide to her that her brothers were still a little wet behind the ears. They needed time to mature and that they'd come around to wanting to assume more of Shushan's responsibilities. His handsome face would search hers, as if trying to see into her very soul. "Don't be so impatient. There's a time for everything," he'd say, playfully stroking her chin.

It was at those moments she'd dive into the pages of her Bible, searching for answers she didn't have a clue about handling. Ecclesiastes 3:1 had become her favorite passage when she felt discouraged. "To everything there is a season, and a time to every purpose under the heaven: A time to be born and a time to die…"

She had expected to get an invitation to Rose and Franklin's wedding. She learned from Doc just yesterday that he didn't think there would ever be one.

"Collina, Mother wants you," Belle yelled.

"Coming!"

The parlor doors closed with a solid thump behind Collina. Mother, clutching the family Bible to her bosom, rocked back and forth in grandma's rocker.

"Lock the door. Now, sit here." Mother motioned her to a chair beside her. Her eyes, however, stared past her to the large french windows framed with crushed velvet draperies. "My lawyer has drawn up the stipulations to Lawyer Farlin's claim that I will agree to. I will not agree to an auction of our existing assets that would jeopardize the estate's productivity. I agreed to acquire one-third of the estate, and you children two-thirds upon Bugie's twenty-first birthday. Mine will include the house and barns."

"Mother, no. Pa wanted you to have it all. That Lawyer Farlin is a polecat, and Pa wouldn't want you to allow him to get the best of you like this."

"My mind is made up. I just don't have any fight left in me. I will not divide this family up because of money and greed. Money doesn't mean that much to me. I want you children happy. But I have to ask you…" She turned, her eyes moist with tears. "Have I ever been unfair to Clem and Myra? Chester and Sarah?"

"Unfair? It's not in your nature to be unfair to anyone. You gave Myra and Clem the best wedding present in the state of Kentucky. That east side of the estate has the best bottom land of all the other sections combined. And Chester and Sarah received an equally fertile portion."

"As I recall, that is the piece Clem demanded."

"What does Clem want now? For us to build him a house on it?"

"Did Myra ever say anything to you about being unhappy staying with us?"

Collina placed an oblong pillow in the small of her back. What Mother had to say would take time saying. She leaned her back against the big-backed velvet chair. "All Myra said was that she missed Clem, though God knows why. Where is she now?"

"Up in her room napping. She's still tired from her trip. I hope Doc can help put some hope in her. She wants a child something awful."

Collina walked to the window seat and pulled back the drapes and tied them with the gold cord to the clasp on the wall. The late sun shone full on her face. It felt good. Shushan's fertile hills rose and dipped like scoops of ice cream on a child's plate. "I think the only thing wrong with Myra is that she married the wrong man."

Mother got up slowly from the rocker, wiping her already clean hands on her red-checkered apron. "Why do you say that?"

"Because Myra isn't happy with Clem."

"Those are my feelings, too."

Looking out over the hills, both were silent.

"I have myself and Ben to blame for you children's strong wills. Both Ben and I are the same. Life is strange. Decisions that mold the course of your destiny are made in youth, when one is too innocent to know what one truly needs. I tried to bring you children up the best way I knew how, teaching you to walk with the only One who could help in your decision-making. But sometimes our own will and desires get in the way, and then we blame God for the mess we've got ourselves in."

Collina turned from the window. "Do you think Myra has lost her faith in God?"

"I don't know. What I do know is that she doesn't seem to care if Clem goes to church or not. It could be nothing. Myra's always been a hard one to read. She's never confided in me like you other girls.

"You know, sometimes I feel people never want to stop fighting. Why would anyone want to assassinate President McKinley? You know Abraham Lincoln was assassinated. Your pa often confided in me that during the War Between the States, he often felt he was battling Satan himself. Satan wanted to kill the idea of these United States. He would recite the Gettysburg Address. I'll never forget how he would say it: 'And this nation under God shall have a new birth of freedom…' Like those words had become his words and not Abraham Lincoln's."

Collina hadn't moved from the window. "A nation under God— the idea is something every American needs to uphold, though some would like to deny that."

"Feels that way at times, and some people act like the war hasn't ended. What with southerners calling the northerners Yankees and northerners calling the southerners Rebs and rednecks, it doesn't seem that these states will ever be united again."

The parlor door rattled violently. Ruby's voice spoke from the other side. "What are you doing in there with the door locked?"

Collina rushed to open it.

Ruby's sun-streaked hair appeared around the corner, her eyes as large as saucers. "Why did you lock it?"

"To make you ask." Collina gave Ruby an affectionate hug. "I thought you were with Stephen."

"We got back early from Emerald and you'll never—"

"We saw Clem in Emerald at Lawyer Farlin's." Austin and Stephen stomped into the study.

"That's what I was trying to tell you. I saw Clem go into Lawyer Farlin's office, and Austin hounded him until he confessed his foul deed," Ruby said.

"Lawyer Farlin wanted to take Jacob and Prudence's land from them, and your pa stopped him dead in his tracks," Maggie said.

"Yeah, and if I recall, Lawyer Farlin swore revenge. Now he's acquired it through Clem." Austin glanced away, as if embarrassed by what his distant cousin had accomplished.

"What do you mean?"

Stephen knelt before her mother. "Mrs. McConnell, did your lawyer already file those papers?"

"I believe so. Why?"

Austin swiped a lock of his hair off his forehead. "You can't trust a snake like Farlin. Clem doesn't understand what he did gettin' in cahoots with that lying cheat."

"Mrs. McConnell, you just have to contest this and fight for your rights. I'm afraid Farlin will demand an auction for one-third of the entire assets of Shushan. That could wipe you out." Stephen slammed his fist onto the end table.

Maggie sighed. "You want this fight to go on for another three years? It takes money to contest a court verdict, and usually the only ones who win in the end are the lawyers. No, we just have to pray that my lawyer can negotiate a settlement that will be agreeable to all."

"The only thing Lawyer Farlin will agree to is for the McConnells to be a ward of the state!" Collina said.

Chapter 15

ollina pulled the hat brim lower across her forehead. President McKinley dying from an infection on September 14 due to an assassin's bullet jolted her into the reality of her and her country's situation. *There are no guarantees you'll live to attain your destiny.* Theodore Roosevelt's words spoken as vice-president and president of the senate echoed in her heart.

"We are a young nation, already of giant strength, yet whose present strength is but a forecast of the power that is to come…And as keen-eyed, we gaze into the coming years, duties, new and old, rise thick and fast to confront us from within…A great work lies ready to the hand of this generation; and thrice happy is the generation that to it is given such a work to do."

Collina's duties, the old one being the promise she'd given Father. Yes, Shushan had survived her poor excuse of managing, but for how long? How long before the next generation of McConnells was ready to put their hand to the plow? Jessie and Robert were showing fine management skills. She could see Pa's common sense in their every business action. She prayed fervently that greed would not overtake their God-given sense of justice, that the Lawyer Farlins of the world be snuffed out of existence by the righteous hand of His elect.

The rain pelted her with jabbing pokes. She petted Betsy's head while Betsy's calf nuzzled her pockets for the carrot she had hidden there.

The last week of September wasn't wasting any time in predicting a wet autumn. She drew the collar of her raincoat toward her face and stamped her feet, partly to warm them and partly in impatience to be rid of this humiliation.

"Sold to Dave Parkins for ten dollars!" Pete O'Riley's gavel came down haphazardly on its wooden cradle. His voice trailed off under the heavy pounding of the rain against the metal roof of the barn. "Shouldn't even have an auction in this kind of weather."

She shrugged. "It's not a good day for anything else." She nudged Betsy and her young calf toward Farmer Parkins's heavily loaded wagon. It had been raining continuously now for nearly a day and a half, and their driveway had become a pattern of deep ruts and large tributaries of muddied rainwater. The calf bumped her, and her rubber boots slid across mud and water. She clung to the gentle Betsy to stay upright.

"Collina," Belle yelled from the front porch, "do you need help?"

Collina shook her head, wiping her sleeve across her eyes. Old Betsy was the first cow Pa had allowed her to milk. Betsy wouldn't hurt a fly. "She likes her bran mash with some carrots chopped up in it." She handed Farmer Parkins the rope. He hurriedly tied it to his wagon.

"Always had my eye on Old Betsy, but now that I think of it, don't know if I'll keep her."

Collina swallowed, running her soiled hands down her yellow rain slicker. "She's a good milker, Mr. Parkins, and gentle as a lamb."

"She's a'gettin' old. Really got her for the calf." He stroked the stout neck of the heifer. "She's going to be a beaut."

Collina wrapped her arms about Betsy for the last time. "Bye, girl," she whispered. Betsy mooed sadly as the wagon slowly made its way down the road, the calf nudging her mother's side.

"Where are they taking Betsy?" Ruby said. She was dressed in Mother's slicker and one-size-too-large boots. "I thought you'd decided to keep her?"

Collina buried her fists deep within the large pockets of her slicker. "I had, but Chester convinced me that she was getting too old and we didn't need her."

"Collina, Ruby, Mother wants you," Belle yelled over the rain.

As they trudged through the mud to the large veranda, Belle handed Collina and Ruby warm mugs of coffee. "How's it going?"

"I've got some warm blueberry muffins ready to come out of the oven," Mother said.

"Thanks," Collina said. "Almost done. At least, I hope they are."

"I want you to stop the selling when you feel we can. We need all the livestock and equipment we can keep," Mother said.

"Can I help?" Belle asked, sitting down next to Collina.

A knock on the kitchen door interrupted them.

"Why, it's Doc and Big Jim. You both come on in here," Mother said.

"Could you spare some coffee?" Big Jim's lopsided grin reminded Collina of Joseph. She glanced out the rain-drenched windowpane. She felt so alone. She missed Joseph and Franklin. She bowed her head and gulped down the brew. They were always there when she landed in a pit she couldn't climb out of. Who was going to save her now? "Mother, I've been watching the money box. It's up to two thousand, isn't that enough?"

"You know Clem will want his part in cash, so will Chester. Most likely need three times that."

"Mine goes back into the farm," Collina said.

"Mine too," Belle and Ruby echoed.

"No, you girls will need your share. I won't let you give away your only hope for a future."

"Shushan is our future," Collina said, "and we've just about sold all we can without losing productivity."

"What have you got left that we could spare?" Mother said.

Pa's tall, grey thoroughbred came to mind, the offspring of his first stallion, Caedmon. "Proud Lady, she's our last hope," Collina said. "There's no time to get her ready to race any more, nor the funds to do it with."

"Is she healed up from her last race?" Belle said.

"She's as sound as she'll ever be." Collina said, "She could race again, or she could make some breeding farm a great brood mare. And now with Raymar gone there's just the five-year-old Caedmon, grandson to Pa's original sire, left." Painful memories caused a lump to form in her throat. Joseph's gone. All her prize horses gone. Mary Blaine, her confidante, dead. What's next to go?

"We're farmers now, and not part of the social picture anymore."

"Don't say that, Maggie." Doc shook his head. "Styles come and go, just like societies come and go, but class, true class withstands life's trials. Class is what you and yours possess and the only style worth noting."

"Thank you," Maggie whispered, giving Collina's hand a squeeze. Mother was consoling her.

"Besides, Aunt Louise will never allow society to forget us, Mother," Belle said with a wink at Doc and Big Jim.

Maggie dabbed at her eyes. "What am I going to do with all of you?"

"Not give up," Big Jim said. "You're the best thing that ever happened to Ben and MacDuff County."

"Thank you," Maggie said. "I know it cost you a lot to admit that."

"Nah, it's I who should be thanking you." Big Jim bowed his head. "I've been holding this grudge too long. Should have told you long before this. You did what you could for my wife and young'un staying there a week and all. Guess I had to blame someone. Forgive me, Maggie."

"Why does it take a hardship in our lives for us to wake up to the real things that matter in life?" Doc said. "I guess I won't know until I enter those pearly gates myself. We'd best be getting back to the auction."

"Here, take one of these warm muffins with you and allow me to fill your cups up. This dampness can chill one to the bone."

"Much obliged, Maggie," Doc said.

As the kitchen door thumped to a close, Maggie turned to Collina. "You'll have to get Proud Lady's price as high as the good Lord allows."

"I'll need money for seed in the spring and feed to get us through the winter. Will there still be enough to pay the lawyer?"

"I'd forgotten about him," Maggie said.

"Best be on our way, Sis," Ruby said.

"Are you sure you want to go? It's not very pleasant out there, seeing Pa's cattle and horses being sold."

Ruby smiled, coaxing her into a lighter mood. "We'll buy them back, once we get back on our feet again."

"And there'll be less to tend come winter," Belle said.

Collina laughed in spite of her depressed mood. Looping her arms with those of Belle and Ruby, they trudged three abreast in the mud.

"You can tell them about the hot coffee and blueberry muffins, Belle, while we get the next horse ready," Collina said.

"Look!" Belle exclaimed pointing a finger toward the auction block "Isn't that Jude?"

Collina and Pa had worked for days on the whites, coaxing them into pulling the huge iron combine. Only when they'd placed the intelligent Jude in the lead would the others pull the strange contraption. Shushan couldn't survive without him. "Wait!" she cried, running as fast as her clumsy rubber boots would allow.

"Stop the bidding," Ruby yelled, trying to keep up with her long-legged sister.

Pete gave a sigh of relief. "Sorry folks, mistake's been made," nodding his head in the direction of the barn. "Take him back to his stall, Jess."

"You bet." Jessie said, muttering under his breath. "That was a close one, for sure."

"Wait," Clem said.

"No, you wait." Collina worked her way through the crowd until she could look him in the eyes. "Did you tell them to bring up Jude?"

Clem turned away from her gaze.

"Now, Sis," Chester said, putting a hand on her shoulder. "'Twasn't Clem. I thought it would be okay." Chester turned to Clem. "Sorry, I made a blunder."

The corner of Clem's mouth curled as he moved to place his hand on Collina's shoulder. She dodged him.

Austin caught his arm. "No, you don't." He thrust Clem's hand behind his back.

"Let me go." Clem struggled.

Austin gave Clem's arm another pull.

"Ouch, that hurts. I wasn't going to do her no—"

"What's the matter? Are women the only ones you can beat?"

"I'm not like that," Clem snapped back at Austin. "Butt out. I was just going to tell Collina that I didn't mean—"

"Watch it," Austin hissed. "You make me any madder than I am, I'll break your arm right off."

Austin's large body engulfed Clem's. Collina didn't want Clem's injuries on her conscience. Besides, he was Myra's husband. She reached out to stop Austin. Ruby pulled on her arm and whispered. "Austin won't hurt him."

Austin twisted Clem's face upwards, staring into his face. "If I ever hear you even touched a hair on Collina's head, I swear you'll wish you were dead."

"What's the matter?" Clem gasped. The pressure Austin was applying to Clem's arm had to be excruciating. His face constricted into a menacing snarl when he looked at her. "You got a hankerin' for that skinny gal."

"All you know is dirt; you wouldn't know good if it married you. I don't know how Myra can stomach you."

"Collina," Pete O'Riley said. "Come up here."

She avoided Austin's glance and took a deep breath as she and Ruby headed for the platform in front of the stables. "You think Clem's been abusing Myra?" she asked Ruby.

"We need to talk to Myra. If Clem is, she needs to leave him."

Collina stroked Proud Lady's silky mane one last time and stepped onto wooden platform. "Folks, this is Proud Lady. We've saved the best for last. She's the granddaughter of Caedmon. She's won most every race she ever ran and has lots of potential as a brood mare. But don't take my word, you can check out some of her get in our stables."

"Let's start the bidding at —"

"One thousand!" Doc Baker yelled.

"I've got $1,000." Pete spoke so fast Collina couldn't understand the rest until she heard—

"Two thousand!" came the booming voice of Big Jim.

"Three thousand!" a man yelled out.

A murmur went through the crowd. Collina held her breath. Could it be true? Her eyes sought the voice of the man standing beneath the maple tree near the tool shed. Who was he?

"Three thousand, five hundred." Doc Baker said.

A pause followed. Pete O'Riley slapped his gavel down again. "Going once, going twice."

"Five thousand."

All eyes turned to the tall man standing beneath the large maple tree. Collina stared at the figure through the mist of rain and fog that had descended like a thick blanket. She looked around for Big Jim. He wasn't anywhere. Could this be Big Jim?

"Wait." Collina rushed forward before Pete O'Riley could strike the gavel down a second time. "It's too much, Big Jim; I can't let you do it."

Big Jim walked out from the tool shed with a pickaxe in his hand, his head cocked to one side like an old hoot owl. "It wouldn't be too much for Joseph. He'd be pleased to know that his father did a kindness to his girl. But I don't have that kind of money, lass. Sorry, wish I did."

A man wearing an oilskin coat with a dilapidated cavalry hat folded over his forehead and the collar of his coat covering half his face, approached the auction stand and slapped down the money. "I'll have my man pick up the horse next week."

Collina clutched the auction stand and whispered, "Thank you, sir." Then whispered to Pete, "We can stop." Taking a breath of the rancid air, she raised her arms high. "Whoopee! We can stop selling off our livestock now, and we have enough money left over for seed come spring and have our tax money to boot." Tears welled from her eyes like she'd struck an artesian well. The man looked back at her over his shoulder, chuckled, then limped heavily away.

Stephen took another look and gasped. "Say, aren't you—"

The man clutched Stephen's shoulder and steered him through the sea of onlookers, muttering to him and then they both turned to watch.

Pete slapped down his gavel with relish and in his booming auctioneer's voice said, "That's all we've got to auction this day, folks. Much obliged for coming."

Big Jim stepped forward, then Doc Baker. She hugged each and thanked them for their support, then wipied her nose on her sleeve. What she'd give for a hanky right about now. The man in the slicker stepped forward and handed her a freshly pressed one.

"Thank you. You must be a stranger in these parts." She looked up at him curiously. He pulled his hat even farther down over his grey-tinged hair, but she managed to see a glint of a scar that ran from the corner of his eye straight down to his mouth. Was this the man who bought Proud Lady? She hadn't gotten a good look at him because she'd been too busy counting the money. She extended her hand. "Thank you, sir."

"My pleasure." He accepted her hand, warm and firm and so like…She met his gaze. Then gasped. He immediately dropped her hand and limped away, lost in the sea of men congregated on the lawn. She stared down at the handkerchief. In the corner were the initials *FL*. No, it couldn't be.

"What's wrong, Collina?" Austin asked.

"I guess…nothing." After all, other people had the same initials and what reason would he have to be afraid.

"Just a minute," Pete yelled as Belle's hands waved frantically. "I have a pretty gal here that's got something to say."

Belle blushed, giving her already rosy complexion an added hue, her striking blue eyes and blond hair putting a ray of sunshine into the bleak day.

"There's hot coffee and blueberry muffins straight out of the oven for any who would like one. Head to the front porch." The wind whirled about her, and she hugged her slicker close.

"Now that's a gal for you, Austin," Clem said. "She's full-bloomed."

"Aw, you're just scum," Austin said in disgust, seeing Collina's embarrassment. "Git. I'm tired of looking at your ugly face." He shoved Clem aside.

"Hey, I nearly fell face down in that mud and you can't tell me to get."

Austin rolled up his sleeves. "I'm primed for a fight; you want to oblige me?"

Collina frowned. Fights were a part of Austin's life. It was clear he wanted to appear more genteel, but she didn't see that happening soon enough for her liking.

Austin chuckled. "It would've been an improvement on your looks if you did muddy up that ugly snout of yours. I'm planning on getting some of that coffee and muffins, and right now I'm embarrassed to be seen with you, let alone know we're related with you sashaying with that polecat Farlin."

Austin and Clem had caught not only Collina's eye but a number of others.

"You always were a hot head, even when you were a kid." Clem glanced at Austin's dark swarthy face and paled. "Aw, I need a drink, anyway." He turned, almost running in his attempt to put distance between them and yelled, "Austin, you're a hot-head."

"Why you…"

Collina held Austin back. "Please." She didn't want more fighting. How could she explain this to him? Her voice coaxing, she whispered, "I need you to help me."

Austin's expression swallowed her whole. He took her hand in his and squeezed it as his lopsided grin bounced his charming dimples to front and center. "About time. It took you long enough to admit it."

So that's how the wind blew. Franklin burrowed deep into his oilskin. What did he expect? After all, Collina must be around nineteen now.

Stephen bit his lip, glancing at him.

Collina came through the front door carrying a tray filled with cups.

"Aren't you going to—"

"Remember your promise." Franklin said, "I'll know when the time is right."

"But she thinks you and Rose are sweet on each other? You need to tell her the truth about your feelings. She wouldn't give Austin a thought if she knew you cared."

Collina set the tray on a low table on the porch. Her thick dark hair, curly and moist, fell about the yellow slicker she wore. Then she retreated to reappear with a steaming pot of coffee. Austin had noticed her reappearance, too.

"Say, Bo, how's the courting going?" Austin said.

"Humph." Bo looked up. "What do you think?" Bo surveyed his competition, arms crossed, hat pulled way down over sober eyes.

"Does Mrs. McConnell know of your intentions?" Austin hadn't taken his eyes off Collina.

Franklin smirked.

"I'm not aiming to start off wrong with a potential mother-in-law," Bo said. "Now is as good a time as any."

"Could I have a cup of coffee, Collina?" Austin said. "You know you did a silly thing riling Clem like that."

"Riling? Would you like cream or sugar?"

"Both."

"Would you like a muffin?"

"No, but I would like a reply to my question. Clem could have caused trouble. I was glad I—"

"Like he hasn't? Clem had it coming." Collina looked up. Franklin had a glimpse of flashing green eyes. "You were right in telling him to go. I completely agreed with your actions."

"I didn't say he didn't, but Clem's got a mean nature to him; you'd be wise not to provoke him. The McConnells don't need more trouble."

"He'd better be careful he doesn't get me provoked."

Austin shook his head. "Collina, you'd better learn to get a hold of that temper of yours, or it's going to get you in a peck of trouble."

Collina was too busy refilling the empty cups thrust toward her to enter into much of a conversation with anyone. Franklin stepped forward. This might be his last chance. He picked up a cup and waited for his turn.

Maggie came through the front door with a steaming pot. Bo stood in the doorway smiling broadly. "Here's more coffee. Hi, Austin, how are your children doing?"

"They miss their ma. Still, we make do, best as can be. I'm glad to see Big Jim is out and about. When Joseph was killed in Cuba, I was wondering if he'd ever get over his grief."

"I know." Collina looked up at the hills. "Sometimes I think it's still just a dream and he'll be galloping over that ridge. I even hear his voice sometimes, just before I'm fully awake."

Franklin bowed his head. Joseph had been safe behind Roosevelt, but he came back to help yours truly and got himself killed. What was he doing here? Turning up bad memories he thought he'd buried? He should leave.

"Collina, there's a church picnic the week next. Would you like to go? I could pick you up," Austin said.

"Thanks, but I've got—

"She'd love to, Austin." Maggie smiled back into Collina's irate face.

"What time should she be ready?" Maggie said.

"How about half past ten?" Austin's voice brimmed with anticipation.

He's falling for her in a big way. Franklin glanced away.

Collina crossed her arms, and huffed. "Would half past ten be all right, Mother?"

Franklin bit down on his bottom lip and rubbed at his scar. He'd noticed her staring at it. Collina hadn't recognized him. What if she had? After all, his initials were on that handkerchief. What made him think she would want him back in her life now?

Austin jumped up on the porch in one leap of his muscular legs. "Here, let me take that pot of coffee; it looks mighty heavy."

Franklin slapped his bum leg. He could do that once. Now he couldn't even mount a horse without someone's help. Maybe with a few more months of therapy he'd be able to mount a horse properly. Eyeing Austin, he hoped it wouldn't be too late. Too late to tell her that he told Rose countless times before all they could ever be was friends? That he still was very much in love with Collina? That he'd built his home around her—to carry his bride across its threshold?

"Sir? Would you like some coffee and a warm muffin?" Collina asked.

Franklin swerved. His eyes gazing into hers.

The fog enveloped Collina like a wet sheet. The man was gone, and she was left to ponder if he was Franklin or some figment of her imagination. The cornfield! If that was Franklin, he would hasten there.

As she rode to the cornfield, the sunset radiated the western sky with pale pinks, golden yellows, and gentle pearls through a sheer veil of white, like a bride before her groom. The cornfield, stripped of its green foliage and fruit stretched out as dejected as she felt. The only thing alive here was the occasional squirrel hustling acorns. She turned her horse away to leave. Then a neigh from her horse told her she was not alone. From out of the shadowed trees rode Franklin.

Snatching a deep breath, she hoped to steady the rapid beating of her heart. "It was you, wasn't it, who bought Proud Lady?"

"Yes, it was I."

The saucy smell of horseflesh and wet bark assaulted her nose. She squinted her eyes for a better look at him, the mists rose from the damp earth and mingled with their sultry breaths. He laid his arm across his saddle horn and watched her like a wary warrior might. Was he smiling or sad? She couldn't tell.

"Why? Why didn't you say something? Why did you run away?"

He rested back in his saddle, tilting his head slightly, as if observing the question from a different angle. "I thought it best, under the circumstances. I have a train to catch back to Detroit in the morning. I have a factory there, Collina, and that's my home."

"I see." What had she expected? For him to give up everything to become a dirt farmer for her? "Well, I will pay you back when Shushan is back on her feet."

"That's not necessary. I was glad to repay the favor. You were there for me when I needed someone."

"I? You mean Rose, don't you?" Her voice caught. She hoped he hadn't noticed the hurt behind the words.

"Rose and I are, and always have been, just friends."

Her heart leapt.

Tall and stately, he rode closer. What was he saying? Her mind didn't want to hear what her heart yearned, hoped to hear, that he had always loved her. But if what he said was true, then he had led Rose on. She had confided to Collina that she was in love with Franklin.

Then what Luke had suspected about Franklin was true. He was capable of using women for his gain.

His eyes penetrated hers. Deep and vibrant blue, they would not release her of the truth. Wooing Rose had enabled him to get into the best rehabilitation facilities Doc could afford.

"Believe my reasons as you will."

It was as if he could read her mind.

"What others say about me, I have little control over. Look to my actions; see if they are not plain enough to mirror the truth." He sighed deeply. "I wanted to know before I leave, do you have enough money left to run Shushan?"

"Yes. We shall do fine, thanks to you."

"You have plenty of able men to help you? Austin looks very capable."

She smiled. "He has become the McConnells' right-hand man and in some ways has taken dear Joseph's place."

The tip of his mouth rose upward ever so slightly. "That will set my mind to rest. Words can little express the grief I felt when Joseph died in my place."

A cry escaped her lips. "You must not blame yourself for Joseph's death. I had always hoped, I mean prayed, that you would someday come back, and it could be the way it was before the war with us."

A few drops of rain dripped despondently off his cavalry brim. "I am no farmer. My talent lies in industry." He gazed over the rippled rows of dejected corn stubs. "We are past that moment of our lives." He turned toward her, allowing the last rays of sunlight to fully expose his scarred face. I feel twenty years my senior at times."

Had he given up all hope of them ever being together? "Have you forgotten what we learned here, the mustard seed?" She hastened to dismount. "We need to—"

"No, please do not dismount. I cannot remount without aid. You see, that is the problem. I have a bum leg that causes me humiliation and embarrassment."

The scar on his face deepened. She imagined the pain he had endured. Lord, give me Your wisdom.

A man's heart deviseth his way; but the Lord directeth his steps.

Yes, thank you Lord. "You are as handsome as you ever were. You're still the cavalier, for you came to the aid of this distressed damsel again."

She rode closer, her eyes merrily capturing his. "If you have faith as a grain of mustard seed, nothing will be impossible unto you..."

"Humph!"

She shrugged off his disbelief. "Anything is possible with God orchestrating our lives. God is still directing yours, though you give Him little credit for this."

"Anything?" He chuckled. "Does that include leaving Shushan to marry me and live in Detroit?" He rode toward her until their stirrup irons clicked. "I've built a home for you, with every pleasure imaginable at your fingertips. I have waited these three years to make enough fortune to ask you to marry me." He leaned forward, his look pleading, searching her face. "Don't think about anyone else but us. Our happiness. Come with me, Collina, we can be married tomorrow."

She gasped. "I…can't. I gave my promise to Pa. Besides, my brothers are not ready for this responsibility—especially after the auction." Leave her beloved hills for concrete and dirty alleys?

"Then your love for me is not enough." He closed his eyes briefly, as if gathering up strength for his next resolution. Leaning forward he caressed his lips upon her moistened cheek.

"Oh." She covered its warmth with her hand. She never wanted to lose the feel of his lips. "I do love you. But my commitment to my family must come first. I can't desert them. Please try and understand."

He took her hand in his and kissed it. His eyes met hers. "I must leave before we wound ourselves beyond hope."

Deeply, almost musically, he uttered the words she would never forget. "I will always love you."

She watched him gallop away as unabashed tears streamed down her checks and onto her hands. He stopped and turned to wave a last farewell, and then he was out of sight.

Unashamed, she cried until the valleys echoed her sobs, until she had no more tears to shed. She knew he had spoken from his heart as she knew she would never love another man like she loved Franklin.

Chapter 16

October 6, 1901

*I*t had gone better then she expected. The harvest was in. Collina drank in the sweet fragrance that lingered in the attic just over her bedroom. She was glad she'd dried the apples early this year.

At haying time Chester, Skeeder, and Austin had proven useful. With the extra help, the tedious work had been accomplished quickly. Austin had been there during the tobacco curing, too.

Absently, she traced the bonnet top of her highboy with her index finger. Austin had wanted to pick her up for church this morning. She'd made a lame excuse about needing to ride with her sisters. She felt guilty, fibbing just before church—a little lie was just as bad as a big one. She knew that to be true enough. She sighed. She wouldn't do it again, the pain her conscience was causing her not worth the experience.

Austin had more than fulfilled his promise for when she had helped Mary during her birthing. Skeeder, being a sharecropper, would get his share to sell. She told Austin so and asked why he was still helping the McConnells. Did he want a share of the sell? Austin had said no. He seemed upset that she'd even asked the question. Well, he'd certainly proven himself a strong and able worker.

She'd best hurry. Her eyes traveled to the feather bed in dismay. There lay the newest creation of Belle's and Ruby's talented fingers—a bright yellow dress with matching hat. "I wish I could get out of this." The two had chosen her to be their protégé. How Collina had warranted such an honor was a mystery to her. Ruby told her the mutton sleeves alone had taken two and a half yards of material. The front of the bibbed dress was complete with flounce. She said a hasty prayer as she stepped into the layered folds of material. "Dear Lord, please have it fit and stay together long enough for me to get back home in it."

She tied it snugly around her corseted waist, for the dress called for a snug fit, much to her discomfort. Ruby had done the tightening and had left her enough room to breathe. Good. They gave the dress a small bustle. She set the bright yellow bonnet on her dark hair. "Humph." *I feel more like a misplaced canary.* But she knew Mother would approve.

Mother's words from earlier in the day rang in her ears. "I've allowed you to wear your coveralls. I've even allowed you to miss Sundays to finish up the harvesting while the weather held good. But now, daughter, your commitment to our Lord can no longer wait. It's time for you to become a proper Christian lady."

Collina opened her parasol, rested it on her shoulder, and smiled back at her image in the mirror. "I may look like a lady, but that doesn't mean I can't do some business." In the pierced-scroll mirror, her large green eyes looked all the larger with her thick hair layered on top of her head. Her finger traced the fashionable pompadour, touching the small, golden earrings that jingled from each ear lobe. She'd contacted Farmer Parkins, and he said he would meet her after church.

Collina missed her best milkers. She hadn't realized how many of their prime cows had gone on the auctioning block. They had been hard pressed to fill all their milk orders. "I'll rectify that today."

She set down her parasol and picked up her silk gloves absentmindedly. She couldn't have their best customers going to another farm for their produce. "I'll buy Betsy back and get Pa's bull to doing what he does best! Now where did I put my Bible?" A knock on her door made her jump. Belle's head popped around the now partly opened door.

"Hurry up, we're all waiting for you. Mother still isn't too happy that you refused to go with Austin, either. So you'd better hurry down."

"Have you seen my Bible?"

"Try looking on your bed stand."

"Of course. Belle, remember Betsy?" Collina reached for her Bible, which was still open to the pages she had read the night before.

"You're not talking about that old cow again, I hope?"

"When you see Farmer Parkins after church, tell him how much you miss her."

"Why would I miss her?"

"Just widen your eyes and look at him real sad like. Then I'll offer to buy her back at a lower price. Belle, now don't forget."

Belle's mouth gaped open in horror. "Collina, remember this is Sunday, the Lord's Day. It's sacrilegious to be thinking about business."

"It is?" Collina opened her Bible. "Show me. That's not one of Ten Commandments, is it?"

Belle shrugged. "If it's not, Pastor Bates will say it should be."

The stained-glass windows along the sides of the tongue-and-groove walls painted in soft white were a sharp contrast to the deep-brown mahogany wooden pews. As the last stanza of "Onward Christian Soldiers" echoed to a close, the congregation rose like one human wave pulled by the tide toward the bright morning sunshine illuminating the open doorway.

The sun warmed Collina's face as the sermon had warmed her spirit. Yes, it felt good to be back in the house of the Lord. "That was a good sermon, Pastor Bates; I truly enjoyed it."

"Thank you, Collina." The pastor patted her hand. "I missed seeing that sweet face of yours." His kind eyes searched hers.

A shadow lingered for a moment over Collina and a deep voice said, "Enjoyed the sermon, Uncle."

"Collina, there's someone I'd like you to meet. This is my nephew, Bill McBrian. Bill this is my favorite girl, Collina May McConnell."

By now the doorway was elbow to elbow with parishioners, but Pastor Bates seemed oblivious to this small technicality. The pastor's brown eyes twinkled with merriment, which only made Collina shift from one nervous foot to another. As she tried to remove her hand from his, he gave her a merry wink, and Collina couldn't help thinking that he reminded her of Robin Hood's Friar Tuck. "She's the flightiest of the McConnell girls. You've got to keep a hold on her reins, or else she'll spook."

"Pastor." Collina pulled her hand away. A bellowing laugh from Bill McBrian followed.

She whirled around, losing her balance, and if not for the quick reflexes of Bill McBrian, she would have fallen head first down the steps.

"Anyone that's as pretty as you shouldn't be in such a hurry," McBrian said, his arms looped like a lariat about her waist.

"Thank you, sir. Now if you would please release your—"

"I'm afraid I quite forgot myself." His small, well-kept mustache and goatee masked the square chin beneath. But it was his eyes that captivated a person, his mischievous brown eyes danced beneath quizzical brows. "Please accept my apology."

Collina didn't need a mirror to know her face was as red as a ripened tomato. Turning, she descended the steps as quickly as her heels allowed. Her large hat with the yellow plum on the top bobbed with every movement, and most embarrassingly of all, she could feel her bustle hit her rump with every rigid clump, clump of her heels. Now, which sister forgot to baste my bustle?

She made her way with what little dignity she could afford herself to the sanctity of God's good soft earth, feeling more than seeing the eyes of Bill McBrian following her. Good, there's Sarah. She half-walked and half-ran toward her sister-in-law, turning just in time to see the stranger stopped in mid-stride by Austin. Austin! She'd completely forgotten about her promise to him.

"It looks like you'll have two bidding for your box supper," Sarah said.

"What?"

"The box supper. It's become quite the social affair. Remember, Maggie said—"

"No, I'm not staying. I've got to go home." Collina turned to leave. There'll be other times she could go to church with Austin. She needed to return home and get some chores done.

"But Maggie told me you were staying."

Collina put a finger to her lips. "Shh, don't give Mother any ideas."

Sarah laughed, placing a hand on her bulging stomach. "That got a response out of Junior."

"When are you due?"

"Sometime around Christmas there'll be a little brother or sister for Little Gill and a new arrival to the McConnell clan." Sarah's large blue eyes sparkled with anticipation, and the blond hair surrounding her heart-shaped face glowed in the autumn sunlight.

"I hope I'll look as good as you do when..." Collina could feel the heat rise to her cheeks.

"Yes, Collina, first the bonds of matrimony, then the family way. But you'll have to stop running and let yourself get caught before that can happen." She turned Collina in the direction of Austin and Bill, who had kept their attentive eyes fixed in their direction.

Oh no. She needed to get home. "It was wonderful seeing you. You could pass for an angel; you're so beautiful." She saw in the distance Mother and Ruby lifting out boxes tied in bright ribbons.

Sarah laughed at her woebegone expression and glanced toward the two men, whom Chester momentarily joined on his way to Sarah. Bill McBrian tipped his homburg hat to her and bowed.

"My, that Bill McBrian is handsome and so gallant. Isn't that wonderful, your box just might win the prize, what with two men bidding for it," Sarah said.

Collina peeled off her gloves and twisted them in her hands. "Men bid money?"

"This will be the first time for Pastor to do the box supper. But in Lexington, Presbyterians and Baptists alike are doing it. They brought in close to $200 last time for their churches and it's a way for everyone to get together and enjoy some entertainment."

Collina gnawed on her nails.

Sarah patted her hand. "You do look lovely. That dress becomes your figure, and that canary yellow looks beautiful on you."

"This dress would look prettier on—"

"I doubt I could fit into it." Sarah patted her stomach and laughed.

"You feeling okay, Sis?" Chester said.

"Why, don't I look okay?"

"Then what's this I hear about you nearly swooning into some stranger's arms?"

"My, news travels fast. Just wish it would travel true." Collina turned on her heels and walked away. She was going to find Mother and get this whole thing cleared up.

The ground, wet from the previous day's rain, was clearly not ready for expedient travel. *How is it that Belle can walk as dainty and light footed in heels as slippers, and I clump like an oversized draft horse?*

Ruby was sure in a giggly mood today. Her sister's face contorted into humorous expressions that she attempted to suppress.

"What's your hurry?" Bill McBrian said, his voice mildly concerned.

"Going back to her cows, most likely," Austin said.

"I believe I've upset you," Bill McBrian said.

Collina pinched her lower lip with her teeth. *What must this stranger think of her?* She looked up, and there was Mother. Collina had best remember her manners before Mother reminded her of them. She turned and smiled at Bill McBrian. "I do not wish to appear rude, but I have an urgent need to return home." There was a moment of silence. She sensed her mother's disapproval.

"Have you met my sisters, Belle and Ruby?" she said. Suddenly a loud, bellowing voice broke into Bill McBrian's retort.

"Miss McConnell."

Everyone turned to see who was calling. There stood Farmer Parkins with a crate full of baby turkeys. "Sorry to be disturbing you all on your day of rest, but Collina and I have some business to tend to." He motioned for her to step forward. Collina's mouth suddenly felt dry.

"Please excuse us, Mr. McBrian, Austin." Her mother lead Collina away. "Just what is the meaning of this?"

"Mother, I'll explain in one minute." She held up her index finger. Farmer Parkins pointed to his wagon and they walked over together.

"Miss Collina, I decided to make you a present of these here turkeys. Soon they'll be big enough for eatin', you mark my words."

"Turkeys aren't all that easy to keep," Austin said. "Hard to keep in a coop. Prefer the woods for their layin', and they're dumb. I've known them to go for a drink of water and fall into the tub and drown themselves getting it. Just a passel of stupid birds."

"Now, you ain't got no call—"

"Please," Collina said, frowning at Austin. Why hadn't he stayed with Mother? What business was this of his? After all, the birds were free, and she had just gotten through counting them, twelve. Mother said that was the completed number. Whatever that meant, Collina was sure it would prove lucky for her.

"Should bring a sizable profit when they reach maturity," Farmer Parkins said, squishing the brim of his hat. "Good for folks' Thanksgiving and Christmas dinners."

"Yes, I'll take them off your hands, and thank you," Collina said.

"You'd take a rattler if you thought you could sell it," Austin muttered.

Now, there was just one other thing that needed clearing up. "Mr. Parkins, about Betsy, I'd like to buy her back. She's getting old, probably be a burden to you in a year—"

"She's not for sale."

Austin folded his arms across his large chest and gave Mr. Parkins glance for glance.

Mr. Parkins shifted uneasily from boot to boot. Austin was good humored. That is, till something or someone got him riled. Clearing his throat, Parkins said, "Truth is, my little Tom took a heap of liking to her. I thought he'd like the calf. But when old Betsy let him pull her udder without even a backward glance or a tail a jerking, there ain't no separating the two now."

Collina sorely missed the gentle cow. But what could she do? She understood how little Tom could have drawn a fondness for the gentle cow as she had. "Let me know how she's doing now and then."

"I'll be talkin' to ya later." Mr. Parkins got into his buckboard and drove away.

"I'll carry the crate to your wagon."

Why was Austin being so accommodating? "Okay, what are you after?"

Austin chuckled deep down in his throat. His face clean-shaven, she could see the deep crevices of his dimples playing across his cheeks. "You best show me where you're tethered."

Collina noticed as they passed Mother that Bill McBrian was getting acquainted with her sisters.

Austin watched her, his thick brows rising quizzically, framing his dark eyes. "Does that bother you?" He nodded his head toward them.

"Not at all, why should it?" She pointed to the back corner of the family wagon. "Put the pens down here."

"Collina, you look like one of those models in them fancy store windows up in Emerald," Susie said. Becky nodded, running her fingers along the outline of one lace fringe.

She laughed, bending down, oblivious of the wet ground, giving Becky a bear hug. "Thank you." Then, observing Susie's woebegone face, she reached for her, too. "Come here and give me a hug."

"Daughter, what in the name of heaven do you have there?"

"Turkeys."

Mother started to count the birds. "Whose are they?"

"Mine. I mean ours."

"Haven't we enough birds to tend?" Her mother clicked her tongue. "Pastor is planning a full day for us. Don't give me that look. The crops are in, and you're staying at this social just like you promised me."

This was not going according to her plans. Then she thought of the winning argument. She smiled. "But Mother, I didn't make a box."

Mother turned, still holding onto Austin's arm. "I made one for you."

Austin had won the prize of a silver dollar and her picnic basket—his smug expression revealed an air of conquest. He had outbid Bill McBrian, winning her undivided attention for an afternoon of sitting on her quilt eating chicken, potato salad, and apple pie.

Grinning from ear to ear, his dimples playing across his face like an accordion, he leaned forward. "Come on, Collina, it's one afternoon. Let's make the best of it." He crossed his long legs, tilting his knees up to leave enough room for his two daughters. She sucked her mouth into a rosette, and nodded her head to her left. "Ruby is enjoying this."

Her sister's lovely face was a rosy pink from the sparks and glances she was receiving from both her admirers. Not too far away slumped Stephen. Stephen had tried to outbid Bill McBrian who proved the more determined of the two. Collina envied her sister's ease and confidence.

"Seems like I remember someone swooning into Bill McBrian's arms right at the top of the church steps."

"Is that what he told you?"

Austin rubbed the his jaw. "Naw, but that didn't take none of his enjoyment away." He nodded toward Bill. "He was real taken by you."

Is that what the two of them were talking about, her? She looked away.

"Looks like Stephen's got his hands full."

Collina nodded. "Bo's asked Mother for Belle's hand in marriage the day of the auction. Did I tell you?"

"I was there when Bo asked me if it was a good time." Austin's laugh encouraged companionship and she found herself laughing along. "Yep, I told him he'd better pop that question, before what happened to Luke happened to him and Belle."

"What question?" Becky queried. Her hands were folded demurely in her lap as she stroked her new dress. The wide, flaring skirt covered her small legs and only her leather shoes peeked beneath.

She grinned at these two proper young ladies sitting alongside her. "That's just grown-up talk."

"Propose to her before someone else marries her," Susie said. "Then when you accept, he gives you a ring that tells other gents you're taken." Susie smiled. "You ever been married Miss Collina?"

"No." Collina could tell by Susie's monotone that this was going to be the first of a series of questions she had no wish to answer.

"My Pa was once. But Ma's in heaven now. Did you ever have a boyfriend?" Becky asked.

"Yes, I know, dear; and no I haven't." She would have to think fast. She never did like questions, especially when they were directed toward her. "Would you children like to go for a walk?"

"Might be we could walk off some of that chicken." Austin was on his feet before Collina realized it. She set the plates back into the box. Then Austin's large hand reached down for hers. She hesitated. The girls stared at her. "I don't need any help." But her legs were tangled in her long skirt. I'm as helpless as a newborn babe in this dress.

"Don't worry, Pa won't drop you; he's strong," Becky said. Her little face was scrunched up like she was watching a pig stuck in the mud. Austin laughed. He was enjoying himself. Collina was glad someone was.

"I don't know, Becky. She ate a lot of chicken."

Austin couldn't keep his mirth hidden. I just hope my face isn't as red as it feels. He looked down at her, his expression unreadable. Then his hand engulfed hers in a grip that was solid. His other arm seized her waist, and she was suddenly airborne. The aroma of shaving cream and soap engulfed her senses.

"Come on, girls," her voice quivered like her legs.

"Look," Susie said. "They've started the games. Come on, Becky."

"I thought you said you wanted to go for a walk?" She pushed herself from Austin's circling arms.

Susie shook her head. "Come on, Becky, I'll race you down the hill. We'll come back and tell you when the dancing begins."

She watched as the two girls ran down the hill. "It is beautiful up here." Her hand went to her throat, feeling the small locket beneath her dress. A light breeze blew her hair, and she closed her eyes for a moment, the soft murmurings of the conversations below, like hummingbirds, fluttered around her, yet were distant enough to make her feel apart. Franklin's handkerchief was safely tucked inside her dress pocket.

"Let's go," Austin said. "You've got to see this brook I discovered once tracking a deer. It's just up the hill a piece." His hand reached out for hers. She stepped away. She didn't want to be alone with him. Not now. A sea of regrets engulfed her thoughts. "Let's watch the games instead."

His right hand nabbed her left. When she stopped struggling, he stroked her ringless middle finger as gently as if she was a sparrow caught in a trap. "You want to know why I've stayed on working your fields and doing your bidding? Because you've got too much to offer a guy. I'll not let you die like a shriveled old maid because of some lost love." His husky voice vibrated with a passion that stirred the innermost strings of her wounded heart. He searched her face. "You might not care what happens to you—but I do."

Chapter 17

December 16, 1901. Detroit, Michigan

New snow cloaked the pavement, the brown roofs, and barren ground. Franklin blinked. He rubbed his hands across his eyes; the bright sunlight and glaring whiteness had momentarily blinded him. He pressed his cavalry hat on his head.

"Franklin, why must you always be the first one in that awful building and the last out?"

It was Melissa, the daughter of Clyde Slinger, his toughest competitor in the tool and dye industry. The same man who had wired him the money he needed for Collina. He patted his pocket. "I have the rest of the two thousand dollars I owe your father.

"Oh, I didn't come for that."

He figured that much. He'd grown accustomed to her waiting for him. As accustomed as seeing the strange three-story brick houses pressed so close together that one could scarcely believe they were solitary homes.

One family was taking full advantage of this closeness. A woman in her fifties with a small frilled muslin cap waved a handkerchief at the window across from her. "Mable, can ya be hearing me? Mable?"

The sash went up on the window across.

"Yes, I be hearing like the rest of Mill Street be hearing."

He laughed. Melissa joined in.

Curiosity piqued, he said, "How do you manage to be here at exactly the precise time I do? Are you a lovely spy come to pilfer secrets of my struggling company to your father?"

Melissa's dark lashes peeked out of aqua blue eyes, made all the more blue from the lining of her hat. "How could you think such an appalling thing? Oh, why do I bother with you?" she said, clearly distraught.

He scrutinized her closely. Everything matched. The satin collar and cuffs of her long, tapered coat flared out about her skirts just hinting of the small black Dongola Kid boots. She was smartly dressed, attractive, and she knew it. Why did she bother with him? Why could he not get Collina out of his heart?

Austin's words whipped like a lance into his thoughts. Collina... that man's old enough to be your father. He can't be Franklin. Stephen had turned beet red, ready to defend him. Or was it his memory? After all, Stephen didn't argue.

However, in the cornfield after the auction, Collina looked at him as if he was still her knight, her dashing soldier before the effects of war had their will on his life.

He didn't regret losing his cash. It had been worth every penny, just to see Collina's eyes light up with hope that day of the auction. God keep her safe.

He realized after seeing her with Austin that love was not easy to deny. It was ferocious in its passion and as elemental as death itself.

Returning to Detroit, he had sought the Bible for strength. From his constant reading, he'd memorized Song of Solomon 8:6–7. "Set me as seal upon thine heart, as a seal upon thine arm: for love is strong as death; jealousy is cruel as the grave: the coals thereof are coals of fire, which hath a most vehement flame. Many waters cannot quench love, neither can the floods drown it: if a man would give all the substance of his house for love, it would utterly be contemned."

Maybe with Dr. Chadwick's aid, his leg would heal and he could return to Collina.

He cupped Melissa's arm in his. Both momentarily lost in reverie.

"It's slippery here." Melissa, losing her balance, grabbed him tightly.

They slid a good foot; he seized the light pole just in the nick of time before he and Melissa landed unceremoniously on their bottoms. He slapped his bum leg with his walking stick. Austin was right. Lieutenant Long died at the battle of San Juan Hill.

His destiny lay in the soot-filled city of Detroit, and Collina's in the green hills of Kentucky. It was best. How could there ever be a right time for him and Collina? Her words about the parable of the mustard seed came to his thoughts unbidden. Yeah, right! Nothing impossible…

Melissa, noting his preoccupation, stooped down and picked up a handful of snow in her mittens. She flung her arm behind her head and threw. The snowball went singing past his ear by two inches. She stamped her foot angrily.

Chuckling, he scooped up snow, forming a large ball, and as she bent down to form another. Franklin's hit her upturned rump.

"How could you?" Melissa said.

Franklin chortled, winking at two boys who had stopped to watch the snowball fight.

She had another snowball ready and threw it at his face. He dodged it easily. Then he threw his, hitting her in the chest.

"Look what you've done." But the gleam in her eyes gave her away. She was pretending to be angry.

"You started it."

"But it wasn't my intention for you to take advantage of me like that." She brushed off her chest and backside, then tucked her hand around Franklin's arm. "I should be mad at you for that."

Franklin smirked, resting her hand in the crook of his arm. "I believe the real Melissa lies somewhere hidden securely beneath the visage you are always careful to display, my dear."

She blushed.

"Someday I shall know the real Melissa…but perhaps, it is best I never do."

"Will you take me home now? I believe it's about to snow again."

"I've got an appointment at Bi-County."

"I'll go too." Her lips puckered prettily. "I'd follow you anywhere. All you have to do is ask?"

He had hoped to hear those words coming from Collina's lips.

His leg buckled. Melissa helped him straighten up. "You should use that cane more."

"Soon I won't need it." He mounted the steps to the hospital, more confidant with every step. "That new therapy is doing wonders for my leg."

"Then you'll go back to Kentucky?"

His heart leaped at the thought, but he ignored her question, pretending he hadn't heard. Stepping into the corridor of the large hospital, he made his way to room 234.

"Come right in, Franklin," Dr. Chadwick said. He nodded to Melissa standing in the hallway, then firmly closed the door. Dr. Chadwick pushed his spectacles up the bridge of his nose. "You know, there's talk of Roosevelt running for the presidency."

"He'll need the support of conservative Republicans in Congress in order to win the nomination," Franklin said, unbuttoning his shirt. "Teddy's a bit unorthodox, but he has the people's interest at heart. He stepped in quickly and handled the reins capably after McKinley's assassination."

Dr. Chadwick placed his stethoscope to his ears and listened to Franklin's heart. "Heart's good and strong. Drop your pants so I can examine that leg."

He palpated the leg and examined the deep scar that ran from thigh to knee. "I think the progress on your leg is miraculous. I never would have thought such a medical endeavor like this possible if I hadn't seen it with my own eyes."

"You mean I'm free to go? No more rehab?" Franklin sprang off the examination table, pulling up his pants.

"Major ligaments and nerves were severed and though they have mended the best they could, you'll always have a limp. And strenuous work might aggravate that leg more. You'll be the best judge of what your limits are."

"But I thought with time my leg would heal completely. Can't ride a horse or do strenuous work dragging this along." Franklin slapped his leg.

"I don't even like it that you're standing on that leg eight hours a day. Can't you find a way of sitting and doing your job?"

"You mean, I'll always be a cripple?" He didn't expect this answer. Dr. Chadwick had extinguished his last ounce of hope. He must let Collina go—from his heart. Jealousy is cruel as the grave…Austin is qualified to meet her needs. Collina's dedication to her beloved Shushan was unpurchasable. For his beloved's sake he must step away and move on.

Doctor Chadwick patted Franklin's shoulder. "Count your blessings. You're one of the lucky ones. You returned home walking on your own two feet, not in a pine box."

The wind whipped around the corner of the building with a vengeance. "What did the doctor say about your leg?" Melissa said.

"That I'd always have a limp." He pulled the collar of his coat closer around his ears.

"Will you be able to ride again?"

She was really quite a tiny thing. He felt like a giant next to her at times. Yet, when her tongue began to waggle, like now, he felt smaller than a mouse. "Whatever made you ask that? Why do you presume I can't ride?"

She took his hand in hers.

A man ringing a hand bell cried out, "Muffins. Warm muffins." He paused in front of Franklin and smiled. "Would you like a good hot muffin? Only two pennies." The shabby suit, the faded grey waistcoat, the gloves with holes in the fingers, and the merry eyes were things Franklin was used to seeing on the streets of Detroit.

"Where're you from?" Franklin had found that Detroit housed more immigrants than citizens. Then, feeling somewhat abashed at his manners, he muttered a hasty, "Sorry."

The man waved this aside, reaching up and bringing down two muffins. "England was my place of birth; now America is my home. Someday I'll have a big bakery, my name across the door."

"Franklin owns his own tool and dye shop, and he was one of

Roosevelt's Rough Riders, though he tries to keep it a secret," Melissa said.

The muffin man thrust the two muffins into Franklin's cold hands. Franklin reached into his pockets for change.

The muffin man wagged his finger. "A gift. One patriot to another."

"That's not necessary." Franklin handed him the coins.

"You have already paid. Everything worth believing in has a price. You have paid me by fighting in the Spanish-American War when I was not able to."

Franklin watched him as he walked on down the road.

"Was it bad there?" Melissa's high-pitched voice broke into the dusky stillness.

Franklin's long fingers balled into fists. He was nothing but an illegitimate half-breed, and as for that patriot stuff, if that muffin man knew how he'd let his friends down, he wouldn't want to be "one patriot to another," at least not with him.

Wealth had bought him a toehold into well-to-do society, and he'd felt certain his past would matter little to him now. But it mattered more. All he had gained with his hard work and material gain was loneliness and dissatisfaction with his inconsequential life. Everything worth believing in has a price. Collina believed in Christ Jesus. He believed, but not in the literal way she did. Who was right?

"I've made you angry. I can tell when you try to out walk me." She ran to keep up with him. "I bet you were hard to catch when you didn't have that limp."

He lifted his face to the descending flakes of snow. Melissa could be so aggravating at times. Other times, she proved a welcomed diversion from painful memories. He faced her, mad at himself more than at her. "Why do you prattle on so?"

She shrugged. "Because I haven't got anything better to do, and because," she said softly, taking a step closer. "I love you."

"Sure you do. You tease me, poke fun at my limp, talk about me behind my back, and then have the nerve to say you love me?" He walked on, paying little heed to her.

"I can see where I stand with you." She ran to catch up, pulling at his coat. "Stop." Tears formed pools in her eyes. "You certainly know how to hurt people."

"Yes, I've had lots of practice."

Her small fists pounded on his chest.

"Melissa." He cupped her gloved hands into his large ones, searching her tear-stained face. "What has come over you?" He gave her a shake. "What's wrong?"

Her tears dripped down her cheeks and onto his bare hands.

"I'm sorry," he said gently.

She searched his face, her soft brows lifting as if expecting something. "If you only knew, I love you, I do. If you gave me a little time, I could make you love me, too."

A flicker of affection for her infected the temperate corners of his lips. Then he turned his face away. "I don't love you, Melissa."

"I don't care. I love you enough for both of us."

He looked at her evenly. "What about Jane and Dawn?" He knew Melissa cared little for the dark-skinned Jane and her daughter, Dawn, but he had promised Joe to take care of them, and he wasn't about to go back on his word.

"You could buy them their own home, right next to that big house of yours."

"Is it because they're Indians? Tell me the truth."

"Yes…no. I…Come for Christmas dinner. Mama wants you to come."

"Sure, give your father this. I'll not come as a beggar to your doorstep."

"Can't you try and love me?" Melissa's eyes beseeched his, her long dark lashes wet with tears. She drew him into an alleyway.

"There, there. Sure. You—"

Her lips sought his. She intoxicated his senses and she folded into his needs with every wave of his desire.

Could he find fulfillment with her? Or would she become his Delilah?

"You would make me the happiest woman alive if you proposed." Tears dripped from her eyelids like dew drops.

"None of this. You will freeze your pretty face." Marriage with Melissa might not be such a bad thing.

"You could bring your money, then ask my father for my hand in marriage. I will make that mansion of yours into a palace fit for a king." He didn't want a palace. He wanted a home. He had sought material gain and now, on his pinnacle of success, he felt—alone, with no one to share his accomplishments. As he cradled her chin, her eyes glistened back at him. He gasped. They resembled the eyes of that tiger he'd seen at that circus last month.

Nonsense. She's a tiny little thing in love with me. He imagined the society page of the *Detroit Tribune*. Franklin Long to wed Melissa Slinger, daughter of Cyle Slinger, a wealthy businessman from Detroit. No longer would he be associated with the stigma of an illegitimate immigrant. Yes, society would recognize him now.

Her fingernails grazed his cheek as she drew his face toward hers. He was sharply aware of their length. Then she drew his lips to hers. Why did the story of Samson come to mind? How silly. Still, there was something about Melissa that eluded him.

Chapter 18

December 28, 1901. Lexington, Kentucky

Ice-covered trees twinkled in the starlight amidst the glow of lanterns hung on tree branches. Collina gazed in awe while her thoughts swirled like a Ferris wheel. Kentucky didn't get ice like this often, but when they did, it was spectacular. The chatter of her sisters kept the carriage in a gala atmosphere on their way to Aunt Louise's ball. The ice tinkled like crystal chandeliers to the gentle strokes of the wind as Collina searched her heart.

Austin had told her his main desire to be at Shushan was because of his affection for her. How did this happen? She stole a glance his way. He'd hardly spoken to her, driving his team carefully over the terrain, both horses wearing the cleated shoes he'd devised for them. The horses pulled Mother's carriage easily along the icy roads. Austin remained distant. Bo had to repeat himself twice on their trip over. She'd felt Austin's eyes on her, but when she glanced at him, he looked quickly away.

They parked their buggy next to the high-step entrance made just for buggies at the side of the wide veranda of Aunt Louise McCullen's mansion and dismounted.

"Yes, yes, come in. So good to see you, Collina." Louise McCullen's tall, slender profile etched a gracious shadow beneath the pavilion. Her long fingers blotched with the brown stains of age and distorted slightly with the pains of rheumatism, gracefully enhanced the impeccable beauty they served. She smoothed a strand of her silver-grey hair dislodged by the wind and smiled at Collina and then at her sisters emerging onto the tiled coach entrance. Aunt Louise's Christmas ball was always a gala event.

Old Tom helped each of her sisters to the well-worn steps that had seen many generations of fair young damsels dressed in billowing evening gowns. He turned to Louise. "Don't you think you should go inside now? I can do my job without you overseeing it."

"Tom, it's not your place to talk to me like that," Aunt Louise said. A smile crossed the eighty-some-year-old face, displaying the many laugh lines she'd acquired throughout her years.

Old Tom hobbled back to his post at the carriage entrance. "You should be indoors. This night is too damp and cold for you to be outside."

"'Tis yourself that should be inside."

He shook his curly white head. "I've got to show this young buck here," nodding in his grandson's direction, "how to greet callers proper. Only the good Lord knows it might be my last time to see young and old alike kickin' up their heels having fun."

Aunt Louise laughed. "I never have won an argument with him and there's no reason to think I shall now. Let us retire our conversation to the front foyer." They moved to the foyer and Aunt Louise continued.

"Now, my dears, let me take a look at you." She scrutinized their ball gowns with inordinate frankness. "Belle, that deep blue taffeta becomes your eyes,and the fair highlights of your complexion.

"Ruby, your tiny waist is emphasized the more, like a dainty glove in your ball gown." She touched the gown, feeling the fabric, "A lovely soft rose and the deep maroon embroidery brings out the bloom of youth to your cheeks and the delicate highlights of your rich flaxen hair."

Louise swerved her attention to Collina.

Collina's countenance did not convey the elegance her gown displayed. No telling what Aunt Louise's response would be.

"Why, darling, you look like a premature valentine in that dress."

Collina chuckled. Exactly what she had thought. "It was a surprise to me. But then most of Belle and Ruby's dresses are."

"Puffy sleeves done in red velvet, and gentle folds of fabric sweeping the floor. What a lovely complement to your slenderness, my dear." Aunt Louise cocked her head like a wise owl. "That emerald-green ribbon about your waist touches off the ensemble perfectly."

"I know my eyes can't help but linger," Austin said as he approached them. His chest appeared wider in the starched white shirt of his tuxedo, his shoulders broader, and next to slender Aunt Louise his tallness more apparent.

"Those long hair curl things shimmer on that red dress, and that touch of green sure brings out the glow of her eyes, doesn't it, Miss Louise?"

That was enough scrutiny from Austin. She diverted their attention to the full-length window. Whatever ailed him before had dissipated. "From Shadow Lake Crossing we didn't know what to make of this." Collina pointed to the lanterns shining through the ice-laden trees.

"One would think we've arrived at a palace fit for a king," Belle said.

"That large magnolia tree is beautiful with that blue lantern shining within its glistening limbs," Ruby said.

"Look at that." The moon had worked its way from a wayward cloud, and its rays shone with brilliance, creating a prism of colors amidst the icy trees. Aunt Louise sighed. "If God can work such beauty on earth, think how beautiful heaven will be."

Dear Aunt Louise, how she loved to put the Lord in her everyday life. They had grown up hearing it, accepting it as much a part of Aunt Louise as her engaging smile. It must please the Lord, for everything within Louise's gentle touch wove an enchanting domain of love for all who came within its borders.

"Where is your dear mother? I hoped she would come and give me someone to talk to while you young things dance off into the moonlight."

"She planned to come," Collina said, "but Chester's wife decided to have her baby. So mother went to tend to her. Bugie went with her to play with Little Gill."

Austin politely offered her his arm and they walked farther into the large, brightly lit entranceway of the grand hall. The long, impressive stairway curved gently upward to the second and third levels, and above it a pickled dome of stained-glass windows that Aunt Louise's late husband, Blake McCullen, the well-known architect, had designed.

Louise paused in the threshold of the dining room, turning a switch that sent the globes above their heads alight. The gold and diamond necklace around Aunt Louise's neck now sparkled as gaily as the trees outside.

Belle looked in wonderment. "When did you install gas lights?"

"I got the house done in time for this ball. I'm trying to get used to them, though I'm behind the times. There's a light called electricity Thomas Edison invented. You press a small button and they come on."

"Yes, we've heard about it," Belle said.

"He's also invented a music machine called a phonograph," Ruby said.

"I wager he'll be inventing a lot more things before our good Lord takes him home. God gave that man a special gift. Come see what I've done to the ballroom." Her thin form artfully maneuvered Collina and Ruby about the crowded foyer. She came to the closed double doors that led to the ballroom and glass-domed sunroom.

"Children, over here," Louise said to the milling crowd of dancers. She relinquished Ruby's hand to clap her own in stern reprimand above the soft murmurs of the room. "Let's not waste time, children; I have a full evening planned for each one tonight." Taking a firm hold on the doorknob, she jerked it opened. "There."

Through the french doors, the colored lanterns glowed against the icy prisms of glass. The large stone fireplace at the end of the circular room gave off a soft aroma of hickory and drenched the room with added romance and warmth. In the center of the ceiling draped a large crystal chandler, its domes sparkling with the soft glow of candlelight.

Ruby pointed to it and whispered to Louise. "Where's the new light?"

Louise gave her shoulder a hug and whispered, "Candlelight is more romantic, dear."

Collina marveled at Aunt Louise's ability to create. People said that Blake McCullen's artistry and talent for building bordered on genius. But Mother said Blake would always shake his head and reply, "Yes, my hands did the building, but the creativity wholly belongs to Loe." Louise would shake her head. "No, no, dear, I only put into words what you were thinking." He would smile back at her, his eyes burning with love for her.

Stephen Meir appeared beside them. Ruby's eyes glistened into his.

"I wish I could have driven you," Stephen said. "Are you upset with me, meeting you like this I mean—"

"Not at all. After all, you had to complete your semester at the university. I'm happy you were able to make it, with the ice and all. How did your studies go?" Ruby said.

"Stimulating, in more ways than one would expect. I'm planning on going into the motion picture business."

"The what?"

Stephen chuckled. "I see I have a lot to tell you."

"Hurry, dears," Aunt Louise said, "the moon is just about to break again." She brushed their questioning looks aside with a motion of her hand. "Come."

As they stood inside the dome-shaped sun room, the moon made its escape from the fickle clutches of clouds, casting its glow on oaks and maples.

"It's beautiful." The soft melody of the violin began its rendition of a Viennese waltz, and the combination of movement and music overpowered Collina's heart with memories she had hoped were long forgotten.

"This is my favorite place." Louise eased down into a wicker rocker, one of many white wicker chairs that adorned the sunroom.

"Miss Collina, Miss Ruby," Old Tom said, "would you care for an hors d'oeuvre? I thought you might be hungry."

"Why, how thoughtful of you, Tom." Louise smiled, drawing her shawl snugly around her shoulders.

"There you are," Belle said, followed by Bo. Brighter than usual, Belle's eyes were a liquid sky blue. She disclosed the small engagement ring that had been in Bo's family for generations. "We are officially engaged."

"Belle, it's beautiful." Collina and Ruby hugged their sister warmly.

Bo, with a sheepish grin on his face, said, "Thought this would be the perfect place to give Belle her ring."

"Tell me, Austin, what have you been doing lately?" Louise's shrewd eyes met his. "I see the years have been kind to you. You haven't lost any of your charm."

Austin smiled. "Thank you." He popped another hors d'oeuvre into his mouth. "I've been trying to stay out of trouble mostly."

Self-assurance of his good looks and a genuine zeal for the women had encouraged his reputation of being a ladies' man. What bothered Collina was that Austin felt no embarrassment about this. She respected Louise's opinions. She never failed to ascertain a situation.

"Those girls of yours are in need of a mother right about now," Louise said.

He shrugged, glanced at Collina, then said, "I guess, but then that would mean I would have to settle for just one gal." He raised his eyebrows in an attempt of humor.

Louise did not return his smile.

"Do you know Jesus?" Old Tom quietly said.

"Don't see any reason to get the Lord involved with my troubles," Austin said. "Yep, always felt it would prove more advantageous not to make God too happy, nor the devil too mad."

Old Tom dispersed the tea and punch, then said, "You means to tell me you ain't freed yet?" Old Tom shook his snow-white head. "I ain't talkin' about Lincoln's freeing; I'm talkin' about real freeing. The liberty that only Jesus can give. Why, without that liberty, you ain't free at all. You can't be, because that old nature," he said, tapping Austin on the chest with one of his gnarled fingers, "will draw you down every time."

Austin smiled at him unabated. "I've survived the Southern Pentecostal and Baptists' submerging. Don't you worry about me. God and I do better if I keep my distance."

Ruby glanced at Stephen, her puckered brow displaying her skepticism. "Stephen, Aunt Louise and Old Tom are right. I realize our family and yours have known each other for two generations, but all I know about your religious affiliations is that your father never went to church. What are your feelings about Jesus?"

Stephen didn't take his eyes off of Ruby. "He's my friend, my confidant, my Almighty Savior. Without Him, I am nothing. With Him I am capable of anything."

"That's the way I feel," she whispered.

"Me too!" Bo replied. "I couldn't have said it better myself. And not half as eloquently."

Louise rose and, leaning heavily on her cane, walked over to them. "Join hands, Belle and Bo." Then handing her cane to Collina, she laid one hand on Stephen's and Ruby's clasped hands and the other on Belle's and Bo's. "Dear God, bless these couples. Give them a keen ear to always listen, obey, and be guided by Your wisdom of the Holy Bible throughout their wedded lives. Amen."

"But, Aunt Louise, we're not—"

"I, I'm not ready," Stephen stammered.

Louise chuckled. "I believe Jake's about to begin, now skedaddle out of here and go kick up your heels before the rheumatism sets in."

Old Jake began the notes of Strauss's *Blue Danube*. A half smile played across the dimples on Austin's face. "I'm not very good at waltzes, but I'm willing to try, Collina, if you are."

The notes weaved a melody of their own as she and Austin dipped and swayed to the music.

Waltzing around the room with Austin's arm about her reemphasized the painful memories of dancing with Franklin to this same music years before. Why could she not embrace the present? Why must she wallow like a pig in the mud pits of the past? Why could she not let go of Franklin? They had said their goodbyes. Myra had written her that she had seen Franklin on the arms of the society debutante Melissa Slinger. And rumor had it they would soon be married.

Why did that not surprise her? So, he'd found another woman to help him with his ambitious dreams of wealth and position. Then why am I measuring every man by his standard? It was evident Franklin Long was far from perfect.

As the waltz concluded, her eyes implored Austin. "Please excuse me for a moment." There could never be anything but friendship between them. The problem being Austin's faith, she'd tried countless times to witness to him and to no avail. She needed to be alone to think. She stepped away from him and ran toward the haven of the dark veranda.

"Collina May."

Closing her eyes, she willed him gone. The admonition of 2 Corinthians 6:14 came to her thoughts vividly. *Be ye not unequally yoked together with unbelievers: for what fellowship hath righteousness with unrighteousness? and what communion hath light with darkness?*

"Go away."

"Sit down," Austin said. One eyebrow lifted in mock distress, he offered her a seat on the black wrought iron bench.

He was so confident. So sure his natural good looks could attain him anything he desired. She sank onto the seat, her knees feeling like jelly. "I can't pretend with you. I have nothing in common with you but our mutual labor at Shushan."

He sat down next to her, running his fingers through his thick, wavy hair. She had seen him do that once before. Then it came to her. It had been that day at his cabin, when Mary was in childbirth. Mary had said, "You'll see, he can be very charming if he has a mind to be. And if he gets a notion to have ya, he will."

"It's because of the answer I gave to Aunt Louise, isn't it?"

She jumped to her feet and walked nervously to the banister. Mary had begged her to give Austin a chance. That deep down he was a good man. She felt the full moon's glow on her face and though the ice beneath her arms felt cold and wet, she rested them there.

Gazing out over the glistening grounds beneath, she wondered why God allowed this to happen to her? She didn't love Austin and she'd prayed that the memory of Franklin would dissipate like the fog on the valleys after an early morning rain. He rode out of her life. Pray let it be out of her thoughts as well.

Austin's outstretched hand held one long-stemmed rose bud, encased in ice.

She picked up the stem carefully, caressing it in the palm of her hand and stroking the ice-covered thorns, then the petals. "Poor thing, it didn't have a chance to blossom."

"True, but if it had, it would now be like the rest over there, only brown stems. You couldn't stroke its thorns because they would have

166

pricked your fingers. No, this one had a mission to accomplish. To fulfill that mission, it needed to wait. So it endured the hardships of being alone and out of its domain to fulfill it."

Bringing the rose up to her nose, she said, "Yet it has lost part of itself, one of the most beautiful parts of a flower, its fragrance, that meaningful part that confirms it's a rose."

"Yes, the lucky ones acquire it all. The rest accept what they're handed."

"It is our choices. There are fewer, the older we become, then we accept what is left. The choice whether we lose our God-given conscience and our emotions—"

"I'm not without emotions, Collina." He gazed down at her, amused. "In fact, at this moment, I am experiencing too many feelings, none of which you care to experience."

She hurried to the farthest side of the balcony.

"You need to wear dresses more often and your hair like that. It shows off your sloping neck line and—

"You're so, so, earthly!" Collina turned. Ready to hurl her best sermon at his carnal head. Only she was ill prepared.

His eyes bathed her with a look so warm, so…no, it was just her imagination. Just the wind causing the trees to sway long shadows across the veranda that caused his eyes to yield and soften.

The moon's rays displayed a glittering fairyland of illusion so bright amidst the dark backdrop of night that she felt their sudden interlude, merely a dream, an allusion of love that Austin knew all too well.

"You don't love me. That's good. I always hurt the women who love me." He walked forward, taking the rose from her hand and placing it behind her ear. Bending over, he placed one hand beneath her chin, tilted it, and looked deeply into her eyes. "Who are you truly angry about? Me or you?" he whispered, then bent his head toward hers. She turned away. He drew her face to his and kissed her gently on her moist cheek. "You think you are in love with that soldier from your past; yet, for some uncanny reason, feel more for me than you care to admit."

Chapter 19

January 6, 1902

"Arrogant and egotistical, that's what he is." Collina went about her chores, her thoughts a maze of confusion. "Who was she angrier at? Herself or Austin? Was he right about her? The horses neighing outside brought her out of her reverie and a familiar sight came into view.

Her mother reined up Jude, then nudged the sleeping Bugie and Little Gill lying in the bed of the wagon behind her. Jessie and Robert came running out of the barn.

Collina reached Mother first and took the sleeping infant from her arms. The front door banged wildly as Belle and Ruby ran out.

"Land sakes, children, don't wake the baby. Someone help me down off this wagon seat." Mother's legs buckled; she clutched Robert's arm. "My poor legs have cramped up something awful. Help me into the house, Robert."

Jessie looked down the winding drive. "Where's Sarah and Chester?"

Mother sat in the first soft chair she came to. "Sarah's gone."

"Oh, Mother, not Sarah. Sarah's too young, too beautiful, to die," Belle said.

"It'll take a miracle for this child not to follow her mother." Her mother eyed each of them in turn.

Collina caressed the small hand in hers, bending down to kiss her tiny head. The little babe seemed satisfied, her bright blue eyes opening an instant before closing them sleepily and pursing her lips. "But

Mother, why wouldn't she live?"

"Poor little thing," Belle cooed. "She's perfect. Look at that little yawn. Let me hold her now."

"Don't worry, Mother," Collina said. "Doc thought I couldn't bring Betsy's calf around and I did."

Robert nodded his head. "That's right; I remember."

"It was too cold to send an infant out in a buckboard across rough roads, but I had no other choice. That woman that wed Sarah's Pa wouldn't let Little Sarah stay until she could be weaned off that goat's milk she was used to. Understand, children, don't go getting too attached."

"I'll go take care of Jude for you, Mother." Jessie left without waiting for a reply.

"Wait, we'll help." Robert and Scott followed him out the door.

Belle and Ruby had tears in their eyes. Neither one said a word.

"Could one of you girls get Bugie and Gill something to eat and cleaned up? I expect Gill here will be living with his grandma for a time." Deep cavities beneath each eye showed her mother's exhaustion. She smiled into the little boy's woebegone face encouragingly. "Would you like that?"

Gill nodded. "Papa?"

"He's bringing your mother home, child." Mother rose and walked to the stairs. "One of you girls bring me up a little something to eat. I'm going to bed."

Ruby grasped Gill's little hand. "Come on, Bugie; let's go show Gill how we wash before we eat."

"I'll bring that food right up, Mother." Belle handed the baby to Collina.

"But, Mother," Collina said, "what do I feed her?"

Mother stopped, one foot on the step. "She's been on goat's milk, and I gave her the last bottle an hour ago. We'll just have to try cow's milk and hope Little Sarah will accept it. We can ask Doc if he knows of any woman nursing."

The Chippendale rocker swayed rhythmically as Collina sang a lullaby to Little Sarah to calm her crying. It was just past the dinner hour, and she prayed Doc Baker would be coming up the gravel drive soon. Mother, sick with a migraine, was resting up in her room.

Collina was confident that at any minute Jessie and Doc would come bounding through those oak doors. Doc would know what to do. He had a remedy for just about everything. She patted the small baby's backside and listened for the predictable burp. But more than just a burp erupted. Vomit washed down her shoulder.

"Not again." She gently moved Little Sarah onto her lap, wiping the sour milk from baby's mouth. Heavy steps on the veranda and mumbling voices brought her to her feet. "Doc, I'm so glad you're here."

"No, Collina," a deep husky voice retorted. Austin's dark head appeared around the corner. "Heard David might be here."

"I've sent Jesse out looking for him."

Austin plopped down onto the well-used camel back sofa. "How's Little Sarah?"

"Not good. Why are you looking for David? Something wrong with your girls?"

"They've both come down with a bad cold and cough. Thought I'd better ask David if there was anything contagious floating about."

Horses neighing, and mumbling voices brought Austin to his feet.

"What's this I hear, Sarah's dead?" Doc Baker's grey head looked thinner and greyer. His shoulder sagged beneath the weight of his black leather bag. Jessie followed.

"This is Little Sarah." She cradled the infant in her arms and tilted the baby up for Doc to see. "Isn't she beautiful?" Little Sarah's golden hair circled her head like a halo, and she opened her large blue eyes with interest at the strangers.

Doc smiled. "She is, and she's awful little to take a half-day journey from Boone Creek to MacDuff County in winter."

Jessie shuffled his feet. "I'd better go and tend to the livestock."

"Little Sarah was doing all right on goat's milk but can't seem to handle the cow's milk. She's got a little cough and some congestion. I can hear it rumble sometimes in her chest."

Doc dropped his black bag on the side table, his face drawn up in an angry smirk. She watched in surprise. What had come over Doc?

"Here it is 1902, and you'd think people would be more concerned about lives than machinery. When are the medicines and hospitals going to keep up with the lives lost up here in these hills?

"When the day comes that women can stop having their babies at home and have them in hospitals where sterilization and practiced surgical procedures can be administered, that will be the day my work is made a whole lot easier. Here, lay her down in that crib, Collina."

Obediently she laid Little Sarah down into Bugie's old crib.

"Hmmm, this little girl wasn't due to arrive so soon." Taking his stethoscope, he listened to her heart and lungs. Doc Baker shook his head. "She's got pneumonia. Whatever prompted your mother to take her on such a journey?"

"I had no choice in the matter." Maggie clutched a water bottle to her head. "I was lucky to get the three bottles of goat's milk for the trip here."

Doc Baker's eyes softened. "I swear people are getting meaner by the day. No wonder there's so much sickness about. Got one of your migraines?" He reached into his black bag and produced a small box of pills. "Here, take one every four hours; it'll help you rest. Now, you go back up those stairs and lie down. That's the only thing that will help a migraine."

"And what can you give me for Sarah's baby?" Collina said. Little Sarah pursed her lips. Collina swallowed down her tears.

"I'll see if I can find a surrogate mother to nurse her, until then, try boiling the cow's milk, then adding a little cane syrup to it. Might be Little Sarah's stomach would have done the same way if she'd stayed at her grandpa's," Doc said. "She looks a little yellow. She's got a touch of jaundice. That should go away. If it doesn't in a day or two, set her crib by a window so she can get some sunlight. What did Sarah die of?"

"Inflammation," Mother said.

Doc Baker listened to Little Sarah's heart and lungs for a second time. He removed his stethoscope. He clicked his tongue against his teeth. "She's congested and too young for me to give her much in the way of drugs. Keep her warm. Well, come on Maggie." He guided her toward the kitchen. "Take that pill with something hot. It'll help it to work faster, and you can give me some hot tea with a teaspoon of whiskey to warm me for the long trip home."

Collina hugged the infant to her breast. Had dying become more normal than living? With a consuming need for activity, she struggled with moving the crib toward the south window.

Strong hands lifted the crib as if it was merely a basketful of flowers. "Will this do?" Austin said.

She nodded. She had little faith in her voice not to edify grief. Laying Sarah down in her crib, she busied herself with folding the mounds of cut-up linen Ruby had made to use as diapers. She'd keep herself busy, so busy she couldn't think.

"I'd better go ask David about my girls before he retreats out the kitchen door. You want me to come back and help you?"

She shook her head, not taking her eyes off the diapers. A fierce desire to prove everyone wrong burned in her chest. She'd show them. God wouldn't want her to lose heart. Yes, she'd show them. She'd done it with the calf; she could do it again.

"She'll live, Austin, you'll see. God wouldn't want Little Sarah to die." He reached for her arm. She pulled it away. "You have to believe. Wait, I forgot. You don't believe in God or know Jesus, the Great Physician. Too bad for you."

Austin grinned. "Maybe I need you to show me how."

Ruby worked diligently on the pieces of fabric she'd make into gowns for Little Sarah. Her fingers worked expertly with needle and thread as she thought of Stephen. She'd never felt this way before for a man.

She patted her apron pocket that held Stephen's letter. How would Mother take the news of her asking him to be her escort at Belle's wedding? Suddenly impatient to get the conversation over with, she hurried through the back door.

In the kitchen, she stole around the large wooden table, hoping not to disturb Belle as she bustled about, starting the supper meal.

"Ruby, not so fast, just where do you think your heading? I need some help here."

"Sis, I promise to be right back. But right now, while I've got my mind made up to do it, I need to talk to Mother about your wedding."

"My wedding?"

"I mean to ask Stephen to be my escort, and I've got to ask Mother first, don't I?"

"Stephen's a university man." Belle grinned, giving the dough she was kneading an extra punch. "I've got to hand it to you. A rich college man like Stephen is quite a catch."

Ruby blushed and hurried up the stairs. Her heart was pounding clear up in her ears as she knocked on Mother's bedroom door, then opened it without even waiting for an invitation.

The shades were drawn and the room dark. "Mother, you're not asleep, are you?"

"No."

"I need to know something. It's about Belle's wedding. Is it okay if I ask someone to be my escort?"

"Whom do you have in mind?"

She swallowed hard. "Stephen Meir."

Her mother lifted the cool cloth from across her forehead and raised herself slowly.

Shoving her hand into her pocket, Ruby's fingers closed on his letter and held it out to her mother. "See, he's written me. He was the one that mentioned I should ask him."

Her mother took it hesitantly. "You want me to read it?"

She nodded, her breath coming out all at once.

"He writes an eloquent hand. I've known his family ever since your father fetched me here as a bride. Ruth was very kind to me, helped me set up housekeeping. She was a good Christian woman. Though when she died, I didn't care for the hard hand Meir used on his son, but spoiled Julie Ann, that twin sister of Stephen's. She could do no wrong, and Stephen could do no right."

"Mother, can I ask him to be my escort?"

Mother got up from the bed and walked toward the window, lifting the shades. "You're a young lady; keep that in mind." She sat down in her rocker and urged Ruby to sit next to her. Taking her hand, she placed hers on Ruby's soft cheek. "Daughter, men will always be men. They'll try to trifle with you as much as they can."

"Yes, Mother, I know."

"He's probably half drawn to you because of your sweetness and the other half because of your innocence. It's up to you to show him there's more to you than a soft body. You've got a strong mind and a steady heart. Don't be in a hurry to fall in love, and remember our good Lord's rules. They're there for your protection."

"How will I know the right man when I meet him, Mother?"

Mother smiled. "I remember another time ages ago when I asked my mother that same question. I can recite my mother's exact words. 'When he puts your needs before his, true love waits.'"

Collina held Little Sarah's hand, so perfectly formed, and gently kissed her soft head. "God, please make her well. Let her live, Lord." Little Sarah's mouth curled upwards, then her bright eyes closed. She placed her in the crib and fell back into the big Chippendale rocker.

"Collina, Collina!"

She woke with a start, nearly falling out of the rocker. The first rays of sunlight pierced the quiet stillness of dawn with sudden clarity. She rubbed her eyes. She was alone, but for the sleeping infant. She had thought for sure someone had called her name.

"Little Sarah." Collina smiled. Little Sarah had slept through the night. Surely this meant she was getting better.

The infant was lying as Collina had left her. Her small cheek nestled comfortably on the white sheets, her little head covered with blond hair shining softly in the morning light.

She touched the small fist. Mmm, feels a little cold. She reached for the comforter. Little Sarah is lying so still. Fear gripped her heart, a sickly tight sensation wrenching her stomach muscles. You know the signs; you've seen them enough. Collina shook her head. She's too beautiful. God would want her to live. She placed her hand before the infant's mouth. Her lips were cold to her touch. Tears formed in Collina's eyes and dripped despondently onto the crocheted blanket that dear Sarah had made for her little daughter.

Suddenly, her mother's arms wrapped around her like a warm quilt. Mother had been right. Was she there to gloat?

"Little Sarah is dead, Mother." She thrust her mother's arms aside.

"I warned you not to become too attached." Mother's shoulders slumped forward, pulsing with unshed tears.

"From the start you acted like it didn't matter whether this baby lived or died."

"I guess I understand it better than anyone, what with three still births and one two-year-old lying in graves next to their father. I understand how you feel, daughter. That's all any of us can do. Understand a person's heartache. With matters like these, you have to leave it on our Lord's shoulders. Now, why don't you go up and get a little rest?" Her mother coaxed.

"You were against her surviving from the beginning."

"Death is part of living."

Collina's pent up emotions demanded empathy. "How can you be so callous?"

"How's—" Belle stopped, seeing Collina's pain-stricken face. She buried her hands deep into her apron pockets. "She's dead?"

Mother nodded. "She died sometime in the night." Her mother got a sheet and began wrapping Little Sarah in it.

Collina stepped forward. She wanted to snatch the rag from her mother's hands. Don't cover that beautiful head. Don't.

"Should I start breakfast?" Belle said.

Mother nodded. Wrapping Little Sarah gently.

Collina ran up the stairway with tears fogging the steps beneath her.

"Should I make sausage or use the last of the bacon?"

"Use the rest of the bacon, I guess."

"Don't bother making me a plate," Collina said from the top of the stairway. "I've lost my appetite." She ran to her room and slammed the door behind her. "Oh God, why? Why did You let her die?"

Chapter 20

*D*eath and dying, sickness and more sickness, Collina had had her fill.

"Collina, are you in there?" Mother did not wait for her to reply, but opened the door and stepped into the room. "You blame me for Little Sarah dying."

Collina didn't know why, but for some reason, she did. A vision of the small grave next to the larger one of Little Sarah's mother's blurred before Collina's eyes. Her heart ached to hold the baby, feel the soft golden head, touch her tiny fingers. With the first shovelful of dirt hitting Little Sarah's coffin, she had run, back to the solitude of her room.

Mother sat down on the bed, rubbing her temples. "Blame who you will, but get over this. Mourning is a luxury we can ill afford when there are others needing care. I know how you're feeling. Don't you know I wanted to blame someone for your father's death? But no amount of crying or wailing or blaming would have brought him back." Mother stood up, her eyes clear, her countenance determined.

How strong was the grit that lay beneath her mother's soft veneer? She had a way about her. Grace and dignity were her crown, compassion and valor her clothing. She had seen a nation divided by war and had prayed for its unity. She had witnessed her father eaten up by hate and had learned empathy and how to forgive. Forced from her childhood home, Spirit Wind Manor, her mother had taken an Irish immigrant's hand in matrimony, believing in his dream, and had turned up dirt alongside of him and begun anew.

Yes, Mother had persevered, and like a lighthouse beacon shining amidst the storms of life, her faith had shown the way for her offspring. She wrapped Collina into her arms.

Collina collapsed within the folds of their strength and cried. Laying her head on Mother's shoulder, she said from her choked throat, "But it's so hard, this life. Is it better not to love? Not to feel?"

"No. If you feel this way, it means you do not love enough."

"Mother, how can you say such things?"

"Little Sarah is with her mother. I can't explain to you why this terrible thing happened. Was it ignorance and lack of care for Sarah that caused her untimely death? What I do know is that both Sarah and her daughter are in paradise with Jesus. God's reasons are not always clear." Mother's look affirmed her words. "God doesn't need to explain His actions to us. He shields us from death. You see, life is our destiny—to be forever happy and carefree with God and His loving Son, Christ Jesus. Sarah and her daughter have reached their home, safe and secure."

Collina cried, Mother gently patting her back. "Get your grief out. What God asks of us is to trust in His wisdom and believe. To walk with faith on that wind-tossed pathway lying before our footsteps! Just pray as I do that the wind is at your back. It makes climbing uphill a lot easier."

Collina blew her nose and blinked.

"Now wash your face and pack your things. You're needed elsewhere. Austin's girls have both come down with a bad case of the measles. Doc Baker asked me to see if you'd go and tend to them. Knowing Austin, he'll more than repay us in helping you plant your crops come spring, and you know we'll need all the help we can get."

"Mother, we can't start using people like that." Then she noticed it—the dark circles beneath Mother's eyes and the exhausted lines around her mouth. "What's wrong?"

"I never dreamed how much you were doing until this past week. Daughter, we need all the strong hands we can lay hold of. I'm going to let Austin know just what a sacrifice it is for you to go and help him when we need you here. He's bound to feel guilty and promise us two months of planting time."

"Mother, if the preacher heard you say that, he'd tell you're doing this charitable thing for all the wrong reasons."

"I know. Be back by sundown. I don't want the neighbors talking any more than they already are about you."

It was good to be out. Her horse's shoes clicked an eager tune on the partly frozen clay path. The early sun caressing her face added to her uplifted hope. The day was not as bitter as last week's temperatures, though she did feel a tinge of moisture in the air. She'd best return before nightfall. She didn't want to risk a chance of being caught at Austin's cabin by an ice or snow storm.

Would he gloat over the fact that God hadn't answered her prayer to save Little Sarah? What had he meant saying he needed help in finding God. "Maybe you can show me…?" Nonsense. She shrugged this off.

Collina patted her bulging saddlebags, heavy with clean sheets and warm gowns for the girls. Mother placed little faith in a man's ability to clean, so she had bidden Collina to take cleaning things. On her horn rested two big baskets of vegetables, fruits, and meat. Austin was a mountaineer, and what the girls needed now more than anything was a balanced diet.

She had nursed Ruby and Bugie through their measles and felt confident the task would not be difficult.

"What a disarray," she said to no one particular as she arrived. The garden patch unkempt, woodpile full of logs yet to be split, the barn door slapping the wooden planks on one hinge. Inside the cabin wasn't any better. She gazed about the room much like a sea captain would on a turbulent ocean. The room was askew with tossed-off clothes and heaps of unwashed linen. The floor was thick with dust, the kitchen sink full of dirty dishes, and the room smelled of dust, smoke, and sickness. She felt partly guilty. It was evident now that Austin had ignored his homestead to help the McConnells with theirs.

She walked toward the closest window and drew back the curtains. Dust particles floated in the air about her. Fumbling with the latch, she shoved it open, inhaling the cold air. "It's better to let in a little cold than breathe this staleness any longer."

The cabin was too quiet. Where were Susie and Becky?

"Hello? Anyone home?" No reply, she walked cautiously toward the closed door. Lord, what if—just last year the McCoys found the McDermitts all dead in their beds from the fever. She threw the bedroom door open so violently the wooden planks pounded on the logs of the wall, startling the two girls out of their slumber.

She let out a sigh of relief, seeing two pairs of eyes pop open. "How do you feel?" She placed a hand on each forehead. Susie's felt feverish with an alarming abundance of sores on her face and arms. "Are they itching, sweetheart?"

Susie nodded. "I can hardly sleep at night."

"We're thirsty, and I've got to go to the outhouse," Becky said. "Only Pa said not to move until either he or you come. And now I've got to go bad, badder 'n thirst, and I'm plumb parched."

"I'm here now." Collina took her small hand. "Where's your Pa?"

"Out getting a deer," Susie said. "He didn't have anything in here to eat cuz we've been sick and he couldn't leave us."

"You can't eat venison. Both you girls need a bland diet and lots of liquid until your fevers are down."

Once done with Becky's needs, and relieved to see her sores were not as many as Susie's, Collina warmed the chicken soup she had brought and spoon fed it to the girls. Neither one could hold the spoon without spilling it. She sponged each off with tepid water she had first boiled, wishing Austin would consider putting in a well. She didn't much care for getting drinking water from a stream where others washed their dirty clothes. She gave special care to sponging down Susie's spots, applying a poultice to the worst ones, and replaced the dirty nightgowns for clean ones. She shook her head at how threadbare the girls' nighties were.

She stripped the bed and remade it with the fresh-ironed linens she had brought. Their smiles and giggles said more than words, as they wiggled beneath the clean sheets.

"I can't recall when I felt so clean," Susie murmured before falling into a fitful slumber.

Collina rested her body on the doorpost and gazed at the slumbering children. Mother was right. She must never pine for what she couldn't control, when much lay to do that she could.

Now that the girls were comfortable, she warmed the creek water and got some dishes washed.

She had thought it odd for Mother to pile so much on her saddle. She wished she had taken the buggy. Then she could have packed more greens and fruits and cleaning things. She would have to make do.

In her frenzy to get the housecleaning chores done, she'd forgotten to watch the sky. Stepping out onto the porch to shake a few rugs, she noticed it had grown colder. A sleeting rain was falling. She'd already unsaddled her horse. Magic was safe in the barn. Collina ran out and gathered what firewood she could. She stoked the fire until it blazed, and every corner of the dim cabin leaped with warmth.

After hours of work, she surveyed the room with satisfaction. The clean wooden floor gleamed, the dishes were displayed like peacocks on their pantry shelves, and her bread awaited the cooking stove. Heavy rain pelted the cabin. Oh dear, the livestock. She reached for Austin's heavy coat resting on the peg by the door and ran to take care of them.

After giving more hay to Magic, she milked the cows and fed the cattle, chickens, and pigs. Perhaps Austin had decided to take shelter.

The icy pellets of sleet pummeled her face, hands, and legs. With only the rays of the setting sun to light the way, she turned the final bend in the wood toward the cabin, groping tree limbs frantically to keep from falling. She slowly made her way up the ice-covered hill toward the cabin's sheltering walls and just as she reached for the latch, she heard someone hail her name.

"Isn't he a dandy?" Austin waved his hand toward the six-point buck he'd laid on his pack mule. Swinging his leg over Indian style, he slipped down, landing on the icy ground, then fell to his bottom. His coon hat fell across his broad forehead above petulant, dark arched brows. His lips bared themselves beneath a thick black beard, making his mouth look wider and frightfully stark. His leather fringed coat he'd not bothered to fasten, and he blinked at her from the ground, smiling broadly like the bold scoundrel he was as spray after spray of icy rain pelted him.

Could he have found some mountain man's still and gotten some moonshine? Well, then, he deserves more than just a good fall on his bottom. She wrapped her coat tighter about her neck.

"You'll catch your death in weather like this. Mother always told my brothers to keep their coats fastened, or they'd be sure to get themselves one dilly of a chest cold."

Austin laughed, sliding on the ice. "Not me, got me a second layer. See." He tore at his loosely tied cloth shirt, laying bare his black chest hairs thick as a ram's coat.

She gasped, embarrassed at his boldness, and turned before he could see the warmth spreading like sunburn from her neck to face. "Seeing how you're already soaked to the bone, do you mind saddling up my horse? I'll come back in the morning. I'll bring some cleaning things, maybe some more greens and soup. The girls loved Mother's soup."

"You didn't come here alone, not on a day like this?" Austin's eyes were boring a hole in her face.

Silly man. Like the McConnells had an abundance of manpower. "I can take care of myself. No one needs to come with me, especially when there are chores a-plenty to do back home. We can't afford to spare a second pair of hands to nurse two little children."

"You can't go. Not if you value your horse any. It's as slippery as wet glass. That's why I'm so late."

"You made it, and so can I."

A slow smile crept across Austin's sober face. "I should have known better. Whatever a man can do, you can match or better." Austin chuckled, shaking his head. "Look, I'll bed down in the barn. You and the girls can have the cabin."

Is he mocking her independence? It ignited her temper like the Fourth of July fireworks. "I'll make it home just fine." The steps of the cabin were now covered with a glassy sheet of ice. Still, she wasn't going to stay here a minute more. If Austin could make it up that hill, she could make it down. Even if she had to slide down on her rump. She was mad at him and mad at herself and mad at—this day had turned out an awful mess and now... She felt herself slipping. Thud. "Ow." The noise of her bottom landing on the ice echoed in her ears. "Ahh."

"Ouch. I heard that from here. Did you break anything? That whack was loud enough."

She glanced up. That grotesque beard of his was vibrating. He was holding back his humor with difficulty.

"Ice is not your best dancing partner. I may come second to last, but you've got to admit, I'd be a lot softer to fall on!"

Collina frowned, rubbing her bottom...and laughed. She laughed until tears came to her eyes. She thought again of the small mound where Little Sarah lay, and she let the tears flow.

Austin laughed with her, his eyes growing sympathetic as her tears sent tributaries down her reddened cheeks. For some reason, his deep-throated bass gave her solace and closure to Little Sarah.

"Okay, you can tell everyone you meet, you ran me out of the cabin." His hands warm, reassuring, as he helped her up. "I know I surely deserve it, it being so dirty and messy to boot. Housekeeping isn't my best attribute."

"I quite agree!"

He smiled.

Avoiding his eyes as he helped her up the steps, she attempted to loosen her hands from his grasp. "But what will the neighbors say?"

"Neighbors? What neighbors?"

She looked around. Nothing but hills and trees as far as the eye could see. She felt a chill trickle down her spine. She was quite alone here with this mountain man. His black eyes stared into hers, her thoughts picking the strings of time remembering that moment on the lane when Franklin had rescued her. There'd be no Franklin or Joseph to save her now. Just what were Austin's intentions?

"God help the man or woman who tries to make anything out of this." Austin muttered. Seeing her safely inside, he turned sharply away, and led his horse and the tired pack mule with the buck to the barn.

I'll have to make the best of a bad situation. She started up the stove, reheating the little bit of broth that was left from the chicken soup. She added a few bits of meat and noodles, more water and seasoned it to her satisfaction. It wasn't half bad. She put the bread in the oven, and the aroma filled the little cabin. Austin's boots climbing the wooden planks of the porch busted into her thoughts as the cabin door opened to a downpour of pelting ice.

"It's a bad one out there," Austin said. "Mmm, something smells good." He discarded his leathers in one stroke of his large shoulders, hanging hat and coat on the wood stove, his large boots striking the wooden floor in a volley of masculine tones. She turned, puzzled. Why was Austin's presence so abhorrent?

He stopped. Watching her as keenly as she him, his shirt was wet, and his fastens were undone. "You need to change that shirt; it's wet."

His square jaw worked itself into firmer lines. She turned back to the sink, chopping the onions.

He moved like a cougar toward her, taking one of her curls in his large paw. His voice low, he said, "Do I dare tell you how fetching you are? Your hair damp and curly about your face and neck, thick ringlets like Irish wool on a sheep's back."

She stepped away to the stove.

He followed her and smiled back at her sheepishly, his fingers drawn into tight fists next to his sides. "Food smells good."

Turning, she nearly hit him with the ladle. "Excuse me." Backing away from him, she hurried to set the table. "The girls are both sleeping, but maybe after you eat your soup and side meat you can go in and see them. They should be awake by then."

"Is there anything I can get you before I bed down in the barn, more wood? How about some water for bathing?"

She jerked herself away from the table, setting down the last plate with a thump. "More water for washing dishes would be good, wood too. But it is much too nasty out there right now. Best you sit and eat while the food is still hot."

She held her breath as he took the first mouthful. She looked away. Why? He'd tasted her food before, and why should she care what he thought about her cooking? She sat down across from him and watched his beard as he bit down on the meat. Neither her father nor her brothers had ever had a beard. They were clean-shaven. Perhaps that was what disquieted her. Yes, that must be it, she decided, and felt better for the insight.

"Got any coffee made?"

"Yes." She hastened to the stove, carrying over the pot. The steam rose about her head. "Be careful. It's steaming hot," she warned.

"I can see that." A bold finger reached up to touch a loose curl that brushed his cheek.

Her hand grazed his shoulder in her haste to get away. "I didn't mean…your, your shirt is very damp, Austin."

What would Mother do? She would tell Pa to go and put on a dry one. She had tried that. But then, had she a right to order Austin?

He had stopped eating and was returning her gaze.

"No use you getting sick on top of everything else."

He smiled, his dimples still evident beneath his thick beard, and she marveled at this small knowledge.

"Did anyone ever tell you that you worry too much? I'll be fine. This soup and coffee will warm me inside and out." He turned, taking a big bite out of the bread. "Besides, I haven't got another shirt that's dry, and I doubt you want me to stroll about these here cabin walls bare chested." His bowl was empty before she knew it. She filled it up again.

"I'm hungrier than a new-born calf. Any more of that bread?"

He eats more than Jessie and Robert combined. I hope I made enough.

His eyes swept the room and landed like a hawk on her. "I don't know how you found time to cook with all the work you've done in here."

"I'm happy to help; you've been such a help to the McConnells." She felt like a hen caught in a coop with no escape. She peered through the window into the darkness. "Mother isn't going to like me staying here. It's been darker than this, and I've gone home in worst."

"Out of the question. In case you don't recognize it that means no. And you do remember, don't you, the most recent time when you refused me?"

He was referring to the last ice storm, when Mother demanded her to come indoors and not out on the slippery hills trying to get her turkeys back in their coop. "Don't bring that up, I warn you." She knew exactly what he was thinking. How he'd toted her up the hill over his shoulder. If he thought he was going to bully her now, he could just think again.

He studied her for a moment, then wiped his mouth with his napkin, and pushed his chair aside. "I'll go see my girls. Mind you now, don't go leaving my hospitality."

When he advanced toward her, she backed away from him.

He chuckled. "It appears we work together well when bad weather hits; that Cheboygan River excursion we survived, and we'll come through this, too. You've nothing to fear."

She shrugged. "Are you forgetting Aunt Louise's ball?"

"No, are you?"

In spite of her resolve, inexorably, Collina's thoughts returned to that evening and his kiss. Burning warmth worked its way to her cheeks. She placed a hand to each cheek, attempting to hide her emotions.

"Was it that bad?" His eyes glinted with pure masculine interest. Daring and rugged, yet sensitive and restrained, the intense physical awareness of one to the other pulsated about the cabin walls.

She shook her head, then gasped at what she had admitted. No, no, she couldn't be attracted to Austin. "I, I expect you to remember whom you are addressing and be a proper gentleman."

He bowed. "Yes, Miss Collina."

What a fine mess she'd gotten herself into this time. A volley of sleet peppered the pane. This is going to be a long night.

Susie and Becky perched like two magpies, one on each of Austin's shoulders, came through the doorframe. He placed them on the long sofa, then walked back for blankets and pillows, which he spread before the fire on the clean floor. "They'll be warmer here, Collina, and you can have the bedroom."

"No, I can take the couch."

He acted like she hadn't spoken. "Now, girls, you be good guard dogs and keep the bad wolf away from Miss Collina."

"Austin!" She'd love to box his ears.

"Here." From a cabinet he brought out starched and ironed linens. "Mary kept these in case we had special company sleep over. You put these on the girls' bed."

The sheets showed signs of yellowing at the edges. Crochet edges of the pillowcases displayed tiny wedding loops, and on the corner of the sheet, Mary had scrolled, "Austin and Mary, married June 11, 1890." The thought had cost him much.

"I…No, this is too much trouble."

"Mary would want it." His eyes looked deep into hers. "The girls will stay here with us till I go to the barn. You sit here." He motioned for her to sit in Mary's rocker. "You've got to be tired, and I've got something I want you to hear. I've been holding it back long enough. Time you see the other side of me."

She just knew her worst fantasies would be realized.

He looked back at her over his shoulder and laughed, shaking his bearded head. Then he opened the large chest along the window seat and brought out a wrapped object and carefully cradled it in his arms. The girls squealed in delight.

"Pa, it's been ages," Becky and Susie exclaimed.

The banjo came to life within Austin's skillful fingers, and his deep baritone filled the small cabin walls with a melody she'd never heard. The evening wore on with Austin playing such lovely ballads, which on occasion, made her laugh.

It was funny to see Austin so comical. His dimples played across his face, his teeth gleaming in the firelight as this other side of Austin flooded the room with merriment. More than once she had to make the girls stay on their pallet before the fire, for their feet, like her own, wanted to jump up and dance to the lively folk music his talented fingers played so easily.

"Now for my closing song before retiring to my barn." His mood turned serious. "Or, perhaps, our guest might concede I could slumber on this plush couch before the warm and cozy fire?"

Her mouth drew itself in ridged lines. She listened to the sleet pattering the window panes. Should she relent? What had she to fear, after all, the girls were here? "I suppose—"

"This song has your name written all over it, and I dedicate it to you! 'My wild Irish rose, the sweetest flower that grows. You may search everywhere, but none can compare with my wild Irish Rose. My wild Irish Rose, the dearest flower that grows, And some day for my sake, she may let me take…the bloom from my wild Irish Rose.'"

"In your dreams!" She jumped up and crossed her arms, hugging them to her chest. "You may take a blanket with you to the barn."

He tilted his head back and laughed.

Chapter 21

June 20, 1902

Almost done. She felt a farmer's sense of accomplishment knowing that first cutting was finished. She snatched in a deep breath, enjoying the lusty odors of sweet timothy and alfalfa, the breezes from the apple orchard blending with the clover.

"Belle's wedding!" Collina yanked her glove off and frowned at her hand's paleness next to the beet redness of her arm. *I just knew it. She'd be as red as one of Mother's radishes at Belle's wedding tomorrow.* Perspiration stung her eyes. She blinked. *Austin would be there because Bo had asked Austin to stand up with her—or was it Mother who had demanded Bo ask Austin to be part of the bridal procession?* She wiped her face. "Ouch!" *I must be burned to a crisp.* Now she knew what a tainted woman felt like because ever since she spent that night in Austin's cabin, the neighbors hadn't stopped talking about it. She could just imagine the embarrassment she'd encounter at Belle's wedding tomorrow.

Everyone in MacDuff County was planning on attending. It was the talk of the county. It would do her little good to worry about her looks now. Crimson hues streaked across the horizon as the hot June sun made its slow descent past the rolling green spirals of newly cut hay. Robert and Jessie were gathering the last of the sweet-smelling timothy and alfalfa into windrows, their bare backs and shoulders moving in unified rhythm to the sound of their pitch forks.

Jessie paused, straightening slowly. He twisted his back from side to side.

"What are you doing now?" Robert said. "I asked you nice to hurry up and you commence fooling around."

"You just hold your horses, little brother. Just cause Sue Ellen's broke up with you, don't mean you can take your anger out on me."

"Really now, what about your Mary Lou? I hear she's wants to break it off with you."

Jessie chuckled. "That doesn't mean a thing. She's still going with me to the wedding."

"That's not what Sue Ellen told me, said that she and Mary Lou were going there together."

"Isn't so. You make it sound like she wants a look see at those dandies Stephen's bringing from that slick university, and it isn't so."

They stared at each other across the sweet-smelling hay they'd just rolled. Daring the other to take a step towards the imaginary line of demarcation that would declare this an official fight.

"Come on," Scott coaxed. "It's too hot to fight. Those girls aren't worth the trouble. We've got to finish this row, and I'm too tired to stay out here any longer than I've got to."

"We've done a good day's work; we'll finish the rest tomorrow," Jessie said.

"Why put off for tomorrow what we can finish today?" Collina said.

Jessie thrust his pitchfork into the rolled grass angrily. "Sis, if you want this done so bad, you can finish it." He started down the hill.

"Jessie!" Collina yelled. The six whites thumped the ground with their big hooves. The wagon, full to the brim with hay, moaned under its heavy load. "Does it look to you like Jude is limping?"

"You can always spot trouble better than anyone. It's the right foreleg," Jessie said. Jessie wiped his moist hands on his coveralls, picking up the big foot by the fetlock. "Picked up a stone." Jessie removed it.

Collina produced the red bandanna that had been Pa's and patted her brow. "Thanks."

"Collina, your face is as red as that bandanna. What's Mother going to say?" Robert grinned up at her, but beneath the brim of his straw hat, his eyes looked worried.

She shrugged as if it didn't matter. After all, nothing she could do about that now. "I forgot and left my hat at home. It can't be helped." She let out a big sigh. "Now we can all go and enjoy Belle's wedding without worrying about the hay."

Jessie threw another bundle of hay onto the already full wagon with such force that three bundles rolled off the wagon from the impact.

"Aw, what did you go and do that for?" Robert said, slapping his palm on his forehead.

"Don't start, Robert, unless you want to find yourself on the top of that hay stack."

"You think you're the guy that can do it?" Robert's long legs spanned the distance between them.

Collina jumped down and rushed to hold back the impetuous Robert. "Robert, come on, Jessie didn't mean it that away. Jessie, tell Robert you didn't."

Jessie turned, walking to the barn. Collina had never seen him so angry. Jessie was usually the good-natured one of the bunch. What could possibly be wrong?

"Jessie," she coaxed in between breaths, running to overtake him. She reached for his bare shoulder, feeling the sweat and grit thick on his skin. "What's wrong?"

Jessie's face, reddened by the sun, was drawn into a patchwork of pain. "You really don't know, do you?" He shook her hand loose of his shoulder, his eyes full of hurt. He turned as if to ward off any sympathy she might give and walked away.

This couldn't be happening. She and Jessie were close. At least she had thought so, until now. She ran to overtake him, and this time she ran ahead of him and blocked his way. "What is wrong with you?" She thought he was going to hit her. His hands flew to his head, instead.

"All right, Sis, you asked for it. Because of you, I'm the laughing stock of the county. Even Mary Lou wants nothing more to do with me, said she's 'got to find somebody with promise.' Promise! Can you believe that? Why, in case you didn't know it, all of MacDuff County is buzzing about you. They say you'll never get married. Why would you?

You like wearing Pa's coveralls, pretending to be him, bossing your brothers around. They say you don't want to lose your freedom, having some man lord it over you. Is that true, Sis? Aren't you ever planning on getting hitched?"

Her eyes masked the pain Jessie's words inflicted. Not want to marry? Was there any woman alive that didn't dream of a love she could spend her lifetime with? A man to protect her, care for her, a man whose strong shoulders could carry the burdens she felt too weak to hold? How could she tell Jessie that once she knew a man like that?

Collina forced a laugh to her quivering lips, shaking her head. "You can tell the county for me that these aren't Pa's coveralls. Their mine. Ruby made me my own. As for that girlfriend of yours, I'll set her straight tomorrow when I see her. Why, if it weren't for you, there wouldn't even be a Shushan. In fact, I think it's about time for you to begin the duties of foreman. I'm…getting much too old for this field work."

"Really?" Jessie's scowling lips turned into a grin. "You mean it? I can't wait to tell Mary Lou."

Collina felt a sinking feeling in the pit of her stomach. Still, she managed to smile and nod her head. "We're almost done here. You could get the barn chores started on."

On her way back to the wagon, Robert's tall lanky form shadowed her face. Did he hear what was said? Probably didn't need to. He had a pretty good idea of the way it ended.

"Sis, it's about time you left the farm work for us to manage."

How long has Jessie felt that way? Does everyone else think the same about me?

"You work like a man, Sis, and you're the best foreman Shushan could have. It's that girl Mary Lou. She's the flirting kind and it's got Jessie's heart tied up in knots." Nothing got by the sensitive Scott.

Collina remembered Mary Lou, and Scott was right.

"Yeah, she's a real looker all right. You think that anyone that looked like that couldn't think a mean thing if she had to," Robert said. "Too bad, I was getting to like the idea of having such a looker in the family. Why she's got more curves than Snake Pass. Well, making

Jessie foreman of Shushan might tip the scales in his favor of her other suitors now."

Her brothers laughed as they loaded the last of the hay on the wagon. Collina climbed up, feeling satisfied they had gotten the haying done on time. For now patches of small white clouds appeared on the empty canvas of the darkening sky. Scott and Robert walk effortlessly down the hill toward the house, laughing, anticipating tomorrow and the dancing and the coquetting they would do with their girlfriends.

Her whip curled responsively above the heads of her whites as they descended the hill toward the barn. She wished she hadn't promised Belle that she would be one of her bridesmaids. That's just what the townsfolk needed to poke their questions at her like a pin in a pin cushion. "When are you getting married?"

She felt her face turn a deeper red, remembering that night at Austin's cabin. God had performed the impossible in Austin's heart. She recalled Aunt Louise's Christmas ball and the rose encased in ice. Austin's heart had once been encased in an icy prison of hopelessness and regret. She understood now…his heart had been set free—only, hers was not.

Tears moistened her burning eyelids, smelling the sweet clover, seeing the soft breezes whispering across the tops of the maples, just beyond her reach. Myra had mailed the picture of Franklin and his new bride from the society page of the *Detroit Tribune*. Would it always be that way? Would happiness always be beyond her reach?

Chapter 22

*C*ollina would tell Austin the truth, that her feelings for him hadn't changed. She'd been powerless in this arrangement of bridesmaid and bridegroom. She could spend a dozen nights in his cabin and have no claim on him, or he on her. Collina inhaled the sweet aroma of the roses in her bouquet.

Her mind now at ease, she smiled warmly at Belle's image in the mirror. "Sis, you are a vision of loveliness."

Myra nodded, spreading out Belle's train. "You are. You look—so in love."

Belle blushed and surveyed herself in the big glass mirrors that filled three corners of Aunt Louise's dressing chamber. She gave her cheeks a pinch and smoothed her golden curls. Suddenly, she looked ready to cry. "Mother, am I doing the right thing?" Belle twisted the ribbons of her bouquet Myra had just handed her.

"When the big day came for your father and me to, well, you all just might not have been here if it weren't—"

"For me," Aunt Louise said, entering the room.

"What?" Myra looked over at her, astonished. "Mother, you never told us you had doubts about Pa."

"I did for one brief moment." Mother laughed. "I was on my way out the back door when Louise stopped me and told me that if I didn't wed him, she would." Her mother and Aunt Louise hugged each other.

"Collina?" Belle said.

Collina turned to look at Belle quizzically. "What?"

"Aren't you going to say you'd wed Bo?"

Collina guffawed. "Bo has licked every boy that even looked at you from here to the Tennessee line ever since you lengthened your skirts. He doesn't even know there are any other women in this world but you."

Belle's elation was evident in the smile that crinkled her full lips.

"How does it feel to know you are the only woman he'll ever want?" Aunt Louise said.

"Wonderful."

"Sort of like Adam and Eve?" Bugie said.

Ruby opened the door of their room and slammed it shut, leaning on the solid walnut, as if she'd lost her strength. "Guess what?"

"Well, you have my attention," Myra said.

"Austin bought a new surrey with the money he made working extra, just so he could show off at Belle's wedding. And he asked Bo to pick him for a bridegroom because he wanted to walk Collina down the aisle. Told him it might be his only chance ever to do so."

"Collina," Myra said. "I do believe you're blushing."

"Ruby, I don't like to hear this kind of gossip," Mother said. "This could prove embarrassing to Austin."

Austin? Collina turned away. What about her feelings?

"And to Collina, too," Mother quickly added.

Collina traced an imaginary line across the Chippendale dresser with her index finger. Even Mother thinks that no one in his right mind would be interested in me. So why worry about my reputation?

"Collina, your face is as red as a tomato," Myra said.

Belle frowned as she pinched her cheeks again. "Wish I had just half that color. But I've got news for Ruby. Why do you think Bo picked Stephen for you?"

"Why?" Ruby said.

"Because Stephen wanted to make certain he'd be your escort."

Ruby's mouth formed an O. "I never dreamt…he did? I was going to ask him, but I sort of lost my nerve."

"Oh, I love weddings." Bugie jumped up and down.

"Who do you suppose will be the next one married, Collina or Ruby?" Belle said.

"Collina—my, your skin looks burned." Her mother gently touched her face. "You're burning up. Might be you've got a touch of sun poison."

"Collina could be the next down the aisle," Aunt Louise said. "Austin is considering matrimony. That is, if I'm not considered too senile to notice such things anymore."

"But Collina can't marry," Bugie said. "Who'll run Shushan?"

"Carrie says Austin looks ever so handsome in his new suit," Ruby said. "Why just the other day—"

"Hush, Ruby, you've done enough damage," her mother said. "Austin's not right for—"

"That's just what you said about Clem and me; that's why I had to go and elope and miss out on all of this." Myra spread her arms to include the room and Belle's wedding dress.

"Myra, are you happy with Clem?" Collina whispered. Myra and Clem had run off so fast to Detroit after the auction, she hadn't had an opportunity until now to talk to Myra regarding her overpowering husband. Collina squeezed Myra's hand. "Your family is always here for you."

Myra squeezed her hand back, giving her a weak smile and nodded.

"Just who is right for Collina?" Belle said. "She's not getting any younger, and soon all the men her age will be married."

"You shouldn't enter matrimony just because you're afraid you'll be an old maid." Her mother hurried to her side. "Now, Collina dear, don't look so hurt, you'll find the right man."

Myra let go of Collina's hand and sat down on a chair, crossing her arms around her abdomen. Collina squared her shoulders. "I could care less one way or the other about Austin. I'm more worried about Myra."

"What are you all doing in there?" Scott yelled.

"I swear, getting the McConnell women together in one room is like trying to out sing a bunch of bees!" Mother hastened to the door.

Myrtle was warming up, her fingers running through the keys. The mellow notes of the grand piano playing familiar tunes drifted up to them. Scott's eyes widened in surprise. "Golly Jehosephat. I've got the prettiest sisters in the whole state of Kentucky."

Aunt Louise surveyed the group critically. "Let's show the guests downstairs how a real wedding is done. Scott, escort your mother to her seat, please. Bugie, hold your basket of petals this way. Good. Now wait for us at the top of the stairs. Myra, you will proceed right after Bugie. Collina, remember; you're to wait until Myra gets to the bottom of the stairs before descending. You will find Austin waiting for you. He'll explain to you further what to do. Now Ruby, you're next. You stand, well, you know where to stand.

"Yes, Belle, right. Oh, you are lovely! Myrtle will wait for my cue, and then the wedding march will begin.

"Collina," Ruby whispered. "You needed to be here yesterday and practice with the rest of us."

Collina nodded, pulling on her gloves, shuddering as her burnt skin came in contact with silk.

"Here, let me help you with those," Aunt Louise said, seeing Collina's attempts at fastening the small pearl buttons beneath her wrists. "There. Collina you look picture perfect from head to toe."

"But my sunburn." Collina felt her skin go hot, then cold, for a chill now spread itself across her body.

"You'll be fine, dear; you're just a little nervous," Aunt Louise said.

Belle pulled her veil forward and arranged the folds of her long satin gown. Aunt Louise arranged her long train.

Tears formed in Belle's eyes. "I will never again belong just to you."

"Oh, my," Aunt Louise muttered.

Collina rushed forward and gave her sister one last hug before she would become Mrs. Barrett and cease to be Belle McConnell forever.

"It'll never be like it was." Belle rested her head on Collina's shoulder.

Myra shrugged. "It's either that or live as an old maid. And you don't really lose a family, you gain another. Remember, Belle, no one wants an old maid around."

Down the long, velvet-covered stairway, Collina kept her head high and her shoulders erect. Timidly she touched Austin's extended arm. His white satin shirt set off handsomely his dark hair and clean-shaven face. His black tuxedo fit snugly about his broad shoulders and tapered about his waist. She had never realized just how big he was. Standing next to him, she barely came to his shoulders. She looked up at him and smiled.

Concern creased Austin's black brows. "Hey, your face is really burnt." He took her hand then, squeezing it, as he wrapped it around his arm. "You've too pretty a face to let the sun wrinkle it. You'd best leave that fieldwork to your brothers. They're big enough now to handle it." He chuckled. "I know it'll be hard not being there to boss them, but you'll get used to it by and by."

"They need me." Then Jessie's words echoed in her thoughts. You don't want to get married because you like bossing us too much.

"No, they don't," Austin said. "Is that why you're letting Belle go down the aisle before you? Cuz you'd miss the whip?" He jested, teasing her into looking at him.

She tilted her head to one side. There was more than just humor in his eyes. There was need. She looked away, impatiently tapping her foot.

Austin frowned. "The wedding march hasn't begun, and you're already getting bored with me?"

Myrtle had left the piano. Murmurs started up and down the aisles.

"Lighten up. Maybe you'll marry someone that enjoys bossy females. Don't recall any myself, how about you?"

Myra's words, like a resounding lyric, rang in Collina's ears. No one wants an old maid around.

"That's it, isn't it?" Austin bent over her and whispered. "You know as well as I you could have been married a half-dozen times, if you had a mind to."

Collina's skin felt like it was on fire. Is everyone saying the same things about me? Jessie wants to run Shushan. He could, too; he's hardworking, and both he and Robert can manage things. She'd given over the reins to Jessie. Where did that leave her? Oh, it was hot. Her sunburn throbbed beneath the tight-fitting gloves. Her face grew warmer by the second.

"That's Collina," she heard Carrie Carson say. "I didn't recognize her at first. Funny, can't remember seeing her in a dress, only thing I ever see her in is overalls."

Austin glared at Carrie. She laughed, pursed her lips, and sent him a kiss. Others turned in their seats and looked into the hallway.

"What's happening?" someone yelled.

"Don't know, but something humorous tickled someone's funny bone in yonder."

Mr. Burns got up and stepped into the hallway, then turned and went back to his chair. "It's Collina." He turned in his chair to look at her. "Yes, it's she," he retorted, laughing.

Burns's teenage son yelled over his shoulder at her, "Hey Collina, heard tell you sleep in your overalls. You got them underneath your dress?"

Collina closed her eyes, but their laughing faces haunted her closed eyelids. I'm nothing more than a clown to them.

Myrtle returned, and the notes of the grand piano appeared to move the very floor beneath her. She felt dizzy, the jeering faces in the garden growing hazy. Her fingers shook, feeling cold and clammy in her tight silk gloves. Her heart felt like it wanted to beat clear out of her chest. "I can't." She felt her knees buckling beneath her. "I think I'm going to—"

"Their jesting has gone too far this time." Austin caught her around the waist. He'd turned as white as the Conferderate Soldier Monument in Lexington, and just as hard, his mouth firm, an unyielding line of defiance.

"Austin, I can't—"

"Steady, Collina, it's only a few steps. Lean on me."

Her legs shook beneath her weight.

He turned, facing her, clutching her to him in an embrace others were sure to misread. "You can do this. I'm going to be right there with you. If I have to carry you every step of the way, I will. They're not going to embarrass you, because I won't let them. Do you hear me? I'm not standing for it any longer."

The pounding of her heart nearly drowned out the notes of the march and Austin's words. Her sunburned face felt like it was on fire. Weakly, she leaned her head on his shoulder, feeling the coolness of his suit, comfort for her hot cheek. Aunt Louise was there.

A moist cloth thrust its way into Austin's hand, and he gently moistened her sunburned face. "Here drink this," Austin muttered, putting a glass of water between her lips.

She drank, feeling revived.

They had lost the note with which they were to begin their walk through the widely arched entranceway to the gardens. Myrtle stopped playing. The curious heads of the neighbors turned, craning their necks backward. All staring at Austin and her.

"I've made a fool of myself again." She moaned, pulling away from his grasp. But his arm held her close; there was no loosening it.

"What's wrong?" he said. His breath tickled her ear.

"I can't walk down there; they're watching me."

He gave a low grunt. "Don't think about them; think about me." He tilted her chin up and gazed deeply into her eyes. "What's a little walk like this to you?"

"Are you ready, Austin?" Aunt Louise said.

He kissed the top of Collina's upturned nose, then nodded, not taking his eyes off her.

Louise smiled and held her arm up in her commanding, authoritative way as if this had been planned from the beginning. She lowered her arm, and the music began.

Collina, baffled by his sudden gentleness, smiled. But his eyes were staring straight ahead at every onlooker. Austin glided her down the long, satin covered archway as if she was a porcelain doll.

A cool breeze met her hot face. She noted the sudden respect of the neighbors for her with Austin by her side. She liked the feeling. But she mustn't lead him on. "Austin, you need not worry about my reputation. I don't care what people think. There's nothing between—"

"Us? Hmm. We'll see about that."

Chapter 23

ou lovely things, all nurtured and protected, safe and comfortable in your little pots." The exotic recluse was what Collina had sought. Here, amidst the foliage of bright ornamental orchids, she walked down the stone aisles examining the beautiful plants. She breathed deeply, closing her eyes to drink of the sweet smells in Aunt Louise's conservatory.

What did Austin think? That she would become a backwoodsman's wife? Spend her life rocking on that unpainted front porch of his cabin, with a corn-cob pipe stuck out of the corner of her mouth? She put a hesitant finger to one silky bud. "It will prove quite a shock to you when you're plucked up and placed on someone's dress and paraded about until you wilt with exhaustion and die from the climate you are so unused to."

"Now, Collina, don't go scaring the poor things."

She spun around. Aunt Louise walked slowly toward her, leaning on her cane. "They do better when talked to, but just what they understand of the conversation, I truly am not certain." She laughed. "So we should guard our tongues while we are in their midst."

"Really, Aunt Louise, I'm not a child and can hardly believe that you think flowers have ears."

Louise shrugged. "Many botanists would argue the point with you. But for me, they are a means to an end. I need a profitable hobby at this time, and these little lovelies are providing that for me."

Collina picked out a familiar figure standing beneath an apple tree. "Yes, indeed, it must be profitable," Collina murmured bitterly.

"What's the matter, dear; you're not enjoying yourself?"

Through the clear glass enclosure, she could see Austin, and he was swinging Carrie Carlson. She clutched his arm, imploring him with her eyes, her mouth puckered into an oval red cherry. An impish grin spread across his handsome face. He bent over and kissed her soundly on the cheek. Then, like the scoundrel he was, seized her about the waist and flung the swing and her high amidst the gnarled branches of the apple tree. Carrie squealed with delight.

"So that's what's bothering you."

Collina spun so quickly that she nearly knocked one of the orchids crashing to the brick floor. "I don't care who he kisses." She pointed a finger to the two. "It's none of my business."

Susie and Becky clamored into the room and came skipping to her side. "Have you seen our pa? He promised he would play with us."

"Why, yes, darlings, I have." Collina opened the conservatory door and pointed to their pa and Carrie Carlson. "There you are, dears. Maybe your pa will swing you, too. Go ask him real nice like."

The girls ran out to him, and as Collina watched, Austin bent down and grasped each of his girls, lifting them high in the air. The girls giggled and pointed a finger in Collina's direction. Austin bowed gallantly from the waist, tipping an imaginary hat on his forehead and removed Carrie from her perch. "Now, Carrie, remember, I told you you'd have to vacate the swing when my girls arrived." He motioned for Collina to join them.

Aunt Louise laughed uproariously at Austin's comical expressions. Holding her side, she said, "Why don't you go?"

Carrie stood to the side and glanced over her shoulder at Collina and chuckled. Collina slammed the door shut. How could he? During the wedding march, he led her to… "I don't care to compete with young pretty women." She nodded toward Carrie.

Aunt Louise leaned on her cane, surveying the man across the grassy landscape. "Austin enjoys the easier side of life. There are some good qualities there that might, with the right woman cultivating them, sprout up if given time. But Austin is not the man your heart desires. Who is it?"

She dipped her head. "No one." The handkerchief with the initials FL had been soaked so many times with her tears it had become stained. She'd placed the newspaper clipping Myra had handed her today of the society page with his and Melissa Slinger's picture in her pocket. What does it matter? Rose Baker had moved on and had married a prominent surgeon. She should move on, too.

Face it, Collina, you conjured up a make-believe ideal man that never existed in Franklin Long. She avoided Aunt Louise's shrewd eyes.

"Austin's worst downfall is his strongest attribute—his magnetic influence on women. Amazingly, he is unaware that his captivating charm will end up capturing him."

"What do you mean, Aunt Louise?"

"Some men would envy him. But good looks like Austin's are not an asset; they're a handicap, a deterrent toward true happiness."

She gazed out the window. "He enjoys crooking his little pinky and watching women flock to his side. He grows handsomer the older he gets. Just look at him; he'll tell you he's never been happier."

"I disagree." Drawing her gaze away from the window, Aunt Louise's eyes swept her form, lingering on Collina's sunburned face and sun-streaked hair.

"You're strikingly attractive now, but, my dear, I know how quickly the outdoors can age the soft skin of a woman. I hate to see you work your best years away at Shushan."

Aunt Louise reached for Collina's hand and stroked her worn and calloused palm. "You already bare the trademark of a dirt farmer." She patted her palm tenderly. "I understand more than you realize. Just be sure there isn't something inside you that doesn't care a little about Austin. I know he's not your first choice, but he's your chance to have your own—"

"I really do want to get married, Aunt Louise." She drew her hand away. The only reason Austin would want to marry her would be to cook, care for his children, and work in the field alongside him. "I'm just fool enough to think someone could want me for me and not for a work mule."

"And you think that's the only reason Austin would want to marry you?"

"Yes."

"Do you think every man and woman marry for love, Collina?"

"I should hope so."

"Life's biggest decisions are made when youth is too young to know true love and the burdens that come with time. How does youth know when love is forever? Or is it commitment, one to another, that binds the heart after romanticism is replaced by reality?"

Like a harp, her thoughts picked the strings of time as she walked out of the small conservatory door. The night at the cornfield after Pa's funeral, Rose's ball, memories of Lady's Lake. Franklin had been the model of her make-believe hero, the knight of her dreams.

Austin, a flesh and blood man, was prone to faults, like she, like Aunt Louise. Still, who was she to point the finger at his faults? Her own stubborn and prideful nature was the reason she had reaped what she'd sown. Galatians 6:7–8 came vividly to her mind: "Be not deceived; God is not mocked: for whatsoever a man soweth, that shall he also reap. For he that soweth to his flesh shall of the flesh reap corruption; but he that soweth to the Spirit shall of the Spirit reap life everlasting."

Her brothers were chomping on the bit for her to release the reins of Shushan she clung to so desperately. Her pa's words floated on the summer breezes and into her heart. They can take over when they're mature enough. Only a false sense of worth prohibited her from shouting out that she was no longer needed as overseer of Shushan. Jessie had proven his worth and maturity over and over to her. Only she refused to see this. "Jesus, please forgive me."

What was the next part of Galatians Pa would read? Yes, she remembered, verse nine: "And let us not be weary in well doing: for in due season we shall reap, if we faint not."

The night had dawned clear, and though the colored lanterns that dotted the trees of McCullen Manor were beautiful, they could not compete with the heavens above. She leaned on a large oak, staring at the stars. The smell of orange blossoms and honeysuckle filled the air as the first pleasant notes of the violin began their gentle sounds across the shadowed shades of evening.

Austin, coming up softly behind, startled her.

"What do you want?"

"Belle wants us. They're going to begin the wedding dance. It's that stupid kiss I gave Carrie that got you in a huff, isn't it?"

"No." Collina turned.

His strong fingers wrapped her wrist like a chain. "We've got to dance this waltz together, then afterward we'll talk."

"No, we'll not." She was finished with men. The gall of Austin, acting like he cared about her and then kissing that loose-lipped Carrie. "After this dance, I'm through with my commitment."

"Your commitment?" He smirked. "After this dance your commitment to me will begin."

It was too dark for her to see his face. She struggled to free herself, then realized it was useless. Besides, she could not let her sister down.

As the waltz began its second stanza, Austin said, "Come now, I've said my apologies. Carrie doesn't mean a thing to me. Are you planning on pouting all evening? Say…" His lips close to her cheek, now whispered in her ear. "Could this be jealousy?"

"Over you?" Collina guffawed, then slammed her hand into his chest. He laughed. His arm tightened against her desires to be loose of him. She pounded on his chest again. He grinned. His eyes swept her face hotly.

"I could kick you in the shin; that would loosen your grip."

"You mean like Ruby did to Stephen? You should see the welt."

"He must have had it coming," Collina said. "I told Ruby to kick only when necessary."

"You did, huh? Well, she followed her big sister's orders to the letter." Austin grinned. "Now, just tell me the truth, are you jealous? Did a stab of feeling for me strike that heart of yours?"

"No." Collina chose to change the subject. "Are you enjoying your new church?"

"I stopped going. The girls are going, but I still say God and me do better from a distance. No use making the devil too mad; I'd hate to get on his bad side like you McConnells have."

"What do you mean?"

"Living a solid Christian life is hard work. The devil doesn't bother with his kind or fence sitters like yours truly. That's why you McConnells have had it so rough."

"I'll have you know we're on the winning side—God's side."

"There's no doubt in my mind you and yours are on God's side. You don't wear your religion on your sleeve, because you don't need to. It envelops you like a glowing shroud. After all that has happened to your family, not a one of you has faltered in your beliefs. No wonder the devil is as mad as a hornet with a tail full of stingers."

Carrie and her dancing partner waltzed near them. Carrie batted her eyelids at Austin.

Collina felt the tightly fitting corset dig into her ribs as she tried to smother her rage. Carrie's earlier remarks were still vivid and painful. She was tired of having others think she didn't possess feelings, and sick of them not caring if she heard their biting words. She jerked her chin up and flashed Carrie what she hoped was a confident smile.

Around and around the dance floor Austin spun her, her long skirts billowing about their forms like the wings of a dove awaiting flight. Then, when the mellow notes of the waltz began to tremble to a close, Austin danced her to the wooden plank steps.

"What do you think you're doing?"

"I want to show you something."

Austin swooped her up and carried her across the bridge. "Austin, put me down."

He tipped her comically back and forth as he made his way across the length of it.

"You'll drop me—"

"Never." Austin gently set her down on the gazebo overlooking the sloping shores of Catfish Lake. Lit with aqua lanterns, the small, white dome-shaped building took on a strangely nautical look. Like the bow of a ship misplaced on the banks of a freshwater reservoir. She leaned over the banister and gazed into the still waters that reflected her frowning brows above round, glistening eyes. This must be the way a fish feels about to grab the baited hook.

Austin's hand slapped the wooden railing near her. She jumped at the sound and turned. His coat and tie he had flung onto a chair, and his long, tapered sleeves were rolled up, as if ready for a fight. "Just what are you up to?"

"You don't mind, do you? I felt restricted in that coat."

"Why should I?" Why should anything he did bother her? She moved to the other side of the gazebo, bending over to examine the stream that ran its tributaries around the framework. The only entrance to the small building was by the wooden bridge Austin had used, for the small enclosure was built right over the lake. "Amazing, I never noticed this gazebo before."

"That's because it's brand new. I built it. There'll be a real bridge with rails when I'm finished."

"You did this?" His own cabin came to mind. "But you have so many things of your own to do; how did you ever find time?"

He shrugged. "I needed a favor done by Aunt Louise, and that was the only thing I could think of she needed. You know Aunt Louise is a very prosperous lady." His voice low, he moved a step closer to her. "She wants for nothing and I want for everything."

His hand went to her arm. She stiffened automatically as he turned her to face him.

"Is my touch so offensive? Other women do not find it so. Still waiting for your knight in shining armor? Waiting for him to come charging over that hill after you?

"God never intended for man to live alone. At least not this man. The years will soon not be kind to either of us." Taking her left hand, he traced the calluses, etched like granite on her palms. Then bending his head, he kissed first one, then the other.

She closed her eyes, his lips not unpleasant. His lips met hers before she had a chance to recoil. Soft at first, caressing hers gently, then his body pressed closer, demanding more. She struggled to free herself. His strong arms pulled her closer, and with every wave of his thirst, she felt herself being swept further out on the sea of his desire. "No!"

"Collina, I love you. Marry me. Say you'll marry me."

"No." She pushed him away and ran to the opposite side of the gazebo. "Is life with me so repulsive? Is becoming an old maid more desirable than becoming my wife?"

"Austin. You deserve someone better than I." She turned, hiding her face as she choked back her tears.

She felt his fingertips gently on her shoulder, turning her. "I didn't mean to get out of control like that." That jesting smirk swept his face. "You're a hard one for me." He touched her chin with his fist, then dropped his arms as he turned from her. "I can't woo you like the other girls. I respect you too much. My Mary was right. You're a lady from inside out."

Collina had never seen Austin embarrassed. Uncertainty oozed from the slump of his shoulders to the shuffling of his boots. "I do love you, don't know exactly when I realized it. I recollect that man at the auction, the one with the eyes like that Franklin guy you wanted to run after. I realized then I was jealous." He sighed.

"I never wanted to see you hurt like that again. I know I'm a poor substitute. I'm not that gallant soldier that never returned." A sad, dreamy look came into Austin's eyes. "You deserve better than me. Only, what you don't deserve is to live out your life alone. You've got too much love inside for that." His eyes were boyish in their eagerness. "My girls want you as their new mother. You'd learn to love them, if you don't already."

Collina placed a hand on his cheek and smiled. "I'm not in love with you, Austin. I only wish I was because you deserve that. You're a wonderful man, and any woman would be proud to share your name. Proud to be mother to such fine girls like Susie and Becky. You deserve a woman who can love you back."

"Honesty. It's the one attribute above all your others I cherish the most. Wouldn't you know it would be the one that cuts the deepest?"

"Austin." She turned away. "I'm not honest, least of all, with myself, but I'm working on it."

Only the sound of the June bugs hitting the brightly colored lanterns disturbed the silence. "I'm not sure if loving me would be good for you. I always seem to hurt the ones that do. I'll not rush this decision on you, Collina. Just think over what I said."

Kneeling down before her, he took her hand and kissed it. "I'll love you till the day I die. Whatever you decide, even if your decision is no, I won't try and change it. Because I want you to be happy, and if you're happier not being with me, then that's what I want. But no matter what hand destiny may deal you, know this: that you were loved, Collina; you were loved by me."

"Austin!" She buried her head into his shoulder and wept for what seemed an eternity. He just held her, cradling her head against his broad shoulder. Aunt Louise's words echoed in her head. Life's biggest decisions are made when youth is too young to know love. How does youth know when love is forever? Or is it commitment, one to another, that binds the heart after romanticism is replaced by reality?

She looked up at him. He had tears in his eyes. She'd never seen him this way before. "And you promise you will go to church? Promise you will accept Jesus Christ as your Lord and Savior? For I'll have no husband of mine not enter the pearly gates of heaven."

"Yes, I promise. And may God Almighty hold me accountable." He swept her up into his embrace and swirled her about. "Yippee! We're getting married."

Chapter 24

March 4, 1905

ollina hummed "Amazing Grace" as she moved about the
kitchen. Throwing away the remaining sudsy dishwater on
her lilac bush, she stopped to survey the landscape of wood and hills.
Being married to Austin had been an adventure. The sun peeked out
from between the sprouts of the budding oaks, and the air met her
face, fresh, and alive with life. "What a beautiful day. And just think,
today Theodore Roosevelt will be inaugurated."

Where had the years gone? Aunt Louise had supplied a beautiful
wedding for her and Austin. And Austin had surprised her with a fresh
coat of paint on his cabin and an indoor pump. Jessie and Robert had
taken on the operation of Shushan and made it into a fully operating
dairy farm. No wonder time had spun out of control for her.

This morning Austin had gone to pick up their new bull and should
be home soon. She wanted everything right when he returned. She
glanced down at the picture in the newspaper. Roosevelt, dressed in
full Rough Rider's uniform, was sitting on his horse. The article said,
"This inaugural celebration promises to be the most diverse of any in
memory." A sudden noise outside had her rushing to the window. No
sign of Austin yet, but she knew he would be appearing soon.

She flew about her domain as her mind skimmed over the events of
her visit with Doc Baker. "Looks like being pregnant agrees with you."

She must have blushed, because of Doc's next comment.

"You were always so slender; the added weight is hardly noticeable to an untrained eye." Then Doc had grown serious. "Saw Austin in the mercantile just the other day. Thought for sure he'd be beaming. You haven't told him have you?"

"The time hasn't been right yet."

Doc laughed. "Wait another three months and you won't have to; it'll be written plain enough for a blind man to see. I'm not sure how Austin will feel if he's the last to know."

"Everything has got to be perfect." She dropped the sausage in the skillet. She would make some gravy, too. The wheels of her husband's wagon grated up the drive. The heavy thumping of his boots on the porch followed. Her heart beat to the rhythm, as if attuned to his every step.

The door creaked opened and a shaft of sunlight fell like a cloak around him. Grinning broadly, he reached for her and swung her about the room. "Come see our new bull."

"My breakfast?"

He kissed her smartly on her upturned lips. "Where's Becky and Susie?"

"Sleeping in, they deserve a rest at least on Saturdays."

"Hmm." A knowing grin swept his face. "It sure was a lonely night I spent in that hotel. Been thinking about you night and day."

She laughed. She'd gotten accustomed to his spontaneous bursts of affection. "What about breakfast first?" She planned to tell him afterwards that she was pregnant. "I've prepared something special."

His arms went around her waist. "Say, have you been eating too much of your own good cooking? Keep it up. You're becoming downright dangerous."

Now was the perfect opportunity. "I'm—"

"Hello, anyone home?"

Two wagons pulled into the drive. Austin walked over to look out the window. His brows met in an ugly scowl.

That wasn't like him; he usually liked visitors. Collina peeked out the window. "Why it's Clara and her mother. Katie Lue probably stopped by to see if the girls wanted to go to Emerald City together."

"Yeah," Austin muttered.

"Who's the other wagon?" Collina said.

"Don't know, but I'd better get that bull in a stall before he pulls loose and hurts someone."

Collina opened the window. She could tell by the thrust of his shoulders, he was mad.

"Morning, Austin." Katie Lue fairly sang the words. "Here, Clara, take the reins for a minute; I need to talk to Austin." Katie Lue jumped down from the wagon seat hurrying to head off Austin.

He turned his face in an ugly scowl. "My wife has some coffee made in the cabin." He strolled to the wagon behind hers.

"Morning. What can I do for you?" Austin said to the man and woman in the second wagon.

"I never," Katie Lue said.

"Mama?" Clara said.

"Hush, child; Mama must think."

"But Mrs. Blaine is here."

Collina hesitated.

Katie Lue turned, her face contorting like she just bit into a lemon. "I declare you're getting prettier by the week. What are you doing to yourself to stay so pretty looking?"

"Clara, Susie's still asleep. Why don't you go on in and surprise her? Katie Lue, I've got gravy and biscuits made; won't you come in and eat?" She said that loud enough to include the wagon behind and motioned with her hand that the strangers were equally welcomed.

"Maybe I could help put that bull away first," the man in the wagon said.

"Sure." Austin shrugged. "Just got him; he's not too good on manners. Besides that, he's fully matured and knows his strength, so be careful."

"Austin, that bull has horns."

"I know. At the cattle auction no one would bid on him, so I got him cheap. Guy that brought him said the bull came from Texas. Said he's been used for breeding and that most of his get don't produce horns." Austin reached into his pocket and placed a wad of bills into Collina's palm.

She couldn't believe it. Hardly any cash had been spent.

"Told you I got him cheap."

The stranger jumped down from the wagon, turned, offering his arm toward the woman on the bench beside him. She, like him, had an olive complexion and black hair.

Collina walked toward them, smiling at the woman, then a half-gasp escaped. The woman was merely a girl. Her well-built curves had deceived Collina. The girl looked to her husband. Austin and the stranger had their hands full with the obstinate bull.

"Hey. Whoa there." Austin pulled with all his might at the stubborn brute whose horns curved around his broad wooly head. "Push his backside; he'll come if I have to carry him the distance."

The man looked hesitant.

"Go ahead, I've got him."

Katie Lue sighed. "No one but Austin could handle that bull. You've got yourself one powerful hunk of man, case you didn't know it."

Collina had been introduced to Katie Lue during their wedding reception at Aunt Louise's.

Katie Lue laughed nervously. "Guess being a widow has made me respect the opposite sex more." She fidgeted with her blouse, following Austin with her eyes. "It's good to see Austin home and not off on one of his hunting trips."

How did Katie Lue know about Austin's hunting trips? Her husband's trips always coincided with their often-heated arguments.

Katie Lue swerved away from Collina's direct look. "I won't have time to eat with you. I've got to get to Emerald, just came to see if Susie wanted to come along."

The front door banged opened with Susie and Clara bounding down the wooden steps.

Seeing the girl from the next wagon walk up, Katie Lue said, "Just what would your name be, and where do you hail from, child?" Sarcasm tinged her voice.

A slow smile crossed the girl's large lips. "I think we both know I am not a child. My name is Rosa Botticelli. We, my uncle and I, are from Sicily."

Collina bit her bottom lip. "Sicily? Isn't that in Italy? My dear, farming is not an easy profession, especially up here in the hills. There are many jobs to be had in Emerald for you and your uncle."

Rosa's large dark eyes, generously shrouded with thick lashes, swept her with a chilling look that resembled a late March thundershower. Collina felt it from her fingers clear down to her toes. *My word, Rosa's such a tiny thing. How can she give out such strong emotions?*

The girl arched her back, announcing her full figure.

"That one will get what she needs from some unsuspecting gent," Katie Lue mumbled to Collina. She pointed a finger at Rosa and said, "How do you like MacDuff County?"

"It will take a little time." She smiled. Collina followed her glance.

Austin strolled toward them. Rosa's uncle, only five feet tall, resembled a hairy dwarf in comparison to Austin's six-foot-four build.

"The men here are quite large, are they not?"

"Not normally as large as Austin," Katie Lue said.

Collina didn't see any reason to stand in the driveway observing her husband trying to wrestle with a bull when they could be sipping on some fresh coffee and having a piece of coffee cake. "Come on in. You can observe the goings on just as easily sitting before the window. I'll go and make us a fresh pot of coffee." She ran up the hill ahead of them.

She snatched up yesterday's newspaper and hesitated before dumping the early morning coffee grounds on the photograph. Roosevelt was sitting on his horse with San Juan printed across his shoulder and down his chest. The paper wrote there would be cowboys, six Indian chiefs, as well as coal miners, and, of course, the Rough Riders attending the inauguration. A picture of Franklin that night he rescued her dressed in his uniform came unbidden to her thoughts. She heard the front door open.

Rosa entered. Boldly, she looked around and snorted like a young filly might do in a new pasture.

Uneasiness washed over Collina. She ripped out the article and tucked it into her pocket, then emptied her coffee grounds. Would she ever feel confident in her new role of being Austin's wife and now— mother of his child?

Franklin felt the excitement exploding around him. Indians, Rough Riders, musicians tuning their instruments, horses neighing, people talking, and singers stretching their voices. It was loud, unorthodox, and exhilarating! All invited by their twenty-sixth president of the United States. Theodore Roosevelt was the youngest man ever to hold that office.

"There are over thirty thousand people in the inaugural parade alone, Melissa. Just think of that."

Melissa's wide brimmed hat adorned with a massive amount of blackbird and peacock feathers fluttered in the breezes like a furniture duster. Franklin stifled his chuckle. Dear Melissa, she'd taken severe care in her toiletry, and she looked exquisite except for that hat. Jane's headpiece had undone her.

"My, it is impressive." She gave her bishop sleeves a fluff. "I much prefer the gidget sleeves of the Gibson Girl era to these things. Does the back of my skirt look right? I don't believe my seamstress fit it as I had wished. I might need to replace her."

She turned slowly. Franklin admired his wife's slender form. The slight bustled back formed an *S* curve that draped her corseted waistline admirably and brought out her finest features. Even her draping bodice in pink silk chiffon added just the right amount of fullness and gave color to her cheeks. "My dear, you take my breath away. I've arranged for a cavalry soldier to accompany you to your seat."

She tapped her parasol on the ground. "Do I have a say about this?"

"No, my dear, you do not." Franklin took hold of Dawn's pony and helped her up. He smiled encouragingly back into the timid black eyes of the seven-year-old, her long, sweeping black hair layered in thick braided pigtails on either side of her buckskin dress. Dawn's tiny beaded headdress of white feathers matched the beadings on her dress and set off her complexion and high cheekbones.

"Jane, where have the years gone?"

Jane was wearing an ivory white dress with tasseled pants beneath. She rearranged her headdress of beautiful white and red feathers, which traveled down her back like a flowing tapestry.

"Franklin, you should ride over there and pay your respects," Jane said. He followed her line of sight to the six Indian chiefs she would be traveling with in the parade. They stood by themselves beneath a tree. "I believe the one on the left is the Apache warrior Geronimo."

"Really. Why did President Roosevelt invite him?" Melissa said. "He's already gotten criticized inviting these chiefs, now Geronimo— he's massacred many Americans."

"He wanted to give the people a good show," Dawn said.

Melissa placed a gloved hand to her bodice. "My word. Let us hope no one wishes a demonstration as to their talents with the knife."

Franklin chuckled. He walked to the mounting block, swung his stiff leg over first and jumped onto his horse.

"I think you care more about Jane and Dawn than me. I told you, I want you to stay with me."

"Darling, I'll be back before you miss me."

"I doubt that. And I doubt all this fanfare will make me anticipate four more years with this rogue." She waved her perfumed handkerchief before her nose. "Ghastly smell, these barbaric renegades."

He ignored her derogatory comment. "Teddy will be good for all Americans. His plans are moving forward to establish more national parks like the one he did in Oregon. He has all the people's interests at heart. Red, black, white, and he'll not pad some stuffy politician's pocket with greenbacks or pompous power."

A soldier saluted Franklin and said, "Shall I accompany Mrs. Long, to her seat, sir?"

Franklin saluted him back. "Yes, please." He rode closer to her and, bending low, drew her to him, blowing the bird feathers from her hat out of his way, and kissed her smartly. "You're very fetching, my dear."

"Humph. I'd attract more admiring glances if I had worn a war bonnet and beads."

The soldier led his wife to her seat. Franklin followed Dawn and then after making his greetings with the famous chiefs, he skimmed the parade grounds, looking for his regiment.

He spotted his group and joined them. Polo friends from New York that he hadn't seen for years, buffalo soldiers, hunters, prospectors, even an occasional gambler. From forty-five states across America, they'd ridden here, rode freight cars, whatever it took to get here. Yep, that was his group. Franklin bit down on his lip. At least what was left.

Along the parade route as the Indians approached, he heard gasps of surprise and awe. Uproarious applause and cheers followed as people waved miniature flags at them. Their horses pranced down Pennsylvania Avenue toward the east front of the US Capitol. President Roosevelt, seeing them approach, jumped to his feet and clapped enthusiastically. You would think they were the honored dignitaries, and not him. Franklin smiled. No, Teddy hadn't changed.

"My fellow-citizens," Roosevelt began his inaugural speech, "no people on earth have more cause to be thankful than ours, and this is said reverently, in no spirit of boastfulness in our own strength, but with gratitude to the Giver of Good who has blessed us with the conditions which have enabled us to achieve so large a measure of well-being and of happiness…Much has been given us, and much will rightfully be expected from us. We have duties to others and duties to ourselves; and we can shirk neither. We have become a great nation, forced by the fact of its greatness into relations with the other nations of the earth, and we must behave as beseems a people with such responsibilities…"

Franklin's thoughts reverted to that bloody battle up Kettle Hill at San Juan, knowing Teddy's thoughts must have been on that same battle when he wrote his speech. Then there was that incident in Morocco. Franklin chuckled. Perdicaris alive or Raisuli dead. That had become the popular chant during Roosevelt's campaign for the White House. Roosevelt's favorite slogan now that he had won the Republican presidency was, "Speak softly and carry a big stick."

Roosevelt looked up from his paper. The wind whistled through the trees, and the feathers of the chiefs' headdresses fluttered in the breezes.

"But we have faith," Roosevelt said, "that we shall not prove false to the memories of the men of the mighty past. They did their work; they left us the splendid heritage we now enjoy. We in our turn have an assured confidence that we shall be able to leave this heritage unwasted and enlarged to our children and our children's children. To do so we must show, not merely in great crises, but in the everyday affairs of life, the qualities of practical intelligence, of courage, of hardihood, and endurance, and above all the power of devotion to a lofty ideal, which made great the men who founded this Republic in the days of Washington, which made great the men who preserved this Republic in the days of Abraham Lincoln."

Franklin mulled over what Teddy said. "The everyday affairs of life…" Are my works showing the devotion to Almighty God and His son, Jesus Christ, who bestowed so great a blessing on me?

Just when did my devotion to God become so difficult to manage? Did my quest for financial independence blind me to the true meaning of life? What did Billy Sunday read from Ben's Bible so long ago?

Read your Bible, choose godly pursuits, show through your actions that you're following the Good Book, not your I Will book. The choice was his.

Chapter 25

April 28, 1905

ollina was powerless to stop him. "Austin, I don't see the need to help the Botticellis. Do you realize it's the end of April? You've spent more time there than here for the past three weeks."

"I'll stay home, gladly. I planned this to be my last week anyways. Anthony should be able to manage now."

A knock at the door made them both jump. "Who could that be this early in the morning?"

"Many apologizes." Rosa hugged her arms. Her dress, loose across the bosom, sashed tightly about her slender waist, showed to perfection her most tantalizing attributes. "Will you come? Anthony cannot manage the plow. It goes here, there."

As Rosa imitated Anthony's troubles, bending first to one side, then the other, Collina could only imagine the view her pantomiming gave Austin. "It does not stand the way your strong arms had it do yesterday."

"Look, I've got my own chores." Austin looked to Collina, imploring her with his eyes to defend his words.

Rosa's bottom lip protruded, her large eyes gazing at him between thick lashes.

Austin shrugged. "I'll come over in a spell."

Rosa fanned her face with her hand. "My, it is so hot. May I have a glass of water before I return?"

Moving a chair for her to sit in, he motioned for her to sit down.

"Would you like some breakfast, Rosa?" Collina said.

Austin gave her one of his beware looks, grabbing the glass of water Collina had poured for her. Did he expect her to eat in front of Rosa? He cleared his throat, a flush coming to his cheeks.

"How do you like your eggs, Rosa?" Collina laid down the egg she was about to break. It was too quiet in the girls' bedroom. "I don't believe Susie and Becky are up. Please excuse me."

Collina woke the girls, then prepared breakfast. She fixed plates for the girls and set them aside, then sat down with Austin and Rosa. The three of them ate in silence. Austin was bent on inhaling all the food his large body could hold for the exhausting chores that lay ahead of him, ignoring their company. Rosa appeared indifferent to his coolness.

"My, you appetite, it triples Uncle Anthony's," Rosa said. "How do you manage to keep enough food for him?" She spoke to Collina; however, her pert smile was for Austin.

Giggles and skipping feet announced Becky's and Susie's hurried entry into the kitchen. They filled their mouths with bacon and a biscuit then headed for the door.

"Aren't you going to sit down and eat?" Collina said.

"Can't." Susie scooped up hers and Becky's lunch buckets. "We'll be late for school."

"And if we're five minutes late, we have to clean the chalkboards." Becky frowned at Rosa. "You here again?"

"Becky," Collina said, "where are your manners?"

Susie shoved her sister toward the door, and just before closing it behind her said, "Doc said for you to come in this week."

"Doc? When did—" Collina coughed. She just knew her face was now as red as that sliced tomato sitting on the table.

"He came over to the school. I forgot until now to tell you. Said you're a week overdue. Becky cried, said she didn't want to lose her new ma. Then Doc laughed and told her not to worry, that it wasn't that kind of sickness."

"I cried only a little." Becky ran over and kissed Collina on her cheek, then whispered, "I'd like a little sister."

"Come on, Beck, we'll be late."

"What she'd say?" Austin watched giggling Becky run out the door. "Becky, what's so funny?"

Collina pushed her bacon around. The scraping noise of her fork on china sounded like a shovel on rock in the quiet room. Austin's eyes felt like they were drilling a hole in her head, and the pounding of her heart pulsed in her ears. Tell him, tell him, it beat. No, she wouldn't. Not in front of Rosa.

The smell of Rosa's perfume wafted past her noise and mingled with the aroma of bacon and biscuits. Now was not the time. Maybe there would never be a right time, what with all his hunting trips and going to the Botticellis and…

"Collina hates to admit when she feels sick." Austin cleared his throat. "What day do you want to see Doc? I could drive you down in the wagon. Need to go and get some things at the mercantile."

Rosa's eyes stared into hers. Wherever Collina looked, there was Rosa. Collina jumped up and ran to the stove. Grabbing a rag, she dipped the breakfast skillet into sudsy water. Austin's chair gritted across the wooden floor, his slow, heavy steps made their way across the room, pounding their steady rhythm in her ears. "Collina," he whispered low. "What's wrong?"

She swerved away, trying to avoid him. It was his fault. Firm arms were placed on either side of her. She fought, but he turned her easily.

"Becky was worried she'd lose her new mama." Concern and fear curved the corners of his lips. They quivered ever so slightly. She looked away.

"I don't know what day would suit me. I have so much to do here. With you—"

"When are you due?" Rosa said.

Collina blushed before Austin's gaze.

"Is that all this is?"

He didn't care. Her face burned with humiliation.

Her inhibitions to tell her husband had only dramatized a normal act as pregnancy. Normal? Not so normal for Mary. Dear, precious Mary. "Austin, I wanted to tell you, but I was afraid. I wanted to make sure." Lowering her voice to a whisper, she added, "About us, before I told you, if you wanted my baby."

The muscles along Austin's square chin vibrated. She didn't know whether to cry or scream with delight that this secret was now out.

"Were you ever going to tell me?"

Collina swallowed. Motioning her head toward their guest. "That day, remember? I was going to tell you—"

"The day I brought the bull home?"

Collina nodded. Her eyes pleading, remembering what Doc Baker had said about telling him before anyone else. Knowing she had not. After all, he was part of this living being within her. "I…" She stopped, not wanting to say the words that came to her mouth, not wanting to bring up again the eventful day he had left her on the eve of her conception.

Rosa scratched her chair across the floor. "Maybe I should go, yes?"

Austin paid her no mind, then seeing Collina's look, turned and said, "Yes. Leave us alone." He reached for Collina's shoulders, his eyes pained. "Go on."

A haughty smile appeared on Rosa's sensual lips. "Congratulations."

Collina heard the cabin door creak behind Rosa. Her laughter, explosively scornful, rained over her head its forewarning as her steps tapped out a sonnet of doom to Collina's heart.

She shivered. She was no competition for Rosa, nor the Katie Lues or Carries of Austin's world.

Austin shook her shoulders, bringing her back from her premonition with a jolt. "How long have you known?"

"I found out from Doc Baker when I was three months along. I was going to tell you then, but you went on your hunting trip. Remember?"

He gasped. "You knew then? Still, you acted so blasted independent. I didn't know what to do with you." His hands were drawn into fists. "Collina, tell me the truth; do you want my baby?"

His face blurred before her eyes as she choked the words out from her tear-filled throat. "How can you ask such a question? I love you, Austin. He, or she, would be my treasured baby, even if we—"

"My darling." His soft lips blended with hers. His arms wrapped her like a loving blanket, caressing, strong, caring arms. She prayed it would last forever.

"Austin, you'll just never guess what else."

"What?"

"It's a secret. So don't tell anyone. Ruby has fallen in love with Stephen Meir. Isn't that wonderful?"

Confusion crossed Austin's face. He looked down at her bewildered, then smiled. "Yes, darling, it is." He crushed her to his large chest.

"Ruby says Stephen's twin sister, Julie Ann, is trying to break up their relationship." Collina buried deeper into Austin's shoulder. "But love is stronger than death." Now why did I say that?

Chapter 26

June 10, 1905

*R*uby shoved open the front doors of the Meir mansion and propped them open. "Stephen hemorrhaged, right on Main Street."

Julie Ann gasped.

Robert and Karl, carrying Stephen between them, barged through. "Where do you want us to put him?"

"How on earth…?"

Eyeing Julie Ann's flushed face, Ruby led them to the kitchen. Throwing everything on the table onto the floor, she said, "Lay him down but keep his head elevated. We need a pillow."

Julie Ann handed a pillow to Karl. "What happened?"

"We'd been working on Stephen's movie projector. Then out of the blue this issue of blood from his nose and mouth happened," Karl said.

"Has Stephen had attacks like these before?"

Karl shook his head.

Ruby gently placed the pillow beneath Stephen's head. He just mumbled. He was in a sort of slumber.

"Everyone out," Doc Baker said as he rushed into the kitchen, his black bag in hand. "You all can wait in the parlor until I call you in."

Dear Jesus, please don't let this sickness be bad. If it is, please heal Stephen. Ruby paced back and forth, praying.

"Can't you sit down? You're making me nervous." Julie Ann had her own way of handling a crisis.

It was deep into the afternoon before Doc Baker, his forehead dripping with perspiration, came into the parlor. "Ruby, he's asking for you."

Ruby jumped from her seat as if she'd been sitting on springs. She swept past Julie Ann and toward the opened doorway.

Stephen rested in the bow-back Windsor near the kitchen's hearth, a blanket on his lap. He held out both his hands to her. She rushed to his side and knelt down before him. "I was so worried about you."

"I don't want you to worry about me, darling." Taking her hands in his, he kissed them gently. "I'm fine."

Robert's head appeared around the corner. "Why that Casanova. Sick, my foot. Hey, Doc." Robert pointed a finger to Stephen. "Tell him to let my sister loose. He's just pretending to be sick so Sis will feel sorry for him. Hey, Meir, that's a low blow even for you."

Stephen acted distressed, but Ruby suspected it was more like pretend indignation. "Doc," Stephen yelled, "keep the riffraff out a while longer."

Robert smiled. "I'll stay where I'm at and protect my sister."

"Doc, I need a little more time, please, before…" Stephen pretended to pass out. One eye opened to see the results of his dramatic act.

Doc Baker laughed. "Do your own dirty work, Meir."

Karl followed Robert into the kitchen nook, and soon the three were laughing about the experience. Ruby took that moment to sneak out to ask Doc about Stephen's illness.

He was comforting Julie Ann, in a joking sort of anecdotal way all Doc's own. "Julie Ann, life's not planning on giving us any breaks."

Julie Ann pressed her hands together in a tight grip. "Bad news, I just knew it, first dear Pa-pa and now my brother."

It was as if Julie Ann was hoping Doc would say it was terminal.

Doc Baker glanced at Ruby. He, too, noticed the exasperated expression sweeping across Julie Ann's plump face. "It's not bad. Stephen will need to take it easy for about a month, then we'll see how he does."

Julie Ann wrung her hands. "That's like telling the ocean to stop beating the shoreline. Stephen can no more relax than I can do pushups."

Doc Baker chuckled and patted her plump arm.

Though they were twins, neither shared the same temperament or looks. Stephen was a man of action, and Julie Ann the opposite.

Ruby noticed Julie Ann's ample arms. Stephen and Julie Ann were nearing their thirty-first birthday, and that was where the similarity ended. For nothing in their physical or mental anatomy resembled one another. Stephen was a total optimist, while his twin was a diehard pessimist. So much so that she had become a chore to be around. Marriage to the right mate could perhaps do wonders to somewhat alleviate the sad situation, but no new prospects of potential husbands sat on the front porch swing these days.

"I don't like it. It's just like Pa-pa's strange illness," Julie Ann said.

"It's too early to tell what might be causing this." Doc said.

"So he has no restrictions in diet, just no strenuous activities?"

"That's the summary. I've got a few more patients to check on before I'm done. Just let me know if Stephen has any more hemorrhages."

"Hey, gents." Stephen reached for Ruby's hand. "I'll meet you outside in a minute."

Robert and Karl looked at each other and smiled. "I should have known that whatever ailed you wouldn't last for long," Karl said.

"Just don't go downtown without us." Robert's long legs made the distance between chair and doorway in quick easy strides. He turned to give Ruby one more be-careful look. "That new machine you brought back with you from the East is so amazing we don't want to miss out on seeing it in action."

"Don't worry. I won't leave without you two. I promise." He impatiently brushed back the blond strands of hair that had fallen into his eyes. He gave Ruby a cheeky grin. "I could use a glass of water."

Ruby hastened to the sink. The pump handle worked easily, and soon the cool water spilled over like a fountain. The back door banged shut. Suddenly, she felt a strong hand on hers.

"Here, I can do that," Stephen said.

Her heart beat all the faster at the warmth of his touch. She moved her hand away. She walked across to the pantry to retrieve a glass. *Why is Stephen having such an effect on me?*

Stephen was looking at her queerly. The water continued to sputter from the pump in a flowing funnel of liquid gurgling down the drain in the sink. She hesitated. *What if Stephen had…?* She woke up every morning excited to see him. His jesting eyes, his laughing mouth. He'd become the best part of her life.

"I don't think I can get this water in that glass unless you bring it a little closer."

Ruby blushed, hurrying back to the sink. Handing him the glass, she held her breath as his fingers lingered on hers.

"Would you like something to eat?" She turned so he couldn't see her face. Moving to the icebox, Ruby picked out a slab of cheese and a shoulder of ham. Confused, she stared up at the rows on rows of china decorating the cupboard. "Which plate is for everyday use?" The Meir kitchen was as different as Windsor Castle would be to Buckingham Palace. But that idea had not even crossed her mind; her own thoughts were not on what she was doing.

Stephen's tall frame obstructed her. He was looking down at her, concern written in his eyes. "What's the matter, Ruby? Have you become afraid of me?" His hand rested on her chin and gently raised her head to meet his. "Can you tell me what's wrong?"

Tears flooded her eyes. "It's just that I was so worried about you. I didn't know what I would do if something should happen…"

"Ahh, is that all?"

He wrapped her in his arms. Her head rested so comfortably on his chest. He stroked her hair, and she could feel his lips ever so gently graze her forehead.

"I'm sorry I put you through that. You're so little, so fragile, too young and sensitive to—"

"Now see here, Stephen Meir." Ruby's head poked up, dislodging herself from his grasp. "It's not me you need worry about, try thinking about yourself. What if that should happen again?"

Stephen's blue eyes laughed into hers. "What a little spitfire I've got myself." He captured her in his embrace.

She struggled to free herself, though she truly enjoyed being there. But hot tears wanted to escape, and this just wouldn't do. Besides, what made him think that she was his anyway? Freeing herself, she walked to the cupboard. "You need something to eat. Go sit down at the table, and I'll make you some bacon and eggs to go with that ham and cheese."

He sat down at the table as she asked. His eyes didn't leave her form as she bustled about the kitchen fixing his plate. Her face grew warm from the heat of the stove, or was it the heat from his eyes? Finished, she placed the plate before him and sat down across from him, exhausted. She blushed, noting Stephen's amusement. "What's so funny?"

A smile crawled to his lips. Still chewing on his first mouthful, he said, "You." His eyes now serious as he gazed into hers. "You're going to make some man a good wife, when you've grown up a bit."

"I'll have you know, Mr. Meir, I'm nearing twenty-one and aware of life, and when Mr. Right does come along, I'll know him."

Stephen put his fork down and cleared his voice. "You're that confident of yourself?"

Confident? Was she? The reality of what she'd said slapped her in the face like hail falling from a clear blue sky. She'd thrown her words out like cards at a poker game, haphazardly onto the table of life. However, unlike the game of poker, words were final, especially words spoken between a man and a woman. Several verses from Hebrews 10 whispered in her mind: Cast not away therefore your confidence...For ye have need of patience...the just shall live by faith.

The warmth of Stephen's hand on hers comforted her escalating emotions. What hurdles lie in the years ahead? Now faith is the substance of things hoped for, the evidence of things not seen.

His eyes probed hers. "Ruby, I do love you. What do you say about us getting married?"

"I..." What would it be like with him always beside her? What would her life be without him? "Yes! I love you." But, Lord, why have you given me these verses at such a time like this?

Ruby's knuckles pounded on the oak door of Collina and Austin's cabin. The noise echoed across the hillside. Since Stephen's proposal six days ago, she'd felt some unrest in her acceptance. Why? Collina would know what was bothering her.

Hmm…No answer. That's not like Sis. She knew I was coming.

A large gust of wind whipped her hat off. She ran to retrieve it. She heard the grating of gravel and the tinkle of harness; a wagon pulled by two draft horses turned the bend in the drive, lumbering up the hill, laden with hay. The girls were sitting on either side of Austin on the front seat.

"Ruby, what are you doing here? Can't you see a bad storm is brewing?" Austin said.

"I promised Collina I'd come over and help her with her dress pattern. I wanted her to be the first to know—"

"I see." Austin rubbed his whiskered chin, his dimples popping up like potato eyes across his cheeky grin. "You're not going to tell me this earth-shattering news until my wife hears it first, huh?"

Ruby felt her face grow warm. Collina must have told him. "I can see you already suspect the truth. Well, Stephen and I are engaged to be married. We're planning an August wedding, and I want Collina as my matron of honor."

"In two months?"

"It will be next year. Mother would never agree—"

"If you become half the wife your sister is, Stephen's getting himself a wonderful helpmate. And hopefully, President Roosevelt will deliver what he promised, and it'll be a profitable year for us farmers." Austin removed his hat and wiped his brow, glancing at the potential thunderclouds, and heaved a sigh of relief. "I'll be up at Shushan to help Robert and Jessie next week. Now that Collina's six months along in her pregnancy, I'm toting the load for us both." He pointed to the one light, like a lighthouse beacon guiding them to safety, shining in the kitchen window. "Go on in and take my girls with you. I'll get this wagon put in the barn. Bet Collina's got a good dinner for us already made. I'll feed the livestock. That is, if your sister hasn't already."

"Ma, Ma!" Becky yelled as they entered the cabin.

Ruby fingered the silverware. The table's set, food's ready, but the stove's gone out, and the food is cold.

"I can't find Ma; she isn't anywhere." Becky ran to Ruby and swung her arms around her waist. "Ma wouldn't let our supper grow cold unless something happened." She buried her head in Ruby's skirts, her words muffled, and cried. "Unless something awful happened."

Susie swayed from one foot to another. Then she, too, ran to Ruby for comfort. "Do you think she tried to have her baby alone and died?" Susie sobbed.

"No. Now, you children stay put inside." Ruby knelt down and placed her most confident smile on her face. "I'll go find your pa. Most likely your mother is outside bedding down the livestock. After all, a storm is brewing and it's just like her to do something like that."

Ruby snatched her shawl, leaving her ill-fated hat inside. She heard Austin before she found him, brooding over an empty paddock.

"Strange, Clover isn't in her corral; she might be out trying to have that calf." Then he pointed at the cause of his brooding. "The bull's not in his stall." Together they walked out toward the bull's paddock. Leaves and branches had spilled across the lane. Then Ruby noticed it. A big limb of an old oak had cracked in two—right over the bull's paddock. A cold chill crawled its way up her spine.

"Don't let your imagination run wild, Ruby. She's probably in the chicken coop."

"You think so?"

Austin struck a match and lit the lantern. "It's the most likely spot. Or else, she could be out looking for Clover." Austin smiled. "You know Collina. She thinks nothing about storms and such."

Through the trees Ruby scanned the darkness. Black and bleak was the lane to the chicken coop. No lantern shined warmly through the coop windows. She felt her arms grow numb, as if her feelings were suddenly paralyzed, remembering the night when after Pa's funeral, she had prayed for her sister's safety, recalling Joseph's words to her sister: "You've got more courage than rightly belongs to a female." Had fate chosen revenge?

The door to the chicken coop creaked open. Austin swung his lantern. The chickens were asleep on their roost.

Ruby walked over to the setting boxes. The eggs were still there. That was not like Sis. She gathered the eggs, a prayer on her lips. "Jesus, keep Collina safe. I claim the promise of Psalm 91:9. Collina has made You her refuge, no evil will befall her. You have given Your angels charge over her."

"Pa, where is she?" Susie, out of breath, pulled on her father's arm.

He turned, his face a mask of pain. "You get back to the house, and help Ruby take care of Becky. I'm going to saddle up Sagebrush and ride to Shushan for help. I'll be back directly." He turned to her. "Ruby, you'll be all right till I get back?"

Ruby had gotten the girls to bed and cleaned up the dinner plates. She left Austin's dinner beneath a towel on the counter. The night wove on endlessly. Austin and her brothers were scouring the countryside and it was long past the midnight hours.

Rosa Botticelli had appeared on the doorstep with Anthony. With misgivings, remembering her sister's fears, Ruby politely let her in and resumed her pacing on the cabin floor. Rosa's flippant conversations grated on her nerves. Finally, she could stand it no longer. She brewed some coffee and cut the cake she had baked into neat little squares. She eyed the sassy girl. Was that makeup on her eyes? She shook her head and said, "Rosa, you stay here with the children."

She picked up the coffee and mugs, and with the sack of cakes in her fist, she hurried toward the barn like the demons from hell were after her.

"Look what we found." Robert and Scott dragged in Clover, her new calf by her side. The bull came shortly later. Collina's partly torn dress layered the brute's horns and neck.

Ruby covered her mouth. No one spoke.

Austin took charge. "Anthony, get my horse saddled and go get Doc Baker. You hear? Go! I don't want any time lost when we find my wife."

Anthony hesitated. "That bull could have carried her clear to the next county."

"You don't think I know that? Go!" Austin wiped his forehead with the back of his hand, watching Anthony gallop down the hill. "She'll need doctoring." Then he started toward his tool shed. "I'll put a bullet in that sorry brute's head."

"Wait," Ruby cried.

Austin stopped dead in his tracks.

"We need to pray." She took his hand and then her brother's. They formed a circle.

Big plump tears rolled down Scott's cheeks. "Go on, Sis. You pray."

The only verse that would come to her mind was Psalm 23:4. But, Lord, we say that over people's graves. God's answer was the same. Ruby snatched a huge breath, "Yea, though I walk through the valley of the shadow of death, I will fear no evil; for You are with me. Lord, be with Collina, and please be with us to find her alive. Amen."

As if his legs could no longer hold his weight, Austin fell to his knees. He bent low to the ground, hiding his face. "Lord, it's me You're angry at. I know that. Please Lord, forgive me of my sins. I'll worship You. I'll read Your Bible. I'll follow the straight and narrow until the day I die, if You let my wife live and let my baby live, too. I promise I'll never doubt You again, so help me God." Austin nodded, tears streaming down his face. "Lord, show us where to look."

Everyone stood silent.

"Let's try the swamp. This time let's spread no more than five feet apart." Jessie said.

"I think you've got something there, Jessie. Let's be as quiet as possible; might be we can hear more than see," Robert said.

"I'm going, too," Ruby insisted.

Through the miles of swamp they plodded. She and Austin

searched with their ears and their eyes, praying under their breaths that somehow in the deep hidden waters, they would find Collina.

Austin stumbled. Must have hit a log, he caught hold of a limb before falling head first into that cesspool of murky and muddied water. A groan, soft and agonizing, reached Ruby's ears.

"Collina!" Austin cried, waving his lantern amidst the low-hanging moss. The darkness of night lingered like the shroud of death.

"Look out, Austin."

A movement, a slash just two feet away from him—a water moccasin had just missed him. Austin was on his knees, crawling, feeling for—

"I've found her!" He scooped Collina into his arms.

"Austin," she cried.

He hugged her and wept openly. "God, thank You." He looked up at Ruby. "I would have missed her again, if I hadn't stumbled."

Doc's headlights lit the dirt road before them. "I'm not too good at driving this contraption. At least no one else is up this early besides us."

Ruby cradled her sister's head in her lap. Doc had gotten the blood from her leg to stop oozing. But the other bleeding…Austin turned around in his seat to gaze at his wife.

Judging by the condition of Collina's body, it had been a battle. Somehow that bull had gotten her over his head and carried her to what could have been a watery grave. It was amazing she had survived that. Yet still more amazing was the fact that if Austin hadn't come when he did and stopped the blood, it would have been certain death for Collina.

"With the Lord's help," Doc said, "just maybe she'll pull through."

"The baby, too, Doc?" Austin said.

Doc shrugged. "My biggest worry is her leg. I'm afraid gangrene might have already set in. And if not that, lockjaw."

"Doc, you think she lost the baby?"

"That's the least of your wife's worries."

Austin reached back and stroked the bruises on Collina's cheeks and chin. A couple of her teeth were bleeding, her forehead gashed. "Doc, will her face be all right?" Drops of blood rolled down her neck from the cut, and Ruby hastened to dab it away with her already soaked handkerchief. How much more could the cloth hold?

Doc Baker glanced over his shoulder. "If you can, reach my black bag and grab some gauze. Those are mostly superficial wounds. They'll mend in time. She might lose a tooth or two. We all do sometime in our life. Now her leg, well, we'll see what the surgeon says about that."

The room they ushered Ruby and Austin into was void of anything but a few chairs. Austin walked aimlessly, unable, though exhausted, to rest. "Ruby, Doc didn't say it, didn't have to." He stopped in front her. "Collina's lost our baby." His mouth contorted, fighting his emotions.

Ruby wrapped her arms around him. "There, there, if she has, there will be other children. Look at Myra and Clem. They keep trying."

Austin slumped into a chair and covered his face with his hands. "I wish I could wipe away the memory of her bleeding face. I should have shot that bull the first day I brought him home."

The waiting room door opened. Doc Baker and another doctor walked in. "Mr. Blaine, I'm Dr. Madison."

Doc Baker walked over to Austin and placed a hand on his shoulder, "She's going to live."

"Yes, we've managed to stop all the internal bleeding," Dr. Madison said. "Your wife will have full use of her leg and arm again. She did lose the baby. Her womb was so badly gored I had to perform a hysterectomy."

"You mean, my wife won't be able to have any more children?"

Doc Baker's eyes beseeched Ruby's. "Austin you've got two beautiful girls. God's given you back your wife. She'll recover nicely from all her scars, with time. If it hadn't been for Dr. Madison here, there was a possibility we would have had to amputate. She probably won't be able to perform…you know, intercourse, for a good two months, maybe three. She'll need your love and support to get through this. But you both have a good life ahead of you, just a few hurdles to climb over."

"What was it, boy or girl?"

Doctor Madison looked at Doc Baker.

Doc Baker patted Austin's shoulder. "It was a boy." Doc cleared his throat. "The nurse will come in soon and take you to see Collina."

The door closed softly behind the doctors. Ruby blinked away her tears. Austin stood and looked out the window. The clock on the wall clicked loudly in the quiet room. Ruby sat down, folded her hands, and thanked God for her sister's life. The clock ticked away the precious moments. Austin turned, his face hard and expressionless. "Why do I always destroy everything that loves me?"

"Destroy? You gave my sister a reason to live. She's alive. Praise our good Lord." Ruby stood up and smiled into his woebegone face. "I've never seen her happier these past months. And she will be happy again, with you by her side."

"She's an unusual woman. She was just waiting for someone to love her." He sniffed and glanced at his hands. "God's punishing me. He only gave me half of what I wished for."

"I remember what Mother told me once. Seems like a lifetime ago… It was the day after that terrible auction…'Ruby, you can't expect life to always go your way. You're fooling yourself if you think it will. God's not your fairy godfather. He's our Master, Savior, and Comforter all rolled into one.'" Ruby bowed her head as tears temporarily blinded her sight.

Her voice shaky, she continued. "God's the Creator of the universe; He created us in His image. He loves us unconditionally, Austin, and refuses to treat us like puppets on a string, but rather as beings with a mind and a soul who can choose to love Him and obey Him or else to live our lives as we choose."

Austin shrugged off her hand and slapped the windowpane. "Oh, God, why?" Austin yelled. "Why my baby? Why my wife?"

Ruby reached out to console him. He sidestepped. God, help me. What was it Solomon wrote in Ecclesiastes? "To everything there is a season, and a time to every purpose under the heaven…A time to weep and a time to laugh; a time to mourn … But Collina is alive. She will recover from her wounds. Rejoice in the Lord…Be anxious for nothing, but in everything by prayer and supplication—"

"I don't want to hear that stuff anymore."

"You must listen. Philippians 4 tells us to rejoice; Collina is alive. She will recover. Allow the peace of God—"

"I'm through with God!"

She walked over and thrust him away from the window and glared up at him. "If you're going to look for the bad and ignore the good in life, you'll never find true happiness, and the devil will use your apathy to get a foothold into your heart."

"That seed thing again? Mary talked about that the night of Ben's funeral, then she died. Collina read from the Good Book, and I did believe. Well, I've planted and cultivated and believed until I've worn calluses on my hands and bunions on my toes and for what? To have my wife mauled by a bull? To have my son die in her womb? Where was God then?

"The Almighty, omnipotent master of the universe couldn't even stop a bull from mauling a Christian, God-fearing woman." He crouched down, covering his head, crying, his shoulders racked in pain. "You Bible thumpers are all the same. Get away from me!"

Chapter 27

April 21, 1906

The drops of rain poured over the cabin's roof, forming a reddish-brown reservoir around Collina's flowerbeds. "Feels like April for sure with all the rain we've been gittin', I mean getting."

Honestly, instead of my grammar rubbing off on the girls, theirs is rubbing off on me. However, her speech wasn't the only thing that had changed. Since her accident, she hadn't bothered to go to church much.

Austin had refused to step into any church. She usually read the Bible after dinner; he refused to listen and would stomp outside, snorting like a bull on the loose. So she'd stopped her Bible reading. It had been a trying year. Not even Mother could persuade him different.

Taking Austin's old blue hat from its perch on the wooden peg, she tied it about her head with a bandanna. She bent down and pulled up a corner of her long skirts, looping them securely about her belt. Stepping off the porch, she avoided the puddles as best she could. Good thing Susie and Becky were already at the Botticellis'. They'd have a fit if they saw her looking like this.

She couldn't understand Austin's feelings about her coveralls. They protected her legs and looked neater than a skirt after a day's work. Wearing dresses didn't stop the gossipers wagging their tongues. She rubbed her stomach absentmindedly. A part of her always felt alone. Though Mother and her sisters tried to make her feel better, she couldn't seem to get out beneath that rain cloud of depression and hopelessness.

When someone did try to penetrate her self-erected wall, she pushed them away. Why hadn't she been hospitable to Pastor Bates and Widow Tomkins? What had come over her to act that way? She had used the excuse she was doing her barn chores when they pulled up and had left them sitting in her lane and walked away. Deep down in her heart she knew that wasn't the reason she didn't invite them into the house for coffee. Ever since the accident, she hadn't wanted visitors.

Austin's attitude toward her had changed, too. She felt it when he lay beside her at night. She was only half a woman now. Mother would come by every so often to pick her and the girls up for church. That heaped the guilt on her head even more. So the family had missed church a couple of Sundays. A couple? She bowed her head. But why did Mother and Pastor Bates lay this on her shoulders about Austin? He'd made his mind up; what did they think she could do?

The rain had let up. The sound of her rubber boots squishing the mud and splashing in the puddles mingled with the birds chirping in a nearby tree. Her horses' shrill neighs greeted her. She walked them into their stalls, grained them, and picked up the empty buckets she left just inside the barn's entrance and headed to the stream. "I bet the pastor expected me to stop milking and pour them some tea and give them something to eat the way Mother always did when the congregation stopped in after church."

Collina's thoughts recalled those Sunday dinners Mother would fix after the service. It had been okay when Pa had been alive. But when Pa died, that was different. Why some weeks she and Mother could barely scrape up enough for their own family, let alone the congregation. But Mother was always glad to serve, always willing to share her last morsel.

The gurgling brook lapped the shoreline at her feet. It had been a wet and humid spring. The stream had overflowed its banks, and her rubber boots sunk deeper into the muck. She would have to be content to scoop up the water close to the shoreline. She dipped her buckets, her throat dry for a drink of water. She swished the water in her bucket and scooped up a handful, drinking it down thirstily.

After climbing back up the hill, she poured her water buckets into the baby steers' water trough. Austin had purchased them a week ago.

Come autumn, they should bring a sizable price at the auction.

Reaching the barn door, she gave it a hard shove. The side door squeaked loudly on its one hinge as it banged against the barn wall. "I'll have to fix this myself, I guess. I think I like the Scripture that says 'charity begins at home.'" But she was beginning to think that there was no such Scripture. She had sought that verse last night, so she could read it to Austin this morning, but couldn't find it. The only one that kept popping up too many times was Luke 8:14 "And that which fell among thorns…"

That certainly described Austin and her. Thorny, looking to prick one another each chance they got. How did the rest of that verse go?

I can't recall. It was something about not bringing any fruit to perfection. She sighed. Mother said there were over two hundred passages in the Bible that talked about praising and singing to the Lord with thanksgiving, and Collina always seemed to see that parable of the seed or the "Thou shalt" ones. Perhaps God thought she needed to focus on those.

She picked up a pail and her three-legged stool, then tied up Clover. "Easy girl," she said, nudging her over. Grasping her udders, she pulled one then the other rhythmically. The warm milk sent out steamy vapors when it hit the metal sides of the bucket. Collina rested her head against the cow's warm flank.

Her mind went back to the conversation with Austin and the girls this morning. She tried to coax them into staying and helping her finish some of the repairs needing done around the cabin after a hard winter. Austin was determined to go, saying he owed it to Rosa for all the work she did during Collina's recuperation. Susie reemphasized Austin's declaration, bragging about Rosa's attributes until Collina agreed to let her go, too.

Susie had taken a peculiar fascination for the foreigner. She absorbed everything Rosa told her about Italy. Collina had lain helpless in bed, her right leg bandaged from ankle to hip, listening behind her partly opened door to Rosa's peals of laughter echoing about the cabin walls. Yes, Rosa had managed to win the teen over in a way Collina envied.

The wagon rolled out of sight that morning with not one of them glancing back at her standing on the porch. She had hoped Becky would say something in her defense. "Bugie would have."

Clover mooed. That's all Collina had these days, the companionship of her animals to confide in. That and her Bible.

Ruby's wedding was in four months, and she had agreed to be her matron of honor. Austin wanted her to go to Shushan for a couple of weeks. Why? Was it for her benefit or his?

The other day, Emma Glaser had stopped over to tell her she had seen Austin and Rosa up at Willow's Bluff. "Both in separate wagons, mind you, but still together just the same."

Collina laughed off Emma's words. Only the slurp, slurping of the milk hitting the pail from her second cow broke the stillness. She urged her fingers on faster and soon the second bucket was brimming with rich, foamy milk.

She remembered that night after Emma's visit. Unable to sleep, she had watched as the curly black hairs of Austin's chest heaved rhythmically, rising and lowering with his every breath. He didn't deserve to sleep if she couldn't. Besides, she could always get the truth out of him better when he was half-awake. So with the moonlight filtering through their window, she shook him awake, telling him what Emma Glaser had told her.

Hesitant, not turning his face to hers, he'd asked what Emma had seen. "Nothing, I expect."

He said Rosa was giving him a list of supplies for the barn raising. Collina had to be content with that. It seemed a logical reason. Though she didn't rightly see the reason behind Rosa bothering Austin with something she could have done.

"I owe her for taking care of the girls and you when you were recuperating."

"Carrie Carlson was here about as much. I swear, you attract women like apple blossoms do bees. Besides, Austin, it's my debt. Not yours. I'm healthy enough now to pay both your women back."

"Rosa's wants my—help not yours."

She placed a hesitant hand on his chest and whispered shyly. "Doc says everything's healed up. That I can start being a wife to you again."

He turned, placing his hand on her cheek. Her face growing warm, remembering how his earlier attempts in lovemaking had hurt, she hadn't meant to shrink from him, but her inadequacy had taken its toll on her.

He slid closer to her. The old hurt in her abdomen came to rest there again. "I could ask Doc what's wrong with me."

He lifted himself on his strong arms and lowered his head, kissing her forehead, then her upturned nose, and finally her lips. Then…

Panic swept her. "I, I feel a little sick."

"Nah, it's just your nerves. Don't worry, we'll work this out. I heard tell a little wine at night might be all you need."

Magic neighed. She shook herself free of her thoughts and looked up. Magic's probably bored out of her mind, she hadn't ridden her since the accident. "I've got one more cow to go, the chickens and turkeys, and cattle to feed. Oh, I almost forgot," looking down at the new wooden stockade, "the lambs to hay."

Becky told her there would be a dance after the barn raising. Collina secretly hoped Austin would miss her so much he would come back for her. She glanced toward the barn door, envisioning his shoulders bowing down to climb through the small side door of the barn to surprise her, calling out her name as he gathered her to him. Collina sighed. He hadn't done that in ages.

"I bet Scott, Jessie, and Robert will be there, and most likely Belle and Bo along with their little boy. Ruby and Stephen too and maybe Mother." She was glad to hear a voice in the empty barn, even if it was her own. I wonder if Chester is still seeing that woman up in Boone County? "It would be so nice to get fixed up and just have some fun."

When was the last dance we went to? I can't remember. There had been plenty of barn raisings last fall that Austin had attended. But she stayed home. Most of them had been Austin's friends and too far away what with the livestock to feed and tend for her to go anyway. Yet, he had mentioned Rosa's homemade pies and how good they tasted.

Collina walked to the livery pegs and peeled off the blanket. There perched her saddle on its peg as she had left it. She stroked the smooth leather with her fingertips, then noted her hands. What had Austin said that night when he'd kissed them? Yes, she remembered. "You need to do more with your nails. Rosa showed Susie and Becky how that new shop in town even paints them and does something called a manicure. You could ask Susie about it."

Rosa this and Rosa that. Now even Austin was singing the same tunes Susie and Becky were. Collina opened her mouth to snap out another rebuke, only hot tears suddenly filled her stormy eyes. She'd only herself to blame. How many times had she wished she'd stayed put till Austin came home? It was her hard-headedness that caused her to go after that bull. She'd lost what she had all these years valued too little—her femininity. And now she stood to lose what she loved more than life itself…Austin.

What a fool she'd been all these months, wallowing in the mud-pits of her own self-pity. Magic nickered. She looked up. "You're right, girl; it's not too late." Bending down to grab a brush and curry. "Girl, get ready; it looks like you're going out tonight."

Collina surveyed the reflection of the woman in the mirror. She smiled. Her teeth gleamed back, white and straight, she hadn't lost a one. She frowned at the scar just above her brow, then dusted it with powder and stood back to survey herself.

Her face glowed with excitement, giving her a healthy, youthful eagerness. Her sun-bleached curls surrounded her oval face, falling thick and softly about her shoulders the way Austin liked it. Her dark lashes set off her large green eyes, the tiny blue flecks as bright as emeralds and robin eggs as they shone back at her. "Won't Austin be surprised?"

As the sun set, the sky became an aura of color. Floral pinks and velvet hues of blues streaked across the horizon in a vivid cast of artistic strokes, lighting a pathway for the sun to make its descent. Though her emerald green riding habit would not be the dress the other ladies would be wearing, she didn't mind. She really had no choice. Austin had taken their only wagon. Gaily, almost childlike, she opened the wooden door of their barn and jumped forward.

Magic neighed, striking the dirt of her stall impatiently. "Ah, Magic, the years haven't dampened your zeal, nor your memory. You haven't forgotten, have you, girl?" She stroked her mane lovingly. "There hasn't been much time for riding lately."

Austin had understood about her mare, not allowing her to be used for anything but riding. "A good riding horse is hard to find," he'd say when she saw a need for another pulling horse in the field.

"He was right about that." She cued Magic into her easy rocking-chair canter. Her right leg was still a little stiff, but she ignored the pain. "God's been good to us, girl."

Her heart ached for the child she had lost, and the womb that would never be able to bear another; yet, John 15:5 came to mind. "He that abideth in me, and I in him, the same bringeth forth much fruit: for without me ye can do nothing." How she would bear fruit, when she was now barren, was beyond her knowledge...but nothing is impossible with God.

Beneath the sure strides of her horse, the miles disappeared. Magic's dainty hoofs hardly touched the sodden roads still wet from the day's rain. The lights of Botticellis' homestead blended like the stars in the dark sky. Magic's head bobbed up and down, like a boat anchored all too quickly from the enchantment of the water. Collina stroked the arched neck, consoling her mare with soft words, not truly conscious of her actions as her eyes strained to see past the darkness into the open doors of the barn.

Through liquid light that spewed on the mud-caked straw came the soft wailing notes of banjos, guitars, and violins. Jude gave a welcoming nicker to her, and Collina noticed approvingly the leaf of hay Scott had placed before the hungry horse. Before she could turn up her saddle irons, she felt strong arms encircle her.

"Sis!" Robert's big lanky form looked taller and leaner in the lantern light. "It's good to see you."

"I can't believe how you've grown. And so strong, too," she said, rubbing her arms where Robert had hugged them.

"You're a sight for sore eyes, and so pretty, too. I think you grow prettier every year you grow older."

"Robert, you Casanova. I can't believe you're still single."

"I'm not ready to settle down. Jessie's engaged. I guess when I find someone like my favorite sister, maybe." Walking to the back of his wagon, he lifted another leaf of hay and placed it before her horse. "Only then will I consider giving up my freedom. I told Mother you'd be here."

"You did?" Robert had been watching for her. "How is everyone at Shushan? Are you getting the crops planted all right? Austin can help now that the Botticellis are settled in. Now that I'm back to health, I can help—"

"Yeah," he nodded in his slow, thoughtful way. "We're all doing fine. Mother's been praying for you nonstop. You've been in our morning and evening prayers, Sis."

"Me?" She glanced away from his penetrating eyes. "How did you know I was coming, when I didn't know myself until this evening?"

"Guess you could say I have a personal connection with the One upstairs. Besides that, I know you better then you know yourself. I keep telling Jessie and Ruby they don't appreciate me enough." Robert's eyes liked to dig a hole into her face; what did he think he'd find?

"We miss you back home. Scott's sick with the typhoid, and he keeps calling for you. Mother told me to tell you to not drink out of the creek and boil your water if need be. Typhoid's bad this spring."

"Dear Scott. I'll go see him. I've meant to before now. The chores at my place are burdensome."

Robert wrestled a stone with his boot and kicked it high in the air. "Yeah, I can just imagine."

"Have you seen Austin?"

Concern crossed Robert's sensitive face. "Saw him come in, can't say I know where he went." His large hand rested protectively on her shoulder. "Come on, Sis; let's show those crackers in there how to dance."

Seeing the dear faces she had missed eased the ache in her heart and made her feel like she belonged. But where was Austin?

As Robert, then Jessie, spun her about the dirt floor of the new barn, she stole shy glances at the figures of the people standing about the premises. Feeling someone watching her, she turned. Carrie Carlson's smirk grew wider. Her eyes gleamed at her like two cat eyes in the semi-light of the lantern-lit barn.

Collina shivered.

Carrie's eyes swerved toward the barn's small door, a beam of light. There he was. She'd know that silhouette anywhere.

Austin was holding the door open for someone. Then as their hands touched, she noted the smile that floated across his face. She couldn't see the woman clearly; she was in the shadows. Austin's face, however, was beneath the lights. She hoped Jessie hadn't seen what she had, but he had. Then Robert was by her side.

"Want me to go over with you?" Robert said.

Austin hadn't seen her. She half wished he had. His back was to her, his hand leaning up against the oak walls where Rosa lounged gracefully. She saw Collina and smirked, then swayed her large liquid dark eyes to gaze into Austin's. She leaned forward, resting on his arm. He bent down to meet her lips. She laughed in his face and whispered something in his ear. Her breath must have tickled her husband's ear, for he rubbed it with his hand. Or was he refusing to believe that his wife was just behind him?

"Husband?" Collina whispered. Had he heard her or chosen not to?

Rosa tossed a strand of thick hair off her shoulder defiantly. Her fingers fluttered her handkerchief heavily scented with perfume. "Don't look now, Austin dear, but your wife is standing behind you."

"What?" Austin spun around. "How did you get here?"

"I meant to surprise you, Austin. I guess by the look you're giving me, I did."

"Say, what's come over you? This morning you didn't feel up to a barn raising?"

"Commitment, Austin."

It was as if Austin's thoughts were linked with hers. He pulled a piece of timothy out from the haystack and chewed it thoughtfully. "You think that's all that's left of our marriage?"

Pain and humiliation washed over her like water. She turned toward the safe haven of the brightly lit barn and to her family.

Austin guided her outside. "How long have you been here?"

Rosa followed them out the door. She clung to Austin's arm. He removed her roving fingers. Rosa clawed her nails across Austin's chest. "Ow." He looked down at the marks she'd made in his shirt. "You're a wildcat when crossed, aren't you?" He gave her a shove. "You'll have to excuse me. I need to give my wife a whirl."

So that's how it is? Austin seized Collina's arm just before she stomped away. She struggled, attempting to shake his hand off. "I've seen what I came to see. It was a mistake me coming here tonight."

"The mistake's mine, for allowing you to have your way." His voice was gruff.

Jake's violin strummed the soft notes of a waltz as Austin dragged her into the barn. His arm went around her waist; his eyes, dark and unreadable, stared into hers. "I didn't want to rush you. I thought you'd come around in your own time. But I see now I was wrong. I should have made you mingle sooner." Austin paused, hesitating, watching the crowded dance floor, glaring back at the knowing stares. He sighed. "You look lovely, Collina."

"I guess I should consider that a real compliment, coming from a ladies' man like yourself."

He coughed, clearing his throat. "Rosa was a big help to us when you were laid up."

"You can't imagine how hard it was for me hearing you and her outside my bedroom door."

He bowed his head and whispered. "I'm sorry. I didn't mean it to go as far as it did." He spun her about in silence, his strong arms easily maneuvering her about the crowded barn floor. He'd hurt her.

He needed more than what she could give him physically, but how about the spiritual? She hadn't done her part there either. "We need to go back to church, as a family. There's a lot we both need to learn if we want to make a success out of our marriage."

His grasp turned hard. "I don't need that crutch anymore."

"How can you say that when our Lord has been so good to us?"

254

"Good? You call what happened to you good?"

"That wasn't His fault. It was mine. I should have never taken it on myself to save Clover, or to try and fight a bull. Don't you see, the Lord carried me through my mistakes?"

"Why didn't He see our baby through them, too? You're only half a woman, and I've got no hope of ever having a son to pass my name to. Don't ask me to go back to church. I've given up on God because He's given up on me."

Both had gone through the same heartache, the same trials. She had witnessed the good that had come from her blunders, he only the bad. Dear Jesus, forgive him and show me how I can help my husband.

Austin danced on, unaware of her feelings. Collina couldn't help noticing, as did Carrie Carlson, who hadn't batted an eyelash since she'd entered the room, that Rosa hadn't taken her eyes off him. He spun her in and out of the couples that dotted the floor. Dust sprang from his leather boots, creating a small cloud wherever they went.

"I'm glad you came," he said, wiping his forehead with his handkerchief.

"Are you?" nodding her head towards Rosa. "Looks like you wouldn't have been too lonely."

He took a deep breath before placing his body obstructively to limit her view of the girl on the opposite side of the room.

"I haven't violated my vows. You need to know that." Austin snatched a strand of timothy from a hay bale and started chewing on it. "Look, I'm a red-blooded male, and I can't help playing along with a filly that likes to kick up her heels." He nodded his head toward Rosa. "She's like a burr; once you come within ten feet, she attaches herself so tightly, you need a pair of pliers to pull it loose."

One thing she did know about her husband, he didn't sashay around the truth. "Really, Austin." She laughed. "Burrs are like minute porcupine quills. But they sometimes leave their quills behind. Best you watch out, lest she leaves a few in that can't be removed."

He glanced down at her upturned face. "That scar on your forehead you can hardly see. Not much more than a tiny crow's foot." He stroked one ringlet that had fallen over her forehead. "Black and thick, your hair glistens like a blackbird's wing in the lantern light. I'm going to borrow a bottle of wine from Botticelli. I've done enough work for them to deserve it. He caught her up into his arms, swinging her about as he had done the night he proposed and she accepted. Laughingly he kissed her hard on the mouth. "I'll meet you at home!"

"Ah," Anthony said, "hate to intrude, but can you stay after the dance a while and help me get that side door knocked in place?"

Austin hadn't released his grip on Collina, "Not tonight. Got plans."

Anthony rubbed his hand over his stubby chin and looked over at the side opening that gaped like a cavity. "Guess I could ask Ben and Joe, but I hoped I could get you. You're as strong as them put together, and it'd save me at least one bottle of whisky just having you do it."

Austin laughed, his chest rising with self-importance. "If you put it that way. Okay, Collina? You and the girls could ride home in the buggy, and I could come back with Magic."

She looked over toward the door in question, where Rosa now leaned. A shiver crept across her spine. "No, Austin. Come home with me." She lowered her voice to a whisper. "Can't you see, Anthony's playing on your cockiness? Remember Proverbs? Pride goes before destruction. You're going to get a mouthful of—"

"Don't worry about me." He picked her up and kissed her soundly. "I'm too strong to let that happen. I'll pull out those quills as quick as a jackrabbit."

"Not all jackrabbits jump free—some get caught in snares." She hugged Austin to her, recalling Billy Sunday's words the day of Pa's funeral: Temptation is the devil looking through the keyhole. Yielding is opening the door and inviting him in. James 1: 14–15 clearly followed: But every man is tempted, when he is drawn away by his own lust, and enticed. Then when lust hath conceived, it bringeth forth sin. "Come away with me, Austin—now. Don't look back!"

Chapter 28

August 3, 1906

*R*uby surveyed her rehearsal dinner from the second floor of the Meir Mansion. *Isn't that Carrie Carlson latching onto Austin's arm? I didn't invite her, must have been Julie Ann.* Ruby bit down on her bottom lip. *Honestly, Collina managed to uproot Rosa Botticelli, and now another woman pops into Austin's life. Will he never see the folly of loose women?*

Julie Ann hooked her arm around Carrie's and pulled her away from Austin, then waltzed her around the room introducing her as if Carrie was the bride.

"Humph." *With gossips turning up the soil between her sister and Austin, did they have a prayer of making their marriage work?*

What about Stephen and her? It was no secret that Julie Ann was against their marriage. Ruby pressed her hand to her fluttering heart. *Hopefully, no one was aware she felt as strange as her sisters in the cold and forbidding Meir mansion. Could she ever call this gleaming cathedral-shaped building home?*

The large, high-domed ceiling with chandeliers that dripped from the ornately scrolled ceiling, and the doublewide banister staircase that swept to the second floor, had her wedding procession in awe. Walking down the stairway, she envisioned herself gliding down the staircase adorned in her satin-white wedding gown tomorrow. *Hope I make it down gracefully.*

Collina, seeing her descend, waited. Her eyes brimming with tears, she hugged her close. "I pray God richly blesses you not only with material wealth, but undying love, health…and children. I'm anticipating lots of children using that handrail as a slide and me becoming an aunt again."

"Again?" Ruby laughed. "Oh, how could I forget Myra's pregnant?"

Stephen held up his glass of punch. "I second that wish, darling; and by the way, you did a beautiful job organizing our rehearsal dinner."

He turned to Collina. "Who would have thought that day you introduced me to Ruby at Doc Baker's ball that I would end up marrying your freckled-nose sister?"

"Just consider yourself fortunate," Luke Baker said.

Collina smiled. "Luke, you took the words right out of my mouth." Luke bent low and caressed her cheek with a lingering kiss, taking her hand in his, he kissed it.

She blushed scarlet beneath his gaze, her green eyes sparkling like gems amidst the blues and whites of the foyer. Her thick curls had caught the glow of the light flickering from the chandelier. She pulled away, but Luke had her hand firmly in his and brought it to his lips a second time, his voice rich with feeling. "You are a remarkable woman. I must admit I shall enjoy this brief interlude we shared standing alongside of you at the wedding rehearsal. And I eagerly look forward to the wedding—"

"Yes, I can see that." Austin took Collina's hand out of Luke's grasp.

"Austin, Luke is kidding." Collina gave her husband a no-nonsense frown. "This is Ruby's—"

"Sis, I willingly share my moment with you." Ruby beamed at Luke, not caring that Austin knew how happy she was that Luke's adoration of her sister was well received. "I am so very glad you accepted Stephen's invitation to be his best man." She glanced at Julie Ann and sent her a flippant look. Julie Ann wanted Stephen to pick Karl.

While the men conversed, Collina leaned forward, whispering in Ruby's ear. "Did you and Luke plan this to make Austin jealous?"

Ruby allowed herself the luxury to glance about the room like a gaily fluttering hummingbird, noting the murmurs and looks. "Luke needed no prompting on my part. You are lovely tonight, Sis, and deserving of every compliment."

She was flooded with well-wishers, and the hours melted away on succulent food and good fellowship.

Glimmering moonlight replaced the rays of sunset and twinkling chandeliers. Stephen and she strolled arm in arm, basking in the stars and moonlight transforming the day's green grass into a halo of fireflies. Tomorrow would be the day she would forever belong to her beloved.

Stephen patted her arm. "I was able to grab a few moments with Luke, or should I say Dr. Baker?" Stephen laughed. "It is hard to believe that my old school chum, Luke Baker, is a full-fledged doctor and practicing in one of the most prestigious hospitals in Detroit. He says there might be a cure coming for this strange problem with my lungs. Only, he still hasn't ruled out consumption—"

"I hope it doesn't include leaving for a dryer climate, like Luke's father suggested."

"That will be our last resort, my love."

"Whatever happens, Stephen, know that I shall always remain by your side. If the only pathway is to the prairies of Colorado to improve your health, then, that is where we will live."

Stephen lifted her chin and stepped closer. Aftershave and the rose on his lapel intoxicated her nostrils as his lips drew closer to her, engulfing her senses with his longing for oneness. "I want our love to be your basis for happiness, never to be a burden to be borne."

Ruby looked off into the distance. Collina and Austin were strolling through the gardens, a short ten feet away. Coming up next to them, she couldn't help hearing part of their conversation.

"Collina." Austin's voice grew louder. "I've tried farming, and I can't say I enjoy it any more than I did the first five years I tried it. And with you always worrying about Shushan, leaves us no time to enjoy life. Why not hightail it to the mountains? I can build us a sturdy cabin. I can hunt game and live off the land. I can give you and the children everything we have down here and freedom to enjoy life."

"We could move in with Mother and sell our farm. Robert's enlisting in the Army and Jessie's getting married. Jessie's fiancée wants her own house. We have Skeeder to help us, and I wouldn't be abandoning my promise to Father."

"Your promise again? I am sick of hearing about it. Shushan is your brothers' responsibility now. It's the sons, not the daughter that should be given your pa's inheritance. What do you think is going to happen to your precious Shushan when your mother and you are dead? Heaven only knows. Because of your accident and God's damnation, I will have no sons to leave my name to. At least your pa had that."

"And what do you want me to do? Learn how to chew tobacco and rock back and forth on the front porch from morning until night in some mountain cabin? I know I can't have any children, but we've got your daughters to consider. They need a proper education and to find worthy husbands for and—"

"Collina?" Ruby touched her sister's arm.

"We're talking a bit loud, aren't we?"

"I'm glad." Austin's pent-up anger needed answers. "I would like to know your opinion, Stephen."

"That's hard, because I am not you. But I am reminded of what President Roosevelt has said. 'Knowing what's right doesn't mean much unless you do what's right.' Collina, I'm not sure, but I believe your father never intended for you to dedicate your adult life to Shushan. You did fulfill his wishes by keeping the homestead together so your siblings could grow up and move on to their own destinies."

"But because of Lawyer Farlin, when Bugie comes of age, we still might lose the homestead and—"

"My lawyer is contesting what Lawyer Farlin is demanding, and the court verdict." Stephen swiped away her concern.

"Ruby and I have already fallen into the trap of what if. We need to trust in the Lord and not rely on our own insight."

"I'm not planning on asking His help." Austin's mouth contorted like a corkscrew. "God doesn't hear my prayers."

Stephen lit his pipe and inhaled. Puffs of smoke, white and irregular, floated upward. "I have often wondered if our destiny is woven within, or in spite of our shortcomings."

"Does anyone know what lies beyond the bend of years?" Collina's gentle voice filtered through the night wind. "President Roosevelt said, 'Nothing in the world is worth having or worth doing unless it means effort, pain, difficulty'...He is an example of his words. As a child he was a frail, lily-white boy who suffered from asthma. He was weak eyed, but that didn't stop him from going out west and competing with the badland cowboys."

"And he didn't quit there. He went back into the arena of political life," Stephen said.

"Our purpose might not be as heroic as Roosevelt's," Collina said, tapping Austin on the chest. "Still, we are equally important in God's plan. Who knows? God might want Stephen to learn to use his hands pulling a plow instead of pushing a pencil. Maybe in Colorado, Stephen will command the next Rough Rider group?"

"Stephen, watch out." Austin stepped away from her and held his hands over his head in a gesture of surrender. "Now she's after you to become a farmer! And worse still...a soldier!"

Collina took a deep breath as she mounted the stairway and entered the room assigned to her. The day shone bright and clear for Ruby's wedding day. The stairway quickly became a flurry of activity with bridesmaids and bridegrooms hurrying to get dressed. Musicians, waiters, and cooks rushed to their stations.

"Ah.." The ornate décor of the Meir Mansion's main bedchambers spoke boldly of Julie Ann. The sitting room of the chamber was adorned in yellow daisy wallpaper and coral stemmed flowers. A pink baby's breathe ceiling and cherubims on the four corners of the room completed the gala splendor.

"This can't be Stephen's bedchambers."

"No, it's Julie Ann's. Now get undressed, you're late." Mother said.

She hoped her sister could embellish her unique charm within this flamboyant interior. But she had little time to dwell on this as Mother pushed her toward the dressing room.

Corset loosely about her waist, she held onto the high-backed chair. "Mother, do you think Ruby will be happy here with Stephen…and Julie Ann?"

"I think it will take a little adjusting. Okay, now relax."

Collina sucked in her breath as her mother pulled her corset stays. "I had a lot of adjusting to do when I married Austin." She chewed on her bottom lip. "Do you think Austin, well, does he—"

"I must admit, I thought he married you for your ambition and just wanted a mother for those girls of his. But I was wrong."

The corset felt more what she imagined the jaws of a shark might feel like. "Me…too…Oh, Mother, stop. No…loosen them some…more."

"That good?"

"Whew…Yes. Austin will be duly impressed with my appearance in this frilly dress."

Mother hugged her close. "It's not Austin you need to impress, but your rivals. He does love you. He told me so." Maggie turned her. "It's up to you reacquaint him with our Good Lord. Only through God's Word can Austin hope to beat temptation."

A creeping uneasiness made its way to her heart.

"He's a looker. Or should I say he has many lookers desiring him? You knew that when you married him."

Irritated, Collina changed the subject. She swept the lavishly furnished room with a hand. "Ruby says Stephen's father left Julie Ann with a cute little bungalow. I doubt she'll be happy to live there after living here."

Maggie chuckled. "That's Ruby's problem." Her mother stroked her cheek lovingly. "Just remember, fretting leads to no good end. Prayer brings results. I have the utmost confidence in my girls to handle with faith and hope any situation their husbands may burden their marriages with."

"Not easy, Mother, but what is?" Myra breezed through the open doorway in pink chiffon and handed Collina a bouquet of white baby's breath, pink tea roses, and white lilacs. "They romance us and woo us and then totally baffle us. Sometimes I think God gives us our husbands because no one else could have stood a chance to help them become better men. Then again maybe it is for us to become better women and mothers." She rubbed her stomach gently. "To test our character and keep us grounded in God's Word so we can endow the next generation with God-proven principles."

Myra embraced her mother, "You are my example, my Christian model, and my confidante. You were right in calling me headstrong. And though my stubbornness has taken me down a rocky road of tears, it also has made me determine not to quit."

Myra's voice vibrated with emotion. Not pity, but wisdom edged her words; a wisdom born of deprivation and God's redeeming love. "I must tell you the news before I burst. Clem has repented of his sins and has vowed to be the husband and father he says I deserve. He's going to tell Lawyer Farlin not to contest what Stephen's lawyer is asking for. So this nightmare will soon be over. Mother, I am sorry, for all the heartache Clem has caused you."

Mother covered her mouth. "What a blessing to know Clem has repented of his ill doings and has accepted the Lord as his God and Savior."

Ruby danced into the room, her satin dress floating and rippling in the gleam of sunlight and breezes flowing through the open windows. "I feel so surreal."

Collina remembered how she had felt dressing for her wedding. Shyness and joy had mingled with anticipation of becoming Austin's wife.

Myra stroked the gleaming satin gently, as if afraid it would disappear. "I heard one woman exclaim how lucky you are to be joined with one of the wealthiest families in Kentucky."

"I don't look forward to life in this big old mansion." Ruby's eyes landed on her mother, like a baby sparrow uncertain of her wings. "What if Luke can't stop Stephen's hemorrhages? What if—"

"No one knows but God what lies ahead for any of us." Her mother spoke with resolve. "Do you love Stephen?"

"Yes. He is the only man I would every consider marrying."

Mother patted her hand. "Stephen is a godly, Christian man and that type comes once in a lifetime. It is better to have known love, daughter, through heartbreak and sorrow. For where hope prevails, there is always another sunrise."

"A sunrise without Stephen seeing it with me, would be one I cared not to witness."

Chapter 29

*C*ollina watched Ruby stroke the soft silk covering her waist and floating like the wings of a dove to the carpeted floor. Then she put a hesitant finger to the veil fastened securely to her hair.

The soft practicing notes of the wedding march echoed through the house. What is one's life worth without someone to share your joys, triumphs, and tears? Joy filled Collina knowing Ruby had found that special someone.

"My heart is fluttering like a canary," Ruby said. "I love Stephen with all my being, but can any woman understand a man's heart—"

"Austin loves me. He just doesn't love me or Jesus enough. He allows his carnal nature to overtake his good, God-given soul. I don't blame Austin. I blame Satan, and fear for Austin's plight."

"Unresolved sin can lead to," Ruby gulped. "Separation from God—"

"I won't give up! I can lead him back to Jesus. He swore he'll never cheat on me, said he'd leave me first."

"Really? That's consoling...I think." Ruby grabbed Collina's hand and squeezed it.

"I will not allow my past to control my future. I am determined to trust God. Something Aunt Louise said now makes sense. 'Life's biggest decisions are made when youth is too young to know love. How does youth know when love is forever? Or is it commitment, one to another, that binds the heart after romanticism is replaced by reality?'"

"Ouch?" Ruby shifted uneasily. "That is an eye-opening thought. I think I prefer the happy-ever-after ending in the fairy tales. You know, wedded bliss, no arguments, no crying babies?"

"Knowing you—"

"I'm kidding." Ruby sighed. "Wouldn't it be wonderful if marriage could be that easy?"

Collina laughed. "Knowing you, you'll get close to wedded bliss. Our good Lord tells us to rejoice and in everything give thanks. 'Delight thyself also in the Lord; and he shall give thee the desires of thine heart.' Didn't He tell us that 'Death and life are in the power of the tongue?' I've been brooding over my troubles and not praising my blessings. I am equally to blame with Austin. A pair of horses pulling apart doesn't get anywhere. I've been an obstinate plow horse, pulling against the harness."

"Only Austin doesn't want anything to do with the plow or harness. Aunt Louise is right—it will be commitment to my husband and my God that will bring me safely through the battles of life—besides whatsoever things are lovely."

They turned to gaze down the stairway. There stood Austin, his arms crossed, resembling a colossus with his eyes staring upwards, his lips crooked in his handsome, dimpled grin. Behind him stood Carrie, her dress of blue water silk denoting her full bosom and tiny waistline. Her upswept curls bespeaking her long sloping neck.

Ruby sighed. "Stephen isn't so tall or half as good looking as Austin, and I'm glad. It must be hard for Austin, with every woman giving him the eye."

"We need to pray for you and Stephen." Collina grasped Ruby's hands. "'Set me as a seal upon thine heart, as a seal upon thine arm; for love is as strong as death.' Solomon 8:6." Excitedly, Collina gave Ruby's hands a shake. "I sincerely feel God has told me that you and Stephen were born to be husband and wife. There will be trials, only not to worry. Your love will carry you through. God will work everything out for His glory."

"Oh, Sis, thank you. That's exactly what I needed to hear."

Robert hurried around the corner of the parlor. His shoulders looked even broader in his brown dress uniform. His long legs took the steps two at a time.

Shame about those pit marks. Collina chuckled. Still he was handsome, despite them. Robert kissed her gloved hands.

"I hope the army realizes what a fine man they're getting."

"I'm just another doughboy from Kentucky, Sis." He turned and extended his arm toward Ruby, giving her a quick kiss on the cheek.

"Robert," Ruby said, "what if there's a war?"

The ridged cloth of his uniform beneath Collina's fingers reminded her of his implacable commitment. "You could return like Jake did after the Civil War, bound to a wheelchair for the rest of your days. Or worse, not return like Joseph…" Tears wet her cheeks. "You just remember the mustard seed and what I told you."

His eyes searched her face. "A man's got to do what a man is called to do. Thanks, Sis, for being there during my growing up years and for setting a good example."

"The Wedding March" resonated in Collina's ears as she descended the winding stairway. One hand held her bouquet, the other the railing. Then she felt Austin's hand. Her heart leapt. Could it be possible she and Austin might experience what they had before her accident?

If you have faith as a grain of mustard seed…Nothing will be impossible.

Collina walked down the white streamer and to the front, then waited for Ruby. There would be no turning back once her heels landed at the bottom of Stephen's winding staircase.

Myrtle's strong soprano sang, "Here comes the bride…dressed all in white…Radiant and lovely she shines in his sight…"

Ruby gracefully descended the stairs, as if floating among the clouds of her sweeping skirts.

"Gently she glides graceful as a dove, meeting her bridegroom, her eyes full of love. Love have they waited, long have they planned, life goes before them, opening her hand."

She watched as Ruby broke into a radiant smile at seeing her bridegroom. Her face glowed with love. The lyrics of "The Wedding March" rang clear, like a church bell heralding Christ's resurrection.

"Asking God's blessing as they begin life with new meaning, life shared as one entering God's union, bowed before His throne. Promise each other to have and to hold."

Collina smiled inwardly as Stephen's strong fingers wrapped Ruby's trembling ones. His deep blue eyes swept his undying love into hers.

Stephen's strong bass rose above the murmurs in the room like sunlight breaks the pitch of night.

"I, Stephen Meir, take thee, Ruby McConnell, to be my wedded wife, to have and to hold from this day forward, for better for worse, for richer for poorer, in sickness and in health, to love and to cherish, till death us do part, according to God's holy ordinance; and thereto I pledge thee my troth."

Ruby and Stephen—and the Lord were the only ones in the room, for everything else had blurred beneath the solemnity of the moment.

"I, Ruby McConnell, take thee, Stephen Meir, to be my wedded husband, to have and to hold from this day forward, for better for worse, for richer for poorer, in sickness and in health, to love, cherish, and to obey, till death us do part, according to God's holy ordinance; and thereto I give thee my troth."

Ruby removed her glove, and Stephen reached for her hand, placing a large ruby ring with a cluster of diamonds surrounding it. A wing-tipped smile creased his full lips. "With this ring I thee wed, with my body I thee worship, and with all my worldly goods I thee endow."

The collage of years swept past Collina's mind's eye. Pa died when she had just turned sixteen. She didn't know how she could work the land without him. He had replied, "Hardened people, nursed on God's Word, endure. Collina, above all, ye must take up the armor, the shield of faith to quench the fiery darts of the wicked one."

And then Pa had said something she still did not understand, perhaps never would understand. "Do not allow the legacy of Shushan to end." She knew now it wasn't just the farming of Shushan. Franklin was right; whatever it was, it had to do with those three mustard seeds brought over from Ireland.

Would she ever fully understand? Yes, when God chose for her to know.

As God chose her to see through Ruby and Stephen's marriage vows, she belonged to Austin and he to her. Life with new meaning—shared as one. A threefold cord is not easily broken. Faith is the substance of things hoped for, the evidence of things not seen.

Austin's look to her was radiant, full of love. The scents of her bouquet perfumed the air. Yes, Austin understood too.

People rushed to congratulate the bride and groom. Austin ran to Collina's side. His eyes gleamed before her tear-strewn lashes. "According to God's holy ordinance; and thereto I pledge thee my troth…my lovely wife, thank you for your faith in me." His arms folded her into his embrace, a seal on her heart.

Prologue

*A*h… " Collina cried. "I'm so thirsty." Her tongue touched her cracked and bleeding lips. "Water." She felt her eyelids fluttering but lacked the strength to open them. So hot. She had to find Austin. She had to tell him it wasn't his fault. That smell…The swine were back. They were everywhere, pulling at her skirts, keeping her from Austin.

Face down she fell. She had tripped. The swine were walking on her! Their smell was horrendous. Gagging, she clutched her throat, spitting out the mud…no, phlegm. She had to find Austin—but the swine wouldn't let her up.

She couldn't yell. There was no escape but through the mud, through the long dark tunnel, to that flickering ray of light.

"Collina. Collina, wake up; it's Mother."

Austin was waiting for her. He stretched out his arm, his palm open to her. "I know I'm a poor substitute for a husband; you deserve better…always remember you were loved by me."

"Come back!" She was a fingertip away from him. He leaned closer, his handsome, dimpled grin, his sparkling eyes glowed into hers. Someone shoved her away. She was falling. Twirling into the blackness.

"Oh, you're so hot. Dear Jesus, please, I can't lose her, too." The cool water Mother bathed her face with felt good. "You're burning up. I'll go see if Bugie can overtake Doc."

Mother's footsteps pounded to the beat of Collina's throbbing head. So quiet. The pigs had stopped grunting. Franklin was here. His eyes as blue as the stripes on the flag, his hands comforting. "Don't ever take true love for granted, Collina." Tears formed pools in her throbbing eyelids and the salt stung her eyes.

Austin stretched out his hand. "You're my wife." Far, far away she fell into the awaiting abyss.

She was in the cornfield; Franklin was there with her, holding the mustard seed. "Nothing is impossible—if you have faith and believe."

She was dancing, dancing in a flowing gown made of starlight white and glistening gold. In a faraway distance, bagpipes played "Minstrel Boy." "Love, like a budding rose can never too quickly reveal the flower, that is, if it is to last, for all things worth having are worth waiting for…." Back, back into the fog Franklin rode, galloping up Shushan's hills until the mists engulfed him.

Chapter 1

April 7, 1917

Sunlight swept across Ruby Meir's face, and a roar like the rumbling Cumberland Falls vibrated through her as the rolling caravan of horses neighing and voices singing echoed through her windowpane. Truck motors raced above the humdrum, mingling with screeching brakes. Trucks at Shushan? No, I must have been dreaming. Her hand touched Collina's letter. She'd fallen asleep reading it.

She and Stephen were in Amarillo, Texas, on their way to Colorado to homestead a section of land near Pikes Peak. Drums pounded in the distance, followed by a duet of trumpets. This must be the preparations for the parade.

The year announced itself with Stephen's illness getting worse and the chain of war events in Europe reaching America's ships. The Great

War did not concern her. Her husband and son did. How was Stephen's fancy book learning from the University of Louisville going to help him out on the Colorado prairies?

Where had the eleven years gone? It seemed like yesterday when they had spoken their vows of love and commitment. She snuggled into her blankets, thinking how neither she nor Stephen had any idea where they would live once they did reach Las Animas. Evidently her husband had acquired an itchy foot in spite of the doctor reports and his peculiar illness.

Cold air swept the bedchambers. She blinked. The silk curtains fluttered like the colors on a sailboat, the shrill notes of a big trombone, followed by more instruments playing a patriotic tune outside the Grand Hotel, caused her husband to raise his voice an octave. "Are you up?"

"Hmm…" She lifted her head sleepily. "I am now."

"You want to go down and watch the parade? It's about to start."

"It's cold out there." Amarillo's wind had been unrelenting last evening. She wished she hadn't taken little William out to see the cattle show. The snow was deep in spots, and five-foot drifts had piled up along the roads and walkways. "If you do go out, bundle William and make sure he wears his hat with the ear muffs."

"Give Mommy a kiss."

Little sloppy lips, followed by Stephen's larger ones, found connection with her cheek. William, who'd been riding his father's back, squirmed uncomfortably, his small fist finding solace in Ruby's face.

"Oh me! That's some kiss."

"Ha! Not even eleven months old and already swinging a wallop!" He lifted the squirming infant off his back and swung him into his arms amidst the elated laughter of his son. She opened one eye, attempting to focus, and smiled, then swung her legs over the end of the bed and watched the antics of her child and husband.

William's peals of laughter mingled with the commotion of the parade's preparation outside their window. He was a miniature version of Stephen. His blue eyes and light hair were the same shade. Both heads came together like two bear cubs romping amidst a clover field.

Only William's short legs were not that of his father's.

Ruby frowned. "Do you think that by some quirk of nature William mistakenly acquired my legs?"

Stephen glanced up, one large paw placed firmly upon his son's chest, he took one look at his wife's woebegone face and laughed. "Son, I don't think there could be a mother alive that can worry as much as yours." He jumped up and giving her nose a playful thump, said, "Be glad he didn't get that."

"Oh dear!" Covering her nose with her palm, her feet glided across the thick hotel rug. She clutched the edge of the bureau, staring into the mirror. An oval face, large eyes, and thick curly hair that bounced to her shoulders and down her back. Carefully she uncovered her face. "Has my nose grown since last night?"

He burst into merry bliss. "Hon, don't take what my sister said to heart."

"How can I help it?" She stared back at her image turning her head from side to side, wishing she hadn't eavesdropped on a conversation between Stephen's sister and Emma Glaser. "Your sister's right, my nose is…predominate, and if noses do grow the older you get—oh, why couldn't your sister be wrong?" Ruby pointed to her face. "But she's not. Here's the proof."

"All kidding aside, you have nothing to fret about." He walked over to the bureau with the squirming William wrapped in his arms. "Let this be a lesson to you, son, never kid a worrier."

If she was a worrier, it was because she married the star kidder. "Ever since I confided in you, you've been ribbing me constantly about my poor schnozzle." She wagged an index finger in front of his, giving it a thump. "Is that what a loving husband does?" Her hair fell into her face, and she blew one curl away, huffing now like an over-worked steam engine. Honestly, just when she needed her husband's sympathy, why must he continue to joke?

"You look more like a misplaced angel than a mother of a ten-month-old." A mischievous gleam surfaced to Stephen's laughing eyes as he lavished them upon her. "No, come to think of it," he said, placing little William down on the carpet. "You are absolutely right. A loving husband should be…" grabbing Ruby in one lunge, "making mad and passionate love to such a succulent and beautiful damsel."

She laughed as he swung her easily into his strong arms.

The sounds of trombone, tambourines, and marching feet boldly announced the parade was moments from beginning.

"I forgot." He kissed her smartly. "I'll get him dressed." He hurried to William's room.

Before she could grab her heavy wool skirt from her trunk, her toddler came in dressed in a winter coat, mittens, scarf, and Stephen topped this off with his woolen hat with ear muffs. "Good."

"I might need to stop by the enlistment office. If the rumors are true, the Selective Service Act will require every male over twenty-one to register, only unlike the Civil War's conscription law, this will strictly forbid the use of any substitutes." He sent her a cheeky smile.

Stephen's love for adventure was nearly equal to his dedication to her and William. Blinking, she said, "Are we one or two on your list?"

Stephen laughed. "You and William are and will always be first. Now hurry."

The glass panel doors banged against the ivory-colored walls.

"You're a grand old flag."

"I think the parade has started."

"You're a high-flying flag."

He swept William up. His footsteps pounded like a Cherokee war drum on the balcony.

"And forever in peace may you wave."

Stepping into her wool skirt, she glanced out the window. Snow slapped the glass pane with a vengeance. Oh, men and their fights for valor and honor. When will it end? Once dressed, she joined him on the balcony, hugging him to her.

"You're the emblem of the land I love, the home of the free and the brave."

"Look at them, son. Remember you're seeing a page of history unfold before your very eyes." The young men below them pounded the pavement with their combat boots. Their stance bold and unyielding, their steps attuned to one another. So many, so willing.

"Robert has already left to go overseas."

"Your brother? Yes, Europe's war became America's when the *Lusitania* was torpedoed by a German U-boat off the coast of Ireland and this year, five American ships were sunk. That war's too close to our shores and has gotten every red-blooded American in an uproar."

The radio on the next balcony reiterated President Wilson's words. "It is a fearful thing to lead this great peaceful people into war."

Ruby shivered, not due to the cold, though she wish it was. Robert had written her from a foxhole in Europe that war was terrible and frightening beyond words.

President Wilson's words blared out: "The right is more precious than peace, and we shall fight for the things which we have carried nearest our hearts."

"Come on." Stephen took her hand and they rushed down the stairway. Bus boys arrayed in flashing red and gold braided suits greeted her. Crystal chandeliers twinkled gaily about the lavishly decorated lobby of the hotel, accenting the deep red and gold drapes and rich mahogany furniture in the lobby.

The doorman opened the outside doors of the Grand Hotel; a gust of cold air greeted them. Snow lined the newly shoveled walkways. The horses' neighs and the tinkling of sabers clashing against the soldiers' stirrup irons mingled with the elated cheers of the crowd.

A regiment of the cavalrymen rode before them. An insignia of the crossed swords was displayed on their sleeves and cavalry blankets. "How dashing." Ruby squealed with delight. "I can vision that gallant Rough Rider Franklin Long there among them."

"Far better it is to dare mighty things…even though checkered by failure." Stephen said, quoting Theodore Rooselvelt. "The United States had become a world power because of the Rough Riders in 1898 when America defeated Spain."

"Ev'ry heart beats true under the red, white, and blue."

The horses nodded their fine heads, and their flowing manes caught the sunlight and glistening snow, as they pranced forward as proudly as the foot soldiers in the snow that had fallen last evening and this morning. "Where there's never a boast or brag."

Stephen's eyes gleamed brightly. "See them, son? I wish for one month with these brave men, just for the experience, the elation of being a small part of this history we are watching march before us."

"Be careful what you ask." One bystander had overheard her husband's remarks. "My son will be unable to purchase another person in his place because of this new law." A plush mink hat covered the attractive lady's powdered forehead. Her thick reddish-brown fur swept her form from neck to boots.

Ruby turned. "I'm so sorry. My husband wants to fight, but he's too sick to go and past the legal age of thirty."

The lady chuckled. "Sick? He's walking isn't he?" Her angry eyes stared back at her. "If this war continues more than a few years, you'll see how sick the enlistment office thinks he is. So, your husband is—?"

"Forty two."

"Well, there's talk about extending the legal age to forty-five."

Ruby pulled on her husband's coat sleeve. "Why would President Wilson sign that into law?" she whispered.

"President Wilson will only do what he must to keep Americans safe." His voice grew louder, she suspected so the lady next to them could clearly hear. "Remember what he said when the crowd below his oval office had applauded after he agreed to a declaration of war?"

Try as she could, she didn't remember. "Was it important?"

"'My message…was a message of death for our young men. How strange it seems to applaud that.'" Stephen looked out at the marching soldiers, glassy eyed. "Such fine outstanding men each and every one. No, President Wilson will only request my service if he must. Americans want the fighting over there in Europe, rather than face our foe on American soil. We want those trenches in France and Flanders, far from our shores—freedom is never without a price." He touched her nose. "Our young men are willing and eager to do what we cannot."

"But should old acquaintance be forgot…keep your eyes on that grand old flag."

She pressed closer to him. She wished she could give him her health and grant his wish. He had sacrificed all he owned for her and William. "Knowing you, you'll hide the fact you are ill in order to ride in that cavalry regiment." She wagged her finger in front of his face. "Remember what happened to Lieutenant Franklin Long?"

"Have you?" He laughed. "I seriously doubt we have seen the last of that good man." He drew her hand to his lips and kissed it. "Shall we purchase our tickets for the train tomorrow?"

"No, you mustn't," the woman's voice vibrated with emotion. She dotted her eyes. Her embroidered handkerchief was moist.

"We—" A chain of coughs followed.

Noting his flushed face, Ruby reached in her pocket for the pills Doctor Luke had given her. "Go inside and take two with some water. I can walk to the train station and get the tickets."

Stephen waved Ruby's words aside, wiped his mouth with a fresh handkerchief, and popped in a Luden's Cough Drop. "My mouth was dry, must be the elevation, don't worry."

The lady turned toward them and waved her handkerchief toward the Grand Hotel. "The porter said the railroad crew just tunneled through a large drift."

Stephen nodded. "Your porter friend told me that Amarillo has never seen a storm of this magnitude."

The woman dabbed at her eyes again. "True and this morning at breakfast, I overheard one of the workers on the railroad crew tell the engineer that they haven't been able to clear all the track, and the engineer said headquarters was aware of this. Said the passenger car could become a steel death trap for those foolish enough to ride the iron horse tomorrow."

Coming Fall 2018

Author's Note

This began in 1976 when I accepted the challenge in *Decision Magazine* to compete in a competition to attend the Billy Graham Decision Writers Conference held in Minneapolis, Minn. The theme: 2 Corinthians 3:17. I was accepted. This poem eventually led to *The Wind of Destiny* which inspired this Destiny four-book series:

Upon the flames of falling embers
Fell their wrath upon December;
But not a foe could waver
America's joy for God and Savior,
Then beside flames and falling embers, I pondered,
Beside those trusting souls, I wondered,
"How did it come to be?
This nation 'Under God' still free?"

Cold and hard fell the sting of evil's plight.
It chilled, yet burned of flint's delight
Upon the barren and treeless rows,
Of faceless crosses and nameless souls,
Thousands filed out upon those hardened hills now stone,
Yet, silently, each faced their foe alone.
"How could it ever be," I mused. "How could it ever come to be,

This nation 'Under God' still free?"
Then strongly pealed the chapel bells,
Again, again, throughout the hills,
Unshackled and unshaken bound,
Freely did their joy resound,
And tall white domes stood boldly staunch
Against the flint of evil's doom,
Against the stagnate, stench of death,
Against the smothering walls of dread.

And rows and rows of crosses lined
Those molded hills of time,
Those rows on rows of faith unmoved,
Those undaunted wills so free and true.
"Oh tell me," I implored above, "how did it come to be?
"Was it a nation that proved to thee?
"Or they that proved to a nation,
"That You could win them victory?"

Discussion Questions

1. What happened in 1898 that made our country decide to go war? Whom were we helping?

2. Ben McConnell wrote next to the parable of the sower in Luke 8:5 "choose godly pursuits, show through your actions that you're following the Good Book not your 'I Will' book. Discuss what you think he meant by this? Which are you following?

3. How does a person know when love is forever? What qualities does that kind of love have?

4. Austin says "always felt it would prove more advantageous not to make God too happy, nor the devil too mad." What does he mean? Can we live this way and still be devoted to God?

5. God allows bad things to happen to Christians. In the book we see, Ben's and Mary's deaths; Collina getting mauled by the bull and losing her baby; Stephen's illness. What was Austin's response to hardship? How did Collina respond?

6. Collina loses what she valued too little—her femininity. She stood to lose Austin. Can you relate to Collina? How did she rise above her mistakes?

7. Mature beyond her young years, Ruby realizes she is in love with Stephen. When Stephen proposes matrimony, what Bible verses does she think of? Why do you think those verses came to her? What do those verses mean to you?

8. Collina promises her dying father that Shushan's legacy will continue, but she is unsure what that legacy is. Look up Esther 8:6 and Esther 9:2. What do you think the legacy of Shushan is?

9. In what ways was Collina May the epitome of Charles Dana Gibson's Gibson girl image? In what ways was she not?

10. September 14, 1901, President McKinley dies from what? Who becomes the next President of the United States?

CATHERINE ULRICH BRAKEFIELD

Catherine is an ardent receiver of Christ's rejuvenating love, as well as a hopeless romantic and patriot. She skillfully intertwines these elements into her writing as the author of *Wilted Dandelions, Swept into Destiny* and *Destiny's Whirwind*, inspirational historical romances, and *Images of America, The Lapeer Area*. Her most recent history book is *Images of America, Eastern Lapeer County*. Catherine, former staff writer for *Michigan Traveler Magazine*, has freelanced for numerous publications. Her short stories have been published in Guidepost Books *Extraordinary Answers to Prayers, Unexpected Answers* and *Desires of Your Heart*; Baker Books, Revell, *The Dog Next Door*; CrossRiver Publishing, *The Benefit Package*. She spent three weeks driving across the western part of the United States, meeting her extended family of Americans. This trip inspired her inspirational historical romance, *Wilted Dandelions*.

Catherine enjoys horseback riding, swimming, camping, and traveling the byroads across America. She lives in Michigan with her husband, Edward, of forty years, and her Arabian horses. Her children grown and married, she and Edward are the blessed recipients of two handsome grandsons and two beautiful granddaughters.

www.CatherineUlrichBrakefield.com
www.Facebook.com/CatherineUlrichBrakefield
www.Twitter.com/CUBrakefield

Lottie's Gift

Memories,
once allowed,
are difficult
to forget.

Available in bookstores and from online retailers.

CR CrossRiver Media
www.crossrivermedia.com

FIND MORE GREAT FICTION AT CROSSRIVERMEDIA.COM

LOTTIE'S HOPE

Jane M. Tucker

After forty years as a world class musician, Lottie has come home to Iowa, where an old home and a new job await. Then the trouble starts. At first she shrugs off the incidents as random petty crimes, but as they increase in intensity, she must face the fact that someone wants to hurt her. Can Lottie sort out her friends and her enemies before it's too late?

SWEPT INTO DESTINY

Catherine Ulrich Brakefield

As the battle between North and South rages, Maggie Gatlan is forced to make a difficult decision. She must choose between her love for the South and her growing feelings for the hardworking and handsome Union solder, Ben McConnell. Was Ben right? Had this Irish immigrant perceived the truth of what God had predestined for America?

ROAD TO DEER RUN

Elaine Marie Cooper

The year is 1777 and the war has already broken the heart of nineteen-year-old Mary Thomsen. Her brother was killed by the King's army, so when she stumbles across a wounded British soldier, she isn't sure if she should she help him or let him die, cold and alone. Severely wounded, Daniel Lowe wonders if the young woman looking down at him is an angel or the enemy. Need and compassion bring them together, but will the bitterness of war keep them apart?

GENERATIONS

Sharon Garlock Spiegel

When Edward Garlock was sober, he was a kind, generous, hardworking farmer, providing for his wife and growing family. But when he drank, he transformed into an unpredictable bully, capable of absolute cruelty. When he stepped into a revival tent in the early 1900s the Holy Spirit got ahold of him, changing not only his life, but the future of thousands of others through Edward.

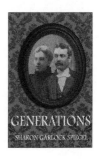

Hostile indians,
raging rivers,
and treacherous trails
are nothing
compared to
marrying a man
she does not know.
Wilted Dandelions
Available in bookstores and from online retailers.
CrossRiver Media
www.crossrivermedia.com

CROSSRIVER

If you enjoyed this book, will you consider sharing it with others?

- Please mention the book on Facebook, Twitter, Pinterest, or your blog.

- Recommend this book to your small group, book club, and workplace.

- Head over to Facebook.com/CrossRiverMedia, 'Like' the page and post a comment as to what you enjoyed the most.

- Pick up a copy for someone you know who would be challenged or encouraged by this message.

- Write a review on Amazon.com, BN.com, or Goodreads.com.

- To learn about our latest releases subscribe to our newsletter at www.CrossRiverMedia.com.

56487503R00161

Made in the USA
Middletown, DE
22 July 2019